Never Come Morning

Never Come Morning

by

Nelson Algren

Fourth Estate•London

First published in the United States of America in 1942
First published in Great Britain in 1958
This paperback edition first published in Great Britain in 1988 by
Fourth Estate Limited
113 Westbourne Grove
London W2 4UP

British Library Cataloguing in Publication Data

Algren, Nelson, *1909-1981*
  Never come morning.
  I. Title
  813′ .52 F

ISBN 0-947795-03-0

This edition published in the USA by
Four Walls Eight Windows
P.O. Box 548, Village Station
New York, N.Y. 10014

Printed and bound in the United States of America.

For Bernice

CONTENTS

AUTHOR'S PREFACE

"I PROTEST against further publishing of this book, for it fosters national disunity and should have no place in our libraries and homes," the president of the Polish Roman Catholic Union instructed Harper & Brothers in 1942, "trusting that you will have this book taken out of circulation and that no books of this character be published by your firm in the future."

The Publisher did not withdraw the novel, but we won the war all the same.

Victory being yet uncertain, however, the Polish daily *Zgoda* opened a second front against Walt Whitman, "The Nazi Information Bureau" (whatever may have been meant by *that*), and the present writer.

"The author leaves a clue to his qualifications," *Zgoda* revealed by quoting Whitman derisively:

I feel I am of them—I belong to those convicts and prostitutes myself,
And henceforth I will not deny them—for how can I deny myself?

adding that "the author is a product of a distorted mentality, for in his treatment of inmates of houses of ill repute he is in an element all his own and no doubt was on a narcotic jag when he concocted this story. It is doubtful whether Goebbels' personal adjutant could have ordered a juicier Pole-baiting tale than this Swede has dared. When free copies begin to find their way into hands of unsuspecting victims it's a signal that this anti-Polish propaganda is definitely directed by Nazi money. At 32, Algren, a Scandinavian, cannot possibly be without malice in his heart against the Poles."

Neither thirty-two, a Scandinavian nor an addict, Algren was at that moment nourishing so much malice in his heart against drill sergeants that he had not a smidgeon to spare 4-F civilians. Yet it was common for businessmen to be more passionate about war than privates that year. It did not come as a traumatic experience to find myself described by a neighborhood newspaper as "a man incapable of producing a book without the assistance of enemy Germans and traitorous Polishmen." The thirty-two-year-old Scandinavian drug addict simply looked about for enemy Germans and, seeing nothing but Americans on their way to the PX, shrewdly concluded that Fort Bragg had not yet fallen to traitorous Polishmen.

I shared the GI faith that Italy would be knocked out of the war any day and Germany would then promptly surrender. Leaving me just time, between KP chores, to earn my good-conduct ribbon for Christmas.

Italy wasn't knocked out for two Christmases and Germany refused to surrender to Santa Claus. This obliged me to transfer my army cot to Düsseldorf with my good-conduct ribbon still unearned. (That I had not made Pfc by 1945 was due not so much to lack of opportunities as to feeling myself unprepared for large responsibility.)

I was still unprepared, while huddled with other no-good-conductors around a small stove in a windy field hospital, when a mail orderly put his head in the flap of the tent to announce, "Kraut *kaput*," then tossed our mail on a cot and went his way in the wind and the rain.

The war was done—yet not one man leaped for joy. For it meant nothing more immediate to us than that the ban on fraternization would be lifted, and we had already been overlooking that ban for months. So there was no cause for leaping—unless someone who felt like leaping just wanted to use the recent news for an excuse. We'd be held for occupation or shipped to Japan, that was the size of matters, I realized.

I was opening my mail while doing this realizing, to find a letter enclosing a clipping from *Zgoda* that returned to my ears the heavy thunder of Milwaukee Avenue artillery forever trained on Harper's:

"Sirs!" was the opening barrage. "Do you realize the instrument that *Never Come Morning* is in the hands of hungry Nazi propagandists against law-abiding citizens of the only stock in the world that

dared brace itself against the onslaught of the tribe of madmen calling themselves *Herrenvolk?*"

And all this while I'd been thinking England was on *our* side!

"Yes, gentlemen, you have now joined forces with those disrupting
the minds of men engaged in defense industry around the clock who
have no time to fight off *Never Come Morning* attacks, while it is
possible for the author—to whom you pay royalties for helping smear
a group of citizens which form a great part of Chicago voters, which
group has built more churches than any other city, whose people
maintain parochial schools and still contribute to the public school
system—to rake in fees while blood is being shed by sons of this
nationality group and sweat rolls off brows of their fathers, brothers
and even mothers in a free country with malice toward none. If he
[the author] were not guilty of prejudice against us he would not dare
smear his pages with the unsavory 'Polack' 41 times or an average of
more than once every seven pages! Certainly if Boston can protest
and ban such a book as *H. M. Pulham, Esquire*, Chicago and particularly its Polish-American residents have a right to voice vehement
objection to this objectionable book."

The German sky was lowering as though sensing its final defeat.
Supper would be Argentine corned beef and breakfast would be
French toast again. It looked like *somebody* was bearing malice all
right.

Yet I found this new method of measuring intolerance exhilarating:
now at last we would be able to tell how much of that wicked stuff a
given soldier or civilian contained simply by striking a mean of the
number of times he wrote or said "Polack." We now had concrete
evidence that, in writing "He smote the sledded Polacks on the ice"
(*Hamlet*, Act I Scene I), Shakespeare had given us nothing more than
another anti-Polish slander.

Thus through the furious logic of illiteracy we had come full cycle.
We had fought in snow and slept in rain because somebody had said
that every time he heard the word "culture" he reached for his gun,
and now we had won him the right of reaching for it. The man who
had lost the war was not necessarily German nor was the man who
had won it necessarily American. The man who had won it was the

man who divides words from meaning in order to make a book serve
a meaning of his own, and never reads the writer's book at all. His
only book is himself, and he reads it over and over.

The victor in any land was the man who feels himself terribly
wronged if his ultimatum on what his neighbors should read, what
they should wear and what they should think is questioned. We had
crossed an ocean only to find that that bore lived on the same street as
ourselves.

So much for World War II. I never *did* get my good-conduct ribbon.

Twenty years have since blown ten thousand novels by as lightly as
colored confetti is blown the morning after the corner carnival
leaves. Two decades have turned *Zgoda*'s pages, once white with fury,
to a wan stale brown. Peanut-patriots hell-bent in their thousands,
living on usury or worse six days a week and saluting the flag from
sun-up to sunset on the seventh—all, all are down, dead or dying. Or
turned to a wan stale brown. The long mindless jackass bray that
once wound down West Division Street—*"Nazi agents may be buying up thousands of copies of* Never Come Morning *to kill growing
good opinion of Poles"*—has been unwound on a Milwaukee Avenue
wind, blown as a handful of colored confetti is blown, as a novel that
was once a best seller is blown. Once readers and gawkers alike have
turned wan brown.

Yet the novel that the rear-echelon patriots and Sunday-morning
Forgive-Me-Lords failed to understand strangely has found understanding on the bookshelves of Europe. *Le matin se fait attendre*,
Jean-Paul Sartre's translation, was the first of a dozen translations. It
is now available in every large city from London to Tokyo, Rio to
Zagreb. That it remains unavailable in the city about which it was
written does not bespeak an active hospitality here so much as the
crocodilism of minds (transfixed around 1903) that conduct the affairs of the Chicago Public Library.

"If you've got the bread you walk" is a Chicago saying. So that
when this story was awarded a thousand dollars, after the war, by the
American Academy of Arts and Letters, hostility subsided. The boys

at *Zgoda* may never have heard of the Academy but they *had* heard of a thousand dollars. Subsequently the writer turned out another neighborhood novel, using a more challenging predicament than that employed in the present story, but no voice dissented then. The local rumor was that Frank Sinatra would play the leading role in the film version, and that did it. The boys might not understand the printed word, but when the name of money was linked with the name of a celebrity they came in with their hands up.

Yet the novel that so infuriated them (and that they were so ill equipped to judge) was nothing more than a thinly fictionized report on a neighborhood where, if you cared to get hit on the head and dragged into an alley, it was as likely as any. The book drew for its details not upon the aftereffects of a narcotic jag but upon the lives of half a dozen men with whom the writer had grown up, as well as upon the newspaper reports of the trial of Bernard "Knifey" Sawicki.

The novel attempted to say, about the American outcast, what James Baldwin has observed more recently of the American Negro: if you don't know my name you don't know your own. I felt that if we did not understand what was happening to men and women who shared all the horrors but none of the privileges of our civilization, then we did not know what was happening to ourselves.

I felt then, as now, that the presence of the YMCA, of settlement houses and of churches, to which *Zgoda* so proudly pointed, could have no greater modifying effect on incidence of local crime than so many loan agencies, so long as the people who run the schools, the people who run the churches and the banks, the people who elect people and get out the newspapers feel no identification with the outcast man and the outcast woman. Anything less than such identification is contempt—and no man is quicker to sense contempt than the outcast. None is more swift to return contempt for contempt.

The source of the criminal act, I believed twenty years ago and believe yet, is not in the criminal but in the righteous man: the man too complacent ever to feel that he—even *he*—belongs to those convicts and prostitutes himself.

And how completely the righteous have failed here is plain enough when we recall that the greatest change that twenty years have brought in our police work is that, while police were then splitting fifty-fifty with ex-cons for whom they set up scores, today they do the stealing themselves.

Nor all your piety nor all your preaching, nor all your crusades nor all your threats can stop one girl from going on the turf, can stop one mugging, can keep one promising youth from becoming a drug addict, so long as the force that drives the owners of our civilization is *away* from those who own nothing at all.

The failure of the people at *Zgoda* was a failure of feeling. A failure to feel

. . . I am of them—I belong to those convicts and prostitutes myself, And henceforth I will not deny them—for how can I deny myself?

And *Zgoda* runs from coast to coast.

NELSON ALGREN

Chicago
November 1962

INTRODUCTION

ACCORDING TO the diary of my wife Jill Krementz, the photographer, the young British-Indian novelist Salman Rushdie came to our house in Sagaponack, Long Island, for lunch on May 9th, 1981. His excellent novel *Midnight's Children* had just been published in the United States, and he told us that the most intelligent review had been written by Nelson Algren, a man he would like to meet. I replied that we knew Algren some, since Jill had photographed him several times and he and I had been teachers at the Writers' Workshop of the University of Iowa back in 1965, when we were both dead broke and I was 43 and he was 56.

I said, too, that Algren was one of the few writers I knew who was really funny in conversations. I offered as a sample what Algren said at the Workshop after I introduced him to the Chilean novelist José Donoso: "I think it would be nice to come from a country that long and narrow."

Rushdie was really in luck, I went on, because Algren lived only a few miles to the north, in Sag Harbor, where John Steinbeck had spent the last of his days, and he was giving a cocktail party that very afternoon. I would call him and tell him we were bringing Rushdie along, and Jill would take pictures of the two of them together, both writers about people who were very poor. I suggested that the party might be the only one that Algren had given for himself in his entire life, since, no matter how famous he became, he remained a poor man living among the poor, and usually alone. He was living alone in Sag Harbor. He had had a new wife in Iowa City, but that marriage lived about as long as a Junebug. His enthusiasm for writing, reading and gambling left little time for the duties of a married man.

I said that Algren was bitter about how little he had been paid over the years for such important work, and especially for the movie rights to what may be his masterpiece, *The Man with the Golden Arm*, which made a huge amount of money as a Frank Sinatra film. Not a scrap of the profits had come to him, and I heard him say one time, "I am the penny whistle of American literature."

When we got up from lunch, I went to the phone and dialed Nelson Algren's number. A man answered and said, "Sag Harbor Police Department."

"Sorry," I said. "Wrong number."

"Who were you calling?" he said.

"Nelson Algren," I said.

"This is his house," he said, "but Mr. Algren is dead." A heart attack that morning had killed Algren at the age of seventy-two.

He is buried in Sag Harbor—without a widow or descendents, hundreds and hundreds of miles from Chicago, Illinois, which had given him to the world and with whose underbelly he had been so long identified. Like James Joyce, he had become an exile from his homeland after writing that his neighbors were perhaps not as noble and intelligent and kindly as they liked to think they were.

Only a few weeks before his death, he had been elected by his supposed peers, myself among them, to membership in the American Academy and Institute of Arts and Letters—a certification of respectability withheld from many wonderful writers, incidentally, including James Jones and Irwin Shaw. This was surely not the first significant honor ever accorded him. When he was at the peak of his powers and fame in the middle of this century, he regularly won prizes for short stories and was the first recipient of a National Book Award for Fiction, and so on. And only a few years before his death the American Academy and Institute had given him its Medal for Literature, without, however, making him a member. Among the few persons to win this medal were the likes of William Faulkner and Ernest Hemingway.

His response to the medal had been impudent. He was still living in Chicago, and I myself talked to him on the telephone, begging him to come to New York City to get it at a big ceremony, with all expenses paid. His final statement on the subject to me was this: "I'm sorry, but I have to speak at a ladies' garden club that day."

At the cocktail party whose prospects may have killed him, I had hoped to ask him if membership in the American Academy and Institute had pleased him more than the medal. Other friends of his have since told me that the membership had moved him tremendously, and had probably given him the nerve to throw a party. As to how the seeming insult of a medal without a membership had ever taken shape: this was nothing but a clumsy clerical accident caused by the awarders of prizes and memberships, writers as lazy and absent-minded and idiosyncratic in such matters as Algren himself.

God knows *how* it happened. But all's well that ends well, as the poet said.

Another thing I heard from others, but never from Algren himself, was how much he hoped to be remembered after he was gone. It was always women who spoke so warmly of this. If it turned out that he had never mentioned the possibility of his own immortality to any man, that would seem in character. When *I* saw him with men, he behaved as though he wanted nothing more from life than a night at the fights, a day at the track, or a table-stakes poker game. This was a pose, of course, and perceived as such by one and all. It was also perceived back in Iowa City that he was a steady and heavy loser at gambling, and that his writing was not going well. He had already produced so *much*, most of it in the mood of the Great Depression, which had become ancient history. He appeared to want to modernize himself somehow. What was my evidence? There he was, a master storyteller, blasted beyond all reason with admiration for and envy of a moderately innovative crime story then appearing in serial form in the *New Yorker*, Truman Capote's *In Cold Blood*. For a while in Iowa, he could talk of little else.

While he was only thirteen years my senior, so close to my own age that we were enlisted men in Europe in the same World War, he was a pioneering ancestor of mine in the compressed history of American literature. He broke new ground by depicting persons said to be dehumanized by poverty and ignorance and injustice as being *genuinely* dehumanized, and dehumanized quite *permanently*. Contrast, if you will, the poor people in this book with those in the works of social reformers like Charles Dickens and George Bernard Shaw, and particularly with those in Shaw's *Pygmalion*, with their very promising wit and resourcefulness and courage. Reporting on what he saw of dehumanized Americans with his own eyes day after day, year after year, Algren said in effect, "Hey—an awful lot of these people your hearts are bleeding for are really mean and stupid. That's just a fact. Did you know that?"

And why didn't he soften his stories, as most writers would have, with characters with a little wisdom and power who did all they could to help the dehumanized? His penchant for truth again shoved him in the direction of unpopularity. Altruists in his experience were about as common as unicorns, and especially in Chicago, which he once described to me as "the only major city in the country where you can easily buy your way out of a murder rap."

So—was there anything he expected to accomplish with so much dismaying truthfulness? He gives the answer himself, I think, in his preface to this book. As I understand him, he would be satisfied were we to agree with him that persons unlucky and poor and not very bright are to be respected for surviving, although they often have no choice but to do so in ways unattractive and blameworthy to those who are a lot better off.

It seems to me now that Algren's pessimism about so much of earthly life was Christian. Like Christ, as we know Him from the Bible, he was enchanted by the hopeless, could not take his eyes off them, and could see little good news for them in the future, given what they had become and what Caesar was like and so on, unless beyond death there awaited something more humane.

KURT VONNEGUT, JR.

New York
October 1986

I feel I am of them—
I belong to those convicts and prostitutes myself—
And henceforth I will not deny them—
For how can I deny myself?

—WHITMAN

Never Come
Morning

BOOK I

BELOW THE BELT

I

The Trouble with Casey

AT THE ten-second warning to the evening's first preliminary, a newspaperman on the apron of the ring stood up to get his slicker off. He had the right arm out and was pulling at the left while watching a Mexican featherweight in the corner above his head. At the bell he left the sleeve dangling: to see a Pole with an army haircut come out of the opposite corner straight into the Mexican's left hand. The army haircut went back on his heels, stopped dead, and glanced unbelievingly at the Mex; then kept coming in.

The Mex backpedaled, mulling his man. Faded from a left, rolled with a right, caught a left and a right on his elbows and let the army haircut bull him into the ropes. When he felt himself firmly packed against them he settled his right glove softly against the nape of the haircut's neck and tied his man up with his left; till he sensed the other dropping his hands for the break. Then he clamped the neck like a vise and threw the left from the knees.

The naked neck started snapping back, trying to roll with the blow; but the bracing glove blocked it, forcing the full shock back into the

1

brain. The Mex slapped his left across the Pole's teeth and skittered sideways, arms at his sides. The Pole's rag mouthpiece popped half-way out, looking like a wad of dirty cotton in the light; the mouth unhinged and he stood drooling under the lights. The Mex looked at the ref.

The ref looked down at the judges.

The judges listened alertly to the crowd behind them.

The ref nodded the Mexican in.

And the army haircut lay on his side with his right still shielding his jaw. At the count of four he rolled gently onto his back and crossed his gloves at the breast innocently, looking vacantly up at the moths circling about the lights. At six the pressman saw the left foot twitch and at eight the boy came around: and put his gloves under his head as though he were home in bed. The crowd saw his eyes clear.

"Get up 'n fight!"

For answer the fighter closed his eyes and did not open them till he was being helped to his corner and the lights were up full all over the house. There was nothing like being certain.

"I only wish that Polack 'd go somewheres else t' lay down," the pressman complained, watching the Mex being assisted into his robe. Nobody was helping the haircut into his and he climbed through the ropes alone; he paused on the apron to rub the back of his neck reflectively.

"You got ever'thin', Casey," the pressman called—"if just you wasn't knock-nutty!"

The Pole hurried guiltily down the steps to the lockers.

The pressman draped his slicker neatly over his right arm and sat down at last. "If I'd of knowed they was puttin' that bum on again I would've stood in bed," he assured the press at large.

Someone was knocking apologetically on the alley door of Boni-facy Konstantine's West Division Street TONSORIAL PALACE OF ART & BARBER SHOP. Bonifacy sat in his barber's chair, facing a narrow tile shelf he had cleared of combs and towels and bottles, dealing a hypothetical game of seven-card stud to five hypothetical players.

He himself wasn't playing. He was just cutting himself in a hypothetical five per cent for dealing. He was just seeing how many cards he could control. He was just trying to deal two pairs to his number four customer while giving the player to his left three queens. At the same time he had to be careful that no one got three kings, three aces, nor a straight, nor a flush. When he could manage that, Bonifacy figured, he was ready to forget what he knew about barbering. He was possessed by an ambition to run a phony card game and wished wistfully now, beneath his calculations, that the neighborhood boys would become as interested in poker as they were in baseball and boxing.

Baseball and boxing that paid money Bonifacy approved. But young Poles with a purely amateur enthusiasm for a wop outfielder or a Jew welterweight angered the barber. Life in the old world had been too hard to permit young men to play games; now, past middle age, he was too old to understand any need that was not the need for money. It was this need that caused him to make obscure suggestions to youths whose natures, in the barber's eyes, were too tolerant.

"When the thunder kills a devil," he liked to tell them in Polish, "then a devil kills a Jew."

They paid no more attention to such allusions than did the four blue roller canaries perched, in four home-made cages, above the barber's chair. Each cage was so small that its bird could barely flutter between its bars. Beneath the cages seed was scattered as though it had been slung at the birds in a rage at their trilling, rather than placed in their feed cups. Bonifacy liked to assure baldish customers: "Hair grow now like bird's feaders. Two-bits shampoo okey?" And he did not, ordinarily, bother to answer any alley-door knocking. He knew who came by the alley door.

Outside, where the afternoon light lay like a flood bearing uncovered refuse cans from telephone pole to telephone pole, the army haircut waited. In a faded red turtle-neck sweater, with a strip of adhesive across his nose. He knocked a second time, lightly. A voice like an aging woman's answered from within:

"Haircut! Haircut!"

But no one came to the sunlit door.

Bonifacy finished his deal absently, reviewing plans for the haircut's immediate future. He heard the haircut's shoes rasping faintly on the alley pavement, doing miniature shuffles as though skipping rope, and listened a moment as though hearing it for the last time. Then he went, lurching, to the door.

His left leg was so twisted—by measles in his childhood—that when he wished to lean backward to gain a fresh perspective of a customer's skull, he had to grasp the arm of the barber chair firmly, with his comb-hand, in order to stay on his feet. The woman's voice followed him to the door.

"Broke a record! Broke a record!"

He gave the haircut no greeting, but returned, lurching, to his deal.

The featherweight paused in the doorway grinning in toothless embarrassment. He had seen this room a thousand days of his life and wished he had seen it not once. In it he had become a bicycle thief when he was ten, a pimp when he was fourteen, and a preliminary boy at sixteen. Now, at twenty-nine, he had come, with the alley light behind him, to learn what the room wished him next to become.

Empty pop bottles were piled to the ceiling in one corner, although no one here dealt in either pop or bottles. Saucers with black flypaper lay on the floor, beneath the unpainted chairs, on the dust of the window sill and between the piled towels; although no flies could be expected so late in the summer. Dozens of playing cards lay between empty shampoo bottles; yet scarcely two had the same back. The late light on the fighter's face slanted across the place where the bridge of his nose had been before Bonifacy had had the bone removed. He stood fingering the loosened end of the adhesive, plastered across the small scarred bump of his nostrils.

"You ain't swept since I turned pro I bet, Barber," he observed nasally, with uncertainty in his voice as though in fear of offending.

"Wrap it up! Wrap it up!" cried the aging voice in the shadowed corner.

"I'm feelin' better awready, Barber."

Bonifacy turned up his number four customer's hand: a straight from the ace. The fellow was cheating. He'd have to watch out for crooks. He hurled the cards in his hand at the hypothetical player and worked the chair around to face his fighter.

"What d' ya say t'day, Barber?"

"Same like yesterday—save your money."

The fighter laughed with an effort:

"Ssss—ssss—ssss. Barber."

Bonifacy removed a snuffbox from his shirt pocket, knocked the snuff off the lid against his elbow, opened it and stuffed a pinch under his upper lip, then sealed the cover as though sealing it forever and had it safely halfway back to his pocket when the featherweight spoke almost boldly.

"How's about a good ol' chow, Barber?"

The barber handed him the can reluctantly. He approved of snuff for old-country Poles like himself, but felt that young men born and raised in America should stick to cigarettes. He watched the dented face above the sweater slip a pinch into its cheek, spit and return the can.

This was Casimir Benkowski from Cortez Street, called Casey by the boys and *Kasimierz* by the girls. He coached the underage youths of the 26th Ward Warriors S.A.C. in baseball, boxing, theft and hoodlumism, and himself preferred baseball and boxing. Not because these possessed larger values, but because they involved less personal risk. He had learned that a boy, on the diamond or in the ring, could bring an occasional ten-spot home to Benkowski, while a boy in the workhouse or the Juvenile Detention Home was of no use to Benkowski at all. Most of all he preferred working with them on the diamond or with the gloves because he understood baseball and boxing as by instinct. When coaching he was a leader of men, and then there was no uncertainty in his manner. Then he could be as canny as the barber was in figuring shady deals; then he was ringwise and confident of himself as he never was elsewhere.

The barber had never learned more of boxing than that ringside seats at the City Garden sold at $1.60 each. He had once witnessed a baseball game between Benkowski's Warriors and the Polish

Wonders, when the Warriors were winning, 17-1. Bruno Lefty Bicek, the Warriors' first-string pitcher and cleanup man, had come to bat in the first of the ninth with nobody on and his sixteen-run lead safely behind him. A slouch-shouldered, slow-moving sixteen-year-old who could slug with his left hand as well as throw with it. The barber, standing behind the backstop had, for some reason, gotten excited when the left-hander had come to the plate. Perhaps it had been the thirteen dollars involved in victory; perhaps it was just that he had lacked his usual caution that day.

"Win your own game, Biceps!" he had cried out.

Lefty Bicek had been Lefty Biceps, in the ring or on the diamond, ever since. And now his manager and pal, Benkowski, stood before the barber trying to work up a touch. He brushed his fists up along his ears, shoving up an imaginary headguard.

"Get me the spik again, Barber?"

His voice was not hopeful. He didn't want any part of the Mex again, and the barber knew he didn't. Bonifacy the barber's lips twisted in a jeering, bitter grin. What did these Americans do with their money? This one had gotten twenty dollars for his dive of the night before.

"I got took in a crap game, Barber," Casey explained plaintively, as though he had experienced a spiritual as well as a physical defeat—"That Mex took me in the locker room. He punches my brains out 'n then gets my end of the purse. You know, them spiks is pretty shrewd, Barber. I'd like t' take him on again."

The barber pretended to misunderstand. "We get him again Monday night. Return match. Okey?"

"No, I just meant with the dice, Barber," Benkowski said hurriedly. He drew up a stool and sat tensely, in the manner of any preliminary boy awaiting the ten-second buzzer: a posture calculated to remind the other of the two-hundred-odd times he had already sat so—in order to soften him for the touch. He did not realize that Bonifacy had long ago observed that the attitude was the tipoff to a touch, and so was always able to prepare himself against it.

"We'll all be doin' better pretty soon, Barber," Casey generalized, "every time, I learn somethin' new. All the time, I'm gettin' the old experience. All the time I'm perfectin' the old technique."

"Like layin' there on your back last night?"

Benkowski leaned forward, speaking fast and anxiously, like a schoolboy explaining tardiness.

"Like not droppin' my hands on the break so soon, like waitin' fer him to lead t' me, like always, always bein' on my toes—" his tone grew slyly ingratiating and he got it in fast—"Borrow me a sawbuck, Barber."

The barber was prepared.

"No more fight. No more borrow."

As though he had not heard, Casey became sweetly reminiscent.

" 'Member the fight I put up against the Greek in Hammond that time, Barber? 'N him the houseman at that? Nothin' c'd stop me, them days."

"Not Hammond. Was Gary. Was not Greek, was Litvok. You was stopped so cold like a popsickle."

"You seen him buckle in the fourt' yerself, Barber"— Benkowski rose, aroused by the recollection; then sank back hopelessly— " 'N look where *he* is now."

"Look better where we are." Bonifacy took a breath to correct himself. "I mean where you are."

Benkowski took the bull by the horns.

"I ain't through, Barber. You get me on again 'n change my name, like they done fer Johnny Paycheck, 'n I'll win thirty-three straight fer you." He came around the side of the chair and laid an uncertain hand on the older man's shoulder. He didn't mind losing a backer nearly so much as losing a meal ticket. The loose end of the adhesive began hindering his vision and he ripped it off; with that gesture both men knew that neither wanted to talk further of fighting. The barber had never liked the game enough—outside of the money he had once thought was in it—to try to understand it. And Casey long ago had wearied of being beaten about the head; the canaries began trilling as though they too felt relieved of a burden.

Casey grinned over at the birds. "It's like a happy ending at the Little Pulaski, Barber—even the birds is singin' ——"

"I got nice big i-dee," Bonifacy said abruptly. "You want ten bucks, you earn first."

Casey reseated himself, white and apprehensive.

"Not strong-arm stuff, Barber? Don't make me do that no more." He was pleading—as only a man with the workhouse behind him can plead. "I couldn't stand another stretch."

Bonifacy rolled his head, laughing mirthlessly at the other's fear, feeling at ease with his man at last. He leaned over and ran his hand over Casey's cropped skull.

"How much you pay for such nice haircut, *Kasimierz?*"

Benkowski lowered his eyes, more afraid of this man's friendliness than of his open enmity. "I paid nothin', Barber. You done it for free. But for other guys it's four bits all summer 'n sixty on Saturday."

"Price has gone up. Is now seventy-five. Is six bits."

Casey's face was clouded by his uncertainty. Why couldn't the greenhorn say right out what he wanted?

"Is forty haircuts, is six bits each, is thirty bucks, *Kasimierz.*"

Casey got it then, dimly. There were forty-odd youths, from every corner of the Triangle formed by Chicago, Ashland and Milwaukee Avenues, who claimed membership in the Warriors S.A.C. They met in a shed under a Noble Street sidewalk and Benkowski's was the only shaven head among them: the haircut marked his leadership.

"You mean all my kids got to get clipped? Where do I come in?"

"For what you ask. Ten bucks."

"Make it fifteen. Some of them kids is vain."

"Ten."

"I'll have to pay Biceps off to convince them."

"Ten."

"Twelve-fifty. Two and a half for Lefty. 'N a free clip to Finger to convince Lefty."

"Okay. Twelve-fifty."

There was a troubled silence in the dim-lit little shop.

"Could I have it now, Barber?"

"Do I look like such a fool? When the hair is in the basket ask again."

"Just a fin then? I need it so bad."

" 'N that's all then—a fin is your percentage?" The barber already had his hand on his wallet and his wallet open. Casey gulped at sight of the fin. The temptation was sore. He thought of the beatings he'd taken. All for this fish-eyed yashek. And put the temptation from him.

"No, not *that* bad," he said. "I'll wait better. I'll start bringin' in them Warriors Saturday mornin'. I'll start roundin' 'em up t'day so's they'll have that much by then."

"Forget 'Warriors,'" the barber advised. "Call better 'Baldheads.'"

Benkowski saw the point: a fellow could hardly belong to a mob called the Baldheads without getting clipped by the barber regularly, summer and winter.

"Only haircuts by Bonifacy count for belong to club," Bonifacy added pointedly.

Suddenly Casey sensed that larger hopes lay at the back of the barber's brain: that perhaps the haircuts were only an opening wedge into bigger money. He shifted restlessly, from foot to foot, made uneasy by his sense of things to come without being able to put a finger on what they were to be or where he fitted in the barber's mind. The barber permitted one side of his mouth to smile: a thin and knowing grin.

Casey Benkowski dropped his eyes to the older man's feet, as though he would be happier shining his shoes than taking such orders. Then turned and slouched to the door, his shoulders looking heavy with worry or fear, and did not turn to face the barber as he left.

Bonifacy remained in the barber chair, clasping his gray and grizzled chin, his eyes fixed on a fallen shampoo bottle with an image of Casey in his mind: on his face beneath the lights with arms and legs sprawled out as though his back had been broken. They hadn't brought him around that night till they were cutting the tape off his hands in the lockers; the barber had never stopped seeing his man sprawled cold beneath the lights.

"There's a Polack on the ropes," he assured the shampoo bottle, "T.K.O. in first." But somehow even saying it out loud like that, with no one else around, didn't make it sound certain enough. The boy was almost thirty, he'd been kayoed twelve times in his last fifteen fights, his strength was gone and his kidneys were gone and his heart was gone and his memory was going. And still Bonifacy couldn't feel sure enough. He could never feel sure enough about anything. They were always trying to cheat him in this country. He lurched to the shadowed corner and spoke in wheedling Polish, bracing himself by his comb-hand against the shadowed wall.

"On ropes, Polly?"

"On ropes! On ropes!" the aging parrot croaked crazily.

The barber bent painfully to pick seed off the floor, and rewarded the bird with a pinch of it: he liked to feed the bird personally, to defer to it and cajole it, and grew angry if one of the roller canaries trilled while the parrot was croaking.

"Washed up, Polly? Washed-up Polack?"

"Washed-up Polly! Washed-up Polly!"

The barber knocked his snuffbox against his elbow, screwed off the top and extended it: the bird dipped its beak in the stuff and croaked its thanks.

Casey Benkowski himself felt less grateful. He felt he was more shrewd than any parrot could know. He felt as full of plans as any barber. "When I start takin' care of number one that dino 'll find I just been too shrewd for him," he assured himself, shuffling up an uncarpeted stair in his Division Street boarding house. "I got the ol' experience, I'm smart as a craphouse rat." He fished for a key and entered his room softly, for the landlady's room was directly below.

A little windowless room was Casey's, with nothing in it but a bed, a straight-backed chair with a gray sweat shirt hanging on it, and a picture of Tiger Pultoric, C.Y.O. light-heavyweight contender, thumbtacked to the soiled wall. Casey took a catcher's mitt from under the mattress and stuffed it under his sweater. "Now if I can convince the Finger to borrow that Chevie, we'll pick up that screwy lefthander 'n start doin' ourselves some good." He shuffled quietly down the stair with the conviction that, with luck, he wouldn't have to avoid the landlady by the time he returned.

"Somebody got to bring that lefthander along. It might as well be me," he rationalized.

The lefthander's Mama stirred restlessly on her cot in the rear of Bicek's Imperial Milk Depot and Half-Price Day-Old Bakery. She heard the lefthander getting empty bottles back into their cases, listened for the faint tinkle that heralded a customer's entrance, and hoped the boy would stay in the store until the driver arrived.

Though it was bright autumn and the sky cloudless, Mama Bicek always felt, in the low-roofed rear of the little store, that outside a cold wind rose and an all-night rain began. She touched the crucifix at her throat and drew the army blanket closer about her.

Bruno Lefty Bicek, ace southpaw of the 26th Ward Warriors, squatted forward on a milk bottle case, as he had seen Benkowski squat in the seconds before the bell, working the fingers of his right hand about a red sponge ball. With the left—the hand that was already strong enough—he filled the cases that happened to be nearest. The fingers that worked the sponge ball flexed regularly, strenuously, with an unremitting ambition; those that handled the empty bottles did so with absent-minded indifference, as though possessed of the knowledge that Bruno Lefty planned higher uses for them than that of pleasing milk drivers.

Bruno Lefty was divided in his ambitions between being a big-league hurler and becoming a contender for the heavy-weight championship of the world. Somehow or other, no White Sox scout had shown up the time he had held the Wonders to a single hit; so he was slightly more inclined to the ring. And why hadn't anyone called him "Iron-Man" the day he'd shut out the Logan Squares and then relieved Fireball Kodadek in the fifth inning of the second game? Why, they'd almost won the second game behind him as well!

That Fireball was through, the boy reflected with satisfaction now. When Bicek was on the mound the boys would play any team on the Near Northwest Side for thirteen dollars a side, and when

Fireball was in there they wouldn't put up more than a quarter apiece, against anybody.

"I hope that Kodadek gets beaned for keeps 'n never comes to," Lefty hoped without malice, as he hoped for any possibility which would clear a pathway to being known throughout the ward as "Iron-Man."

Or maybe the barber would get him a fight with some head-shy boogie, like that Big-Ink Martin from the Savoy, and he'd ice the jig with a punch. Then the *Chicagoski* might call him One-Punch Bicek, the undefeated white hope of Chicago Avenue or something; maybe the *Daily Times* would pick it up and tell just how he did it. The boy had a sort of super punch, they'd say. He sat looking vacantly into space, sponge ball and milk bottles equally forgotten.

When the doorbell tinkled he did not rise; he recognized the black bombazine and pince-nez of the middle-aged caseworker from the Sangamon Street Relief. She hustled past him into the rear, without recognition; she had learned that if she so much as said "Good afternoon, Bruno," he lied to her in reply. She was curing him of the habit by not recognizing him at all. For the boy's part, he didn't seem to notice that anyone had entered, and that irked the woman a little. While sitting with Mama Bicek, notebook in hand, she concluded that she'd better have a heart-to-heart talk with the boy before she left. Perhaps all he needed was Social Guidance. He was leaning on the handle of a broom when she came out, apparently absorbed in his shoes. "I know everythin' she 's goin' t' tell me, like it's a big discovery," he thought. He knew it all by rote, and he listened patiently while she dinned it in his ear anew:

Mama Bicek needed an orange.

Mama Bicek needed meat.

Mama Bicek needed medicine.

Mama Bicek should get sunshine.

But Mama Bicek couldn't have those things from the relief, for she had a son and a store besides. Now if Mama Bicek had no store, and Mama Bicek's boy wasn't old enough to work on W.P.A., then things could be different. Then the black bombazine would take care of everything personally.

Bruno had never taken advantage of the fact that he was a year younger than the woman credited him with being. He enjoyed being taken for eighteen. "At least you don't lie about your age," she had once assured him.

The implication, that he lied as fast as a dog can trot about everything else, was true so far as she was concerned. Why he lied to her the boy didn't know. Perhaps it was, in part, distrust of her notebook and pince-nez; perhaps it was partly her consistent failure to regard him as the Warriors' mainstay; perhaps it was chiefly his realization that she came from the same world as did detectives and truant officers and park policemen. Perhaps too he had sensed that she stopped to question him chiefly in order that she might be able to leave feeling she had been most deliberately, brazenly and wantonly betrayed by a client she had trusted completely.

"You didn't show up Wednesday morning," she apprized him now, "Why not?"

He had promised her faithfully that, when she got him assigned, at fifty-five a month, to a project on the Outer Drive, he would be as certain to appear on the job as the foreman himself. Now he rested his cheek on the end of the broom handle and mumbled sleepily.

"I'm in trainin'. Had to go to bed early 'n sleep late. That was orders."

Seeing the full-grown slouch of his shoulders, she found herself hoping that he'd lie more outrageously than ever before. But she kept that out of her voice.

"Training for *what*? Orders from *whom*?"

It wouldn't pay to let him think she was being fooled for one minute. But one would think, by those shoulders, that he was twenty-one; she surveyed his face to make certain that he wasn't over eighteen: a wholesome, placid, sallow Polish face with cheekbones set high and widely to protect the nose and eyes. And what in the world was he up to, at that age, squeezing a sponge ball?

"For a fight. From my manager."

"You mean you fight pro*fess*ionally?"

"Uh-huh."

Anyhow, he was going to get a money fight pretty soon, wait and see. If the barber didn't get him on at the Garden, Benkowski would.

She jotted something in the book, and he took time out to fancy himself climbing through the ropes at the City Garden. Then she'd see his picture in the paper the next morning and would write him a letter of apology addressed to "*Mister* Bicek." He found himself waiting for her to call him "Mister"; as he waited, among the boys, for someone to call him "Iron-Man."

"What do you earn when you fight?"

The boy had no one to whom he could boast freely but an under-age girl friend, and she didn't count.

"I wouldn't pull on a glove fer less 'n a hunerd," he heard himself saying. And if she had the nerve not to call him "Mister" after that one, he'd raise the ante until she did.

"Of course," he added, looking her squarely in the pince-nez, "there's trainin' expenses, gym expenses, travel expenses, manager's cut, handler's fee, sparrin' partners—they're gettin' harder fer me t' get since I developed my super punch—the word's gettin' around about that——"

"How often do you fight, *Mister* Bicek?"

There! He'd gotten that much out of her. He felt almost grateful. Some day he'd get her a couple free passes to the Garden.

"Ever' chance I get. If I can't get a ring match I pick up a street fight just t' keep in shape. I'm sharp as a razor right now."

He leaned the broom against the counter and jab-jabbed for her with his right.

"How often in the ring?" she asked, notebook poised. If this hunky thought he was going to be able to deny any of this later, he had another think coming. She retreated a step to give him more room.

"And you always get a hundred dollars?"

He leaned indolently against the counter.

"So help me."

"Why isn't your mother getting better attention then?"

As though she had heard, Mama Bicek groaned appropriately.

Bruno hung his head in mock repentance. The old lady had been doing that, sick or well, all her life.

"I spend it all on myself—I guess I'm just a mug."

He heard the door slam behind her, a proper slam; righteousness had been betrayed again.

Well, he reflected, she wasn't going to help the old lady anyhow; now she had a good excuse not to. He heard his mother call for water and brought her a glass. After she drank he sat unconcernedly on the side of the bed.

"T'morrow I get up," she told him. "Do a little work, feel better." She had the peasant faith in work as a cure-all. When a woman got sick all she had to do was work a little harder than usual, till the sick was gone. Not enough work was why she was sick—washing Bruno's dishes and sweeping the floor and selling a bottle of milk— Was that a day's work for a woman? No wonder she was sick. Not enough work to keep her well; not enough work ever to make her well again. If the other children had lived, there would be enough work. She heard a peddler passing in the alley and opened her eyes.

"Obarzanki! Obarzanki!"

A *zyd* selling bagles. Out in front a horn honked, and the boy straightened up, hoping Finger wouldn't honk again. Mama Bicek felt the bedspring give as he rose. All the health that had been denied her three other children had been given this one—it seemed to Mama Bicek—the only one who had lived past ten years. She heard the bell tinkle faintly as he closed the door behind him.

She turned and faced the wall, remembering a time when two policemen had come for him, their numbered badges and the flashlight on the wall. That had been the summer he was fourteen. On the cot on the other side of the room, he had pulled the covers over his head and feigned sleep.

"Get him up, Missis, or we'll get him up for you."

She had yanked the covers back and there he was, fully clothed, with blood on the front of his shirt.

"Just shootin' dice, Mom . . ." he had turned to the officers sullenly: "The fella got me in the game 'n I lost a autograph *Al Simmons* bat, 'n I hold the dice up to the light 'n sure enough, they was missouts, they was engineered, he couldn't have sevened with those in a month."

Mama Bicek had not understood. Two days later, when he was released, he had tried to explain. She had waved him away. Fourteen years old and he had thought nothing of being two days in a jail. She had taken no pleasure in him since. She had never been certain, since, whether his friends weren't detectives when they entered the store.

If they had stayed in the Old World, she felt, her son would have been a good son. There a boy had to behave himself or be put in the army.

"You! Bruno!" She called, to be certain he was gone.

Boys in the army were good boys. The army made them good. She turned painfully on her side and a car door slammed and he was gone again; for a day or two weeks or two months or forever. That was the way with poor folks' boys. She felt in the pocket of the army coat: the forty cents was gone, so he wouldn't be back that day. And the front door open. Well, what was there to take? A few day-old rolls? Would the driver come today or tomorrow? She pulled the coat over her head so as not to hear any who entered. Half in sleep and half in waking, she heard a cold wind moaning to itself through the alleyway. And heard an all-night rain begin.

The boy at the wheel of the car at the curb had a heart-shaped head with hair neatly parted in the middle. This was the Finger Idzikowski, so-called for his reputed ability to jinx anything, from fighters to race horses, by the simple expedient of pointing steadily, with the thumb and forefinger of the left hand, at the jinxee or a reasonable facsimile thereof. He surveyed Bruno critically.

"Jesus, Lefty, don't you shave no more? You look like you been in a battle. No wonder yer old lady got no customers left. Button yer barn at least."

Bruno grinned good-naturedly and shook hands with Casey Benkowski in the back seat.

"We're gonna need a strong back 'n a weak mind," Casey welcomed him. "Climb in."

Bruno clambered in beside the Finger, who gave him one last

disapproving up-and-down look. Finger always became fussy about appearance when he had the loan of his brother-in-law's car.

"Is that a relief shirt, Lefty?" he asked.

Bruno wore a blue workman's shirt from which the sleeves had been scissored roughly, faded green corduroys, and heavy boots re-enforced at the toes with steel washers. In his hand he held a pavement-colored cap with air holes punched in the top.

"It's my Lefty Bicek Helt' Shirt," he explained seriously to Finger now. He crossed his boots and pointed at the steel toes. "You don't like my shoes neither? Well, them's Lefty Bicek Helt' Shoes." He twirled the cap on his forefinger in a concentric circle. "See this? This is a Lefty Bicek Helt' Hat. Where we goin'? Whose jollopi?"

"The brother-law's," Finger answered, looking straight ahead and dawdling with the gadgets on the dashboard as though thinking of something else. "You've rode in her before. We drove you that time we fought the dago kid, that's how we made expenses, they give us bus fare—remember?" And added, without looking at Lefty and without enthusiasm, "Look you what Casey give me."

He pulled a catcher's mitt out of the side-pocket and laid it in Lefty's lap. Lefty recognized it as the glove which Casey had loaned Finger on the afternoon that Finger had been Lefty's battery mate in the victory over the Wonders. Across the thumb an autograph had been cut:

Ernie Schnozz Lombardi
Cincinnati Reds, 1937

"Where we goin', Case?" Bruno asked, full of wonder and doubt. "Do I get a autograph mitt too?"

"You get somethin' better. Start wheelin', Finger."

Finger wheeled down May Street toward Chicago Avenue. "You just tell me where you want to go, Case, 'n I'll tell you how many minutes: twenty miles? That's twenty minutes." He stepped on the gas till the car reached sixty, to illustrate his point. "How many minutes, that's how many miles." He slowed and wheeled around the corner of St. John Cantius onto Chicago Avenue.

Bruno didn't like the way Finger wheeled west, without a word from Benkowski, as though he had made his terms before he had honked for Bruno: here he was, going somewhere but he didn't know where, on some sort of cowboying job he didn't know a thing about. He took his sponge ball out of his pocket and worked the right hand nervously. Maybe Finger was going on a job for the sake of an autographed mitt and maybe he wasn't. But Bruno Lefty didn't do any strong-arming for the fun of it; nor even for a mitt.

"I don't know what you guys got cookin'," he told them both, "but I'm still takin' care of number one. I got a strong back but my mind ain't *that* weak. Where there ain't no payoff there ain't no Biceps."

"There's a payoff in gettin' money fights at the Garden," Benkowski reminded him. "There's a payoff in bein' president 'n treasurer of the Baldheads True American Social 'n Athletic Club."

Bruno looked blank. "What the hell is *that*?"

Casey leaned forward confidentially, like a professional bondsman. "That's the Warriors up-to-date. All a guy does is get his knob shaved by the barber 'n that's his initiation fee too, 'cause the barber's gonna buy us uniforms next year, 'n then the guy is a charter member. By another barber 'r at home don't count. So there ain't no more Warriors."

Bruno studied the Finger's bucktoothed profile to learn how much of this change Finger had already accepted; but the boy's face was a blank. Gently therefore Bruno reached over and raised the bleached yellow straw off the boy's head: the scalp had been shaven clean. Bruno replaced the hat reflectively; Finger's expression had not changed.

"Finger's secretary of the Baldheads, Left',"—Casey explained solemnly—"'n when I get you on at the Garden he's gonna handle the bucket 'n sponge 'n be your official hex-man. You want t' go at the Garden? I can get you on a week from Monday. Four rounds, twenty bucks."

Bruno Bicek felt a warm glow go through him from stomach to chest. But he had his own cunning, and concealed his own joy. "You guys 'r full of promises t'day," he observed, "tossin' autograph

mitts 'n ex-ecutive jobs 'n money fights around so easy. Ever'thin'
but ready cash. How much cut you gett'n off the barber for fixin'
him up with all this business? 'n who's gonna pay him for *my*
hairclip if I go along?"

"I'll take care of that, Left'," Casey said hurriedly— "All I get
out of it is the barber's word about the uniforms—that's my ambition, Left'—to manage a uniform team. I'm workin' my way up.
'n when we win maybe the barber slips me a fin. Politics, Lefty,
politics."

"'n the barber, he puts out for uniforms 'cause he wants us all t'
grow up strong 'n healthy I guess—is that *his* angle, Case?"

Benkowski chose to disregard Bruno's heavy-handed irony.

"Maybe it's the free advertisin', Left'," Finger put in innocently.
"Maybe the uniforms 'll say somethin' nice about Bonifacy on the
back, to vote for him for somethin'."

Casey spat over the side of the car as though in disgust, and
spoke with a wad of snuff working around his cheek.

"Don't let him kid you, Lefthander. He knows the score. The
Baldheads is a social 'n athletic club—like Bonifacy is a barber.
You c'n stay in 'r you c'n get out. If you're gonna get out, get out
now. 'n if you get out, I'll give Finger the Garden fight."

Bruno stayed silent while three images of himself careened upon
each other through the city of his mind: B. Bicek, president and
treasurer. Iron-Man Bicek in a red-sleeved uniform, hurling no-hit
ball against the Logan Squares. Bruno Lefty Biceps climbing
through the ropes in a red bathrobe at the City Garden with a
hurricane of applause coming across the ropes.

The last one did it.

"Count me in, Case."

"In you are. Give him the business, Finger."

"It's a slot machine," Finger explained. "Casey's cased the place.
A couple spooks runnin' a roadhouse with a gas pump out front.
I wait in the car 'n you'n Case go inside 'n when Case gives the
word, you yank the thing."

"What am I—Superman?" Bruno laughed at the image of himself

wrestling with a slot machine, feeling flattered by his appointment to the muscle stuff.

"Take the crank before we go in," Casey directed. "Use it fer a jimmy first 'n fer the convincer later—I'll take the shift extension in case they don't hold still. Have a shot?"

He came up with an unlabeled bottle and they passed it around. The afternoon sunlight flooded the streets. Bruno had never been this far west of the Triangle before, and a pang of anticipation, provoked by the liquor, warmed him. This was something bigger than fruit stealing on Division. This was big time. Then a slow thought broke over his mind, leaving a cold spot of fear in his stomach: What of the men who syndicated slot machines? That was something different than dealing with the police. The slot-machine syndicate was big business, and big business didn't fool.

"What about the syndicate, Case?" He asked as coolly as he could, looking at Finger to see if Finger had thought of that.

"Glad you asked that, Lefty," Benkowski said slowly, "it shows you're on them toes. But this is private stuff, it's a ringer the spooks been hidin' in the back. It ain't been emptied for a month, neither."

Bruno felt slightly reassured. "So long as them big guys don't get the idea somebody's tryin' to muscle in . . ."

"Forget it. I tell you they don't even know the machine is there. You think I'd fool with the big guys?"

Bruno's silence conceded that not even Benkowski was that punchy. But he felt the cold spot below his belt begin to swell as the distance between himself and home grew greater. When Finger wheeled southwest on U. S. 61, Casey said too casually, "It won't be long now," and Bruno reached for the bottle.

"Too much water gives lice on the belly," he philosophized uneasily, smacking his lips. Then he stole a glance at the Finger out of the corner of his eye. The Finger could keep a poker puss when he wanted all right.

"That moldy-lookin' mill up ahead, Finger," Casey said. "Turn in for gas, we need some anyhow. The spooks is footin' the bill."

Over a doorframe a legend read: OLD BLUE MILL. *Ladies Invited.*

And traces of blue still clung to the shingled arms of the phony mill above the shingled roof. The cottage below the mill had been constructed like something out of a Hollywood travelogue, complete with a wooden bridge. The stream beneath had long dried up, so that nothing but a line of tin cans showed where cool shallows once had run. The flies on the screen door hadn't moved in a week.

"Fill her up," Finger ordered the attendant, while Bruno climbed out carefully to conceal the crank in his corduroys. Casey moved ahead of him with two bulges below his sweater at the hips: one where the bottle rested, and one where the shift extension was held. This was an eighteen-inch hard-rubber lever, hollowed to fit over the gearshift, thus constituting a blackjack which the law couldn't call a concealed weapon. Inside, he followed Casey to a table in the rear.

"Give us a little check fer a big beer," Casey asked an over-weight Italian woman with crimpers in her hair.

"That's the spook who runs it," he informed Bruno when she was out of hearing. "Borrow me a greenie now 'n I'll show you the machine."

Bruno found a nickel in his pants pocket, and waited while Casey wound his way among chairs to the slot machine. He yanked the lever of it somewhere behind a mechanical piano, in order to show Bruno where it was, and returned to the table. Outside Bruno heard the gas burbling into the car. "The monkey crankin' the gas is the old lady's kid," Casey told him.

They had two beers and two shots apiece before Casey concluded that it was time. He waved Bruno toward the machine and waited, standing at the table, till he saw him crouching before it and heard Bruno begin prying at the iron base. It wouldn't be long. He took the extension out of his sweater and turned, to see the old woman peering into the gloom, trying to locate the other customer. A single yank of the crank told her, and her mouth opened wide to scream.

Casey slapped the rubber across her teeth. To Bruno, sweating in front of the machine, it sounded like a well-hit cue ball smack-

ing into fifteen pool balls to start a game of rotation. Embracing
the machine with both hands, then bending it back on its single
leg, he brought it off the floor, bringing part of the floor with it,
and stumbled backward holding it. He packed it under his arm
and Casey gave him interference toward the door. The woman
was through the door before them both, holding her apron to
her bleeding mouth and wailing. Bruno saw Casey reach her, pin
her arms, and hold her at the door while Bruno got through it
with the machine. Galloping heavily toward the car he heard a
sort of sickening splash, as though Casey had given it to her in
the gut, and the fall of her body and the slam of the door. The
attendant stood rigidly, pale and tense, against the pump where
Finger had put him.

Bruno hurled himself and the machine into the back seat, felt
Casey fall in beside Finger and Finger giving her the gas; at the
same moment the boy by the pump came up on the running board
with the pump handle. Bruno ducked. It ripped into the upholstery
and banged wildly about as the boy tried to control it with one
hand and hold the car door with the other. Bruno guarded his
head with the slot machine and dropped the boy with his left
between the eyes. He dropped half on the running board and
half onto the gravel driveway; then rolled on all fours onto the
drive with his hair in his eyes like a beaten dog's.

Bruno looked back as they got on the highway and saw him
trying to get to his knees: the sun was behind him and he looked
like a drunk trying to pray.

By the time they regained the city limits the sun had set and
Bruno had the machine apart in the back seat; he began tossing
strips of tin, stamped with lemons and plums, into every darkened
alleyway they passed. He ripped out the coin box and handed
it obediently to Casey, who emptied it behind the dashboard.

"We'll count it in the back by Mama Tomek's," he promised.
"You guys won't be sorry you give me a hand. Guys like the
barber 'r gonna find out: Benkowski ain't through, he's oney
beginnin'. Guys like you 'r good guys. Finger got the car, Lefty
got the muscle, I got the brains. If you guys wanted we c'd al-

ways have change, 'n not be takin' long chances like t'day for it neither. We c'd get them Warriors to quit matchin' pennies. If Lefty was president, that is, 'n Finger was sec'tary, 'n we had a real place t' meet. Then even Catfoot 'n Kodadek 'd have t' toe the line. They'd have t' do like Lefty told 'em 'r they couldn't be in. They wouldn't have no good place to nuts around, like us guys."

"They wouldn't do nothin' I said," Bruno observed reluctantly. "That Catfoot talks up t' me all the time, ever since Kodadek run me wit' the knife that time. He knows he got that screwy spitballer right behind him, he knows I know it too. They 're both older 'n me, Case, they'd do the opposite anythin' I told 'em."

"They got the barber the way you used t' have him, Casey," Finger advised Benkowski sorrowfully.

"I still got the barber," Casey persisted. " 'n better 'n the barber too. I got Frankie Figura. He c'd put that barber out of business so fast th' guy 'd have t' start sweepin' up his shop, t' get some customers in it t' make a livin'. You know, when a guy got a precinct captain like Frankie behind him, it's the same like havin' the alderman hisself."

"Would I get money fights regular then, Case?" Bruno asked.

Casey turned to Finger to assure Bruno, as though he were too weary of assuring the boy further himself.

"You tell him, Finger. He don't believe *me*."

"You'd be fightin' Collyseum windups, Lefthander," Finger said solemnly. "In six months you'd be fightin' Honeyboy Tucker."

"I don't want t' get brought along too fast," Bruno warned them both anxiously. "I won't be eighteen till Christmas, I got time, I ain't full-growed yet."

Finger squeezed Bruno's ribs with his free hand.

"Not a ounce o' fat on him, Casey," he advised professionally. "He'll be the size of Jeffries."

Bruno grunted. He didn't like to be touched by anyone. "I'll give that Tucker the ol' chancery," he mumbled resentfully, "I'll get in close 'n give him the ol' chancery. That's what I'll do. All the jigs, I'll give 'em the ol' chancery." He held the nape of

Finger's neck firmly with his right and feigned to crash the point of the jaw with the left.

"Careful you don't bust your hand on one of them jigs doin' that," Finger warned defensively. "Just use it on white guys best."

Bruno relaxed and spoke to himself aloud. "The ol' chancery's why they don't get up."

"You got to keep in shape more though," Finger suggested cautiously, "You get yourself trued up, 'n lay off that Polish pop by Rostenkowski's, 'n you'll ice that boogie for sure." He nudged Bruno familiarly. "Then the Collyseum fer us, kid—LEFTY BICEPS MATCHED WITH BILLY CONN! WINNER TO GET LOUIS BOUT! How's *that* sound, Left'?"

Bruno brightened. That sounded all right. In the back seat Benkowski maintained a strategic silence. He had lost his desire to talk when Bruno had mentioned "the old chancery"; the back of his own neck was still so sore he couldn't bend it to rest against the upholstery without feeling it halfway down his spine. Never trust a Mex, that was the moral to *that* experience. A Mex 'd give you the chancery and win your money afterward every time.

"Finger," Bruno asked after a minute, as though he had spent the minute arriving at an idea all his own, "Just for the fun— say the Louis one. I ferget how it goes."

"BRUNO LEFTY BICEPS BATTERS LOUIS TO FLOOR! CHAMPION RUNS OUT ON RE-MATCH!" Finger bawled above the traffic's howling.

It took another minute for Bruno to digest that. Then: "Say it the *real* way now, Finger. You know."

"POLISH WHITE HOPE WINS TITLE! LOUIS DECLINES RETURN BOUT!"

Bruno looked thoughtful. "Think of the herrings in *that*. I wouldn't mind gettin' punchy for a cut of *that*. Dames don't care if a guy's puss is pushed in, so long as they ain't no dent in his wallet. I'd open up a fancy poolroom 'n bar 'n all the boys 'd come around 'n spend their *gotówka* 'n there ain't no trouble. Even cops 'd come around 'n Case 'd be the alderman by then, he'll tell 'em they can stay around 'n have a beer so long as they don't try no smart copper tricks, this is Bruno Lefty's place. So the old gumshoes you, they sneak right out 'n never come back, they run 'n tell the Cap, 'Lay off that Bruno Lefty, Cap, he's straight as his own cues 'n doin' fine'. —How's *that*, Finger? I can say it too!"

Bruno grinned from cheekbone to cheekbone, a wide white grin.

"Yeh," Finger agreed, "'n we'd get one of them yachts in the Linc'n Park lagoon you—we'd get a couple movie actresses out there 'n there wouldn't be no heat pullin' up 'n some flatfoot hollerin', 'Pull over, you, the Cap wantsa talk with you,' 'n spoil all the good old fun."

Bruno exulted inwardly: he had just retired undefeated with a wad of twenty-dollar bills, had married that little Sylvia Sydney and had just told the Potomac Street Station Captain, Tenzcara, where he could get off.

"But maybe I ought t' change my name before then," he reflected aloud, "to somethin' like 'Stanley Ketchel Second.' He was a Polack too." He turned to Casey for advice. "What you say, Casey? How's *that* for a good old name?"

Casey had no interest in daydreams. "I say let's get half a dog by Rostenkowski's," he urged sullenly, "'n go whorehoppin' afters by Mama Tomek."

"Yeh," Finger agreed readily, "Let's break the old monotony, Left'."

"I can't t'night, fellas. I got a date with the widow's kid."

"You score yet?"

"Maybe t'night. It looks pretty good."

"Let us know when you do," Finger suggested. "Then we c'n all score."

He had been out of the Triangle and into the world and he had made good. He entered the widow's poolroom first to make certain that both she and her dimwit boy were there instead of upstairs, and bought a five-cent cigar.

"You work?" Widow Rostenkowski asked hopefully, remembering half-forgotten debts.

Bruno considered his answer before replying, chewing the cigar without lighting it.

"I'm bein' managed now, Widow," he explained, "You see, a fella with money back of him is takin' me under his wing."

The widow appeared puzzled.

"This is *business*? Fighting is *business*?"

"Fight business, that's right." It wouldn't hurt to start spreading the word around. "I'm a pug now. There's money back of Bruno Lefty now."

"Is *crooked* business?"

"Ever'thin's crooked, Widow."

The Widow Rostenkowski shook her head dubiously and he left with the deliberate pace of the man of affairs. Once out of her sight he dodged around the back and through an unpainted gate that bore a sprawling warning:

BE AWARE OF THE DOG

And skipped softly up the widow's back steps.

The widow's girl heard his two-step-at-a-time approach and opened before he knocked. She had been sleeping, and the freshness of her met him in the doorway. She grabbed the cigar out of his teeth by way of greeting and he tousled her hair; it was chestnut brown and set off the pallor of her face. Over one ear a bright ribbon flowered.

At seventeen Steffi Rostenkowski was one of those women of the very poor who feign helplessness to camouflage indolence. She had been called upon, as a child, following her father's death, for so many duties, the family's circumstances being then so precarious, that she had early learned evasion. She had, early, found ways of relieving herself of the most unpleasant tasks. Her indolence was that of one who fears that, if she fulfills one duty well and swiftly, she will be called upon immediately for a less pleasant one. So the girl had made it her habit to do all things slowly and halfheartedly where they did not immediately concern her own pleasure. She divided the tasks of the small home between her mother and her brother. Udo did the dishes and she got the credit. Udo washed the floors and Steffi got money for a movie for reward. Udo cleaned the windows, inside and out, and was

then sent downstairs to help tend the poolroom because Steffi
wanted to be alone in order to read.

"Tell Ma the windows 're done," she told him, and Udo told
his mother the windows were done. Later, when someone had to
beat the front-room carpet, Steffi complained, "Let Udo do it, Ma,
I done the windows."

She enjoyed shopping. Though she could neither cook well,
sweep well nor wash dishes well, she could spend half a day
pricing groceries and buying useless trinkets at the five-and-dime.
She had long brown indolent eyes, and all the life of her thin
body was gathered into them. As Bruno's fingers stirred her hair
she smelled his body's strength, and her eyes shuttered defensively.

They had been born two months apart on the same street, had
played Charley Cross the Water and Fox in the Box on one leg
a thousand times down Noble Street. Had saved potatoes together
in the corner fireplug and had hidden maps there too, for treasure
hunting. Had kneeled on winter mornings in the same pew at St.
Bonifacius. He had swung her on the swings at Eckert Park and
had taken her, one night when they were twelve, to Schwante's
Family Theatre—All Seats 10¢, over near Santa Maria Addolorata.
She had preferred the playgrounds and the ten-cent shows to the
streets. He himself had never liked being on a playground, for
fear the fellows would see him there. Playgrounds were for girls
and sprouts.

Now, for the first time, they saw each other. She stood smiling
wryly before him, under a bleeding heart in an oval frame, knowing
why he had come. Somewhere in the room a fly without wings
began beating itself against a screen. For one moment, as she
stood against him, his courage failed and he would have liked
to continue the make-believe of mussing her hair: the recollection
of his acts of the afternoon restored his courage. He put the
unlit cigar back between his teeth and saw her walking slowly,
like a sleepwalker, one hand on her forehead, to the corner armchair. There she sank down weakly, not needing him as he needed
her.

"I feel dizzy," she said, "My head's goin' 'round the world."

There was no other place to go now. There was only the chair, and she waited for him in it. He came to her and placed his hands under her armpits, and she hoped uselessly for the sound of her mother's foot on the stair. She pushed his hands off and averted her eyes: she was crying inwardly, at the accomplished act. Her hands gripped the arms of the chair fiercely, that he might not raise her to him; he could not loosen her grip on the chair.

Outside, the evening's first arc lamp came on. Someone in the street was roller-skating on a single skate; and the single clack of a billiard ball sounded from below. He saw her dimly before him and sensed the city outside waiting for them both. Saw the green-plumed flash of a Chicago Avenue trolley a block away and heard the girl begin to plead indistinctly in Polish. He raised the chair then, Steffi and all, and slung both onto the disheveled couch.

The chair clattered to the floor, like a chair clattering in another room, and she sprawled on her side with her plaid skirt flung to her knees. He caught her hand when she tried to smooth it down and placed both her arms about his neck. When she felt her arms about him she began to draw them back but felt his mouth, hot and sweet, on hers: and let everything be then as he wished. Felt his knee coming up between her thighs and so held him all the tighter, being afraid. He did not loosen the skirt until he sensed that the hands about his neck were there of their own accord.

"I ain't got it in me to fight you off no more," he heard her confess at last.

Later the fly without wings returned. He saw it against the screen and crushed it there with his palm.

"You got blood out of him," Steffi said wistfully, as though thinking of something else.

From her there had been neither blood nor tears. Though inwardly she bled and wept.

The next time he heard the clack of the cueball below he

said, "That must be my manager waitin'." He left her in the darkened room, flooded by the arc lamp's light.

"I'll make it up to her," he planned hurriedly on the way down the back stairs. "I'll take her to Riverview."

II

The Trouble with Daylight

HE WALKED beneath the shadow of the El. Through the sickness and heat of his third summer he had slept quietly only under the shadow of the Division Street station. In the heart of the city, in the heat of midsummer, the platform had sheltered him. Now he remembered the sun as a hostile thing coming between El ties; remembered sunlight as others recall it seen first through trees or climbing vines.

The ties had contracted, expanded in the heat, shimmering down at him all that summer. He had sensed the gleam of the rails, heard the clatter of many locals, and associated that gleam and that clatter with his father's piano-accordion. Both had glittered and blared down at him from great heights, moving constantly, making him want to run a little way off. Later he had learned not to fear the accordion, for all its brave noise.

His preference for shadows remained. Sunlight and daytime were hostile things.

Even by night he preferred the tunnel of the El to the narrow walks of the Triangle. As a child he had learned that the safest place to play was beneath the El. For the streets belonged to streetcars and walks to people who lived in houses and not behind stores or above poolrooms. Nobody but pigeons owned the littered places under the steep Division Street steps. Nobody owned it. And from beneath it a small boy could hear conductors call something in English; different conductors but always the same word; could see feet coming down with no one seeing him watch at all. That was the safest part. Nobody came there to make you play in the sun; nobody could find you when you slept, an underfed, shoeless six-year-old of the cageworked city's curbs and walks. The cars rolled assuringly overhead; in sleep he had heard them pass.

On nights of snow or rain or sleet, when Division was a sewer and Potomac Street a creek, it remained dry under the platform steps. On such nights, when he was almost old enough for long pants and the little room back of the bakery was so crowded with stale loaves and *obarzanki* there was scarcely room to move about, Catfoot or Fireball Kodadek or Finger always had a pair of dice or a deck of worn cards; the light from the bulb midway up the steps came down across their shoulders as they played. For lack of money, they played for chances to mock each other: the loser had to dance foolishly about for a minute with one thumb on the point of his cap and the other on his buttocks, making himself as obscene, before others, as the light from above permitted.

"Funny thing," Bruno recollected now, "how old Catfoot use' t' try t' lose all the time."

On other nights they stole apples and potatoes and what they couldn't eat they stored in fireplugs, in order not to have to go home for supper. They lived on the streets around stove-heated rooms; the rooms were the last place to go at night and the first to get out of next morning. They were in the way in the rooms.

They took short cuts, across the deserted playground, in order to lie on their bellies beneath the El, with a stolen b-b gun between the four of them, waiting for rats to come to the puddles to drink. When a rat was hit he went straight up, four feet into the air, running on air, forepaws going furiously all the way up and all the way down till he hit earth and was gone. Nothing like that could happen on a playground. The children of the poor preferred the crowded adventure of the alleyways to the policed safety of the playgrounds and settlements.

Older men, and women and children, walked hurriedly under the tracks, taking short cuts to barroom and Mass, trying to get back onto the open walks before a train came by. But Bruno Bicek was one who used the open walks only when he couldn't take his time. When he was in no especial hurry, which was always, he felt the roar of the passing cars above like a wall between himself and the world. A long secure tunnel of sound, away from the sunlit or moonlit or rain-wet streets. In the heart of the city, then, he walked alone. In the heat of midsummer or the pit of midwinter. But especially was this so on days of fog or starless nights.

He fumbled in his frayed pockets for tobacco, found tobacco crumbs instead, and chewed them deliberately.

"Next time I get hold of a tailor-made special I won't smoke 'er right off," he planned, "I'll save 'er 'n after a while I'll eat 'er." A "special" was any eleven-cent-per-pack cigarette. "I'll get a whole pack of specials 'n call 'em 'Lefty Bicek's Camels,'" he decided. "I'll write that down right on that good old package."

His life was a ceaseless series of lusts: for tobacco so good he could eat it like meat; for meat, for coffee, for bread, for sleep, for whisky, for women, for dice games and ball games and personal triumphs in public places. Day and night, one or all of these rode him, and was never fully satisfied even for a while; they could no more be satisfied than they could be evaded.

He walked only from the waist down, the whole torso resting, without effort, on the loose-muscled movement of the hips.

Reared in fear of cold and hunger, he retained a wistful longing for the warmth and security of the womb; there it was always warm. It felt like a half-memory in him when he came to any dark windless place; he could not recall a time when he had not preferred silence and darkness to daylight and struggle. He could see almost as well at night, with his pale Tartar eyes, as he could at noon, so that he sometimes boasted, "That's why I'm just a Rover boy, fellas, I like to rove at night."

Now he saw the heavy, regular, riveted beams, and a small junk fire smoldering near Chicago Avenue; closed his eyes as he walked, knowing the way so well. The early autumn dark felt physically good, like a warm bath after a day shoveling snow in open streets, a thing good in itself. When he opened his eyes sparks were drifting down from between the ties, floating toward the littered places where the gray cats lived.

In the half-darkened Division Street *gospodas* beer was a nickel a glass and the big bass jukes played only Polish songs. Three oversize Polish piano-accordions played "I Want Some Sea-Food, Mama," at the same time that the juke played the "Po Zawabie Polka," each trying to drown out the other so that you couldn't hear what the drunk beside you, with his head on the bar, was trying to sing at all. But you could tell what the girls were singing, and if you didn't smile back they stamped their feet angrily at you.

He had once seen a wolf's head in a Milwaukee Avenue taxidermist's window, above a bare varnished floor with nothing around but a couple chairs and an empty paint can lying on its side. He had thought dimly of himself, since, as a hunter in a barren place. "I been hungry all my life, all the time," he told himself, "I never get my teeth into anythin' all my own."

Too hungry for the arid place he'd been born in. For lights, music, the women of the *gospodas*, all these awakened the hunger in a man. The same hunger that might, wolflike, lie sleeping for an hour or a day. Or else waken and keep a man in trouble the rest of his life.

Things you couldn't live another hour without, that were yours and yet not yours: a steady job, a steady girl, a clean place to sleep where you could be with the girl without her whole family and your whole family and every sprout in the block knowing exactly where the two of you were and maybe listening at the partition too. And jeering the girl on the street about it an hour after. These were things that made you a man if you possessed them, or a wolf—if you were born where such things were only to the hunter.

And there were different hunters as there was different game. The informer and the pay-roll bandit were equally hunters. The barber hunted women for the woman called Mama Tomek, and

Mama T. sheltered a little Jew called Snipes. And all were equally hunters; though the Jew hunted only cigarette butts and a place to sleep. The alderman's brother-in-law, at the Potomac Street station, sought convictions; and Bibleback Watrobinski, with his hair in his eyes, sought converts to the church in order to save his own harassed soul. Both were equally hunters.

His thoughts returned to Steffi. If a girl was really a good girl she ought to have sense enough not to bother with a Polack who had barely finished eighth grade, just because he'd been born on the same block. And hadn't had a job, outside of freight handling, since.

And freight handling wasn't a real job, because you never knew from day to day whether you had it or not. You walked over to Kinzie Street to save carfare, with your lunch under your arm, and hung around half a day waiting for them to tell you either to get yourself a truck or go home. So the next day you went with only two sandwiches and a date with Steffi at six, and had to work sixteen straight hours and leave her standing up.

She hadn't forgiven him for that one for a week; she hadn't understood, at first, that he had had no way of getting away without losing the hours already put in. The shippers were never able to tell a man how long he was going to work because they never knew themselves. They unloaded the cars, loaded them again, trying to get everything into the least possible number; it was well worth their while to save one car even though it meant paying six men for an extra hour each. They did not pay for the hours that elapsed while the men waited for the extra hour.

Standing Steffi up hadn't bothered him too much, however. That was good for a dame, kept her from getting stuck up. Nor was it the way you had to work for that forty cents an hour or their way of never letting you know whether you were on the job or not, that had made him throw it up. He hadn't done that until they'd cut the rate to thirty. A few men with families had stayed in the face of the cut, feeling that thirty was better than nothing at all. The others had left, and the next morning the company had a full gang working at the new rate. They had picked men off the street, from the agencies around Grand and Halsted and from the Green Street Shelter—any man with two arms and two legs could learn how to shove a truck, and the right place to shove it, in five minutes.

"*Grzmoty zabili diabla,*" he hummed idly to himself, "*a diabla zabili rzyda.*"

It was the barber's tune. "When the thunder kills a devil." He hummed it without remembering where he had heard it.

Why hang around a crumby relief station, with a mob of crumby greenhorns, for a fifty-five a month pick-and-shovel job, when you could get by never going near the relief, beating some sprout at rotation in back of the widow's for a quarter a game or pitching softball on Saturday afternoons for a dollar a man or league ball on Sundays; or by picking up a half dollar off Mama Tomek for bringing her a couple customers?

Once Mama Tomek had given him a horse called Lonely Road, when he'd had no money to play a horse himself. So he'd given it, in turn, to the ticket taker at the Little Pulaski, who was the wife of the owner of the show. She had played ten across the board, the horse had won in a photograph finish, and Bruno had been awarded ten dollars for his advice.

When that was gone he had stopped by the poolroom and shot a free game with Steffi while her mother was upstairs and then had asked the girl to loan him a dollar.

"Ask your old lady to borrow you out a buck," he had suggested.

"She'll want to know what for."

"Tell her it's for a special intention."

"But she knows I done five 'Our Fathers' 'n five 'Hail Marys' Sunday toward it, so she'll think I really been up to something since if I need a buck so soon afters—she won't let me out of the house all week if I give her that one."

"Don't tell her nothin' then. Just hook it."

"I wouldn't steal from Ma. You shouldn't ask me. I don't earn nothin' for her. Least I could do is not steal off her."

"You'll pay it back. It's just borrowin'. I'll borrow it back to you before she misses it."

"What's the matter with your own old lady? Borrow off her."

"She'd miss it sooner 'n yours. Don't you trust me?"

"Where would you get it to pay back, Bunny?"

"Never mind where. I'd just get it."

"Stealin'?"

"I said I'd get it, didn't I?"

"You always say that. 'n you never have a dime."

"I had a ten-spot last Saturday."

"That's why I didn't see you till it was spent."

"Forget I even said anything." He had thrown his cue across the table and turned away: she saw him going, his cap too far back on his head and his shoulders like a wall.

"Bunny!"

He had turned toward her, in the doorway, waiting; she had seen there was no use moving toward him. She had gone to the cash register instead.

"I'll make that up to her, too," he resolved now. "I'll take her to community singin' on double-feature night. She's a *good* girl."

But what could you do with a good girl once she was yours? You couldn't keep on just sleeping around, above a poolroom or on the beach or in a corner as though she were some Clark Street tramp. If you did you'd make a Clark Street tramp out of her. He decided fiercely that no one else was going to sleep with her ever; as though others, unseen, were already challenging his exclusive right to any girl.

"I'll make it *all* up. I'll take her on the *Bluestreak*."

But he remained troubled. She had put trust in him, who had no trust in himself. He felt irritated with her for that; a girl ought not to trust anyone these days. Why should she trust him any more than he trusted the barber, he wondered as he walked. How could you trust the barber, who was nobody's friend, when you couldn't trust Benkowski, who was anybody's friend? You couldn't trust the barber because he kept Mama T. running a fourth-rate house by the Northwestern tracks, because he never took chances and yet would buy anything, from a bicycle to a radio, if it wasn't too hot. And he always knew, somehow, what was hot and what had cooled off. He knew the right people, he knew too much. And you couldn't trust a Benkowski because he didn't have anything. You couldn't trust the ones with brains, because they had them, and you couldn't trust the ones without, because they didn't.

"All the hoods on Division got guts," Benkowski had once told him—"but they got no brains to go with them. If they had the brains they wouldn't be hoods, they'd be like Bonifacy. How many guys, beside me, you think got brains in the whole Triangle, Left'?" Benkowski had asked.

Bruno considered the answer now: the alderman had brains, the democratic committeeman had brains, One-Eye Tenczara at Potomac Street had brains. Even the precinct captain, Figura, had some brains. And the barber had brains or he wouldn't be getting twenty cents off every two dollars that Mama Tomek's women earned. But that was all. That covered the ward. That's all the brains there were between Chicago Avenue and Division Street. That took care of all the penny matchers, all the jackpot sneaks, all the buck priests, the Gallaghers just off the boat, the bartenders and all the spooks on W.P.A. That took care of the widow and her half-wit kid Udo and that good-looking little Steffi R. That took care of Bruno Bicek's old lady for living her life behind Bicek's Imperial Half-Price Bakery. It took care of Finger Idzikowski for training to be a hex-man by pointing at fellows from the Polish Wonders to make them lose their next game. It took care of Fireball Kodadek for practicing a spitball the year round, with a dime-store rocket against a warehouse wall, when spitballing hadn't been allowed in the majors since the Dodgers had released Burleigh Grimes. That took care of Bibleback for thinking he was going to make a living for the whole year by peddling tomatoes during the summer, when he didn't have either a wagon or a license. It took care of Knothole Chmura from the Viaduct for trying to stay off relief by selling song sheets in front of Goldblatt's with one knee knocked a little against the other to give the impression he was lame without making it look too lame—in case a citizen dress man from the Potomac Street station was on the prowl for an arrest.

It had taken good care of Dumb Kunka and Poor Andy Bogats, the night Kunka had shot the cop. Bruno remembered Andy lying alone in the front room of his mother's house the night after he and Kunka had burned: the yellow all-night flares of the vigil lights and the hoarse sounds of the drinking in the kitchen. Andy's forehead and nose were burned a rust-yellow and the cheeks were sunken, as though he had taken it too hard, and there were great dark pouches under his eyes. Bruno had remembered him as a grinning, high-spirited, round-cheeked eighteen-year-old. The man in the casket had looked forty-five.

The single-car local to Humboldt Park slowed up overhead and clattered lamely west; to the boy's ears the clatter became a crescendo of applause. He jabbed with his right and threw the left—that's the hand they were cheering. A right to the heart and a left to the jaw. He bobbed, ducked, covered, swung and straightened up: the applause was faint and far away and then it was gone. He shoved his hands down his pockets and shuffled on.

There was only the dumb September dark about him and the places where everything looked the same as always and so looked a little like he'd always wanted them to; a fellow didn't get so mad at himself when he was alone like this. This way things didn't seem to matter, as they did at the sidewalk shed when everybody had a pair of dice and nobody had a dime; or when shooting pool with Steffi when the fellows weren't around.

"It's best for a Polack who ain't got much not to think too much about gettin' more," he philosophized easily. "After all, I got a place to sleep 'n there's still a couple cans on the shelf. I'm settin' pretty you." First thing you know, if a fellow got too big for his shoes, he'd wind up with some Dago judge throwing the book at him. "It's a free country. You always got enough to eat 'n a place 'sleep." He felt pleased with himself for having thought of that; it was always easier to think of such answers in the dark. Then you could feel yourself not caring so much after all, like just before falling asleep to dream you were driving a cream-colored roadster like those the state police drove.

Bruno Bicek from Potomac Street had his own cunning. He'd argue all day, with anyone, about anything, in daylight, and always end up feeling he'd won, that he'd been right all along. He'd refute himself, in daylight, for the mere sake of an argument.

But at night, alone, he refuted no one, denied nothing. He saw himself close up and clearly then, too clear for any argument. As clear, as close up, as the wolf's head in the empty window.

That was the trouble with daylight.

He started down the rickety steps, to the shed beneath the walk, two at a time; then paused midway, his head a foot below sidewalk level, to pull up the brim of his cap. Heard dice scurrying across a wooden floor; they would be shooting by flashlight.

A warehouse basement served for a wall on one side and the sidewalk for a roof; the dirt wall facing the street had been re-enforced with planks and the alley side was of dirt. The side away from the street was open, but lay in the warehouse shadow. A flashlight full in his face blinded him for a moment as he entered, then was taken away.

A dozen youths huddled about the dice, but Bruno became most aware of a shadow within the shadows: Kodadek, six feet and five inches, and a bare one hundred and fifty pounds, fondling the catcher's mitt that Benkowski had bestowed upon Finger the preceding afternoon.

"Hi! Fire!" Bruno greeted him. The shadow smacked its fist into the mitt for reply.

Hovering about the players, in faded overalls re-enforced at the knees, was the boy called Bibleback. His hair was uncut for weeks and he watched the dice more intensely than anyone, although he—and the shadow—were the only ones not playing. When the dice came around to the youth who held the flashlight, Bibleback hurried to relieve him of the light while he rolled. Every once in a while he tossed the hair back out of his eyes with a nervous jerk. Bibleback never gambled.

"Not gamblin' awakens certain nobilities in yer mind," he was fond of saying; but since he never had anything to gamble with anyhow, it was hard to tell of what he was thinking. Bruno went to the window that opened onto the underside of the staircase.

"You want the dice, Left'?" Bibleback asked in the dark. He was always one to see to everything. "It's yer turn if you want 'em, after Catfoot."

"I'll sell 'em fer a dime," Bruno offered from the window.

Catfoot Nowogrodski was taking his time; the flashlight beam was held on his palm as he shook, and he shook noiselessly. When he rolled the dice out of his hand at last they went noiselessly across the wood. He sevened. In the dark he was laughing noiselessly.

"Boy, what a greasy shake," someone said admiringly.

"But you can't sell 'em unless you rolled awready, you can't just walk in 'n sell a hand like that, Left'." Bible was indignant. The flashlight went out and Bruno sensed Catfoot moving across the floor; he walked as soundlessly as he rolled.

"You're gonna get yourself shot some day, prowlin' around on yer toes all the time, Cat," Bible admonished him.

Catfoot N., his face sallow and aquiline, with red dice hanging for luck from his belt and his hatbrim turned up in front, paused in the doorway a moment to look pleased at the warning.

"I been doin' things soft all my life," he explained softly. "The old man 'd come in blind 'n I'd be scared t' roll over in bed, he'd be hollerin' so, 'n the old lady 'd just hold her breath hopin' she wouldn't get beat. I got t' be like her, good at stayin' out of sight; before I started in school even, I walked quiet 'n kept out of the way 'cause I found out, that's how you don't get caught."

Bibleback was at his side, advising him in deadly earnest. "You'll get youself shot all the same, Cat. Let them milk bottles alone."

Catfoot grinned. He spoke in a lisping whisper. "I got butter 'n cheese by a place once you, 'n a pint bottle from *whipp'n cream.* You—*whipp'n cream.*" There was a faint creaking midway up the stairs. Bruno turned and Cat was gone.

"You can't sell the dice till you've . . ." Bibleback began.

"I'll give 'em to you for free."

"But I don't play no more, Left'— Don't you remember how I quit all evil ways that time?" Bible was shaking with excitement, as though his salvation depended upon proving his purity to Bruno Bicek. A half-dozen voices murmured irritably.

"Keep it down to a scream, Jerk."

Bruno turned his back on the boy without reply. He didn't feel like arguing with screwloose sprouts tonight. Tonight, right now, he had something to think out. Penny craps was all right for Knothole Chmura and John from the Schlitz Joint, but he'd go along with Benkowski and be playing silver-dollar blackjack with the precinct captain. He'd be playing fifty-cent poker, in the flat the barber kept, while these farmers were still matching nickels on the steps of St. Bonifacius. He listened to scraps of conversation absent-mindedly, troubled by Kodadek's silence. The boys were ribbing Kodadek carefully, their voices jocular and coaxing.

"Ol' Fireball gets this crow t' come up 'n look at his books you— like a Nort'western co-ed she looked, her hair done up in the back 'n ever'thin'—'n dey get in da f——— house 'n dey ain't a book in da f——— place 'n she says where's d' books you? Ol' Fireball he just says O dem—dere out gettin' rebinded. You."

"But wait you—this is the fix—he brings her up t' the barber's flat ever' day almost after that 'n then he finds out her old man is a Pinkerton. So what does he do, he tells her she should meet a friend of his, th' marryin' kind—'n he passes her on t' Knothole 'n don't even tell about the old man. So Knothole says his right name 'n where he lives 'n how the cops slugged him that time. 'n now she's knocked up 'n is Knot nervous you, he got no dough 'n she knows where he lives. A Pinkie you, a guy McMurray 'r somethin', a regular copper you, she's gonna tell him where Knot lives."

"I'd like t' take up fingerprintin' 'n detectin' like them Pinkies— I'd come home with the old magnifyin' glass 'n find Fire's fingerprints on the old lady's fanny, I'd have him dead to rights you."

Fireball listened in the dark, with his fist in Finger's mitt. He had once pitched a shutout for St. John's over St. Bonifacius, when he'd weighed a hundred and ninety-two pounds; calling him anything but Fireball now implied that he was no longer the man he had been that afternoon; it would be the same as asking him what was the matter with him. And there was nothing the matter with him—said Fireball. He was just taking off a little fat from around the waist was all. "I'm on the whisky cure," he would say bitterly, and drain a half pint without taking his lips from the bottle.

Yet he never became drunk.

The more he drank the thinner he got, the soberer he became, and the more desperate in his hopes and jealousies.

"I thought Fireball used t' be mean when he weighed two hunerd," Bruno once complained, "but he gets meaner with every weight he loses." To Bruno, a "weight" was a pound.

Fireball Kodadek's hands were long and almost fleshless; he pounded his fist into the pocket of the mitt, seeing another whole summer come and go without starting a single game, just because he'd taken a little fat off his stomach. He could have been pitching into this mitt himself, and not for just an inning. Not for just fielding practice. For keeps, for thirteen dollars a side, for a full game against the Intrepids or the Logan Squares. Now, when an American League scout walked by, Bruno Bicek would be burning them in to Finger and Kodadek would be sitting on the bench in his street clothes waiting to pinch-hit for some feeb like Bibleback.

Fireball Kodadek, sick in his lungs and sick at heart, longed for one last summer of being alive in the only way he had ever felt he was living: pitching shutout ball for St. John's over St. Bonifacius. That afternoon had been his life, and the big-league scout wasn't coming by now after all. Everyone else would be getting jobs and getting married, getting to be big-time bookies and politicians, getting the women and getting the money, getting autograph mitts and free beer at picnics, going to weddings and dances and parties, getting what they wanted and going where they pleased. While all he'd be having would be a few corny wisecracks from a mob of smalltime crap players until it was time for the shovel in his face. Then a couple of them would toss in a few empty pints with the dirt. That's the only place he'd be going.

If he got any sicker, he decided vaguely, he'd go to a doc. The decision was swamped by a sudden sick rage against Bruno Bicek, so that he hurled the glove into the center of the dice player's circle and turned up the steps after Catfoot. Catfoot knew whether he or the lefthander was the better man, even though the dice players had forgotten.

The players turned their quips and inventions on Bruno.

"When Lefty takes his shoes off you, I bet the widow's kid gets that footy smell."

Bruno defended Steffi. As best he was able.

"I don't take 'em off."

"Wow! He joops 'er with his boots on!"

Finger struck a dramatic pose, playing the flash on his own face, and recited:

> He died game, boys, I'll tell you
> He kept his boots on till he blew

And added seriously, "I do *my* wolfin' by Riverview at the roller rink. No poolroom brats fer me. You c'n bring yer own lunch 'n stay all day you, they never run you off."

"Skatin's no good fer wolfin'," John from the Joint advised. "They go by too fast."

"Is 'at so?—you should see the jump I picked me up once there. The dew was still on it."

"Some of them cherries 'r gettin' moldy on the bough these days."

"I bet she was a deadly."

"Best place fer wolfin' is Danceland," John said authoritatively; he was an undersized youth in his early twenties who lived in winter by setting pins in a Milwaukee Avenue bowling alley and in summer by caddying. "Tell you who goes there. Widows, divorcees, old maids, blimps cheatin' on their husbands 'n boy friends. It's not where they have that innocent act like the Aragon."

"I bet all the old bags go there."

"Yeh. But there's enough to go around."

Finger, offended by the others' oversight of his preference for the rink at Riverview, derided John's Danceland.

"It's just a elephant's graveyard fer whores is all. No original stuff like by the rink. 'n the rink's cheaper too. All they do fer a dime by Danceland is play the title of the song 'n they call that a dance."

"Best time fer wolfin's Christmas Eve—that's the night the quails 'r givin' it out fer Christmas presents."

The game was being forgotten, and the flashlight went out.

"That's right. Save the batt'ry."

"No. Leave it on. Here. Hang it on a nail. When it burns out I'll go by the five-'n-dime." Bruno recognized Corner-Pockets' voice. He hung the flash on a nail against the bricks of the warehouse wall and the beam fell on a pack of cards littering the planks of the floor. Pockets could bring anything out of the five-and-dime small enough to stuff under his shirt. "I c'd do a clog dance 'n the stuff 'd never fall out," he liked to boast. Bruno crouched and began making a deck of the cards scattered in the flashlight's beam.

As he crouched the staircase creaked. Catfoot? Waiting all this time? Listening? To hear what? Their voices came down indistinctly to him; then were gone down Noble Street. He looked at the others to learn whether they had heard: Nothing. Sprouts heard nothing. But he knew somehow, as he resumed making the deck, that he was going to go on needing Casey Benkowski.

"What I wanna know," Finger was persisting, "*is* they really such a thing as a Chink whorehouse? 'r is that a theory?"

"Sure is, down by Nineteenth 'n Dearborn above a cigar store," Punch-drunk Czwartek answered. "They stand behind the cigar counter 'n say 'two-bits lookee, four bits feelee, six-bits doee.'"

"*Boy,* I'd like to go to one of *them,*" Finger said credulously. He never doubted anyone's inventions, yet retained a craftiness of his own. "I'm like a moron you," he added now, "I like a dame with hair on her arms. It arouses the beast in me. Why is that?"

"I dunno. It's like mind over matter sort of. Speakin' of Chinks, where's Knothole t'night?"

"Ain't seen him in three days."

"Maybe he's settin', you."

"Naw, Knothole don't nuts around since the heat give him the beatin'," John from the Joint put in. "I seen him down by the bowlin' alley. Every night he's hangin' around that nickel machine with two nickels in his paw. He counts the times it's played 'n when he thinks it's due to pay off he puts in one of the nickels. Trouble is, he's gettin' so squirrelly he loses count."

The boy with the uncut hair and the intense eyes wandered over to where Bruno crouched.

"The six of hearts 'n jack of clubs is missin'," he offered without being asked.

Bruno did not answer. That was Bibleback for you every time though, giving free advice. He'd get them all in trouble some day with that flannel-tongued trap of his. He had once stolen his old man's W.P.A. check, and after he and Bruno and Finger had spent it together, Bible had confessed to Father Francis and hadn't been in trouble since. But he was still repentant, although that had been six years before, when all three had been eleven.

"Is that my *snus*?" he asked, seeing Bruno's snuffbox on one of the cards. It was his way of asking for a pinch.

"Lefty, tell me somethin' I want t' know," he asked after putting the pinch under his lip and returning the box; he put one hand on Bruno's shoulder to divert him from his counting. Bible pushed a truck, the hand was calloused and cracked; Bruno resented the hard-working feel of it unreasoningly, as though it were a personal reproach. He laid the deck down deliberately, yet with resignation. The sprout wanted talk, he'd get it.

"You still workin' steady for Apex on Kinzie, Bible?"

"Sure. T'ree—four days a week 'n night school I'm goin' to too— pretty soon I am anyhow— Don't you like workin' no more, Left'? Like when me 'n you pushed sixteen hours straight that time fer the Santa Fe 'n had t' eat pushin'? Know what my department is now, Left'?—*Pers'nal effecks in consolidated cars*—it says that over the office now. I'm workin' my way up."

"You still makin' thirty cents though?"

"Yeh, but pretty soon it'll be thirty-five I bet. You know what I was thinkin' all day, Left'? I was thinkin' how all us hoods don't do nothin' but shoot dice 'n raunch broads 'n exercise. Ain't we ever gonna settle down?" His narrow forehead furrowed and his worried eyes held to Bruno's as though they had never seen that face before.

"Yeh. I'm gonna settle down awright. On my farm. I'm gonna marry a actress too."

"If you *could* you mean I guess—huh Left'? You mean what you'd do if you had the old lettuce, huh?"

"You're too sharp t'night, Bible." He resumed his counting of the cards and when he reached forty-two he began hoping to be interrupted; at forty-four Bible obliged him.

"Uh—Lefty."

"Forty-four. Forty-five. Forty . . ."

"I wanta ast ya."

". . . six. Forty-seven—can't you see I'm *countin'*?"

The boy tossed the hair back out of his eyes.

"Forty-nine. Fifty." He recalled that Bible had told him two were missing, and so added hastily, "Fifty-one. Fifty-two. All there."

Bible overlooked a challenge in Bruno's voice for a matter of great seriousness. "I just wanta ask ya, if you had that money you said before, would you start goin' to Mass again regular, Left'?"

That was the kind of question Bruno enjoyed. Something you could put a finger on and hold in your hand.

"Nope, I wouldn't, Bible. I'd buy St. Bonifacius 'n start me up a notch-joint with the sisters, bigger'n the barber's, 'n Father Francis 'd be pimpin' by the Nort'western tracks for me."

Bible drew in his breath with shock. "Don't *say* things like that, Left'. Don't even *think* 'em." He leaned forward and warned the other in a low voice, "Get right with Him, Left'. That's what *I'm* doin' these days. I'm gettin' pure 'n white so's I c'n settle down."

"On thirty cents a hour?"

"On *faith*, Lefty. Goin' t' Communion. Don't you *know*, Left', every Mass shortens yer purgatory? 'n I know where *I'm* headed fer takin' the old man's check that time. I want t' get that part over fast, Left'. Every Mass you go to goes with you t' Judgment 'n pleads fer pardon, Left'. You gotta believe *somethin'*, Left'," he concluded apologetically.

"I believe I got to take care of number one then," Bruno answered. "That's *my* faith."

"Yeah—but what about the hereafter, Left'? Let's talk in the abstrack now— What about the *tomorrow*?"

"The tomorrow 'll take care of itself."

"You mean you ain't gonna pervide fer t'morrow, Left'?"

"Just tak'n care of t'day is all *I* can do."

"Listen, Left'—you carry *in*surance?"

That one was easy. "No."

"Does yer old lady?"

"No."

"You ever put money in a bank?"

"No."

Bruno felt himself growing angry at being put on the defensive.

"Look, Left'—if you had half a buck, 'n it was almost midnight, 'n I asked you for it—oney you had a chance t' go t' that Chink whorehouse Punchy was tellin' about with it—would you gimme it 'n lemme go instead, Left', if I ast you for it?"

The proposition was honest and warranted an honest reply.

"No. I'd go myself."

Bibleback whooped. "Don't you *see* then, Left'?—you're pervidin' fer tomorrow on account it was almost midnight when I ast you fer the half 'n you couldn't get out t' Nineteenth 'n Dearborn 'n rip a hunk without it bein' at least twelve-thirty—'n then it's t'morrow that you were holdin' out the half for on me— Don't you *see*, Left'?" His face was so close to Bruno's that Bruno could smell his breath.

"Keep it down to a riot call," Bruno said, and turned his back to look out the window below the staircase; this bedbug was getting too big for his shoes.

"You see now why you oughta have faith, Left'?" The voice was directly in his ear.

"I believe I gotta take care of myself is all I said."

The voice was suddenly suspiciously humble. "I guess you figure you can take care of yourself all by yourself too? Huh Left'?"

"I been doin' that since I was born."

"Well, if that's the case," the voice observed meekly, "I guess a guy like you don't need God a-tall—I guess you know about as much as Him awready, seein' you get along so good without Him."

Bruno regretted permitting the conversation to go this far. Some hood to have in a mob, a thirty-cent-an-hour Jesus-lover. What if they were playing the Logan Squares some day and this mutt started preaching salvation to the base runners?

"Huh, Lefty, huh? You think you know as much—just answer me *that.*" The voice was overly eager.

"If I get along without God that means I got good sense by myself, don't it?" he asked irritably, and added, "Christ, a man ought to know as much as a spook, shouldn't he?"

"Oh I see—God been around a thousand years 'n you been around seventeen 'n you know as much as He does awready— Boy, Lefty, *you're* sharp—you learn faster'n Him even!" The boy's breath smelled like that of a nervous woman to Bruno.

"How come *you* to know so much, Polack?" Bruno countered, an idea dawning in him— "How come you're so sure I been here only seventeen years? How you know maybe I didn't have a *in-car-nation* somewheres before— How you know I wasn't Jesus Christ before I was livin' in this neighborhood? How you know? Maybe I was *Adam* even."

He was carried away, as well as was Bibleback for the moment, by his own possibilities; his good nature began returning as Bible appeared to be floundering:

"Kelly-Christ! Maybe you *was* Adam!"

The dice players waited, troubled and tense, by the possibilities involved: there was no telling, at this rate, who'd be pitching to Finger the next time they played. Maybe they'd have St. Francis himself in there, burning them in knee-high. Bruno grinned, feeling oddly flattered. His eyes closed till they were mere glints of gray above the grin and his face looked as wide as it was long. This Bibleback wasn't so bad when you tossed back some of the same bull he was always tossing at you. All you had to do was talk like a lawyer and he was licked to a frazzle.

Bibleback's expression was again slyly solemn, instead of frankly

reverential toward a rejuvenated Adam. "Awright, so you *are*
Adam— I'll concede the point. Awright, so you lived a thous'n
years ago. Awright, so God was around *two* thous'n—so you're still
oney a half-wit compared to Him." He hopped onto one leg, clutching his thin shirt over his pigeon chest with one hand and pointing
derisively at Bruno with the other. "Fellas! Here's a guy who says
a half-wit gets along awright by hisself! Fellas!"

"It oney means He's twice as smart as me is all," Bruno pro-
tested—"*Twice* as smart is all 'n I'm not old enough t' vote yet
even . . ." he stopped, resenting the acknowledgment of defeat
which the tone of his own voice was carrying.

"You said you was a thous'n years old 'n now you ain't old
enough t' vote!" Bibleback doubled with joy, and the crap players
were grinning. Bruno rose and moved toward the laughing boy.
Bibleback retreated.

"Don't get sore, Left'. Don't take no picks on me. I was just foolin',
havin' fun. Don't get sore, Lefthander, let's just talk some more."
He grabbed Bruno's arms without strength.

"Bruno! It's fun! Talkin'!"

Bruno wrenched away. He was seldom one to laugh easily.

"Don't shoot no dice, Left'," he pleaded. "Just talk with me. The
guys don't talk t' me. I don't smoke 'r swear no more. I don't have
nothin' left t' do these days but work 'n come down here. I got to
go *some* place, Left'. Left'—listen. What if you was a real dumb
guy the other time—I mean you wasn't no Jesus Christ 'r Adam—
you was just Knothole from the viaduct, you was some dino from
across couldn't talk English even. How about *that* kind of in-car-
nation? How'd you come out matchin' brains with Him *then*?"

Bruno did not reply, so Bible tried another tack, speaking
nervously for the dogged attitude with which the lefthander began
regarding him. "How'd you like to go to that Chink whorehouse?"
he asked. "The Chinks send half their money back to the emp'r'r fer
wars 'n stuff like that—they're great on *that*, Left'. Say—Left'—
You wanna talk in Chink? It's easy, Left', I'll learn ya, it's just
English backerds is all. . . ."

Bruno lowered his head a little, like Benkowski lowered his when he had something important to say. He took off his cap and the light was across his skull.

"Hey! You got a clip like Casey!" Bible was dancing with wonder and joy. "Hey! Fellas! Lefty's got a army clip!"

"So's Finger," Bruno said sullenly, and all eyes turned to Finger, standing with his faded straw in his hand.

"That's 'cause Finger's sec'tary 'n sergeant at arms around here now," Bruno explained. "Just like beginnin' t'night I'm president 'n treasurer." He spoke to Bible just loud enough for the crouched gang to hear. The figures rose slowly, one by one. There was no other place in the Triangle so familiar and tried for crap-shooting and drinking as this shed. Bruno caught his heels under the box in order to sit as if ready to come out of his corner at the bell. "Get on with yer game, hoods," he said steadily—"But just cut the house a nickel on every fifty-cent pass after this. Finger, you take the cut." He saw Bibleback gaping open-mouthed at him, and sensed a chance to rid himself, for the moment, of his fear of Fireball.

"*You* beat it. No sprouts in this org'nization. This ain't no social club, this is a mob. You never wanted to help out wagon-bouncing 'r coppin' by the five-'n-dime, you're never around when we need a extra hand. So scram back to yer Catechism, Holy Harold. You stick by the swings at the playground after this. Now don't stand gawpin'—*scram*—I'm runnin' this show now."

He rose, and Bibleback backed slowly before him to the wall; when his back was against it he tightened his buttonless shirt about himself and said solemnly, his eyes full of reproach for Bruno, "I'll be wearin' the blue scapular when all you crapshooters 'r in Statesville." He turned stiffly and shuffled out, round-shouldered and work-weary as he went, his right hand in his pocket as though clutching the last nickel in Chicago there. He turned at the door and told no one in particular, "I got no other place t' go . . ." interrupted himself and they heard him on the stairs, his step as burdened as a man of sixty's.

"Anyone else who don't want to take orders can scram too," Bruno offered. "There's gonna be some resolutions made, 'n then nobody scrams." He looked about challengingly: there were a dozen of them, of whom at least eight had already seen the inside of the Potomac Street station. "How'd you Polacks like t' resolve t' have yer heads shaved like mine 'n be charter members?"

The boys glanced uneasily at each other, uncertain whether this was an order of the barber's or a bluff of Bicek's. The vainer ones ran their fingers through their hair.

"Well, I'll tell you," Bruno went on, taking his time. "This is the Baldhead True-American S.A.C. So you got to."

"What's the Warriors then?" someone asked. Bruno answered as though reciting the Pledge of Allegiance, standing up, his eyes shuttered.

"The Twenny-six Ward Warriors Social 'n Athletic Club is hereby dissolved by order of me 'n the barber, 'n this shed is gettin' boarded up, 'n the fellas who still want a place to shoot craps 'n bring dames 'n belong to a baseball team with uniforms 'n be in on the ground floor in a big new political-athletic org'nization with a real clubroom with a stove 'n a five-tube radio 'n electric lights 'n a plush sofa 'n a parrot fer a mascot even, you better show up t'morrow mornin' front of Bonifacy's. All we have t' do is clean up his back room. 'n take the Haircut Pledge."

"Who you talkin' for, Lefty?" Punch-drunk Czwartek asked. "Yourself 'r the barber?"

"Fer both. I talked the barber into givin' this mob clips if we c'd meet back of his shop. It's my idea, so's we'll get uniforms. 'One good turn deserves another, barber,' I told him. So you guys better scatter 'n start diggin' up some change. Six bits covers ever'thin'. First come, first shaved, no credit, 'n tell the other guys you can't be a Baldhead by anyone but Bonifacy. The home-made kind don't count."

Bruno Bicek stayed by the window until the last youth had left. Then he stretched out on the plank floor, using his Health Cap for a pillow.

Two brief days had brought him from dependence to independence. From boyhood to manhood. From vandalism to hoodlumhood.

"I like the way I left Casey out of ever'thin'," he reflected dream-

ily. "I'm a ex-ecutive you. I take the credit. Some day I'll leave
the barber out too. I oney hope that Kodadek don't show by the
shop. I oney hope he don't show around here no more a-tall. I oney
hope he shoves that spring-blader into a copper 'n burns like
poor Andy."

And fell immediately into a deep and dreamless sleep.

III

The Trouble with Bicek

ONE week later he was crossing Western Avenue toward the main
gate of Riverview with two silver dollars in his pocket and his girl
on his arm. The gate had a million lights, and he sensed her excitement: each light was burning for Steffi R. tonight. Inside, people
no better than herself were eating cotton candy, playing roulette
wheels you couldn't lose on, and riding a merry-go-round as big as
all Eckert Park. This was the last two-cent night of the year and
there wasn't a ride they wouldn't be taking.

Once, when Steffi R. was ten, her mother had taken her and Udo
on a Ferris wheel at a street carnival on Ellen and Wood Street,
and she'd longed for the sight of Riverview ever since. Now she
was going inside with Bunny and ride anything she liked, just as
though both of them still had papas. She gripped the boy's hand
as she had gripped her mother's at the street carnival—as though
the lights would go out and the music stop and the merry-go-round
slow down forever unless they got through that gate immediately.

But once inside, before the ticket cage to the Greyhound, she
drew back. It was too high. It went too fast. Why were those girls
riding screaming so?

"Let's try somethin' easier first, Bunny," she pleaded. "You been
here before, you're used to hard things. I'm new at ever'thin'."

So he spared her, without coaxing. Though she waited only to
be coaxed. They passed a side show where a barker stood pointing
to an assortment of freaks painted on the show's canvas front.

"Hasn't seen her feet in ten years! Curves like Boulder Dam!
Five hundred and forty pounds of human flesh! Arms like beer
barrels! Biggest woman in the Western Hemisphere! Hurry! Hurry!
Hurry!" Plus the world's deadliest killahs! Alive! Alive! Alive!"

Inside, a stuffed gila monster lay on a roll of cotton batting, and
a young man in a sombrero pointed a stick at it and explained.
"He's sick. They get sick same as you 'r me."

The fat lady had gone to supper.

In another cage a cobra was stuffed. The young man explained.
"He's too dangerous to let run around loose outside." He saw the
brown-haired girl looking skeptical and challenged her: "You want
me to *let* him, Kid? It'll be yer responsibility." Her blond boy
friend with the clipped skull decided they shouldn't take such a
chance. He seemed a surly sort. "Let's get out of here," the barker
heard the boy urge, "I wanna see somethin' alive."

"Fer a dime them Polacks want a zoo," the young man complained to the girl in the ticket cage. A dozen stands down the
Pole and his girl friend were pausing before another barker.

"Three fer a dime! Three fer a dime! Nobody loses! Evabody
wins!"

This one was dressed in a green-and-white-striped baseball outfit, complete to spiked shoes and peaked cap; he was waiting for
them with three dime-store rockets in one hand and a bat in the
other; he pointed with the bat to a row of canvas kewpies.

"Win a Chollie McOtty kewpie! T'ree t'rows fer a dime!"

"You watch the ol' lefthander," Bruno boasted, "This is how
I'll be burnin' 'em in out there against the Logan Squares next
summer." He made her stand back farther than was necessary and
wound up so elaborately that a couple schoolboys paused to watch:
it was for them he hurled the first ball. It dented the doll's stomach
without knocking it off the shelf. He studied it a moment for the
second pitch and tossed a slow ball high against the right shoulder.
The kewpie toppled off.

"I got that ol' confidence now," he told his girl, rubbing the third and last ball against his hip; he studied the third kewpie like a big leaguer peering at his catcher's signal and decided on the left shoulder just to show these schoolroom sprouts how he could cut the corners.

"This is the croosical toss, honey," Steffi said aloud, but her voice sounded far off to him. For Bruno Lefty Bicek was miles away.

He was on the mound at Comiskey Park under a burning July sun with three and two on the batter and the sun in his eyes. Fireball Kodadek faced him in a Yankee uniform and someone else he knew dimly was catching him without a mask. Big Lefty Bicek yanked his cap down over his eyes to see his signals better and glanced out of the corner of his eye to see what size leadoff the runner on second was daring to take. They didn't dare take more than a couple inches with Big Lefty in there. The lights of the great double Ferris wheel behind him came down, so that when he glanced at the runner he saw the white-faced rows of the stands and the striped sun on them. He stepped forward without a windup and gave it his old sidearm slider that even a baby could hit— if only the baby could see it before it dropped. The kewpie saw it and waited, irresolute and wide-eyed, then seemed to tumble backward before it was hit, as though too unnerved to wait longer. The barker grabbed the fuzziest Charlie McCarthy of the lot and held it aloft for all to admire.

"Anotha winna! Anotha winna! Nobody loses! Evabody wins!"

Steffi's fingers reached for it like a baby's fingers reaching: it would be something of her own. She would make a place on the mantelpiece for it, and that part of the mantelpiece would be all hers. It would be the first doll she'd owned all to herself and not half her goofy brother's. She had the natural acquisitiveness of children who have been denied possession of one thing, no matter how small, all to themselves.

"Bunny! Bunny!" she jumped up and down, her red anklets flashing, "We did it! It's ours! Bunny!"

He handed it to her sullenly, seeing her dancing eyes only dimly behind the backstop from where he stood in the spiked sand of the pitcher's box. The green stands and the cropped grass. And the striped sun on them. To be a man out there in the world of men. To be against men, any other men, with a hard-fought game behind him and the hardest hitter in front of him and the trickiest runner behind him; pouring sweat, the breaks going against him, aching in his great left arm every time he raised it; but forever in there trying, not caring that they were all against him because they were making a man of him by being against him. Pitching out his arm and his heart and his life. But in there, pitching. To be a man in the world of men.

He looked around: pink and baby-blue confetti and a thin girl called Steffi hugging a kewpie and calling him Bunny as though it were a baby and he was too. He ripped its grinning head off with a single twist of his wrist and tossed it into a drift of confetti. Steffi stood horrified, as though he had decapitated a child. Suddenly he felt guilty, for a dozen half-forgotten thefts, and shook his head as though shaking off a blow.

"I'll make it up, Steff'." So soon he was repentant. "I'll win you another."

"But I don't want another. I want *that* one. Why you *do* things like that? You scare me."

"I'll take you to the Little Pulaski for community singin'."

He was pleading with her.

She put her hands to her mouth and the gesture hurt him as though she were already crying. He took the hands away and placed them firmly on his hips.

"Don't cry, Steff', I'll make it all up."

He had never noticed how bloodless her lips became when she was unhappy; they had been full and red the night he had left her alone above the poolroom.

"Is it *me* makes you so mad, Bunny?"

He felt she was crying inwardly.

"I just don't like stuffed things no more, Steff'. It's not you, it's stuffed things. Snakes 'n dummies 'n nothin' alive you can get your hands on 'n work on. Makes me feel like a dummy myself, playin' against dummy things all the time. I didn't like seein' you hold'n onto a dummy like it was a real kid, it made you look like a dummy too. I don't want my girl to be no dummy. That makes a dummy out of me."

"I don't feel like no dummy, Bruno. What I think is you need a steady job."

His face brightened and his voice sounded relieved—"I don't feel like no dummy when I'm pitchin' 'r scrappin', Steff"—remember the time I almost win the double-header?"

"I remember, Bunny. I felt so good after that one."

"What you feel like t'night though?"

"I feel like your girl friend." She had caught his tone and sensed that he wasn't trying to hurt her. " 'n I don't care for that dummy. You're my dummy."

He had looked for a man's face and had seen a doll's instead. Now, somehow, he felt he had won something honestly, more than a doll or a dollar, for the first time in his life. They saw a parade of floats coming, and moved to the side to watch; by the time half of them had passed he realized what it was he had and put his arm about her. Instantly her gayety was no longer forced; slowly he felt less troubled.

"I'm *glad* you done that to the damn dummy," she said, "we both want live things—*Don't* we, Bunny?" And the recollection of his act began to amuse them both.

"The way you looked when you tore into Poor Charlie! Was I *scared* you."

He grinned down at her, pleased at finding her no longer afraid.

" 'n those jerks who seen you do it—did they stop 'n give you the dirty eye like it was *their* Charlie, like you ain't got a right even t' do what you want with your own proppity—Boy, if you c'd ever fight like you c'n pitch!"

She doubled with laughter at such a possibility.

"Let's have a beer," he suggested restlessly.

They sat at a table between a dancing pavilion and a bar. Bruno put a nickel in the nearest juke and it played a throaty blues singer, heavy on the bass.

> It's raining all the ti-time
> I'm weary all the ti - ime

They had another beer, and danced, and had another.

"I'm glad you tore hell outa that no-good dummy," she said for lack of anything else to say. "Could you *really* scrap like you could pitch, Bunny?"

He leaned toward her, already feeling the beers, as though he hadn't heard aright.

"You ask me could I *scrap?*"

"Can you, Bunny? For *real* I mean?"

He tilted his chair back and shook his head as though too stunned to do anything but repeat such a question. "Can I *scrap* she asks me. She asks me, 'Can I *really* scrap.' Wow." He blew off foam, took a long self-confident drought, and stood up, "Which you wanna see me do—scrap 'r pitch?"

"Pitch," she said, to be on the safe side.

He wound up elaborately before her—but just as he let his side-arm slider go a whim took him and he went into a kind of reel instead of following through, turning completely about and ending with one finger of his left hand on the button of his cap and his left leg behind him like a ballet dancer's. Steffi followed his movement with wide-eyed amazement, and her mouth hung unhinged for a moment after; then her eyes filled with pleasure at his antic and he held the absurd attitude until he saw the brown lights in her eyes beginning to dance.

"Do it *again*."

So he did it again, not minding the bartender's glances because Steffi was laughing and he was the one making her laugh. The second time it was half a pitch and half a waltz.

"What you *call* doin' that, Bunny?"

"That's my Detation Waltz I call it," he explained obscurely and sat down, feeling greatly pleased with his own humor.

And pleased with his girl too. She knew when to laugh and when not to all right. She knew when something was funny and when it wasn't. Seeing the pallid oval of her face beneath the helmet of her hair, he wanted her somewhere all to himself.

"Let's have one more 'n take in the *Bobs* 'n beat it," he suggested, keeping the words in front of his mouth so the feeling coming up in his throat wouldn't be betrayed too soon.

"That one's too high, Bunny. I'm scared just to *look* at it."

Funny, how fast a guy could get excited. Would it still be like that if he was married to her?

"Let's take in *Pennyland* then," he offered, with an eye to saving enough of his change to buy a pint of liquor. Skyrockets began bursting a thousand miles overhead and showered down a million green and yellow and red petals. In all her life the girl had never imagined anything like that. She stood gaping, her face luminous with pleasure, while he feigned that it was nothing, nothing to him at all.

"I seen it from Sheeny Louie's roof summer before last," he said, trying to sound bored; but she scarcely heard.

"Holy Mother," she exclaimed in awe, "Looka *that* one."

She began drawing in her breath, once her reverence had passed, in sharp, dreamy little hisses, her underlip caught between her teeth. He felt her very breathing exciting him. The thought broke over him like another man's idea: "Get some liquor in her. That's what dames are for." He averted his eyes and said, "That *Pennyland's* over this way." For a moment she felt uneasy about him again; when she saw the wilderness of fortunetelling machines, however, she dismissed her intuition.

"I love mov'n pictures better'n anythin'—even penny ones"—she told him, "Get me a nickel's worth, Bunny."

He bought her a dime's worth, still figuring close, and gave her all but one.

With that one he watched a scarred and faded film of the Dempsey-Willard fight.

Dempsey came through the ropes looking like he hadn't eaten since the last time he'd shaved. With his fighter's heart and his fighter's mind, Bruno sensed the mind and heart of the other. He watched Willard on his knees, swinging his head like a blinded ox, and no spark of pity came to the watcher. "Some white hope," he thought cynically, "what a target for a left." His fingers spread, resisting the urge to get in there for the kill himself. He watched the ref standing Dempsey off, and that bothered both Dempsey and Bicek. He turned the film as slowly as possible. "Get that ref out of there, let Jack get his man," he pleaded softly. "Good Old Jack." Dempsey was circling, circling, trying to get at the beaten man on the other side of the referee's arm. A warmth rose in Bruno: Jack was in on the bum—one—two—left to the heart—right to the jaw —to the heart—to the jaw—and his hand stopped cold on the film. There was nothing before him but a cracked square of yellow cardboard and he was sweating on his hands. "We killed the bum fer life," he assured himself, "I'm a killer too."

"Here Bunny—here I am!" He heard Steffi call. She was unreeling Rudolf Valentino in "Blood and Sand" and he grew impatient. "Lay off that old stuff," he advised, "That guy was just a Dago when he was alive 'n he's only a coppy now."

By the time they came to the roller rink he was walking a foot ahead of her; he paused to let her catch up when, peering through the window at the skaters, he saw Catfoot N., skating wearily; when Bruno called he skated blindly toward the sound of the voice; his shaven skull was damp with perspiration, and he carried a knitted red skater's cap in his hand. Bruno saw he was barely able to lift his feet and hold his head up.

"I been on the hunt here since ten this mornin'," he sighed through the window, "'n ain't turned up a hair. They go by too fast, like John said. That Finger don't know his ear from a bag of bananas. That was all bull about wolfin' 'em on skates. 'n it ain't the haircut, neither, 'cause I been wearin' the cap t' cover that. I been around this rink ten thous'n times 'n I'm gettin' damn weary of it." He lowered his voice. "How's that new jump of yours, Left? You got her with ya? You gonna toss 'er fer grabs? Build me up wit' her, yeh?"

Bruno looked over Catfoot's shoulders at the skaters without replying.

"Say, ain't she even fixin' you up yet?" Catfoot asked suspiciously. Catfoot N. from Fry Street was challenging the manhood of Bruno B. from Potomac and Paulina.

"You think I'd spend *gotówka* on somethin' who wasn't?"

"Where then? Upstairs by the poolroom?" His eyes never left Bruno's face even to flicker.

"Sometimes. One place is as good as another."

"What about when the widow closes? Downstairs by the pool-room?" He winked broadly. "On the rotation table?"

"Go climb the chain."

"Hey, I bet you ain't got a place, I bet you ain't even joopin' her."

Bruno saw Dempsey circling, circling. And needed to prove himself as well.

"Don't worry about me. I got my own place. I got my own technique too you."

Catfoot drew closer to whisper in Bruno's ear: "If you ain't got a good place I'll let you in on one. Me'n Fireball pulled a old bedspring into a corner of the shed after you'n Casey boarded it up. There ain't no mattress, just the spring but . . ."

"By the warehouse?"

There was a long pause. At a respectful distance the girl stood chewing caramel popcorn.

"Yeh."

"Where's Fireball?"

"Who cares? He ain't no friend of mine, Left'. I ain't seen him in a week. I heard they had t' take him t' County. What you think I am anyhow? You think I'd spill a good thing to a bathead like Fire? You know yourself, nobody can tell what that guy's thinkin' of, what he's gonna do next."

"You think Fire is really nuts, Cat?"

"Naw, he's just puttin' that on t' get somethin' he wants."

"He didn't use t' carry no knife. He used t' be friendly-like sometimes."

"If he was nuts he wouldn't keep his trap shut all the time, would he? Only smart guys do that."

Bruno eyed the boy directly as he spoke; Catfoot returned his glance steadily. For a moment no words passed between them while Bruno searched his face. Catfoot did not speak until Bruno dropped his eyes.

"Say Left', 'member that old bob from the N'ort' Av'noo beach I built you up wit' that time 'n you raunched her by the boathouse while I was lookout fer you?"

Bruno glanced uneasily at Steffi R. She was wearing the plaid skirt.

"Interdoos me then just. I'll build myself up. 'Hey you,' I'll say to her, 'I tawt all th' angels was in heav'n'—that goes over big you. You. I'll tell her, 'I'm the marryin' kind.' Go ahead, Left', she seen me before. Call her over. Tell her I patronize her old lady. She seen me shootin' rotation once, she'll remember *me* awright."

"Her Ma don't let her talk to the fellas that shoot pool. She got to stay upstairs 'n take care of the house."

"Don't stall me, Left'. Tell her I seen her in church then. Tell her anythin'. Call her over 'n tell her that now."

Bruno hesitated.

"Don't she got to do what you say?"

Catfoot leered knowingly. It wasn't much of a man whose woman didn't come and go as he directed.

"You damn right she does. Or else."

"Tell you what, Left'—you build me up 'n then I'll build you up afters: I'll tell her you're a executive now you, I'll tell her how you'n the barber got t'gether."

Catfoot crossed two fingers to indicate how close Bruno Bicek and Bonifacy Konstantine had become in twenty-sixth ward politics.

The girl came toward them with the new city light on her old-world face, swinging her skirt innocently at the hips, her hands clutching the popcorn box to her breast.

"You know Catfoot from Fry Street, Steff'? Cat, this is Steffi R. from by the poolroom."

"Glad t' meet ya. I tawt all the angels was in heav'n."

Steffi looked blank and Bruno looked away; when he looked up Catfoot was skating wearily, the red skater's cap stuffed into his hip pocket, the rink lights glistening on his skull, trying to catch up to two girls with billowing skirts skating hand in hand.

To himself Bruno reflected, "I shoulda just said, 'She ain't no old crow like that moldy North Avenue one.' That was my out. I shoulda just said, 'No deal, Cat, this is stric'ly private stock. Knowed her all my life.' I guess I fumbled that one 'n Cat beat it out."

"What *he* want, Bunny?"

"I should borrow him some dough he wanted. But I told him I oney got six-bits left, I couldn't afford."

Why was it that he always thought so fast and so well with her, and so uncertainly with Catfoot and the barber? He'd not only explained everything to her easily, but had thrown in a strong hint that they'd be leaving soon to boot.

Passing the roller coaster she cried out, "I wouldn't go on *that*, Bunny, it's too *high*." And when he took her at her word again she looked back enviously at those waiting for a boat that would lift them higher than Weiboldt's on Milwaukee and then plunge them perilously into the lagoon, faster than the Jackson Park express. "Maybe it's not so high as it looks, Bunny," she observed. "Maybe we'd enjoy."

"Your dress'd get wet through." He was figuring now on keeping enough for a bottle and a quarter for the Sunday collection as well. "I'll go to church with you Sunday," he said abruptly. He hadn't been in months, and she wondered why he was planning to go now. Two more rides, he calculated, was all he could afford and have enough left to contribute.

"Can't we go on just one more ride, Bunny?" she persisted. So he bought tickets to the Greyhound and they climbed, painfully, inch by inch and with the knowledge that, once they reached the top, there would be one breath-taking moment when the car would tip precariously into space, over an incline six stories steep and then plunge, like a plunging plane. She buried her head against him, fearing to look at the park spread below. He forced himself to look: thousands of little people and hundreds of bright little stands, and over it all the coal-smoke pall of the river factories and railroad yards. He saw in that moment the whole dim-lit city on the last night of summer; the troubled streets that led to the abandoned beaches, the for-rent signs above overnight hotels and furnished basement rooms, moving trolleys and rising bridges: the cagework city, beneath a coalsmoke sky.

And there was neither cotton candy in back of Bicek's Imperial Bakery nor a Ferris wheel above Rostenkowski's Polish Poolroom; neither lights nor confetti where the barber's women worked the barber's doors. There the days went by without color or light, nor any happy occurrence that you didn't drink yourself into; the car tipped forward and the women screamed. "The park's a fake," the boy thought hurriedly, "Ever'thin's a fake," and the car dived as though shoved off a roof.

The screams were caught in the scream of wind past his ears. Feeling Steffi pressing against him he thought—"Was that pressing a fake too?" Would it last longer than the next dip of the tracks? Wouldn't she be pressing just as hard against Catfoot if he had bought the tickets? He closed his eyes, picturing her against Catfoot and her hair flying backward—then the hell with her, the hell with Catfoot, the hell with everything. The hell with it all. If he'd spent his money on liquor he'd have something now. "I'll still have a night of it," he decided; and remembered the alley below the El, where southbound locals made shadows on a warehouse wall.

On the way through the gate she pretended to be dizzy from the ride.

"Look, Bunny, I'm on a cheap drunk."

"How about a real one then?" he asked brutally.

She looked at him anxiously. "Ma'll be upstairs by now."

"Forget yer Ma's."

"We shouldn't."

When they transferred, at a deserted intersection, he crossed the street toward a tavern; she followed him up to the darkened door. Then stood, feeling abandoned, beneath a scarlet HOFF-BRAU sign, in an abandoned place. Now all the lights were out forever save the beer ad above her. Stood, alive and alone, feeling unloved. The red legend flickered till its light on the streetcar rails appeared as running blood between the shadowed cobbles. And each time it flickered so she felt it was going out forever.

When he rejoined her, with a pint on his hip and a wad of snuff in his cheek, he did not sense her fear. Despite her arm safely hooked in his, she could not rid herself of the feeling of being abandoned in the dark.

"I'm cold all over," she complained.

"This'll warm you."

He showed her the label proudly before opening the bottle. The label bore a fighter's head and shoulders and an identifying line:

Tiger Pultoric.

Ranking contender for the light-heavyweight title of the world.

She took a timid drink, slowly, hoping for a streetcar down the tracks so she wouldn't have to take another; she drank with him in order to feel less alone. And because he'd spent all that money on her.

"Now all we got left is this 'n transfers," he said, relieved to be rid of his change.

"My girl friend Okulanis from Moorman Street, she makes twenty-four bucks a week," Steffi offered to create a diversion from the bottle.

"Not even a man makes that," he assured her, and took another slug. The streetcar poked into sight, jerking uncertainly forward to one corner, waiting there, for no one, a while; then coming a little farther forward, like some humble sort of bum who had spotted the man with the bottle and was trying to make his approach toward it appear uncalculated.

When they left the car he guided her, one arm about the waist, down the broken walks to the El. Below the Division Street platform they drank again, and he kissed her without caring. She clung to him, wanting to cry for the careless way he had done that; but able only to hold his shoulders and hide her head on his chest.

"What's the matter, Steff?"

"I'm scared. If there was a real place to go maybe it wouldn't be such a sin."

"I know a real place."

"Hotel, Bunny? My girl friend Masurczyk from Ellen Street you, she went once."

"I mean a place to ourselves. Nice place."

She stopped, fingering her locket, troubled by distrust, yet unable to distrust him. "You mean under the sidewalk where the club was, Bunny? I won't. It's a sin there for sure."

He turned her head to the light. "What's the matter, Steff? Don't you *trust* me?"

"I *got* to trust you now. But it's like animals. It makes me cry you."

"I don't see no tears."

"I mean inside. That's how I do it. I don't make tears. I just cry."

He took her arm, and the drink was in him. She moved with him hopelessly. And when he paused to drink she drank with him, because she had no honest reason for not drinking, nor any honest reason for not doing all he desired. "I got nothin', so I got nothin' to lose," she decided.

When they reached the warehouse he guided her down the rickety steps into the pit gouged under the wooden walk. He felt her drawing back, at the last moment, midway on the stairs. So held her there and spoke quietly; till she took the bottle from his hand and drank of her own accord. And went down the steps then, without further urging, before him. He groped for her in the dark, and spread his shabby jacket over the rusted bedspring in the corner.

They sat drinking and spoke in whispers, that passers-by on the walk above might not hear and stop to look down between the cracks. Each time he drank his voice grew hoarser. Once a drunk passed above them singing off-key.

> She came to the door in her stockin' feet
> Said, "Honey, Don't come here no more."

He leaned her back across the crook of his arm. The drunk's last distant chord came faintly to them.

I am safe with my save—yer at home

She was half-asleep in his arms, and they were both half-drunk, when he sensed a step midway on the stairs: it was not a sound so much as a vibration. He tried to shake the drink out of his head. But when he moved Steffi stirred, and nobody should wake up Steffi. He looked at her sallow, wistful face, the lips slightly parted as in wonder and the hair touched with light; the sidewalk's shadow fell slantwise across her shut and dreaming eyes. He wondered foggily how he could arrange to wake, in a bed of their own, in a place of their own, and see her so. The shadow across her eyes and throat passed slantwise across his heart. He looked up.

"You build me up big, Left'?"

Bruno laid his girl's head back, still trying to think what it would be like to be alone and together, reluctant to let the thought go just in order to talk to a stray Polack from Fry Street; but the shadow across his heart remained. He passed the bottle instead of replying.

While the other drank, the right answer arrived.

"No go. She's flagg'n like fount'n, Cat."

Catfoot retreated, bottle and all. Bruno heard him whispering hoarsely directly above and felt himself sobering. He listened for voices: none. But felt Catfoot creeping down again and repeated something he had heard. "The way that guy walks, he's gonna get somebody in trouble some day." And closed his eyes that he might not see Catfoot enter again; he'd just be returning what was left in the bottle, Bruno assured himself.

"Sssss—Lefty Biceps!"

No answer.

"Sssss—Lefthander."

He opened his eyes.

"Don't wake her," he warned.

"Fire says he don't care, flag 'n no flag."

Steffi wakened, startled. "Don't you ever sleep?" she asked. Then she saw the other. "Who's *that* cliff-ape?"

"Just that fellow from the rink. He knows about this place too. He come down for a drink with us."

She did not hear the quiet steps above.

"Tell 'em t' beat it," she heard Bruno pleading, "Cat ol' boy, some other night." Catfoot stood, deaf and peering, trying to make out the girl's face and figure, the stippled light from the walk across his face. To Steffi he looked spotted.

Bruno made his voice tough. "Who you gawp'n at?" He saw Catfoot's narrow face, like a pale alley cat's, deriving courage from those he had above him on the walk. Lefty Biceps wasn't really tough, everyone knew that. He was strong, he could lick anybody in the Triangle of his years and anyone older too—if you didn't count Pultoric himself. And there were those who said that he could lick Pultoric too—if Pultoric went down the first time Lefty hit him. Lefty could beat anyone in the world—if they went down the first time he hit them. If they got up, he didn't look so good. He'd once knocked down a big sick hood called Kodadek, and Kodadek had gotten up with a spring-blade knife in his hand and run the lefthander halfway to Goose Island. Later Lefty had denied owning a spring-blade himself, but all the boys knew better than that. "I reached fer it 'n it was gone," he'd explained; but Catfoot had known it was in his pocket even as he spoke; he knew that Kodadek with a knife had Lefty's number then.

"If I go up there I won't be first, Left'."

"Don't talk t' the president 'n treasurer like that," Bruno threatened, grasping at the nearest straw.

Catfoot smiled smugly.

"Don't gimme that hustle, Bicek. Don't gimme that executive hustle. Go up 'n complain to ol' Fireball hisself if you want, I'm tired runnin' up 'n down steps. This is Fireball's night, he says. You better go up before he comes down, his fingers is itchin' on that ol' spring-blade."

"Listen, Elbow-Sneak, I told you ——"

"I ain't no elbow-sneak 'n you told me a lie. After all I done fer you. After all all the boys done fer you. Fire says I c'd be first, fer all I done fer him."

"Benkowski . . ."

"Benkowski's washed up. Barber's just givin' him kid stuff t' do to keep him from messin' around the big stuff. I know where you was with him 'n Finger last week. You pulled out a slot machine in Stickney 'n got a sawbuck apiece 'n now any time the barber wants he can put a finger on you fer the syndicate ——"

"It wasn't no syndicate machine ——"

"There ain't no slot machine in Stickney that ain't. You think me'n Fire'd take chances like that for what you got? Fire's takin' over the big stuff fer the barber, Fire 'n me is cuttin' in on the barber's women. That's the big stuff, Left', not heistin' a slot machine—that's how guys get theirselves killed. You act right to Fireball t' night 'n when he takes over he'll treat you foursquare."

"I don't take no orders from Fireball. Tonight 'r any night."

" 'n I don't take 'em from Benkowski." Catfoot spat accurately on the steel toe of Bruno's Health Shoe and turned to go. Steffi had retreated to the shed's farthest corner, looking first at one and then at the other.

"Cat!" The boy turned in the doorway.

"C'mere. I wanta ast ya."

"Ast me from here."

Bruno came up and spoke confidingly.

"Tell Fire he c'd be first-string pitcher all next summer. Say, he might get picked up by a scout you. I always liked first 'r outfield best anyhow—I got to save my arm for the rope' arena."

Catfoot called up through the walk.

"Lefty says you could pitch next summer in his place."

There was silence; they heard the girl in the corner brushing down her skirt.

"Bruno, take me home," she asked.

She was through the door and in front of him when Catfoot slipped both arms about her middle and yanked her back; he was laughing soundlessly.

"Wait. My friend upstairs wantsa meet ya. He's th' marryin' kind."

They heard Fireball coming down, as though at a prearranged signal, three steps at a time.

"Hi, Fireball!" Bruno greeted him with hollow enthusiasm, "I was sayin' t' Cat, fer the best int'rests of th' team ——"

"I won't be pitchin' next summer."

"What you gonna play, Fire? You c'd play any position you want, I'll fix it with Casey fer you . . ."

"I'll do my own fixin'."

"Next summer . . ." Bruno began lamely.

"Next summer we'll both be dead." He turned his back on Bruno and offered Steffi a cigarette. She shook her head.

"No. I don't wanna smoke," And caught Bruno's sleeve. "If you don't take me home you'll never see me again," she warned him.

Kodadek stepped in front of her, shaking the package insistently.

"Take one, Steff," Bruno suggested, "If you don't wanna smoke it, you c'd give it to some poor guy."

The girl took the cigarette reluctantly, but did not light it till Kodadek struck a match and waited for her to puff; when the flame was at his fingers she relented, and puffed. "*I'll* see you get home," he assured her.

"Take me home, Bunny," she pleaded, ignoring Fireball's assurance. Bruno heard the fear in her voice like an echo of his own, and took a single step toward Kodadek. Catfoot came up at his elbow, whispering liquidly.

"Fire got that spring-blade strapped to his wrist—I'm yer real friend, I'm tellin' you. He's on the prod fer you, all he's after is to get you sore. Don't let him bait you, Left' ol' boy—he been carryin' it like that ever since he got sick—what's eatin' you t'night, Left'—you in *love*?"

Fireball heard and took up the jeer.

"What's eatin' you, Left'—you in love?" His right hand was buried in his pocket and his breath smelled of sen-sen mixed with canned heat.

What kind of a man would they think him if he admitted he

was? He wouldn't be able to show his face at the barber's, that was sure. What would Casey think of a president and treasurer who was lovesick? What kind of a contender was it who still scribbled with chalk on billboards, "I love Steffi R."? He saw Kodadek begin shoving the girl gently backward; she took Bruno's wrist in both her hands, tightly, the way she had gripped the arms of the chair at her mother's.

"I'm trustin' you," she repeated.

He saw the corner of her blouse in Kodadek's hand and Catfoot watching. Steffi took one hand off Bruno's wrist to pull the blouse right again; Bruno unloosened the fingers of her other hand.

"Let her alone, fellas," he urged weakly.

"Have a shot, Lefthander," Catfoot offered, "Go ahead, keep the bottle, kill it. You're the champ t'night. I knew you was foursquare all along. Go ahead, kill it."

Bruno drank with his back turned to the couple in the corner, feigning not to hear the whimpering protest there. Funny, how a kid like that wouldn't ever bawl outright. And crept up the steps with the bottle in his hand. When he got into the light he saw there wasn't as much left in it as he'd thought.

He drank beneath the arc lamp, asking himself how soon Benkowski would get him the promised money fight, telling himself he had to figure that out for himself now; but able only to hear Kodadek's fevered breathing below. And Catfoot's noiseless laughter.

Knothole Chmura and John from the Schlitz Joint waited by the warehouse wall: shadows within shadows. Bruno offered them the bottle and tried to grin. Then his heart started sickeningly and turned over: Sheeny Louie, Coast-to-Coast, Punch-drunk Czwartek, and Corner-Pockets.

"This one's on me, fellas," Bruno explained, nodding toward the steps to the shed. Knothole went to where the arc lamp stood and got down on all fours to peer through the cracks of the walk.

"Lookit ol' Kodadek you. C'mere. Lookit ol' Fireball go."

A two-car local came clattering past, its lights moving downward, in yellow squares, across the warehouse wall. Sheeny Louie drained the bottle and laid it carefully away behind a telephone pole.

"You leave 'em in the middle of the alley somebody's likely t' get a puncture from it. I'm careful about things like that. If I had a car, I wouldn't want no puncture. How is she you?"

"Skittish as a pony in the Nation'l Guards 'n clean as a whistle."

"Tight?"

"So you'll skin yerself."

Sheeny was satisfied. He walked over and kicked Knothole squarely.

"It ain't no peep show. Get up 'n get against the wall out of sight, like a man. You c'n be after the last guy maybe. You c'n be before Bibleback, he's comin' now."

The shapeless figure of Bibleback stole surreptitiously into line. "I hope them Eckert Parkers don't get word," they heard him hope humbly, "I don't wanna be after some of them."

Beneath them, once, between the passing of El lights on the wall and the chimes for early morning Mass at St. John's, he heard her struggling desperately to rise beneath someone and again he waited, hoping to hear her weep or cry out. And heard only a muffled whimpering. It would be so much better, so much more known and over, if she would call his name or beg to be let be or scream in pain or anger. But even the whimpering faded and he began following the arches of the El toward Chicago Avenue, checking a rising dread by feigning a toughness to himself that he could not feel.

"Dames got to get experience just like fellas," he concluded, and immediately abandoned all further thought in the hope of getting drunk for a week. He had never needed to get drunk so intensely in his life before. There was a great wheel beginning to turn, slowly and heavily, in his stomach, and he had to have liquor to make it go faster and faster, till he was blind with its turning; till its turning was a blindness in his mind for a month. He turned absently on Noble and walked into the widow's.

She was alone in the place; the boy must be asleep in the back and both of them thinking Steffi was asleep upstairs. A picture of

Dizzy Dean had been painted behind the bar since he'd last been in and he asked the widow, "How's about a half-pint on ol' Diz there?"

She shook her head. Nothing on the house tonight.

"How about on myself then? I been workin' is why I need it so bad."

"You work? You not in business no more?"

"Nope. Out of business. Back at the old stand. They're payin' forty an hour again so I went back. How about it, Widow?"

"By Apex you work? Forty an hour?"

"Sure Annie, all week. Started at ten this mornin' 'n worked straight through. How's that for hours? I'll have twenty-four bucks comin' Saturday. How about it?"

The widow nodded cheerfully. She was a square-faced woman with her hair in two brown braids about her head; even so late at night she looked as though she'd just risen from bed. A fresh-faced, immaculate peasant woman with the easy nature of an easy-natured race. She handed him a half-pint of unlabeled whisky and recorded it on a soiled pad beneath the counter; while reflecting that long working hours kept good boys out of trouble with bad girls.

When Bruno returned to the warehouse, a dozen shadowy shapes leaned, like a bootleg bread line, against the warehouse wall. He walked up and down like a reviewing general, taking a new pleasure in his status of president and treasurer. He paused in front of Punchdrunk Czwartek, a youth with forearms as large as a bear's. He'd have to make certain that his pals knew who was fixing them up tonight.

"This one's on me, Punchy."

Punchdrunk Czwartek scratched his skull; the hair was beginning to grow back in a bristling blond crescent down the skull's center.

"I tawt it was on Kodadek. 'at's what Cat said."

Bruno lowered his voice cautiously. "It's on both us. Don't forget."

Suddenly, under the pleasure he was finding, he felt he was

going to vomit. He leaned against a telephone pole, disgust coming up in his throat like a forkful of contaminated meat swallowed
in the dark. "If only Finger 'r one them good guys 'd beat it with
her," he thought miserably.

But Finger hadn't shown up and neither had Benkowski. He
saw Catfoot going down for the second time, a fresh bottle in his
hand. Was it the Pultoric label stuff too, Bruno wondered idly.
Then he realized they were feeding her liquor now, and who could
tell whether she'd be up at all again? A weakness came into his
knees and he sat down with his back to the wall, knees hunched
to his chin, worried lest someone perceive how sick he was feeling.

"You yasheks keep quieter," he ordered. "The heat'll be along.
The word's gettin' around. 'n why don't you keep guys out of line
who ain't Baldheads? What we got an organ'zation for?"

An Italian whom nobody knew got out of line and scurried off
down the alley.

"I wasn't lettin' no wallio in on this," Bruno assured everyone
without rising, "I was just waitin' till it was his turn to run him
off. He knew I was layin' for him."

He could hear, as he sat, a deep and heavy throbbing conducted
by the wires overhead through the telephone pole and down the
bricks of the warehouse wall: the all-night beat of the powerhouse,
half a mile away. As he listened a heavy-shouldered Greek, looking
like Grand Avenue and Halsted Street, shouldered his way in
ahead of the second man in line. Bruno looked at the situation
blankly.

He heard Punchdrunk mumbling something complainingly
about "th' president 'n treasurer." Bruno found time to regret the
absence of the sergeant at arms. Would Punchy and the others
back him up if the Greek got tough?

"All they'll do is holler jigs for me in case the cops show," he
realized. Nobody was going to spoil a good fight by failure to give
both men room, even though one was from out of the neighborhood. Give the guy a chance was the rule; unless it began to
appear that he was doing too well. There was always time enough
to gang up on a single man. Bruno rose and tapped him on the

shoulder. The youth half-turned his head, and a scar went from cheekbone to lip.

"What's this," he asked, "Tag-Night?"

"The heat'll be along," Bruno offered uncertainly, hoping it would work again. The Greek looked him up and down, and laughed easily to himself. "You better run along then," he suggested.

Bruno took a step backward and watched Punchdrunk out of the corner of his eye; this wasn't going so good. How did an executive act in such a situation anyhow?

"How many *us guys* been down?" He asked with the tone he fancied might be employed by a W.P.A. foreman; Bibleback answered, plaintively.

"Five 'n the Catfoot twicet. 'n I ain't a-tall."

"How many waiting back there?"

" 'bout twelve. But I'm ahead of some."

"I thought you was the guy who's so holy he don't even shoot dice."

"I'm gonna do pen'nce for this afters, Left'. I got no place t' go."

Bruno turned on the Greek.

"Beat it, Sheeny, this is a white man's party."

Why had he had to throw that in? What if the fellow had a knife?

The Greek put his back against the telephone pole, his hands at his sides, his eyes narrowed and traveling down the line of shaven heads.

"Make half those gorillas stay out of it 'n I'll show you who the white man is." He unbuttoned the top button of his coat, and a cold wind came down the alley. The line dissolved backward to give the Greek room.

"See what he got on him, Punch?" Bruno asked without taking his eyes off the fellow.

Czwartek came forward and slapped the boy's hip and pants pocket. He carried nothing, and finished unbuttoning his coat, taking his time. As the last button came loose Bruno stiffened with cold: Steffi was calling him from below. No, not him, but calling.

His fingers spread tensely, uncertain that he had heard or imagined it, till it came again.

"Next!" He heard her call. And she was laughing a laugh like a single drawn-out sob, hard as a man in handcuffs laughs.

"Next! Next!"

The Greek's shoulders were bound by his sleeves; as he stretched them back to slip the coat off Bruno smashed at the scar. The boy jerked his hands up in haste and wriggled as he felt himself still bound. Bruno cupped the boy's jaw in both hands as he struggled, set it for the left and swung from the pavement: the head jerked back and the boy slipped down the side of the telephone pole, trying to grasp it with his bound fists. Bruno listened. But she did not call again.

He felt the boys behind him coming up, and saw the Greek trying to raise himself. He got onto all fours, his forehead against the alley pavement, bracing himself with his forehead. When he got his elbows beneath him Bruno heard Bibleback whisper anxiously behind him:

"You goin' down again *yerself*, Lefthander? *I* ain't been."

For reply Bruno brought up his foot as though converting a point after touchdown: the point of the boot caught the point of jaw. They all heard the snap, like the snap of a brittle reed. They all saw the supporting forearms fold and saw him roll on his side. They stood, looking blindly down, a dozen bald-headed Poles with a warehouse shadow across their skulls.

There was no sound from below. There was no sound from above. As though the last El had crashed and the last trolley had finished its final run. Only the beat of the powerhouse, the heavy throb through the city wires: and the blind wall waiting before them. Then they ran.

Fireball and Catfoot didn't run. They didn't know that it was time to run. And if they had known they wouldn't have run far anyhow. For they had the girl between them.

She lay groggily across Catfoot's arms, calling him, in turn,

"Bunny," and "Chollie McCotty." Once she tittered weakly and said the ride was getting too high.

"The dame's whacky," Fireball suggested. And whenever he spoke after that, she laughed weakly. Once she tried pulling her blouse back up over her shoulder, but Catfoot pulled it back down again. She laughed, weakly.

"Cold," she mumbled.

"Fire 'll warm you," Catfoot said. And shoved her off to Kodadek. "I'm goin' upstairs t' take a peek," he added.

"Take a peek," Steffi mocked, and fell against Kodadek.

Fire shoved her off. He was trying to get drunk and couldn't. He had been trying to get drunk for two years, and all he could get was sick. He heard Catfoot pause on the walk above and wondered to himself what they should do with the tramp now that they had her. Well, let Catfoot figure that. Let Cat figure everything.

In the abandoned alley Catfoot's hand touched the broken back of the Greek's neck. He stepped back with neither fear nor surprise; one step, two steps. Looked both ways down Noble Street. Then both ways down Walton. And back into the shadows. Yanked the body over on its back, disentangling the arms from the coat to get at the inside pocket first.

The inside pocket was empty. He cursed. *"Psia krew."* Investigated the side pockets. Empty again. *"Psia krew."* Served the sheeny right for not staying in his own back yard. He rolled it over on its stomach and went through the pants pockets, taking his time. "Somebody was holdin' his arms, looks like t' me," he reflected, and tried to bring to mind the faces he had seen waiting by the wall. A tin can clattered faintly, half a block away, from one side of the alley to the other as though it might have been kicked. He was on his feet and strolling easily before the can had stopped rolling. When he was certain it had been only the wind, he returned.

"Nobody in the world 'll ever catch Catfoot N. at anythin'," he assured himself, turning out the hip pocket. Ah, bubble gum. A full pack. In the other hip pocket he found two dimes. "Lousy place t'carry dimes," he disapproved. "That's how a guy can lose his dough." Deep in the lining his hand discovered a single street-car token; good on any line in the city, day or night. He clamped a stick of the gum into his teeth and returned to the street without haste. What Fire Kodadek didn't know wouldn't hurt him. When nothing had happened you had to trust no one, not even a man like Kodadek. Okay then, nothing had happened. He popped the gum to make that definite and told himself with self-satisfaction: "Me 'n my gum, we'll stick t'gether."

Catfoot tapped his shoe on the loose boards above Kodadek's head.

"Bring the Duchess up with you, Fire," he advised. At the top of the steps he met her, supported by Kodadek, and took her in his arms with mockery, affecting a thousand love scenes he had seen at the Little Pulaski.

"Sweetheart. At last. Fergive me. Marry me 'r be my wife." He thrust a stick of gum into her mouth. She giggled and chewed.

Kodadek grinned. "You oughta be on the stage, Cat. Are you comical you."

She wasn't in such bad shape, Catfoot reflected, taking her about the waist. She was in better shape than Kodadek, he decided to himself. Skinny thing though. Could feel her ribs. "I bet your Ma washes yer clothes on ya," he told her—"uses yer ribs fer a washboard I bet." The wind came up behind him and he had to keep her from falling face-forward. She was drunk as a judge. But they couldn't afford to let her go falling around the streets now, he felt, with that Greek on his ear back there. One thing led to another. If she put a finger on anyone, for anything, it would be for the Greek before it was over. She'd have to have a little private talking to by Bonifacy. And Catfoot was the boy to tell the old greenhorn how to say it, he concluded.

He tried to figure whether she would put a finger on Bruno B. if she knew it meant involving him with a murder. He studied her closely. She was pale as a ghost, but he could tell all right. Not this crow. Not for what that meant. There were women who could and did; but it was in their faces, sober or drunk, if they were up to it. This one wouldn't be up to putting a finger on a man for anything. Not yet. A woman had to go to the wars to get mean. They weren't born that way, any of them.

All the same, someone like Tenczara at Potomac Street could get what he wanted out of a dame whether she wanted to talk or not. If he got his hands on her. But not even Tenczara could do much with one he couldn't find. Catfoot put one arm protectively about her and she clung to both equally. Fire pulled instinctively toward the alley; Catfoot pulled the other way.

"You don't want her picked up in this shape by one of them *Polska* Wonders, do ya?"

Fireball didn't want anyone even remotely attached to the Polish Wonders to share as much as a crumb of what was his. "I'll t'row 'er in th' gutter first," he answered, half-enraged at the mere idea, "One fer all 'n all fer one."

He offered Catfoot his hand and they shook solemnly, while Catfoot pondered what it was that they were shaking hands on. He concluded that he didn't know. So replied, "It's now 'r never, Fire ol' boy, we'll see her through t' the last ditch, come hell 'r high water."

Kodadek's face set with a grim determination to see the girl through. He began to feel that someone must be trailing them, or waiting to jump them out of the next alleyway. At the corner he paused, bewildered.

"*What* we gonna see through, Cat? Ain't it all over?"

Catfoot mocked the barber's tone.

"I got nize big i-dee, boyz. . . ."

Kodadek looked worried a moment. Then his face cleared. He obtained a firmer grip about the girl, and they turned down a street where the last lamps of morning threw a gray glow down a block-long fence. In three-foot letters, green on black, the fence bore a block-long legend:

POLONIA COAL—MAKES WARM FRIENDS

"Walk faster, Duchess," Catfood urged, "I got t' get t' bed some time. I had a big day. My dogs is killin' me." And to himself:

"Somebody's got Catfoot N. pertectin' him now. Whether he knows it 'r not."

The barber was dealing himself five hypothetical hands in his room above Ryan's Broken-Knuckle Bar. He dealt swiftly, one-handed, for he wanted to beat his number four hand in time to get to six o'clock Mass. But the fellow kept cheating; they were all trying to cheat him here.

From where he sat he could watch the curtained windows of Mama Tomek's second-floor parlor. Traffic had been light all night. They were trying to cheat him over there too.

He paused with the jack of clubs between his fingers. Had someone knocked lightly at his door? He limped to it and crouched there, ear to the wood: the sound of two men breathing hard, and a girl or a woman tittering. Then one of them snapped something like snapping a rubber band, and he opened the door on Catfoot, complacently champing bubble gum and looking as pleased with himself as a man could look.

Behind him stood Kodadek, supporting a brown-haired girl. The barber glanced down the gaslit passage, allowing the men to pass into the room with the girl between them. Down the hall the doors were numbered in bright bald tin. All the way down to the fire escape. Some were locked and some were a little ajar, where the wind had tried them secretly in the night. Within them the women slept. He was satisfied that none had seen.

"Come by shop, boyz," he instructed them, urging them out the way they had come. "Tell Mama Tomek come." It took a woman to take care of a woman.

He stood over the girl on the couch, and a desire he had not felt in years shook him. Her helplessness, the very pallor of her and the disarray of her clothes roused the barber; as weakness had always aroused him. It had been so long since he had seen anything so young, so helpless. So wonderfully lost.

Bonifacy Konstantine ignored women possessing strength and health, unless they appeared stupid enough to trick in some easy fashion; there was nothing in health or strength to excite him. He heard a door slam across the street and put a pillow under the girl's head. Then he went to the window.

Mama Tomek was coming across the streetcar tracks wrapped in a green kimono, her hair in her eyes and her eyes full of sleep. The barber decided, watching her hefty hustling walk, like that of a circus elephant hurrying home to supper, that had she been a frail thing, like the frail olive thing on the couch, he would have had more than a business relationship with her. It had been for the best that she was such a horse of a woman, he concluded. She would have cheated him right and left if he hadn't had sense enough to stay out of bed with her. But had she cheated him nevertheless? Had she been cheating him year in and year out like all the others?

A corner of the parlor curtain opposite him raised an inch, and a girl whose eyes were underlined by mascara peered out, following the billowings of Mama Tomek's weaving walk to the barber's hotel door; then she saw the barber himself watching her, and dropped the curtain before he had time to wave his hand at her in disapproval.

The girl behind him moaned as though falling into a troubled sleep. He heard her laugh a little, looking down.

"Next!" she laughed lowly, "Next! Next!"

"*Grzmoty zabili diabla,*" he told her, as though talking to his mad parrot, "The thunder killed the devil."

She smiled softly, as though she had heard and understood.

In the doorway Mama Tomek watched him looking down.

BOOK II

A BOTTLE OF MILK FOR MOTHER

I

"Only Myself to Blame"

THREE months after the Potomac Street police had hauled a Greek with a broken neck into the county morgue, Bruno Lefty Bicek was picked up for the shooting of a drunk in a hallway off a Chicago Avenue alley. He was coatless when arrested, and was wearing a worn and sleeveless blue work shirt, grown too tight across the shoulders, when urged forward into the query room by Sergeant Adamovitch. A full-bodied boy, thin in the shanks, with a loose-muscled swing to the shoulders and too much length to the arms. He stood, with the sergeant's fingers about the back of his belt, in a pair of faded corduroys, tennis shoes grown dirt-gray from snow, and a pavement-colored cap in his hand. He had spent the night in a cell, had slept well, and now his skull and face were shining from a morning scrubbing, the point of his nose glistening between the protective points of the cheekbones.

The two arresting officers, Comisky and Milano, came in behind Adamovitch to form a semicircle about the boy. Behind the desk sat a figure that began fascinating Bruno by the gadgets that clung to his person: sleeve garters and no coat, a leather pen and pencil set protruding from his shirt pocket, an extra button on the pocket itself, and a cigarette behind his right ear. He had a small, fair mustache, but his hat was too large, giving the boy the idea that he was wearing it mostly as a place to make his badge conspicuous. The cap's visor shadowed the upper half of the face to the mustache; the lower half was undershot. Without being able to see his eyes, Bruno felt that the man was shortsighted or deaf: there was that lack of expression about the lower half of the face peculiar to those thus handicapped. When the captain tilted his hat back Bruno saw that the eyes were equally colorless, and equally lightless too; there was that same expression, like a mask of flesh, of unreceptiveness to sights and sounds.

The captain was occupied—as though unaware that three officers and a promising prisoner awaited his attention—making entries in a charge sheet by the desk lamp's fading light. He looked as though he had been tracing the familiar menu of crime all night; the monotonous repetitions of drunkenness, disorderly conduct, forgery, trespass, window tapping, exposure, dice playing, fighting, bestiality and blackmail, dope addiction and strong-arm robbery, crimes against nature and crimes against man.

This was One-Eye Tenczara, eleven years on the plain-clothes detail, three promotions and brother-in-law to an indicted alderman. Above his head a red and yellow wall motto bore a square-faced legend:

I   HAVE   ONLY
MYSELF TO BLAME
FOR   MY   FALL

Tenczara's good eye caught the glint of Bicek's skull, and the pencil above the charge sheet paused.

"What's your name?" His voice was unemphatic.

"Bruno Bicek."

"Come again?"

"Broon-o By-cek."

"Who's Lefty Biceps then?"

"That's me too."

The eye surveyed the pillar of the boy's open throat.

"You're a jack roller," he decided. "You're a strong-arm bandit. You're a hook. Take him away."

The eye returned to the charge sheet and the pencil scampered nervously across the page. But no one took the boy away. Instead, he stood watching Comisky wiping the lining of his cap with his handkerchief as though the barren little room were already growing too warm for him. One-Eye Tenczara looked up: he hadn't expected anyone to take anyone anywhere after all.

"What you here for, son?"

His voice contained a friendliness now that put the boy on his guard.

"Suspicion."

"Suspicion of what, son?"

"Suspicion of walkin' down a alley."

"Picked you up just for walkin' down an alley?" Tenczara's glance went accusingly from Comisky to Milano and across Bruno's shoulder to Adamovitch. "But isn't that illegal?"

"Yes sir. I was on my way to buy a bottle of milk for mother."

"But they can't do that. You're an innocent man."

Silence.

"Well, you weren't up to anything wrong in that alley, was you, son? Tell us."

"No sir. I wasn't."

"Of course you wasn't. You wouldn't steal the sleeves out of your old man's vest neither. Give, Jackal."

There was an edge to the epithet as cold as the edge of a spring-blade knife. Had Comisky or Milano gone into his cell after Adamovitch had taken him out of it? If they had, they had found his own spring-blader.

"I wasn't arrested," he answered, deciding that they hadn't.

"You don't look like you're standing on the corner of State 'n Madison t' me."

"I was just picked up is all."

"For what?"

"For in-vestigation I s'pose."

"Investigation? For what?"

"I wouldn't know that."

"Then you'll need a lawyer to tell you. Are you on parole?"

"No sir."

"Ever been in an institution?"

"No sir."

"Ever have your head examined?"

"No sir."

"Ever been in trouble before?"

"No sir."

"If you don't start talkin' you will be. The officers 'll tell me why you're here if you won't. I'm just tryin' to give you a chance 'n you won't take it. You always carry a thirty-eight?"

He had to think fast: Casey had carried a thirty-eight in the venture, and perhaps he had thrown it away when he had left Bruno to run for the car. He and Casey had followed the drunk on foot, with Finger following slowly in the Chevie. When the drunk had started hollering Casey had fired at his feet and run. Bruno had been pinned, against the hallway wall, by his own grip on his victim. Until the fellow had crumpled. Then he'd run too. Into Adamovitch's waiting arms. With the exhaust of the fleeing car still faintly in his ears.

He knew Casey had made the car because he'd heard him hit the running board as Finger had wheeled it out of the alley—but had no way of knowing whether the officers had found the gun. Perhaps they had both the gun and the knife; perhaps only the gun; perhaps only the knife. Perhaps—with luck—neither. All he could be fairly certain of was that they had seen neither Casey nor Finger up close.

"No sir," he answered, "I don't carry no concealed weapon."

"I'll say you don't. You're too smart. You can get what you want without a gun. All you do is have your pal hold the drunk's arms while you go through his pockets. That right?"

"No sir. I don't believe in that."

"I damn well know you don't. Not with those arms. What you

believe in is doin' the whole damn job yourself 'n save yourself the split. Ever grab a man around his neck till his tongue hangs out 'n starts turnin' black while you go through him with your free hand?"

"I don't believe in that neither."

"Or break a man's neck by kicking him in the jaw when he was on his knees, Lefthander? Ever believe in *that*?"

Somewhere in the room a watch began ticking distinctly. Bruno shuttered his eyes a moment, trying to place that sound. It was somewhere between Tenczara and Adamovitch. Then he folded his arms and looked steadily at Tenczara.

"No sir. I don't believe in that neither."

Tenczara appeared to relax. He sat back, with the oversize hat perched on the back of his head, and grinned at the boy.

"Is this yours, Morning-Glory?"

He flipped a spring-blade knife with a six-inch blade onto the police blotter. The boy leaned forward to see: his own double-edged double-jointed twisty-handled All-American gut-ripper-upper.

"Is it yours 'r ain't it?"

"Yes sir. I'm a scout. Troop 857, the Black Eagles."

Not one of the three officers moved forward so much as an inch; yet the boy felt their semicircle about him tighten.

Tenczara extended his palm toward Milano and Milano placed his billy in it. Tenczara spread the blade across the bend of the blotter before him and clubbed the blade off with a single blow. Then he returned the billy and held the knife's handle upright before Bruno's eyes: there was a scant three inches remaining of the naked blade. He threw the broken inches into a basket and the handle into a drawer.

"Know why I did that, son?"

"Yes sir, 'cause it's three inches to the heart."

"Wrong again. Because it's against the law to carry more than three inches of knife. What were you doin' on Chicago Av'noo with this thing in the first place? Ain't your own ward big enough you have to come prowlin' around down here to get into trouble?" Tenczara feigned irritation, that he should have to undertake disposition of a case that, had the boy stayed on Division Street, would have gone to the North Avenue station where it belonged.

"Like I say, I was doin' a errand for Mother 'n the officer just jumped me. I'm just a neighborhood kid is all, Mother must be pretty worried by now . . ."

"You always do errands down an alley?"

"That way was nearer. Mother was in a hurry."

"Nearer to where?"

"To the dairy. By goin' there I save Mother a penny on a bottle. Mother isn't well, that penny helps to buy medicine."

"Why didn't you take a bottle off your own shelf? You deal in milk."

So they'd been around to the store. The old lady would be sick for real. She'd think he'd killed somebody.

"We was fresh out, Captain."

"You always turn the lights out when you go on these rush trips for Mother?"

"Yes sir. That's to save electricity. We're pretty poor."

He let his head drop slightly toward his chest, to indicate humiliation at his poverty.

"And leave your poor old mother all alone in the dark?"

Tenczara's tone was as false as Bruno's gesture.

"She wanted to sleep."

"Nobody here's going to make you talk, Lefty," Tenczara said, sadly and frankly, like a schoolteacher long resigned to the obstinacy of all schoolboys. "We don't want you to say anythin' you don't want to, 'cause everythin' you say can be used against you." His lips formed each syllable precisely.

Then he added absently, as though speaking to someone unseen. "We'll just hold you on an open charge till you do."

And his lips hadn't moved at all.

"Take him away," Tenczara ordered, and as he said it his pencil was already resuming its scurrying across the charge sheet's endless pages.

The corridor was clean all the way down; but inside each cell lay a carpet of filth. For the first time in his life the boy felt a fear of dirt. This wasn't the flour-and-dust smell of Bicek's Imperial Half-Price Bakery. Nor was this the chalk-and-whisky smell of Rostenkowski's Polish Poolroom. This was a melancholy place, where a thousand young men had lain with the horror of the penitentiary like the weight upon them of an incurable disease caught in a laughing moment: they had sweated here in their horror, and the smell and feel of their perspiration was part of the melancholy place now, for other young men to smell and feel as tangibly as the touch of the spoon holder on the wall or of the bucket by the green-painted bars. As sad as the way the light came down from the streets of the morning.

One such had scratched with a fingernail on the wall above the bucket:

> Louis Anderson
> Drunk and fighting.
> Jan. 2, 1938
>
> Louis Anderson
> Drunk and fighting
> Jan. 8, 1938
>
> No-Good Anderson
> Same old thing

And he couldn't see out. He couldn't, somehow, seem to *hear* out. He took a turn about the cell looking for something besides the spoon holder, the legend by the bucket and the mattress on the built-in cot. But there was nothing else. He paced up and down the carpet of filth, confident that these things could not be all: a picture scratched somewhere or a forgotten, rusted trinket or the warped cover of a cardboard snuffbox or even perhaps an Indian penny buried in the littered dust.

But there was nothing. There were the padded walls, the carpet of filth, the spoon holder and the built-in berth with the threadbare coverlet; and yet he could not feel that there really could be only these. There had always been something, there must be something even in here.

"Jesus Kelly Christ!" he called after Old Adamovitch, "I ain't gonna stay in here! Hey! You! Boobatch!"

Bruno Bicek knew no better word to indicate a church-going, foreign-born Pole than "boobatch." The boobatch made no reply, so he added, "I'll get your job you goddamn Wes' Virginia dino!" And clanged the spoon threateningly against the bars.

"Flannel-mout'l"

Silence. He grew bolder in his contempt.

"*Swinia!* German!"

No answer. Had the boobatch heard and was he feigning that he hadn't, out of fear of Bruno Lefty Bicek? Bruno Lefty flattered himself that he had, and turned his attention to the other cells.

"Call me 'Lefty,' fellas," he offered. "I guess you been hearin' 'bout a little cowboyin' I done up around the powerhouse. The Triangle's my territory. Friend of mine took a couple of shots at a farmer we was rollin', 'n One-Eye's still tryin' to find who done it. He won't find out from Foursquare Bicek though—they call me that too around the powerhouse 'cause I never ratted 'n never will. This jailhouse 'll rot down 'n mold over before I squeal. They call me Biceps in my neighborhood too—you fellas c'd call me that 'r 'Iron-Man,' 'r just plain 'Lefty' if you want. I got lots of names."

He had been placed in an abandoned corner of the basement; it was not until he raised his voice and the whole cell rang that he realized he was alone. That there was no one, above or below or near at hand, or down the corridor to hear. That no one was coming to see him, that no one was feeling badly about his being in here. That Finger and Casey were worried only a little, for fear Lefty B. might talk. That Bibleback was probably saying, "I warned Lefty, I told him so." That there was no one in the whole city but Bonifacy Konstantine with a fighting chance of getting him onto the street again.

When he realized there was no one to hear he didn't sound tough even to himself: he sounded loud and empty, as when he had once cupped his hands to his mouth and called out nonsense to the echoes beneath a viaduct. "I guess they're scared I'll get the other hoods to organize. a delivery if they don't keep me away from them," he tried to assure himself. And squatted, cross-legged and solemn, upon the iron berth.

Later the lockup squeezed a bundle through the bars; Bruno feigned sleep till he heard the heavy door down the corridor close. Then he ripped at the bundle: a faded blue bandanna holding a box of snuff and a ragged copy of *Kayo: World's Foremost Boxing Magazine*. It was all he had had on him when Adamovitch had collared him racing out of the alley. He fumbled in the bottom of the snuff, found a nickel and held it up to the dim whitish light. It had begun to assume a greenish tint, and he replaced it with satisfaction. When it was quite green he planned to make a luck charm out of it by plugging it and hanging it onto his belt.

He groped in the bundle for the belt itself, found it missing and then missed his rag of a tie as well. "I see they ain't takin' no risky chances with Foursquare Bicek tyin' up the lockup," he observed, and smiled knowingly to himself. If they hadn't found the spring-blader he'd have the lockup bound with the belt and be halfway to the street right now. And sat studying the world's foremost boxing magazine. Toward evening he began pacing the cell's gray length.

"Now I'm keep'n in the pink," he told himself, protecting his jaw with his left and jab-jabbing with his right to make his man lead. "Prob'ly be hard as Pultoric th' time I get back on the street."

Hé reassured himself that, if anything went wrong and he got sent to the House of Correction, he'd escape with ease. Knothole Chmura had escaped from St. Charles once, and anything that Knothole had brains enough to do would be a cinch for the Lefthander. "I shouldn't never of voted for Figura that time though," he recollected uneasily, "if they dig that up they'll say I'm old enough fer Statesville by now. I c'd prove by the old lady I didn't have no right to vote then—I'll prove it by that relief spook from Sangamon Street." Before he could recall that he had lied about his age to the caseworker also, his mind was swamped by an image of himself; as though he had been abruptly transplanted before a technicolor movie being reeled a little too fast.

A stirring drama of one Powerhouse Bicek, the Near Northwest Side's new 195-pound white hope. The name, like "Foursquare," was no sudden inspiration, but the result of long weighings and comparisons, talks with Finger Idzikowski and many rejections. They had considered together literally dozens of names for Bruno's career "in the rope' arena," and sometimes, for his assistance, Bruno had allowed Finger to keep one or two for himself in the event that Casey should some day get Finger a fight as well. They had, at different moments, arrived at "Homicide Bicek," "Superman Bicek," "Bombshell Bicek the Cosmic Bomber, the Polish Panther and the Modern Ketchel." In the end they had compromised, simply, on "Powerhouse Bicek, the Modern Ketchel." Because that had seemed most accurate to Bruno.

So now the Modern Ketchel, resplendent in a black and red silk robe strode down a littered aisle between Finger and Benkowski, scorning to crawl through the ropes, leaping the top strand lightly instead: he turned on his ankle in the cell coming down, but scorned the twinge of pain also. He saw himself standing between Casey and Finger, the black of his robe offsetting the great white "B" emblazoned on their red turtleneck jerseys, himself in perfect trim and freshly tanned from his summer as a lifeguard at the Oak Street Beach, shaking hands now with the champ and now returning lightly to his corner in a flutter of red and black, while a great slow roar began filling the vast park. The lights began going off one by one, till only the lights overhead remained.

"And in this cawneh," he bawled to the bars, circling the middle of the ring in white ducks while the managers gave their boys last-minute instructions in the corners—"Lay-deez 'n gentlemen, the manag'munt takes great pleasure in present'n, in the fin'l bout for the evenin', the contender for the heavyweight title of the world, at one hun'erd ninety-eight pounds, the pride of th' C.Y.O. 'n the great Near Nawthwes' Side . . ." Pause. Suspense. Peanuts in the aisles and the five great lights overhead. Who could the wonder in the red and black robe be?

POWERHOUSE BICEK, THE MODERN KETCHEL FROM POTOMAC STREET!

He swung gracefully about the middle of the ring. Cheers. Boos. Hisses. (This Bicek had plenty of enemies out there; gangsters for the most part.) And applause.

As the seconds cleared the ring Bicek watched the beetle-browed titleholder from Roosevelt and Lawndale out of the corner of his eye while scraping his shoes in the resin. This was Pinsky, the Jew who had taken the title off Tiger Pultoric on a fluke, after Pultoric had beaten Louis handily on points. The Jew wouldn't give Pultoric a return match, he was taking on this young unknown instead to be on the safe side; but the night before the fight good old Pultoric had come to Bicek and shaken his hand, saying that it didn't matter to him who held it, so long as it wasn't a Jew or a jig. "Me'n you 'n Ketchel 'r the three best of 'em all," good old Pultoric had reminded Bicek—and he hadn't had to add that all three were Poles. "You got the case of a Jew callin' himself th' white hope now," had been Pultoric's parting words—"seems to me we still need a white hope t' get that title back." And he'd had tears in his eyes when he'd said it. Good old Pultoric.

Bicek's eyes held no tears, however, now that the moment of reckoning was at hand. But under Pinsky's eyes were bags like that John Barrymore in the movies had; he certainly looked like Fireball Kodadek all right. Bicek watched him skulking about in his corner like he was all punched out from the night before. Well, Playboy Pinsky from Roosevelt and Lawndale, you been the dirtiest pug ever to disgrace the heavyweight belt, but now the jig is up so you're caught like a rat in a trap. The warning buzzer, and Bicek, looking fresh as a colt and clean as dew, tossed off the robe with a single shrug, touched the tiny cross at his throat, kneeling; rose and winked broadly down at Father Francis from St. Bonifacius in the third row behind the press table.

Bicek came out so fast at the bell that the Jew hadn't gotten his robe off—was standing there with one arm free and the other all caught up and the customers laughing all the way back at his predicament, urging Bicek to finish him off then and there. He had the right to, they knew, and moreover that was exactly how Pinsky had beaten Pultoric only the month before. But Bicek didn't. Not Bicek the Modern Ketchel. This Bicek was made of better stuff. This Bicek wasn't one to take advantage of man, woman or child. Just a big, clean kid, he'd be a clean champ, and he let the Jew clean free of his robe now. Cheers. Hisses. Catcalls. Applause. Father Francis blessed the boy openly from the third row.

Bicek feinted, took a long left to the head going away, and spun the Jew halfway around with a right that somehow turned into a magnificent hook at the last moment. The Jew's shining mouthpiece went spinning, he dropped his hands and gestured groggily at the referee while his two managers, in black derbies and beards, jumped into the ring protesting volubly and waving their arms. They smelled of fish, and the ref nodded at Bicek, "Go get him." This ref was one good old guy, he looked a lot like good old Casey B. Bicek rocked indolently against the ropes, smiling and relaxed and confident; he had no intention, his manner said, of hitting a man who didn't have his hands up. No title in the world was worth that to Foursquare Bruno.

Cheers.

Hisses.

Applause.

But what was this—had one of the Jew's managers stuffed plaster into his man's left glove in the rumpus of the moment before? Plaster or no plaster, the champ was as tricky as a fox and could hit like a kicking horse with either hand. Wham! Bicek down! Three! Four! Five! Six! Seven! Eight! Gallantly, blindly, Bicek struggled to one knee, putting down his rage in order to think more clearly. Up at nine, and at the bell the crowd was still standing as both boys slugged it out in the center of the ring toe to toe. God, that sheeny could hit! But how that Polack could *take* it! What a heart! What stamina! What courage! A gamester all the way down!

Bicek, collapsed on his stool, rubbed his jaw reflectively, the way he'd seen Jimmy Cagney do it. He still saw the humorous aspect of getting caught that way and grinned affably across the ring at Pinsky. Cagney did that too. He was that good-natured he wasn't even sore at the tricky Kike. But Pinsky, that sullen heel, only frowned in return. Bicek's jaw was swelling, he could feel it coming up between his fingers. That was bad—he had to meet that Sylvia Sydney in front of the Little Pulaski for a double-feature with community singing, and he didn't want to be marked up. She was getting pretty fussy and might throw him over for a millionaire. He'd have to be more careful.

Bicek came out for the eighth swarming all over the demoralized Pinsky, batting him unmercifully from corner to corner and rope to rope, until it seemed that only the bell could save Pinsky from the first knockdown of his career in the roped arena. And the bell.

In the ninth Bicek caught him with a long straight right flush on the button before the round was a minute and a half old and Playboy Pinsky went down for the first time in his career in the roped arena. Up at eight, and down again for another eight from a long left to the short ribs. Up and down for nine, and the crowd calling to stop it—he was rising for the third time when the bell saved him once more. Were his managers bribing the timekeeper? Bicek scorned the thought as unworthy and trotted lightly back to his corner, standing relaxed against the ropes instead of sitting down, and spurning the ministrations of his seconds. But you had to give the devil his due, this Pinsky still had guts, he was losing like a champion should lose after all.

As the late editions remarked, it took Bicek six rounds to recover fully from that accidental first-round knockdown. He had been over-confident then, the editions agreed, and hinted at plaster in Pinsky's left glove. The lighting in the park, too, had hindered the challenger —all right for night baseball maybe—and by the way the new champ was a southpaw fast-ball artist who went around with movie stars. It was the first time he had been knocked off his feet in his career in the roped arena. That proved to the skeptics, who'd predicted he'd never come up off the floor, that he had a heart like Ketchel. They all agreed, now, that Bicek could take it as well as dish it out, and that it was certainly remarkable in so young a fighter that he had been able to slug it out with the champ after such a blow. Not even the veteran Pultoric had been able to do that.

Bruno Bicek, leaning heavily against the wall to catch his breath and sweating from stomach to forehead in a corner of the cold little cell, the carpet of filth still feeling a little like canvas to his feet and still eying Pinsky frankly in the opposite corner, hoped that the champ's manager would toss in the towel. He didn't want Pinsky to have to take any more; and besides he was already well winded, actually, himself.

He straightened his back against the wall and went into a half-crouch—there was something phony here, and sure enough he guessed it—the champ was going to come out tired and slow, but with direct orders to foul his way out: that's what the skulking figure in the black Jew hat was telling Pinsky, bending over the champ and sort of hissing, not talking English at all. Boy, he was a dirty one—Bicek gasped to get his breath back, the bell would sound any second now and foul play was afoot. Pinsky was certain to lose the round anyhow, he might as well foul his way out of it with this green Polack sprout, the black hat was hissing. You couldn't lose a fight on a foul in Illinois any more, he chuckled to Pinsky. Sure enough, still snarling, he caught Bicek a full two inches below the belt and Bicek doubled up; the Polish girls with the field glasses in the back of the park began screaming for fear he might be hurt seriously, and the ref bent over him solicitously— Bicek was getting up, pale and determined, and the house was going wild. He shoved the ref aside and the press could hardly believe it. But Father Francis was standing up, his hat in his hand, and his head bowed slightly, invoking one more blessing on his brave parishioner.

Their gloves had scarcely touched again, when Pinsky tried once more, but this time Bicek was prepared. He took it gracefully as a dancer, on the hip, and then slammed in fast above Pinsky's rotten heart. The champ sagged, trying desperately to hold, and Bicek, seeing he was finished, stepped back as before. He still wasn't one to throw an unnecessary punch. But the ref, that dirty Greek, what did *he* say?

"Fight him, Bicek! For Pinsky is still heavyweight champion of the universe!" Bicek caught a nod from Father Francis: the Father would absolve him if anything happened to Pinsky when he hit him now. The sin would be on the ref's head, that'd serve the Greek right. He began to feel that the ref must have a scar going from lip to cheekbone and worried, as in a dream, because he couldn't see the face clearly enough to tell. He brushed the fear aside and measured the champ coolly, drove a left to the heart and a right to the jaw, being careful to pull both punches so as not to risk killing the Jew outright and getting the ref's soul in real trouble.

The lights of the park came up like a single light, but as the crowd started leaving they flickered uncertainly, as though from a loose circuit; so that Bicek, riding back to his locker in a flutter of black and red atop the shoulders of Father Francis and the ref, saw them wane and brighten above the milling thousands; each flicker lit Sylvia Sydney's face. She was waving a blue handkerchief from the bleachers at him in one flash, and the next was running wildly toward him with arms outspread. He smiled contentedly, knowing there wasn't a millionaire living who had a chance with her now, his heart was that full, and he touched the cross at his throat as he rode, stretching his arms toward her. As their fingers touched, the lights flashed on like a lightning flash, he caught a full glimpse of her face against his and it was Steffi's face—he passed his forearm across his eyes to duck the glare and wiped the perspiration off his forehead with the same gesture; then fumbled forward in the gloom, feeling for his cap.

The Greek. The whole thing had been the damn Greek's fault.

It was growing cold along the floor, he could feel the cold of the street creeping in. He curled up quietly in a neutral corner, shivering a little but still damp from his exertions, and his body began jerking occasionally as the nerves began relaxing from their triumph; and slept, distressed by many dreams. Once in the night a flashlight's dreaming beam came playing across the floor and up across the walls and bars; when he woke he was uncertain whether he had dreamed.

For there was a low, steady, familiar beating beneath the basement floor. As though the city were a drunk murmuring hoarsely all night to himself. "I never heard that in daytime," he thought, and put his ear to the floor. Then he understood. The powerhouse. And listened longer, with eyes half-closed, translating the murmur into long bright pictures of the way the plant, and the street itself and the darkened factories about it looked now with the plant lit up and beating all night long.

He heard the great smash of the open wind down Potomac, the way he remembered the wind down the narrow streets of his boyhood; and saw the cell block's single bulb burning without warmth overhead.

He followed its reflection in the water bucket, shivering as he held the bars: the light moved restlessly deep in the water, though the surface appeared still. He stared at it long and directly, without wincing or ceasing to shiver, till he saw a fringed yellow flower, like a small yellow water lily once seen in Lincoln Park, opening slowly in a shallow pool. It was summer, the flower was blooming beneath the water; he stood holding the handle of a child's baseball bat beside the Lincoln Park lagoon and somewhere behind him Steffi and his mother were taking turns calling him. But he would not reply, remaining stubbornly silent and looking down at his flower, feigning not to hear; let them come to him. The wind turned swiftly, like some hunted thing, some lost and alone thing in the street below; the winter lightning lit the whitewashed corridor. It lit the endless walls and Bruno Bicek's fighter's face between the cold green bars, staring fixedly down at a dented bucket.

He stood so till his eyes blurred, then returned to his berth. When he lay down he felt he was in this cell for life. Felt walls and bars, for the first time, as walls and bars: he would no longer wait for anyone in here nor hope for someone to speak near at hand, inside or out. He knew at last where he was, and it did not seem to him that, even though he were freed in the morning, that he would ever be free again. It did not feel to him he would ever be free again, whether in the Workhouse or on Chicago Avenue.

If he could only find the cap. Somehow that seemed to matter. He began padding about again, feeling his way forward with his fingers, telling himself how much he needed a cap to keep himself from knowing how much he needed Steffi R. Not even the barber, not even Figura, not even Tenczara and the alderman himself, could free him now.

Only Steffi R. could free him.

When the lockup came by in the morning the boy was bent above his berth, his hands folded in his forearms and his forearms on his knees.

In the cell's farthest corner, touched by the morning's first faint light, lay the pavement-colored cap.

"Up in there!"

Bruno unbowed his head and looked at the lockup without interest. The lockup's cat was sleeking herself against the lockup's leg.

"Wash yer face. You're goin' to the bug doc."

The bug doc looked like an underfed poodle; his brows, once dark, were now streaked with gray and so overgrown that he peered at Bruno through many loose gray strands. For a moment Bruno had the uneasy notion that he was facing an older Tenczara, in white coat and gold-rimmed glasses for disguise; it was almost as hard to tell whether the doc was looking at him as it was to tell when Tenczara was. Bruno sat before him working the red sponge ball with his right hand.

"What color is it?" the bug doc asked, nodding at the ball.

Bruno decided to play safe right from the start. He didn't fully understand the question, but, whatever they were up to, he'd give them a run for their money.

"Green," he said with definiteness. The right answers never had gotten anyone out of trouble yet.

The doc glanced over his shoulder and Bruno saw that the lockup waited at the door with the cat.

"What color's this?" Shoving a yellow chip toward him.

"Purple."

The doc began looking interested.

"How much is eight 'n eight, Mr. Bicek?"

"Hunert sixty-six." That "mister" stuff wouldn't get the croaker anywhere.

"Four 'n five?" the doc's voice was overly polite.

"Twenny-two."

"Cut the funny stuff," the lockup warned from the door. "Answer the man's questions. You're not *that* batty."

"Did you like to play with little girls 'r little boys when you were a little boy, Mr. Bicek?"

"Um—little boys."

Now that doc felt he was getting somewhere; he lunged with the next one like a prosecuting attorney.

"Do you still prefer the company of men to the company of women?"

Bruno looked the man up and down.

"If they're big 'n strong I do," he answered steadily.

The doc looked the boy up and down in turn. Then he grinned and printed a single word, in a large hand, on a slip of paper. Bruno saw the lockup glance at it and rose; he read it over the lockup's shoulder. It said, simply, S-A-N-E.

And yet, that night, he wondered whether he had read aright; for the lockup led him to another cell, the last one in the overcrowded tier behind the station, and this one was padded.

"Are they all padded, partner?" he asked the next cell, with an indifference that didn't ring true. And heard others laughing.

"Nope, you're in the only one. But don't worry. They put the ones for Dunning in there. They'll call for you pretty soon. I hear it's nice out there."

"Tell me straight now. I got to know."

He felt himself growing cold with pride.

A leisurely drawl from the other side reassured him.

"It's all right, son. It just means they might take a notion t' turn the hose on you some night. They turn it on a man in an unpadded cell he's likely to hurt hisself against the walls. They just want t' find out a thing 'r two without marking you up—you got a trial comin' up?"

"I dunno. I ain't even been down to Central Police yet."

"That's it then. They're gettin' you set for the Thursday line-up. Where'd you fall from?"

"Chicago Av'noo 'n Noble."

Late that night Bruno heard the same leisurely voice bargaining with the lockup for the privilege of rolling a drunken soldier.

"One third!"

The soldier was paralyzed, down at the far end of the tier.

"I'm in a public place!" he cried out, as though overcome by that fact.

"Fifty-fifty." Bruno recognized the lockup's voice, and saw the shadow of a cat.

"One-third," the drawler persisted.

This time the lockup did not reply, but all heard him hauling the drunk into an unoccupied cell, still announcing his wonder at being in a public place.

"When I'm in a public place," he shouted like a Fourth of July orator—"that's where I am!"

"Okay. Fifty-fifty," the drawl conceded.

A moment later Bruno saw the lockup pass, dragging the drunk, whose arms were going like a comic-strip figure's arms. He was in uniform, but had lost his hat, a boy of perhaps twenty-two, with a fat foolish face. The lockup opened the cage where the drawler waited: Bruno saw his shadow, and the shadow of his keys against the whitewashed wall. The drunk seemed, of a sudden, to sense danger, because he laughed sarcastically at both the drawler and the lockup, as though he were squaring off. "Oh—so I got two against me now—am I scared—" and the dull thud of the fist against his jaw, the grunt of sick pain as he fell. The lockup scurried into the cell, the cat following as though to see that his master was not cheated. Bruno heard them dividing money. After the lockup had left the drawler boasted to Bruno.

"A fin apiece. Not bad, eh? It ain't hay in here. Have a hamburger on me t'morrow, kid. 'n call me Mustang."

First thing the next morning, as though he had lain awake half the night planning its precise procedure, Mustang ordered officiously.

"Two hamburgers 'n coffee back here! Heavy on the onyunz!"

The lockup strolled back to take the order, the gray cat at his heels.

"Two hamburgers 'n coffee," Mustang snapped, "fer me 'n my pal in the next cell. 'n throw my breakfast out the winda on yer way back." He handed the lockup a dollar.

When the lockup returned with the order Mustang asked, "Where's my change?"

"From *what*?—a *dollar*?—What is this, a service house 'r a jail?"

By Sunday morning the lockup had gotten three of Mustang's five dollars, and Mustang was broke again.

When the Salvation Army came in on Sunday afternoon someone down the tier called out, "Save me, brother! I want to get out of here!"

Mustang echoed, "Save me too, brother—'n bring me a drunk t' roll. I wanna get out of here too!"

Bruno lay on his bunk while four thin-voiced women and a whisky bass with a guitar serenaded him:

Were you there when they crucified my Lord?

The buzzer for visitors went all day long on Sundays. On other days, during the lunch hour, Bruno heard the police at target practice in the station basement. At night he listened again for the murmur of the powerhouse. But he could not hear it through the padded walls. He heard the iron rocking of the bells of St. John Cantius above him, the tinny clang of the Chicago Avenue trolley below, and the smooth splash-splash of gas into the squad cars in the station yard. He heard the cars pull out after being refueled, and threads of conversation, coming all day long, through the fog of smoke at the end of the tier. The buzzer was forever coming through the smoke for some woman bringing something for someone.

In later months Bruno Bicek never recalled the Potomac Street station without smelling the bluish smell of cigar smoke and hearing the voice of an unseen woman coming through it.

"Bring to John Smokowski please?"

"How do you say it in English?"

The women were never insulted when they had something to bring to some Smokowski.

"Just John. Big boy. Please. I point. Down."

"I'll say you point. This is the third time you been here t'day."

"I bring—t'ree t'ings. Please. John."

"If I give this to him now will you promise to stay away t'morrow?"

They always promised.

"Stay away long time. You give."

"You told me that yesterday 'n now you're back every ten minutes with another armful of junk—what am I, lady? A errand boy? This ain't no service house."

"Please. John. I point. You good man."

They always won.

Mustang claimed he was "sitting" because a seventeen-year-old girl was conducting a racket with the station police. They encouraged her to sleep around with men with jobs, Mustang said, and sooner or later she came along in a squad car with Tenczara, Adamovitch and Comisky to identify the fellow for statutory rape.

" 'n I guess you know what you get fer windin' up that little ball of statutory yarn," Mustang added.

"You c'd get one t' fourteen," Bruno advised him, "if it's that. If it's just contributin' to delinquency though, they can't do you more'n a year in the Workie. If you don't pay off."

"What's the dif—a year in the Workie 'r fourteen in Statesville?" Mustang asked. "It's the same thing. I'll take the fourteen."

"You could pay 'em off. They'll take anythin'."

"They want twenty apiece. That's sixty right there, 'n a sawbuck for the girl. I ain't got a cryin' dime."

"They'll take ten apiece 'n forget the girl," Bruno assured him. "They been workin' that thing in my ward since the prohibition racket give out. Tenczara got more rackets right now than Joe Soltis ever had."

"Trouble is the girl has sort of caught on 'n the cops can't reason with her no more. I guess they left her out of the deal before— told her t' drop the charges against the guy, that they didn't have no case. So now she says she won't drop nothin', she'll collect her ten-spot or else."

"If she can prove she's underage she's got you in a spot then. I know, a lawyer told me once, always pay off for rape if you can. It don't pay to get tangled up with women, Mustang."

"She's under all right," Mustang observed gloomily. "I checked on that. She looks like twenty-two but she's seventeen."

"Even if she wasn't, Tenczara could make it that she was. He could fix anythin'. Pervidin' she was born around here, o' course. He had a twenty-two-year-old crow work'n that one around Wojciechowski's Tavern on *Div*ision. I know three guys she caught just 'cause she didn't look her age. 'n you know what you—one of 'em married her, the last one, his name was George-from-the-Garage, 'n Tenczara got so burned up at them both that they had t' move over the other side of Ashland so's he couldn't get at her."

Both boys were lost for a long moment in the career of the remote and troubled character called George-from-the-Garage. Then Mustang asked quietly, "You booked yet, friend?"

"They ain't bookin' me till I talk," Bruno answered with pride.

Mustang considered the case of the Potomac Street Police vs. Bruno Bicek.

"All I ever seen of you, friend," he finally acknowledged, "was yer arm when you handed me your snuff once. 'n you ain't never seen me. So it ain't like I'm tryin' to hand somethin' out to someone I know all my life just to make 'em feel good. But I been thinkin' about yer case. 'n yer an innocent man. They can't do a thing to you. They can't lay a hand on you. You got the law on your side, friend."

Bruno was grateful.

"If I make the street before you do," he promised Mustang, "I'll have the alderman take up yer case. I'm a friend of Frankie Figura's. Frankie 'n the alderman 'r just like that. That's where I'm in solid." And added apologetically, as an afterthought, "Of course it might take a little time, the alderman got his hands full hisself right now. They got him indicted, I guess you know."

Mustang was gracious enough not to doubt that even an indicted alderman, with pressure from Bicek, could pull him out of his difficulty.

"What they got him indicted for?" he asked.

"Sellin' police jobs."

"Well hell, a alderman got a right to put his own men on the force, ain't he? Where would law 'n order be if cops had t' be elected?"

"It ain't that so much," Bruno had to admit for the alderman, "it was just the fellas who paid him off didn't get no jobs."

"Them fellas would of made good cops all the same," Mustang consoled Bruno. "That alderman is in his rights."

On Bruno's fourth afternoon of existence on an open charge, Comisky came up with a plain-clothes man named Scully who had once dropped into Bonifacy the Barber's shop the day after the poor box at Santa Maria Addolorata had been robbed. He had been back to the shop several times after that, till all the boys had come to know him. He had come to get unnecessary shaves, and when they had learned that he was afraid of them, they had begun buying him drinks to give him courage. He had been so easy to out-smart that they had begun liking him, had done him small favors to keep him around, upon Bonifacy's advice. There was no telling what sort of fox might replace him, the barber had felt. Whatever the barber had meant, Scully had been fun.

"I just wanta keep my somp'n t' eat, boys," he would complain in his phlegmy voice. "This is the fourt' distric' I been in since the brother-law got me on, 'n I ain't made good yet. Now you boys 'r all good boys, I don't come all the way out here from Englewood lookin' fer trouble. All I *want* is shaves. Polacks 'r the finest people in the world. They got to eat just like us Irish. The Irish 'n Polacks always get along—didn't ya ever *notice?* Irish 'n Polacks live on p'tatoes 'n got it in fer Hitler, that's why they get along so good; all over the world. Never heard of no war between Poland 'n Ireland, did you? No sir, that's 'cause we're all Cath'lics. I go to Mass regular by St. Columbanus, 'n my wife, she's part Polish. Our

kids look just like her, I'm sort of a Polack myself." He would laugh
unconvincingly, looking harassed about the eyes.

The boys had let him have inconsequential information from
time to time; they had given him the address of a basement room
in which a dozen Italian schoolboys from Santa Maria Addolorata
ran card games and dances. Scully and two citizen dress men had
raided the room early one Sunday morning and gotten two squad
cars of young Italians, most of them drunk, to cart back to the
station overnight. One had carried a pair of brass knucks, so
Scully was passing a bottle around back of the barber's the next
afternoon.

On another occasion they had given him another address, and
he had been able to walk in on a dozen Polish business-men watching an obscene movie in back of a photograph studio. The *Chicagoski* had got hold of that one, and the merchants involved had
retaliated by denying the boys credit, and even trying to collect
past-due bills. When Mama Bicek couldn't understand why the
bakery man's driver wouldn't leave *obarzanki* like always, Bruno B.
had understood.

By way of apology to the merchants, therefore, the Baldhead
True Americans had beaten Scully in the back room at the widow's,
while the widow's Udo ran wildly about trying to beat Scully's
brains out with the biggest cue in the house. Udo had been re-
strained and credit had been restored, subtly, to the poolrooms and
taverns of the Triangle. Scully was transferred a fourth time, and
Bruno had not seen him since.

As president and treasurer it had been his privilege, that last
evening, to roll Scully for fourteen dollars and his badge; they had
left him lying, more drunken than injured, in the alley between
Walton and Noble, face down on an ash heap as comfortable as
though pillowed in his own bed. Casey had allowed Bruno ten
dollars and the badge.

The boy had been merely proud of the badge, till the barber
had suggested that "anybody wit' badge scares greenhorns. Badge
is U.S.A. Gover'ment. They pay. You tell 'em in English, I tell 'em
in Polish. They pay."

Bruno felt relieved, now, that he hadn't gotten around to trying that, and hoped Scully had been too drunk to remember much. He lay with his back to the cell wall, eyes closed, wondering however Scully managed to stay on the force; he was the worst cop any of the boys had ever known.

He paid no attention to Comisky's "Up in there!" until he heard that officer fumbling with the keys. Bruno went to the bars rubbing his eyes.

"Hi, C'misky," he offered affably, as though expecting supper, slouching against the bars without seeing Scully.

"Stand up straight, son," Scully asked.

Bruno stood a little straighter.

"They tell me you're gonna be a pug when you get out of this," Scully went on, "but you got to stand straighter if you want to be any good at it. Nobody ever saw a round-shouldered pug get to the top of the heap. Kid McCoy spent plenty of time in the can, 'n he come out straight as a rod. You can still straighten them shoulders, son, you're still a growin' boy you know. What you should get is more sun, eat more greens, cut out them cigarettes 'n lay off that Polish pop. I was by the widow's place the other day but none of the boys was around. They don't come around no more, she told me, but she didn't know why. I thought she was doin' pretty well there for a while."

A lot of good snooping around there 'll do you, Bruno thought. Then realized that the killing of the Greek was doing *him* some good: no girl like Steffi R., no matter how angry she was, would put a finger on a man when that would put him in the shadow of the chair. And there was no way of fingering anyone for rape without involving him with the murder of the Greek as well. For once he had done something right in his life.

"Can I write Mother a letter?" he asked Comisky with all the meekness he could muster. "Could you borrow me a two-center stamp? You aint got a extra smoke 'r two on you, have you?"

Scully pulled out a pack of eleven-cent cigarettes and shoved one into the boy's lips. "I call these Lefty Bicek's Camels," the boy grinned while Scully was holding a match to the cigarette. Comisky slapped it out of the lips onto the floor.

"Now turn your face to the man, Strong-arm, 'n keep that Polack puss buttoned before I take a notion t' beat it blue. Keep lookin' at him till he tells you t' stop lookin'. Or I'll come in there 'n take a look at you myself."

Bruno stared obediently at Scully. Both he and Scully had put on weight in the past months, he saw, looking at the big whitish face, more stupid than Old Adamovitch's and seeming, as always, a little drunken; the eyes were so pale, seeming not to focus directly.

"Where you been in before, son?" Scully asked mechanically, the lips moving flabbily.

"Stickney. Hammond. St. Paul. E. St. Louis. Gary."

"Don't lie!" Comisky threatened. "He's just tryin' to throw you off, Scully—you ain't seen this Polack no place excep' between that poolroom 'n that barber shop. He was in trouble when he was in short pants 'n he ain't been out of the Triangle since him 'n a couple others like him stole a W.P.A. check 'n cashed it. I don't ferget nothin', Lefthander. You don't even get as far south as Lake Street 'cause you're scared one of them Lake Street boogies 'll take after you with a shiv." He confided earnestly to Scully: "These Polacks figure the South-side is out of town."

"Was you one of them kids from around Rostenkowski's?" Scully asked ineffectually, feeling embarrassed by the innocence of the boy's stare. Behind the innocence there Comisky saw the eyes beginning to flare; Scully saw nothing. To Scully the boy looked a good deal like all the other toughs around Bucktown; all these Polacks looked alike anyhow.

Bruno was reflecting to himself that outside he wouldn't be afraid of either of these fat fly cops. But they hadn't yet beaten him, and if they started on him inside here they might not know when to quit. He remembered how Casey had once said that it was better if they beat you in the squad car, when they picked you up, than in the cell; that if they did it in the car they got it all out of their system, without being as accurate about it as they were in a cell. He remembered a time that Knothole Chmura came back from an inside beating with key marks on the back of his head. He'd first begun acting squirrelly after that, and sometimes his left hand would go so numb he couldn't close it to pitch pennies with and had to change to rightie.

"Was you one of them rolled me that time?" Scully asked, trying to sound friendlier than Comisky.

"No sir. But I heard about it next day 'n told them fellas they done awful wrong, you was a foursquare copper from the word go. They was sure ashamed of what they done awright."

"You're the biggest jackal in the bunch," Comisky said quietly, "I ought to come in there to you, keys 'n all."

Bruno got the feeling, all the way down, that Comisky was boiling with rage. Well, that was a cop for you, changeable as a woman. They got sore automatically at anything behind bars. It seemed sometimes that the bars bothered men like Comisky almost as much as they annoyed the men behind them. Once you were in the open Comisky could be frank and friendly; but he couldn't take the look of men between iron and iron. The more humbly a man looked out at Comisky the worse Comisky wanted to treat him. It was part of being a Comisky to believe in no man's humility: humility was a challenge. It was part of being a Comisky to call that challenge.

"Awright, Comisky," Bruno said, still keeping his eyes on Scully. "Keep your shirt on. I was there that night but I got drunk early. Didn't know a thing that happened till I heard about it the next morning—" he turned the corner of one eye toward Comisky— "you better not come in here—I'm a friend of the alderman's."

Comisky banged the boy's knuckles off the bars by a single swift rap of his billy. Bruno grabbed the bruised knuckles with the fingers of his other hand and grinned weakly. It was his left hand that had taken the blow: he felt hurt in his pride as well as in his knuckles. Comisky's mouth looked like a new wound and Scully's was drooping unhappily, as though it were his hand that had been hit. Comisky shook his keys at the prisoner.

"You traded Officer Scully's badge fer that thirty-eight, Jackal!"

Bruno blew calmly on the knuckles, reflectively. He decided that he wasn't talking. He knew now he was going to be beaten, sooner or later, with keys or hose or billy—but whatever he got, it wouldn't be as bad as what he and Casey and Finger would be dishing out to Comisky some fine night. His knuckles hurt less at the thought. When the boys took a toe hold on Comisky they wouldn't have to worry about leaving marks for a lawyer to show a judge, as Comisky would have to worry on Bicek's account. In his mind's eye he saw Comisky on a narrow white bed with a vase of faded flowers near at hand, their odor mingling with the odor of iodine: an interne was joking slyly with a nurse at the door and she was trying not to titter; she was bending over the unconscious man to read his temperature, like in a picture from the *Daily Times*. Well, Comisky had had it coming to him.

"I don't know nothin' about a gun," he said at last.

"You mean you don't know how to fire one, Lefty?"

Bruno sensed danger.

"I don't know that neither," he said.

"All you do is file the numbers off for Benkowski—is that your job?"

"I wouldn't know that neither." He looked through the bars at Comisky when he said that, head to foot, and Comisky's face a foot from his own.

Comisky drew back, laughing good-naturedly.

"Look at him, Scully—he's gettin' mad. Look at that puss, Scully—ain't he a *sweetheart*?" The pair stood eying the boy like eying a strange animal, Comisky shaking his head in feigned amusement, Scully trying to smile, as he knew Comisky wanted him to, without doing so in a way that might make the boy mad at him again. Bruno returned Comisky's glance until the officer took Scully's arm.

"C'mon, let's get back to the office. The baby gorilla ain't talkin' t'day."

Half an hour later Bruno was in his corner, reading an article on Leo Lomski's great fight with Loughran in 1927, when the trusty who delivered bologna and coffee in the mornings paused, leaving his wagon standing down the tier while he fished for something in his jacket pocket. He brought out a single dirty two-cent stamp.

"Scully sent it up," he explained to Bruno. "He says you should write to your mother with it."

So all that December afternoon Bruno sat in his corner, his back against the wall and his knees to his chin, writing with a stub pencil borrowed from Mustang, with a copy of the world's foremost boxing magazine on the floor beside him:

Dear "Question-Box":
I am going on eighteen years of age, am five feet ten inches tall and weigh one hundred eighty one pounds. I have smoked cigarettes eight years but have never been a very heavy drinker. If I stopped smoking now do I still have a chance in the game or is it too late? How can I gain weight fast enough to fight at one hundred ninety eight this time next year?

This he placed carefully across the spoon holder, which had come to serve both as a clothes rack and a mailbox. He was not yet ready to trust the letter to the mails, however; it would have to be reread first. If he got another stamp he might even write the old lady and let her know where he was. He clipped an ad with his thumbnail and read it in the whitish light:

Young Griffo, the Will-O-The-Wisp of the ring—his life and battles— With numerous incidents of his escapades. Send one dollar in cash or money order.

"I better ask the old lady for a soldier when I write her," he decided. "If she ain't too sick maybe she'll hold still."

She'd been soft about money since the old man had died at County. The old man had been afraid to spend even when blind drunk. The tighter he got the tighter he got. Until it was hard to tell which it was that had killed him. Mama Bicek's story had always been that the old man's piano-accordion had turned the trick. He had been sober and hard-working, she always insisted, a home-loving man whose chief pleasure had been the accordion. In the depression years he'd taken it into his head to pick up extra money on Saturday nights by playing the instrument in Division Street taverns. His listeners had been more free with liquor than money, and Papa Bicek took whatever was offered. He had taken to playing every night, tavern to tavern, asking for the drink before it was offered. Till the day came when his job was gone, and the accordion was gone too. Then he toured the taverns begging drinks on the strength of the accordion's past achievements.

He had contracted pneumonia, one February night, by the simple expedient of going to sleep in an open Division Street doorway. And had died at County, twenty-four hours after, singing "Red Sails In the Sunset" to a Polish tune.

"His kid won't be goin' to hell on *that* handcar," Bruno determined, wondering idly what had gotten into the old man to make him start hitting the bottle that way. Night and day, week in and week out, till he'd had the shakes so bad he couldn't lift the glass, but had to put his lips down to it. Or steady his hand by grasping the end of a tie thrown back around his neck. That was the final picture of his father that Bruno bore in his mind. "I s'pose he was just breakin' the old monotony though, same as ever'one else," Bruno concluded philosophically. And resumed the reading of an interview someone had once had with Stanley Ketchel. When he'd finished he went to the bars and called Mustang, with the magazine still in his hand.

"Mustang! Listen t' this, it's what old Ketch said—listen ——"

"I'm listenin'."

" 'I say to my body'—" Bruno read from the magazine—" 'Come on now, we've got to lick this fellow.' I treat my body just as if it were another person, a friend of mine, a pretty good friend, too. So my body gets up and comes into the ring with me, and I say to my body, 'Now, don't get anxious; he's worse scared than you are. And don't get in a hurry; just take your time.' Then maybe my body gets hit, so I say, 'That's all right. Let him hit you. It don't hurt *us*, and it will give *him* confidence. He needs confidence, because then he'll come close to us, and we'll get him. Come on now! There! *Soak him!* '"

Mustang had never heard of Ketchel, and failed to share Bruno's enthusiasm. "Who'd *he* ever strong-arm?" Mustang asked.

Bruno clipped the paragraph carefully, wrapped it neatly, and stored it away in his snuffbox for future reference. Then added a postscript to his letter:

When and where did Ketchel fight Jack Johnson? How long did Ketchel have him on the floor? Was he still a middleweight at that time? Where can I buy a picture of Tiger Pultoric, my "favorite" fighter? Could Mickey Walker have licked Dempsey in his "prime" if they were both the same weight?

That night the cell was colder than ever. Toward morning he dozed, till the clank of keys against the whitewashed wall roused him, frightened and ready. The lockup's great gray cat sprang across the long sink the other side of the bars; she preceded the lockup everywhere and never paused to see who called when a prisoner meowed or called "Kitty!"; and shrunk disdainfully from every hand that smelled of a cell. The lockup went so far as to claim that the animal could tell whether a man had been finger-printed.

"Up in there!"

Bruno recognized Comisky's voice and sensed the others behind him. You'd think he'd heisted an A. & P. truck the way they were on him about that old man. He lay with his shoulders toward them, breathing heavily, like a man in a pleasant dream. Maybe they had come for Mustang.

But when the keys rattled in the door he rolled off the bunk and groped heavily toward the bars. "My body's just like a friend, a good friend," he tried telling himself. "They're just as scared as you are."

Adamovitch. Milano. Comisky.

A Polack, a wallio and a harp. No one was tougher on a Polack than another Polack. The going would be tough. Had someone been talking?

"Dip yer head in the bucket. The Capt'n wants talk with you."

"What time is it?"

"Dip yer dizzy bald head . . ."

Bruno slapped tepid water about his ears until Comisky said, "That's enough. You."

As he straightened up he saw the coiled shadow of the hose against the wall and threw both hands across his eyes, his elbows guarding his stomach and went back in a flood, legs over head, banging into the padding on the far side. Then it was off and the tier was awake, jeering and calling and cursing.

"Let the kid alone!"

"Toin it on in here 'n kill the bugs!"

"Whatsa matter?—Who's the fire department after?"

"Don't you ever sleep, Comisky?"

Bruno lay, doubled up and shivering, trying to get his breath. He heard Mustang roll over on his cot, as though he were listening to hear whether Bruno was hurt. "I'm lettin' 'em get confidence now," he told himself as he lay.

"Up in there!"

He got to his feet, holding his groin, and went downstairs between Adamovitch and Milano with his arms across his belly; he couldn't straighten up till they reached the room. He stood dripping in the doorway and heard someone ask, "What happened to you?"

"We told him t' dip his head in the bucket 'n he overdone it, Capt'n."

"Seems to me you overdo everything, Lefthander," Tenczara observed. "How'd you lose that tooth? Copper knock it out?"

Bruno shivered and daubed his head with a rag. This was a room like any other room; but somehow changed since he had last been questioned in it. It had one small window opening onto Potomac Street and you could hear the early morning trolleys poking past. There was a threadbare armchair and an old-fashioned wall radiator, just beginning to sizzle.

"I never had a tooth knocked out by a copper in my life," he answered, handing Old Adamovitch the rag. "I'm a citizen."

Milano came in carrying a straight-backed chair with both hands and elaborate care; for the gray cat was curled upon it pretending to sleep. When the ride was over she leaped, in a lazy arc, across the wall radiator and out the door, softly down the darkened tiers and in and out of the cells.

Bruno watched Tenczara playing absently with a black silk

bandanna. It lay folded in his black-gloved palm, then bloomed suddenly, as though with a life of its own. The other officers watched with interest. "The guy's a dilly," Bruno thought. "He's forgot what he's here for." Tenczara turned on him as though the boy had spoken his thought aloud.

"You'll get a few knocked out t'night then," he said. "Sit down."

And hanked Bruno's right arm down to the armchair swiftly, as though angry that it had almost slipped his mind that that was what he had intended to do with it in the first place.

"He calls me Lefthander 'n hanks down my right hand," Bruno thought contemptuously. Tenczara seated himself on the straight-backed chair in front of Bruno and drew Benkowski's thirty-eight off his hip. He laid it on the boy's knees like laying down a gift to a friend.

"Now where'd you come on this?"

"A bum sold it to me."

"On Chicago Av'noo?"

"No. In a tavern on *Mil*waukee."

Tenczara turned and reported to Comisky, as though Comisky had not heard. "A bum gave it to him, in a tavern. On *Mil*waukee." He shrugged his shoulders helplessly, took the gun and unhanked his man.

"Just another misdemeanor," he said lightly. "Discharged."

Bruno, rooted to the chair, crimsoned at the captain's ironic disposition of his alibi. Old Adamovitch replaced Tenczara in the straight-backed chair. It was growing light on the other side of the little window. Adamovitch covered the boy's hands with his own. Gently. The old man had wanted to be a priest, when he was this boy's age, and still fancied himself in such a capacity.

Maybe this one wasn't such a bad Polack, Bruno felt. He wasn't as bad as Tenczara anyhow.

"Look, son," Adamovitch said in his too reasonable voice, "nobody here wants to *hurt* you. We just don't want you turning out a criminal, costing the taxpayers money. That's what we're here for, that's our job. Those boys you run with though, they're bad ones. I'm a Polack myself, I know how bad a Polack can get. What you think that Benkowski 'd do if he was in your shoes now? He's older than you, son—he'd do you in in a minute. He'd take care of hisself first. And that's what we want you to do for us now. Protect yourself. You aren't helping him by lying to us, we'll catch up with him sooner or later. But there's still time for you to get in the clear. We don't think you shot that old man. We think he did. But if you don't say so, or even tell us where we can find him, there's nothin' for us to do but hang the rap on you. You remember Poor Bogats, Lefty? He didn't mean to shoot nobody neither. You got this rod the same place Bogats and Kunka got theirs. Somebody's peddlin' those things to you boys. You're a different type from that Benkowski, son. You're better class. You could be an educated boy if you made up your mind to it. I can tell, you aren't cut out for the comp'ny you're keepin'. Were you at Bogats' funeral that time?"

Bruno nodded his head, yes. And pictured Benkowski where he was now, listening mutely as he was, with a Polack cop holding his hand and talking like a mother, like a father, like a real pal.

"Did you buy that gun off the barber, son?"

"No."

The wall radiator tilted swiftly and the window in the wall swung dizzily overhead. Milano was hauling the armchair out from under him. Bruno shook his head to clear it; he was sprawled across the chair and the chair lay on its back; his legs were in the air and the back of his head was touching the concrete of the floor. "It must of been the harp come up behind me," he decided. He saw Comisky's boots as he lay and drew his legs together protectively and got to his knees. He'd have to keep on his feet with a man like that in the room.

"Nobody was goin' to *kick* you, son," Adamovitch assured him.

"Yeh," Comisky put in. "Yeh. Nobody was goin' t' kick you. You must have fell over. You must have fell over backerds."

"Yeh," Milano added, "you must of fainted."

Tenczara coughed into his glove.

Old Adamovitch set the chair onto its legs and urged the boy back into it as gently as a family doctor. His right sleeve was rolled to the elbow and Bruno read, tattooed in blue beneath the fore-arm's hair: *World's Columbian Exposition, 1893.*

"Catch your breath, son," he advised. "It was only to scare you. It wasn't to really *hurt*."

Bruno closed his eyes, a pain in the back of his head making his skull feel like it was coming to a point behind the ears. He felt someone hanking him down once more and heard someone leave. There was a half-audible murmur, now rising, now falling, from somewhere near at hand; his temples felt cold and his mouth dry. He opened his eyes and put his unbound fingers to his forehead; they came away feeling wet.

"Boy, am I sweatin'," he told Adamovitch, and twisted his neck to see the others. The others had gone. He saw the bandanna on his arm faintly fringed with red, then saw the fingers that had just touched his forehead.

"Kelly-Christ," he said half to himself, "I ain't sweatin'—I'm bleedin'."

"Pick up your chair 'n follow me, son," Adamovitch asked him.

He hitched the chair up under him and carried it into the next room with a thin line of blood coming reluctantly down the side of his face and neck. Adamovitch began rinsing the same gray rag with which Bruno had dried himself at a basin in the corner. Then he daubed the boy gently.

"This old bird's the worst of the bunch," the boy began to feel. "At least the others don't put on a act like a Father."

"You say you found that gun in an empty lot?" Tenczara asked.

"It wasn't no empty lot," Bruno said sullenly, knowing they waited to hear him say it. "It was in a tavern I bought it. From a bum."

"Same bum who sold you the spring-blade stabber?"

Tenczara spoke now from behind his desk, seated as he had been when Bruno had first faced him, above a charge sheet with a night lamp burning. Bruno stood before him bent like a beast of burden, carrying the armchair. "Sit down," Tenczara said to the charge sheet. Bruno let himself down into the chair. His back ached and his head began to throb every time he closed his eyes for a second. The lights were too bright.

Bruno made no reply. He knew Tenczara wanted to hear him give that one about being a boy scout again, so he stayed silent.

Tenczara tried another tack.

"Why'd you quit church? Who told you you could?"

"I still go, sir," Bruno ventured.

Tenczara dismissed the reply. "I know. Like you do errands for Mother all day. Why don't you start in morning Mass again and stay out of trouble?"

"I will as soon as I get out of this scrape, sir."

"Where do you go?"

"St. Bonifacius, sir."

"See that you're there t'morrow morning then. I go there too. I'll watch for you. Six o'clock. One of you men get this lad's clothes."

Was it all a lie about the old man catching that slug then? Or was this the same old "discharged" gag? He heard Milano leaving.

"Tell us more about yourself while the officer gets your clothes," Tenczara asked.

Bruno Bicek could feel that it was a windy morning in the streets, but clear overhead after last night's snow. Somewhere out there, faintly, he heard the flowing grind of roller skates over a hollow walk. Roller skates! The snow must be melting! The skates sounded, for a moment, the way skates did over the wooden walk above the shed by the warehouse. Then like they did over cement, across the rink at Riverview——

"Next!"

Had someone called that or had he spoken it himself? They were all looking at him a little oddly, as though he'd been told something he hadn't heard, and Milano was in the doorway with a little pavement-colored bundle in his hand. He made a good-natured toss of it into the boy's lap. Bruno held it with his free hand and looked steadily at Tenczara. Tenczara had his black bandanna cupped in his palm again, but this time he did not let it go, though everyone waited. There seemed to be just one more thing to do before he let it bloom as before and let Bruno Bicek go home for good.

"We're going to forget about that rod," he explained. "We don't think you bought it off a bum. We don't even think it's yours. We think it's Benkowski's 'n he bought it off the barber. We could give you six months in the Workie just for admittin' you carried it, but we ain't even gonna do that. We're gonna let you go home."

He was suddenly overly familiar, as though possessing some knowledge of Bruno Bicek which he and Bicek alone shared. Bruno felt Adamovitch's fatherly Polish arm about his shoulders, and didn't like the old man's touch.

"Tell us who slugged the Greek 'n we'll forget the rod, Left-hander," Tenczara urged.

So that was it. First he puts a finger on half the neighborhood for Tenczara, and then takes the rap for the rod for it after all. "Never trust a copper," Casey had told him often. And he wasn't doing any trusting now.

"Name us names, Lefthander."

Tenczara began consulting his charge sheet as though the names might be there.

"Don't gimme that hustle no more, Capt'n," the boy asked earnestly. The cut in his scalp began burning, and he wanted a glass of water. He saw the three officers looking quietly down at the floor at his feet, so he looked there too. And saw the bundle of his small possessions there; he had dropped it without feeling it fall. Now it lay limply, like a reddish-brown cur he had once seen in the middle of Moorman Street a minute after it had been struck by a truck.

"We don't *want* to hurt you, son." That was Adamovitch's voice, still trying to sound like a priest's. "It's not you we're after so much as them others. They won't never know how we found out, son," he added slyly.

There was something the boy wanted to say now but didn't know how to say it. He wanted to tell them that he didn't trust anything in uniform because he had never met up with any uniform that had ever learned how to deal with a man in any other fashion than by beating him. He felt, with them, as though he were in a ring with an opponent he couldn't see. He sensed his helplessness before them, and felt enraged at such helplessness.

"I'm no crim'nal," he said at last.

"Of course you're not," Tenczara assured him. "But how do you live?"

"I'm a fighter."

"A good one too I'll bet. Make anything at it?"

"Not yet. But I'm goin' to."

"I saw you pitch once over by Eckert Park 'n thought you was headed for the majors. That was last year. You ain't give up pitchin', have you?"

Bruno resented Tenczara's overtures at the same time that he felt flattered by them; the whack knew he was a left-hander after all.

"Yeh. I give that up. I feel more like sluggin' somebody these days than tryin' t' throw a ball past his knees."

"Think you're gettin' mean in here, eh?"

"Yes sir. I am."

"I bet there's more money in fightin' than in pitchin' anyhow."

"Yes sir. There is."

"C'mon, Lefty, name us names." Tenczara's voice was joshing, friendly and pleading, the way a tired man pleads.

Silence.

"Idzikowski?"

Silence.

"Punch drunk Czwartek?"

Silence.

"Morocco? Moochy?"

Silence.

"John from the Schlitz Joint?"

Silence. That sneak Scully had picked up a little information after all.

"Benkowski?"

Silence.

"Baranowski? Nowogrodski? Kodadek?"

Silence. Tenczara was reading them off a list now. If you couldn't trust a dimwit like Scully, how could you trust a man like Adamovitch?

"Knothole? Watrobinski? Coast-to-Coast?"

Silence. He'd gotten down to the sprouts, the five-and-dimers, the penny matchers, the yasheks who'd never come closer to going on a job than to lean against the same newsstand that Bruno Lefty leaned on.

"If you get mean enough you'll make some real money I bet."

Bruno saw the point suddenly and anticipated it: "I'm mean enough right now." He wanted to get it over with; if he was to be beaten, let him see his man and get it done. And felt Comisky slipping a clumsy half nelson on him from behind.

Heard Tenczara's voice, the real voice at last, no longer cajoling but hard and thin and cold and pleased at the way things were going to work out now. And felt relieved that it should be the real voice at last.

"That's all right," he counseled himself hurriedly from memory, "Let them hit you. It don't hurt *us*, and it will give *them* confidence. They need confidence, because then they'll come closer 'n we'll get them all." Without pain he felt Milano beating him about the ribs as he sat. "He's afraid to bust me in the face for how it'll look in court," went through the back of his brain, and felt his own shoulders kick back from a long right hand and realized he'd been on his feet and fighting Milano for minutes. The floor behind him came up like a carpet and rolled him back down with it; he rolled over on his face with one hand protecting his eyes wondering bloodily whether it was just Milano or both he and Comisky kicking him now and would they remember about the court—the lights came up too brightly all over the ring, a thousand lights all little, over a vast and ropeless ring.

And all the little lights began going out. One by one.

When he came to he was handcuffed, and the lights overhead were too strong. It seemed as if it must be night again, for he felt that the morning was gone. Then saw that someone had pulled the window shade, shutting the morning out forever; as though, in this room, no morning was wanted.

Comisky. Adamovitch. Milano. Tenczara.

He felt sick at his stomach and was sweating on his hands.

Adamovitch put a cigarette between Bruno's teeth and lit a match. Bruno didn't want Comisky to slap it out of his mouth again.

"Ready to talk, son?"

Adamovitch lit the cigarette and the boy raised his handcuffed palms to his mouth to take a long drag. Then he held the cigarette between his knees, the smoke trailing over the iron links of the cuffs.

"Yes sir."

"We seen this boobatch with his collar turned inside out cash'n his check by Rostenkowski's," he began. "So I followed him a way. Just break'n the old monotony sort of. Just a notion, you might say, that come over me. I'm a neighborhood kid is all.

"Ever' once in a while he'd pull a little single-shot of Scotch out of his pocket, stop a second t' toss it down 'n toss the bottle at the car tracks. I picked up a bottle that didn't bust but there wasn't so much as a spider left in 'er, the boobatch 'd drunk her dry. 'n do you know, he had his pockets *full* of them little bottles? 'stead of buyin' hisself a fifth in the first place. Can't understand a man who'll buy liquor that way. Right before the corner of Walton 'n Noble he popped into a hallway. That was Figura-the-Precinct-Captain's hallway. So I popped in right after him. Me'n Figura 'r just like that." He crossed the fingers of his left hand.

"What time was all this, Lefty?"

"Well, some of the street lamps was lit awready 'n I didn't see nobody neither way down Noble. It'd just started spittin' a little snow 'n I couldn't see clear down Walton on account of Wojcie-chowski's Tavern bein' in the way. He was a old guy, a dino from across. Couldn't speak a word of English. But he started in cryin' about every time he gets a little drunk the same old thing happens to him 'n he's gettin' fed up, he's lost his last three checks in the very same hallway 'n it's gettin' so his family don't believe a thing he tells 'em no more."

Bruno paused, realizing that his tongue had been going faster than his brain; his story would have to sound straight, but it didn't have to be absolutely straight. He could still leave Finger and

Casey out and have a straight-sounding story. But he'd have to go slower, he was getting ahead of himself.

"I didn't take him them other times, Capt'n," he anticipated Tenczara.

"Nobody said you did. Get on with your story."

"I told him I wasn't gonna take his check, I just needed a little change, I'd pay it back some day. But maybe he didn't understand. He kep' bawlin' about how he lost his last check, please to let him keep this one. 'Why you drink'n it all up then?' I put it to him, 'If you're that anxious t' hold onto it?' He just gimme a foxy grin 'n pulls out four of them little bottles from four differ'nt pockets, 'n each one was differ'nt kind of liquor. I could have one, he tells me in Polish, which do I want, 'n I slapped all four out of his hands. All four. I don't like t' see no full-grown man drink'n that way. A Polack hillbilly he was, 'n certainy no citizen."

"What's Benkowski doin' for a livin' these days, Lefty?"

"Don't know the fella well enough t' say, Capt'n. Is he the one they call Casey 'r somethin'? Yeh, I've seen him around."

"What's Nowogrodski up to?"

"Goes wolfin' on roller skates by Riverview. The rink's open all year 'round."

"Does he have much luck?"

"Never turns up a hair. They go by too fast."

He eyed the cuffs of his corduroys; they were turned up to the ankles and the cuffs were frayed.

"What's the Evil-Eye up to?"

Silence.

"You know who I mean. Idzikowski."

"The Finger?"

"You know who. Don't try stalling, Bicek."

"He's just nutsin' around I guess."

"Ever run into Corner-Pockets any more?"

"Don't know the man."

"How's Kodadek feeling lately?"

"Fireball? He ain't feeling so good I heard."

"What's Knothole got on his mind?"

"Knothole? He just goes around with a rope that got a noose in it 'n hands it to guys 'n says 'Here. Go hang yerself.' "

The captain looked to be at a loss. He glanced for assistance at the other officers, then returned his glance to the boy.

"He does that?"

"Yes sir. It's a joke."

"Oh." Tenczara cupped his chin in his hands; then gave up and referred again to his list.

"Seen Czwartek lately?"

"Punchy? I guess. A week 'r two 'r a month ago."

"What was he up to?"

"Sir?"

"What was Punchy doin' the last time you seen him?"

"Punchy? He was nutsin' around."

"Does he nuts around drunks in alley hallways?"

"Nutsin' around ain't jack rollin'."

"You mean Punchy aint a jack roller but you are?"

The boy's blond lashes shuttered his eyes.

"All right, get ahead a little faster with your lying."

"The old man. I ferget where I was at."

"You said you slapped some liquor out of his hand because he wouldn't stand and deliver."

"Oh. I told him to let me have his change was all. Was that too much to ask? I don't go around just huntin' trouble. 'n my feet was slop-full of water 'n snow. But he acted like I was gonna kill him 'r somethin'. I got one hand over his mouth 'n talked polite-like in Polish in his ear, 'n he begun sweatin' 'n tryin' t' wrench away on me. 'Take it easy,' I asks him, 'We're both in this up to our necks.' 'n he wasn't so drunk then, 'n he was plenty t' hold onto. You wouldn't think a old boobatch like that 'd have that much stren'th left in him, boozin' down *Division* night after night, year after year, like he didn't have no home t' go home to. He pried my hand off his mouth 'n started hollerin' '*Mlody bandyta! Mlody bandyta!*' 'n I could feel him slippin'. He was just too strong fer a kid like me t' hold."

"Because you were reaching for his wallet with the other hand?"

"No sir. The reason I couldn't hold him was I'm not so strong in my right like in my left. 'n even my left ain't what it was. I thrun it out pitchin' a double-header. I c'd still hold half a dozen greenhorns with it though, all day. Zbyzsko couldn't get off my left."

"Only the rod was in your left, was that it?"

The boy hesitated. Then: "Yes sir."

And felt a single drop of sweat slide down his side from under his armpit. Stop and slide again toward the belt. He had cleared Casey.

"What did you get off him?"

"I tell you, I had my hands too full to get *anythin'*—that's just what I been tryin' t' tell you. I didn't get so much as one of them little single-shots for all my trouble."

"How many slugs you fire?"

"Just one, Capt'n. That was all there was in 'er. I didn't really fire though. Just at his feet. T' scare him so's he wouldn't jump me. Plain self-defense, Capt'n. I just wanted t' get out of there 'n go home." He glanced helplessly around at the officers, feeling the inadequacy of his story—"You do crazy things sometimes fellas," he said suddenly—"Well, that's all *I* was doin'."

Then, in an access of desperation, "I just had t' show him . . ."

"Show him what, son?"

Silence.

"Show him what, Lefthander?"

"That I wasn't no greenhorn sprout like he thought."

"Did he say that's all you were?"

"No, but I c'd tell that's what he thought. Lots of people think that. But I show 'em, I showed 'em now awright." He felt he should be apologizing for something but couldn't tell whether it was for strong-arming a man or for failing to strong-arm him.

"I'm just a neighborhood kid. I belong to the Keep-Our-City-Clean-Club at St. Bonifacius. I told him polite-like, like a Polish-American citizen, this was Figura-a-friend-of-mine's hallway. 'No more after this one,' I told him, 'this is your last time gettin' rolled, old man. After this I'm pertectin' you, I'm seein' nobody touches you—but the people who live here don't like this sort of thing goin' on any more 'n you 'r I do. It gives the place a bad name, there's gotta be a stop to it—'n we all gotta live, don't we?' That's what I told him, only in English."

Tenczara exchanged glances with Milano.

"You shot him for keeps, Jackal. He's dead."

Tenczara shaded his eyes with his gloved hand and studied the charge sheet; the night lamp's light brought out lines below his eyes, black as though packed with soot; and a curious pucker came to his button mouth, making it look like a freshly stitched wound.

"Bullet through the groin—*zip*," he added, his words coming flat and unemphatic, reading from the charge sheet without understanding. "Five children. Stella. Mary. Grosha. Wanda. Vincent. All underage. So he wasn't so old after all. Mother invalided since last birth, name of Rose. W.P.A. Fifty-five per. You told the truth there at least."

Bruno Bicek's voice came, full of mild surprise but without awe. "The hell you say. That bullet must of bounced."

"Who was along?"

"I was singlin'. Lone-wolf stuff." He wondered idly whether anyone would call him "Killer" now. It wasn't as good as "Iron-Man" or "Powerhouse." But it was better than nothing. But as he said the word to himself a dryness began coming up in his throat and his stomach started tightening in the first faint touch of fear. It'd take an alderman to straighten this out all right.

"You said 'we' seen the man. Who's 'we,' Jackal?"

"Capt'n, I said 'we seen.' Lots of people, fellas, seen him is all I meant, cashin' his check when the place was crowded. They cash checks there if they know you. Say, I even know the project that old man was on as far as that goes, because my old lady—Mother—wanted we should give up the store so's I c'd get on it. It was just me done it, Capt'n."

"How big a man was he?"

"I'd judge two-hundred-twenty," Milano answered. "Forty pounds heavier 'n half a head taller 'n this boy, I'd judge."

"Where was that bald-headed pal of yours all this time? He run out on you?"

"Don't know who you mean, Capt'n. Nobody got hair no more around the neighborhood, seems-like. The whole damn Triangle went 'n got army haircuts somewheres."

"Just you 'n Benkowski I mean. Don't be afraid, son—we're not tryin' t' ring in any jobs the pair of you pulled before this. Just this one. Did you 'r him have the rod? Whose turn was it to be cowboy?"

Bruno heard a V-8 pull into the rear of the station and a moment later the splash of the gas as the officers refueled. Behind him he could hear Milano's heavy breathing. He looked down at his tennis shoes, that he had been careful to wear at all times since the Greek had felt the toe of his relief boot. He'd have to have new laces mighty soon or else start tying them with a double bow; already they were knotted in two places on the right foot.

"That Benkowski's a sort of toothless monkey used to go on at the Garden around one hundred and eighteen pounds, ain't he?"

Bruno looked up. "Don't know the fella well enough t' say."

"Just from followin' his fights though, what'd you judge he'd usually weigh in at?"

"Oney seen him go once 'r twice is all. He wore a mouthpiece, I couldn't tell about his teeth. Seems t' me he come in about one-thirty-three. If that's the same fella you're think'n of, Capt'n."

"I guess you fought at the Garden once 'r twice yourself, ain't you?"

Bruno sensed danger, but could not see where it lay; he looked down at his shoes.

"Once 'r twice."

"How'd you make out, Left'?"

The temptation to talk about himself was strong. "Won 'em both on kayoes. Stopped both fights in the first. One was against some boogie. If he would a got up I would've killed him fer life, I didn't know I c'd hit like I can."

"Was Benkowski in your corner both fights?"

"No sir."

"That's a bloodsuckin' lie, Biceps. I seen him with my own eyes the night you win off Cooney from the C.Y.O. 'n that was your fifth straight. You can hit all right, you ain't lyin' *there*. You wanna watch out 'r you'll kill somebody some day."

Bruno looked at his shoes.

"Look up here. What you always studying the floor for? Why'd you tell me Casey wasn't your manager?"

"Didn't say he wasn't."

"You said he wasn't in your corner."

"No sir. He wasn't. He just talked t' me from over the ropes. The guy in the corner is the handler."

"Who's that?"

"Him? That's Finger is all. Some neighborhood kid."

"You told me Finger was your hex-man. Make up your mind."

"Finger does both, Capt'n. He handles the bucket 'n sponge 'n in between he fingers the guy I'm fightin', 'n if it's close he puts the whammy on the ref 'n judges. Finger, he never losed a fight. He waited for the boogie outside the dressin' room 'n pointed him clear to the ring. He win that one for me awright."

Bruno daubed at the cut in his scalp with the lining of his frayed cap; then spun the cap in a concentric circle about his index finger, remembering a time when the cap was new and had earlaps. The bright checks were all faded now, to the color of worn pavement, and the earlaps were tatters.

Tenczara began appraising the boy's torso, weighing it in his mind against that of a man over fifty weighing two hundred and twenty. He judged that the boy might really have handled the fellow at that; he was built like a brick backhouse. Bruno sensed what the look sought and began, almost imperceptibly, to swell his chest to proportions equal to the deed he was claiming. When his lungs were full he shut his eyes, like swimming underwater at the Oak Street Beach, and said breathlessly, "I give him the arm alone, I'm rugged as a bull." And let his breath out slowly, ounce by ounce.

"Cross my heart 'n spit t' die, I was on the prod by myself. He was big 'n he was strong, but he was old 'n stiff too. Take my word. Just me on a private flang. But I didn't mean t' plug him. Fer Christ I didn't. I aimed at his toes. Take my word. *Say*—that bullet *must* of bounced!"

"What possessed you to get your head shaved, Lefty?"

Bruno's mind clung a moment to the word "possessed." That had a randy ring, sort of: "What *possessed* you boys?"

"I fergot what you just ast me."

"I asked why you didn't realize it'd be easier for us to catch up with you when you had your head shaved."

This time Bruno saw the danger warning clearly, and anticipated Tenczara. If Scully had told him anything, he had told him that the name of the club had been changed and that the boys had gone to the barber's for army haircuts.

"So many fellas with army clips around, I guess I figured it'd be harder to catch a finger with a clip than without." He stopped as though he had finished his explanation. Tenczara glanced around at the arresting officers significantly, and the boy began again hurriedly. "Well, it was a sort of accident. A fella was gonna lend Ma-Mother—a barber chair 'n go fifty-fifty with her shavin' all the Polacks on P'tom'c Street right back of the store, for relief tickets. So she started on me, just to show the fellas, but the hair made her sicker'n ever 'n back of the store's the only place she got to lay down. The fellas begun givin' me a Christ-awful razzin' then, ever' day. God oh God, wherever I went around the Triangle, all the neighborhood fellas 'n little niducks 'n old-time hoods, whenever they seen me they was point'n 'n laughin' 'n sayin', 'Hi! Baldy Bicek!' So I went home 'n got them clippers 'n the first guy I seen was Knothole Chmura. I jumps him 'n pushes the clip right through the middle of his hair—he ain't had a haircut since the alderman got indicted you—'n then he took one look at what I done in the drugstore window 'n we both bust out laughin' 'n laughin', 'n fin'lly Knothole says I better finish what I begun. So he set down on the curb 'n I finished him. When I got all I could off that way I took him back of the store 'n heated water 'n shaved him close 'n Ma couldn't see the point at all.

"Me 'n Knothole prowled around a couple hours 'n here come Nowogrodski from Fry Street with a spanty-new side-burner haircut 'n a green tie. I grabbed his arms 'n let Knothole run it through the middle just like I done him. Then it was Nowogrodski's turn, 'n we caught Moochy Chekhovka fer him, 'n fer Mooch we got Cowboy Okulanis from by the Nor'twestern viaduct, 'n fer him we got John from the Joint, 'n fer John we got Sheeny Baran, 'n fer Sheeny we got Coast-to-Coast, 'n fer Coast we got Corner-Pockets, 'n we kept right on goin' that way till we was doin' guys we never seen before even, wallios 'n Greeks 'n a flip from Clark Street he musta been, walkin' wit' a white girl we done it to. 'n fin'lly all the sprouts in the Triangle start comin' around, they want t' get their heads shaved too—they thought it was a sort of club 'r somethin' I guess."

He breathed deeply, feeling he had just passed an underwater sinkhole, feeling sandy earth under his feet once more, near shore; and went on inventing smoothly.

"Some of 'em we let do it 'n some we didn't, 'n some went out 'n done it theirselves when we told 'em 'no,' 'n then had t' let it grow back in again fast. It got so a kid with his head shaved could beat up a bigger kid because the big one 'd be scared to fight back hard, he thought the other Baldheads 'd get him."

"Is that why you changed the name of the club, Lefty?"

"Yes sir. We're the Baldhead True American Social 'n Athletic Club now. I play first when I'm not on the mound 'n I went t' St. Bonifacius all the way through. Eight' grade that is. If I keep on gainin' weight I'll be a hun'erd ninety-nine this time next year 'n be five-foot ten—I'm a good-size light-heavy right this minute. That's what in England they call a cruiserweight you. But the dough ain't in *that* division."

He touched his shirt with his handcuffed fingers as though to unbutton it to reveal his proportions—that would show them, too, that he was big enough to handle any dino alive. Old Adamovitch laid a bare hand on the boy's shoulder till he put the hands back in his lap. He decided, in that moment, that he didn't like this kid. This was a low-class Polack. He himself was a high-class Polack because his name was Adamovitch and not Adamowski. This sort of kid kept spoiling things for the high-class Polacks by always showing off instead of just being good citizens like the Irish. That was why the Irish ran the City Hall and the Police

Department and the Board of Education and the Post Office while
the Polacks lived off relief and got drunk and never got anywhere
and had everybody down on them, even their own priests. All
they could do like the Irish, Old Adamovitch reflected bitterly,
was to fight under Irish names at the City Garden.

"That's why I want t' get out of this jam," this one was saying,
"So's it don't ruin my career in the rope' arena. I'm goin' straight.
This has sure been one good lesson fer me. Maybe some day I'll go
to a Big-Ten college 'n make good."

Bruno began hoping that Tenczara might ask him something like,
"*What* Big-Ten college?" Then he'd answer something screwy, just
to throw them off, like "The Boozological Stoodent Collitch." But
not too screwy. Just screwy enough to get by. He scuffed his shoes
uneasily. There was no sound in the close little room save that
uneasy scuffling and the scratch of the captain's pen. Bruno took to
looking steadily out of the low barred window above the I HAVE
ONLY MYSELF TO BLAME motto, where the sun was climbing sullenly
above Potomac Street. Heard an empty truck clattering east on
Chicago, sounding to his trained ears like a '36 Dodge with its safety
chain dragging against the car tracks; closed his eyes and imagined sparks flashing from the track as the iron struck, bounced,
and struck again. The bullet had bounced too. Wow.

"We're just neighborhood kids is all," he began—his anxiety to
regain Tenczara's attention betraying his fear—"We don't do nothin'
'cept fight the Eckert Parkers 'n nuts around t' break the old
monotony."

Tenczara looked up.

"What do you think we ought to do to a man like you, Bicek?"

The boy heard the change from the familiar "Lefty" with a pang.
For once he didn't want to be called "Mister." And the dryness
began in his throat again.

"I don't think you should do a thing, Capt'n. It's self-defense.
I'm just a kid defendin' hisself. I'll plead the unwritten law."

"Who give you *that* idea?"

"Thought of it myself. Just now. It's a first offense."

"It's the first time you shot a man you mean. Remember Bogats?"

A plain-clothes man whom Bruno had never before seen, with a toothpick in his teeth and freshly talcumed face, stuck his face in the door and called, "That's the man, Captain. That's the man." And disappeared.

"This is a differ'nt case, Captain," Bruno assured Tenczara, speaking slowly, feeling shaken by the plain-clothes man's trick and trying to keep that shakiness out of his voice. And as he spoke so he felt a slow thought breaking over his brain. Dimly, then a little more clearly, along with the plain-clothes man's trick, he sensed a greater trick. Then the whole thing came to him in a flash.

They were trying to frighten him into a confession of the killing of the Greek. That's where it had been leading all along; he'd let them take him up to the very edge. And there they'd have him for keeps. Before it was over they'd have Steffi in bawling about the raping. Bruno felt his nerve returning. Casey had fired at the old man's legs. No bullet could have bounced like that. It would have flashed against that wall like a struck match.

Whew. What if he'd let them get the stuff on the Greek down in writing, on some promise of dismissing the shooting of the old man, and had then learned that the old man had walked home, put iodine on his big toe and dropped in at the station the next morning to report it, on his way to work? He'd have to change his line fast, he'd have to let them know they didn't have him after all.

"What's so different about it?"

"Well, in the first place," he said slowly, "It was a copper that Andy and Kunka shot. That makes a difference. Second place, I'm pretty close to the alderman." He paused to let that sink in. There now, he'd told them.

"You mean my brother-in-law, Bicek? That won't get you out of a thing."

Bruno grinned good-naturedly. Then yawned in Tenczara's face with deliberateness, stretching himself effortlessly, and raised one blond eyebrow inquiringly.

"Captain, I ain't been in serious trouble before 'n I don't figure this is as serious as you're talkin'. Fact is I been think'n it over 'n

I don't think that old man got caught by the slug at all. He musta fainted, sort of, that's all. 'r he wouldn't have hollered mad-like like he did. He would've yelped. I heard guys holler when they got a slug in 'em in a bad place 'n they yelp bloody murder fer someone t' come help them, they ferget all about the guy that potted them. But that old man was hollerin' fer someone to catch me. No hurt man does that, Captain."

"What does a hurt man do, Doctor?"

"Screams 'n folds up. 'r just folds up."

"How do you know we didn't find him folded in the alley 'n get him to County before he died? Maybe he wasn't the hollerin' kind."

"Maybe not, Captain. But if he died at County then he's in the morgue now. Bring me there 'n I'll identify him for you." The boy took a breath, knowing he had to stay on the offensive he had assumed though they beat him to death for it later. "Whyn't you bring me to him at County, Captain? Whyn't you have him finger me before he cashed in?"

"Maybe he never regained consciousness."

"Then how do you know it was me at all? Because I bought a gun off a bum? Captain, I don't scare so easy as you think. If that bullet had ricocheted I would of seen the flash of it on the wall."

He looked down at his tennis shoes, humbly, to show he wasn't trying to be smart: would the customers razz him if he came in for a windup in tennis shoes? He'd worn them in five preliminaries and there had been catcalls—but no one had laughed when he'd climbed out of the ring. Maybe they were luck. Like Finger.

"I don't think you scare at all, Jackal," Tenczara admitted, "I don't think you would've scared even if you had killed him. You ain't got sense enough t' scare." He rose from his desk and walked to the shade drawn over the barred window. He raised it, looked out a moment at the yellowish midwinter light, and spoke with his back turned to them all.

"Book him for a misdemeanor 'n ship him over to Central for the showup. Tell them to keep him there. He'll be well disposed of."

As he returned down the whitewashed corridor, with Old Adamovitch's fingers still on the back of his belt, a cold draft came down the tier, bringing the smell of disinfectant up from the basement cells. Outside, far overhead, the bells of St. John Cantius were beginning. Bruno felt the winding steel to the upper tier beneath his feet and heard the whining screech of a Chicago Avenue street-car as it paused on Ogden for the lights to change and then screeched on again, as though a gray cat were dragging beneath its back wheels. Would it be snowing out there still? And what had Tenczara meant by that last crack, 'He'll be well disposed of'? He wasn't out of this yet. But before he was, Casey would know, they'd all know, that Bruno Lefty was regular. Six months in the Workie—"I'll do it on my ear," he boasted aloud, to brace the sinking sensation he felt at such a stretch, in such a place. But maybe, now that he was booked, the barber would get Figura to go to bat to the alderman for him. After all, even though an alderman was indicted, he was still the boss. Or was he? Bruno didn't know.

Behind him Old Adamovitch plodded along thinking, "The kid don't *feel* guilty is the whole trouble. You got to make them *feel* guilty or they'll never go to Confession. Carrying a gun was bad all right, but staying out of church was worse. A man who goes to church without feeling guilty for *something* is sort of a hypocrite, I'd say. Anyhow, he's wasting his time." When he closed the cell door behind the boy he saw the boy pause and go down on his knees in the cell's gray light. The boy's head turned toward him slowly, a pious oval in the dimness. Old Adamovitch took off his hat.

"Run along, Dryballs," Bicek told him, "I'm lookin' for my cap is all."

The old man turned, hurt and tired and troubled and afraid. When he reached the far end of the corridor the boy called after him in a ringing jeer, "I'll see you in hell with your back broke, Adam*OWski!*"

A murmur half of resentment and half of approval came from the other cells. And when the murmur was past Bruno Bicek returned to his corner and fingered the world's foremost boxing magazine.

But he did not read. He sat with his head above the printed

page without seeing either the words or the photographs above them. He had won a victory worth talking about the rest of his life, and it had left him with the same sense of defeat he had had when he had crept up the steps of the shed away from Steffi and Fireball.

For whether that old man was dead or alive, he knew at last that he had killed. He had killed Steffi in his heart, and there was no room for any old man left in the dull pain that was beginning there.

He lay on the built-in berth of his cell with a metallic buzzing behind his eyes, an incessant lurching whirr, as that of a lame foot working a sewing machine. He was on the Eckert Park playground, a nine-year-old among other nine-year-olds, and the buzzing was the sound of the big circular maypole: it was of iron, and had dozens of iron rings attached, to which children clung and were thus whirled in a great arc, their feet sometimes high off the ground, sometimes scraping it dustily with their toes. He himself clung desperately, with both hands, to one of those rings: every moment one of the others would lose his grip and go crashing to the gravel below. "They're gettin' killed 'cause they can't hang on no longer," he realized, and knew then it wasn't a game after all, it was a matter of his life, and tried to cling even tighter. But felt his right hand losing strength, and the buzzing increased to a rushing roar. "If I let myself go now I won't be killed," he decided, "they're goin' to let me off with just havin' a harelip." And in darkness, somewhere flat on his back on a table like a rubbing table, he felt a cord being drawn through his upper lip, drawing it back up over his teeth to make a harelip of him forever.

"Benkowski 'll be up to stitch up the lip," someone told him mockingly near at hand.

The dream dimmed a little, he sat up looking about him in the cell, feeling relieved that it had been only a dream about the harelip after all. Without surprise he saw beside him a stocky youth in a thin blue shirt, shivering a little as he slept, trying to waken from some troubled dream, doubling up to get warmer. Beneath the fellow's head the blanket was wet: he touched it with his finger and it was not sweat, but blood. The touch of it turned him a little sick at his stomach, as though as soon as the buzzing began once more, he would have to go back on the rings. And felt a dampness against his own cheek. Felt the sobbing of his own throat as he wakened at last.

So he went on crying a little more, just to himself and not for Tenczara to hear.

Yet all Bruno himself understood of his own confusion was regret at not having killed the old man after all. "I guess I'm goin' screwy," he mumbled, and got up and went to the bars. "First I find out for myself the old man ain't dead, 'n then instead of bein' glad that that gets me out of a jam, I feel like hell that he ain't—what's gnawin' me anyhow?"

He could not know that his muffled conscience was crying out for a killing that would have been clear and definite and in the open: if the old man was dead Bicek would be punished, there would be no mercy, there would be no way of getting out of it. Bicek would pay all the rest of his life. And that was what, at heart, he wanted. He wanted it so, because of what he had made of Steffi R. He had snuck off with a bottle in his hand while the one human he loved had been turned into a loveless thing. And there was in his nature, so deep it had never before been sounded, the conviction that no punishment was too great for such a betrayal.

Yet there was no way of paying for Steffi. There was no charge against him for that, there was nothing definite he could be accused of by her. She was alive and well, in the way that any woman who worked for the barber was alive and well. So he could not, even to himself, see his guilt clearly toward her. According to his code he had done no more for Catfoot and the others than Catfoot and the others had at times done for him. He had been straight with the boys, he had been regular. And to be regular was all he had ever been schooled to accomplish. Beyond being regular there was nothing expected of a man. To give more wasn't regular. To give less wasn't straight.

"A guy got to be practical about women," he comforted himself. And *hadn't* he been practical? He'd made her, hadn't he? He'd scored and so the other sports had scored—if that wasn't being straight he'd like to know what was. Hadn't Catfoot fixed him up half a dozen times? A fellow had to square himself, didn't he?

He'd been pretty shrewd about it all too, he reflected now. And lucky too.

And even luckier about that Greek! How he'd gotten himself out of the jam about the old dino just in time! He recalled, with a sickening chill, the promotion that had come to Tenczara only a week after poor Andy had been sentenced. Well, he reasoned, the breaks had just gone against Andy. Lucky Lefty!—Three breaks in a row now! What more could a fellow expect?

"He could expec' t' be dead 'n forgot fer good the fourt' time," he answered himself. And added inwardly: "That'd be the best break of all."

When the trusty came past with the wagon, to leave him bologna and black coffee, the boy left the food standing.

"They tol' me t' tell you the doc 'll be up to stick a stitch in yer lip," the trusty told him.

"I'm not havin' any, Pigeon," Bruno answered, "Move on 'r I'll douse you." He picked up the hot coffee threateningly.

"That's up t' you." The trusty moved on.

Alone again, as he wished to be, he sang moodily to himself, a song of his own, all to himself.

> When I burn please bury me deep
> Somewhere on West Division Street
> Put a bottle beneat' my head
> 'n a bottle beneat' my feet

Later he wrote again, with an added determination.

Dear "Question-Box"—
How do you rate Tiger Pultoric? Does Irish Eddie Boyle represent anything but the Irish? What nationality was Ketchel? Do you spell his name with one L or two? Is it true that Jack Dempsey is part Polish? What was Joe Choynski? A boxer has been knocked down and at the VERY SECOND that the ref is saying TEN the round ends. He is ready

to answer the bell for the next round. Did the gong save him from a kayo? What is the decision? What is the best way of protecting teeth in the ring? I have very strong even teeth but have already lost one in the ring again Nash Coony. Is a piece of clean rag almost as good as a regular mouthpiece? Where can I obtain details of the fight between Jack Johnson and Stanley Ketchel? Is it true that Kid McCoy came out against Tom Sharkey with plaster in his gloves? Who won? How can I get rid of pimples? They keep coming out on my chest. What should a beginner in the heavyweight class get per round in Illinois? I weigh 181 stripped right now. How do you rate Casey Benkowski?

He paused, pencil poised and tongue between his teeth, then resumed:

Who invented the trick of pointing at an opponent's shoelaces and knocking him out when he looked down? Can this still be done?

He knew the nationalities of Choynski and Ketchel as well as he knew his own; he merely sought printed assurance that they too were Poles and they too were unbeatable. When they were right. Before he had a chance to beg another stamp with which to mail it, Adamovitch appeared to take him down to the wagon.

"They want you at the line-up," the old man explained. And this time all his false fatherliness was kept out of his voice.

The showup room for the bi-weekly line-ups overlooks the outspread web of all the tracks to Chicago: The Santa Fe, the Nickel-Plate, the Père Marquette and the Pennsylvania, the Wabash, the Monon, the Chicago-Northwestern; the great passenger liners south and the New York Central, the I. C. and the Burlington, the overnight manifests and all the grunting freights.

Bruno Bicek, waiting beside a barred window for the last line of the evening, watched the moving locomotive lights and saw, across the valley of the tracks, the lights of the low-roofed village between Halsted Street and the river; a village in the city, like his own low-roofed streets. Clamorous, like his own, with old-world markets and mid-American saloons, murmurous with poverty, filled with old-world faces and mid-American cries, bound by the laced steel of the railroads and the curved steel of the El. And covered, like his own, with a low slow pall of locomotive smoke.

These are the yards where the dust-covered fruit tramps come in, the off-season bindle stiffs and the punch-drunk veterans; the place where the outdoor workers of the republic hop off the Santa Fe at half past ten of an August forenoon or at 2 A.M. in the middle of March with feet wrapped in rags, in search of the Madison Street Slave Market.

Bruno could see the lights of that street the other side of the upflung bridges: the street where men watch the weather from the windows of louse-ridden rookeries in the hope of a snow-shoveling job before night; where farm boys stand around the corners and curbs all winter reading the employment bureau signs and never go home in the spring. It is here that those who stacked oats in summer are fingerprinted for lack of snow; and never go home in the spring at all. Here for half a century a tired army has shuffled, moving into bread lines at break of day or kneeling in missions to get out of the rain, a moving army by noon or night; wandering, like rain, all night through the streets alone. Or fidgeting in fake agencies, forgetting the weather within the forest of the free-lunch taverns where the mustard goes along with the bread—"to give the boys a thirst."

Most of "the boys," sooner or later, fidgeted a night or a week in the cells where Bruno waited now. It was a short step from the cake flops to the showup room; from the horse-parlors to the cells. Out of the open-door barrel houses, out of the secret brothels; out of the two-bit honky-tonks, out of the stag hotels. Among the men who had already preceded Bruno's line onto the platform, where Tenczara awaited them all, had been a mechanic from Indianapolis, turned panhandler with four fingers gone, a bookkeeper whose lungs had gone bad in the Bronx, and a bearded Kentuckian, the last of his race, in tight-fitting trousers a little too short and smelling like a moldering mission as he had passed. Not one would go home in spring.

Now the door to the platform opened and Bruno, at the end of the line, saw, over the shoulders of the vagrants and gunmen preceding him, half a hundred men and women seated comfortably, as though for a double-feature. Some had been victimized, some were merely curious. Bruno stood blinking in the glare, looking over their heads.

The little man at the head of the line had just been brought in off West Madison; he wore a frayed khaki overcoat dragging past his knees; its seam was muddy, where it had dragged in the gutter while he had rested on a curb, and its top button dangled loosely. As though the last vestige of his respectability dangled with it. He clutched a battered derby in one hand and with the other was patting down a few wispy strands of dishwater gray about the fringes of his skull. To Bruno B. he looked like Amateur Nite at Schwante's Family Theatre. What was a bedbug like that doing in a police line-up anyhow, Bruno wondered. Tenczara wanted to know that too.

The army overcoat answered into the amplifier.

"For protectin' myself."

He glanced quickly at the darkened corner where the captain stood as though fearing he had already given the wrong reply.

"The officers picked you up for protecting yourself? Shame on them. Don't you ever carry anything to protect yourself with? Don't look over here, just talk to the mike."

The oversize overcoat looked at the amplifier with the face of an aging terrier searching a world of alleys, side streets, unlit corners, curtained brothels, padlocked poolrooms and bootleg bookies, with brown-eyed weariness. He looked as if he hadn't walked down an open street in daylight, nor had a friendly nod of recognition, in his life.

"No sir," he answered, "I don't."

"Then what are you doing in front of a tavern at two in the morning with a Lueger under your coat? Don't you know those things go off?"

"I'm a veteran."

"What's that got to do with it? I'm a veteran too. But I don't go prowling around with artillery under my clothes."

The veteran eyed the captain's corner furtively.

"He took hold of me."

"Who's 'he'?"

"A feller. I never even seen him before. First he bought me a drink—because I'm a veteran—'n then he took hold of me."

"You mean he put his arm around your shoulder, something like that?"

"No sir. He *shoved* me."

"Then what happened?"

"He told me to go home."

"Then he slugged you?"

"No sir. He just shoved me. I'm a veteran."

"Into the street?"

"No sir. Away from the bar."

"And then?"

"Then nothing. That's all. I went home like he told me."

The vet backed off from the amplifier, feeling that the interview had been successfully closed, looking sideways at the next man to see whether that fellow thought he'd be able to clear himself as easily and swiftly as he had.

"If you don't mind," Tenczara asked politely, "We're not quite through."

The vet stepped forward once more.

"You went home just like he told you?"

"Yes sir."

"And picked up a Lueger 'n came back to use it on him—is that right?"

"Yes sir."

"You're lucky an officer came along to take that thing off you. You'd be standing up there for murder if he hadn't—you realize that?"

"Yes sir."

"You're pretty cool about it."

"I'm a veteran."

"What the hell *has* that got to do with it?" The captain asked, exasperated at last, "I saw as much over there as you did."

The little man seemed to find Tenczara with his eyes at last. And snapped like a mongrel held where it cannot move.

"It wasn't you who got shoved."

The captain lowered his glance to his desk as though he were the guilty man.

"Man," he said quizzically, half sympathy and half mild surprise, "I'd hate to do something to get you *really* mad."

A pock-marked mulatto in a red bandanna and black Spanish hat was next; he looked as if he'd been picked up for playing Cowboys and Indians.

"What you here for, Tom Mix?"

That got a laugh from a woman toward the back.

"For havin' whisky in my home."

"It wasn't your home. You commercialized it. You're a pander. Next."

The laughter ceased abruptly. Someone was shocked.

Next was a young Negro in a gabardine, heavy in the shoulders and lean in the shanks. The way good welterweights are built, Bruno B. reflected.

"What you here for, Ready-Money?"

"Attemp'."

"Attempt to what?"

"Attemp' t' prowl a cah."

"I'll say 'attemp'.' Attempt to do about everything. You're a hook. You're a flat-thief. You're a wagon-bouncer. You're a vestibule bandit. You're on the boost. Are you on parole?"

"Yes sir."

"Good-by."

While the mike was being moved the captain turned to the audience with the deliberation of a side-show barker at a county fair.

"I want you to look close at this man, ladies 'n gentlemen. This is Hardrocks O'Connor. Meet the folks, O'Connor."

A flat-faced felon in his late fifties with a four-day beard and a bulge for a forehead. The beard was grizzled with gray and the voice was hoarse from a hundred cells. Or from boozing. It was hard to tell. Bruno could tell by the voice that he hit the bottle hard; could tell the man had done his time the hard way. In the hard places. A man who was still trying to do everything the hard way. It was in the lean set of his jaw and across his punched-in mug like a brand.

Hardened by iron and softened by booze. Softened with iron and hardened by booze. No one near him could miss it. Bruno B. could smell it.

"Tell the folks about yerself, Morning-Glory."

O'Connor's mouth split: "Take 'em west yerself."

Tenczara knew when he had a prize: He took Hardrocks west for five solid pages. Danbury, Waupun, Jeff City, Wetumpka, Leavenworth, Huntsville. For a phony bunko game. For a dice game with packed dice. For violation of the Drug Act. For forgery, for the pocketbook game, for the attention racket, for the phony bunko game again, for using the mails to sell packed dice, for bigamy, for vag, for impersonating an army officer, for breach of promise, for contributing to delinquency of a minor, for defrauding an inn-keeper, for statutory rape, for using the loaded dice again, for indecent exposure, for turning in a false alarm and for tapping a gas main. And for the phony bunko game, right back where he'd started, a lifetime before.

Two years, ten days, six months, thirty days, a year and a day, a fifty-dollar fine, a suspended sentence in Texarkana, Texas; only to be run out of Sunrise, in the same state, three days later. A floater out of the state in Lubbock; only to get two years at hard labor on the pea farm at Huntsville for taking a rancher with a phony roulette wheel at a McAllen county fair.

"Why didn't you get out of the state like they gave you a chance to do at Lubbock instead of running on down to McAllen?"

The captain sounded merely curious.

"I had a deal on in McAllen."

Tenczara turned to his audience. He had read five pages and there were five more under his hand. But he was showman enough to resist further reading.

"Five more pages, ladies 'n gentlemen—'n not one a crime of violence. How do you like that? There's a man who'll take anybody, but he never carried a gun in his life. He'll do anything. But you can't make him carry a gun to do it. He'll sell you a little dope, take a little hisself, sell you an oil well 'r take a merry widow for a ride on her insurance money. But he won't carry no gun. He'll con you 'r me 'r his mother. But he won't carry a gun. He'll spot a beggar paddlin' down the street when he has to get out of town in a hurry—but he'll stop 'n try to take the beggar." This spectacle of a man who could steal for a lifetime without once doing so by force irritated the captain.

"What you here for this time, O'Connor? Stealing the sleeves out of your father's vest?"

O'Connor did not reply. Now he was hurt.

"I asked you what you were arrested for."

"I wasn't arrested."

"What they do—send you an invitation this time?"

"I give myself up. I walked into the station 'n give myself up. I can't make it no more. I want 'em t' come 'n get me, I want 'em all t' come 'n get me. I want 'em all t' know I can't make it no more. Anyone who wants me, tell 'em t' come 'n get me. I can't make it no more."

The woman in the back stopped tittering and pretended she'd only been coughing. Tenczara cocked his head to one side. Bruno Bicek looked out over the rows as though the old man were speaking for Bicek's future as well as for his own past.

"I been a stumblin' block, I been a obstacle to the whole country. I done it all wrong, I got hard-boiled too soon. I got kicked around too early. I didn't have nobody, I didn't care. I never had anybody. I'm an old man, I got nobody. I been a stumblin' block to ever'body. Now I don't care. I can't make it no more."

Hardrocks O'Connor was crying.

Next was a redheaded Dane of eighteen, with teeth like piano keys.

"What's your trouble, Red?"

"Left a jimmy in a gas-station door."

"At night?"

"No sir. Daytime."

"Didn't have any criminal *in*tent, did you?"

"No *sir*."

"You weren't going to break into that station after it got dark, were you?"

"I just had it on my mind."

"Where'd you fall from?"

The boy looked honestly puzzled.

"Where were you arrested?"

"Walkin' on the rocks off 39th."

"Where were you going?"

"Home."

"Then you got it off your mind?"

The redhead grinned amiably.

Next was a willowy Jewish youth. The captain sized him up hurriedly.

"What's it for this time, Milton?"

"Exposure."

"Startin' in early in that racket. You'll be knockin' your brains out in a padded cell in about two years. Next."

"What's your trouble, next man?"

"I'm a burglar."

"Just like that. How's business?"

"Booming."

"What you doing here—vacationing?"

"A parole officer asked me to drop in."

"I see. A social call. Perhaps you'd tell us the secret of your success?"

"I just do my best, all the time."

"Thank you so much. Are you staying for tea?"

"Might as well. I've closed up shop."

Tenczara dropped the farce, the edge came back to his voice.

"It's time you closed up. Here it is: Murray Taub, alias Tom Murray. Juvenile Detention Home in 1927, Illinois State Training School for Boys, '28, St. Charles, '29, Pontiac in the same year and transferred to Statesville to finish your sentence when you came of age in '30. In '34 you were charged with a felony and it was changed to a misdemeanor, so you did ten days instead of ten years. In '35 you were charged with a felony and served thirty days for a misdemeanor instead. In '36 you were charged with four felonies and they were all changed to misdemeanors and you did six months for all four instead of twenty years apiece. How do you do it, Taub? How'd you beat all them years?"

"I done my time for nothin' in Joov'nile. I just got a bit of my own back after that."

"You've beat society out of four hundred years."

"Society beat me out of a thousand first."

"How do you figure that one?"

"That's how long the time was at Joov'nile."

"Later on it went faster?"

"Later on I got a good lawyer."

"But don't people ever get mad at you, robbing their homes? Who were they—friends of yours?"

"No sir. Loan shops."

"Did you take them all alone?"

"Yes sir. All loans."

"I said 'alone'—were you alone or with somebody? Don't try playing stupid on me, it won't get you out of a thing."

"Sometimes I had a helper. He stood outside t' give me the dirty sign, someone's comin'."

"Were loan shops the only places you took?"

"I got a dress shop to my credit too."

"To your *credit?*" Tenczara turned plaintively to his audience, as though someone there might help him understand. "He says 'to his credit,'" the captain reported; and turned to the mike with forced scorn in his voice.

"What else you got to your *credit?*"

"I got a butcher shop. To my credit."

"You're a snowbird. You're on the wiz."

"No sir."

"No sir *what?*"

"I ain't on the wiz."

"They didn't send you to Alcatraz for stealing weenies."

"No sir."

" 'No sir.' 'No sir.' You set there four years for running a stop light?"

"No sir. For sodomy."

The captain took a breath and relaxed, leaning his cheek on his palm, elbow on desk, his face to the spectators registering relief.

"Just one more misdemeanor," he told them lightly, "Next man." The women tittered. The women loved it.

The "next man" was a blond boy of perhaps twenty-two, half-leaning, half-crouching against the rule-marked wall.

"Stand up there!"

Tenczara sounded like a public school principal on examination day.

The boy stood, swaying with the effort, the knuckles tightened white, the tip of the nose as white as new snow. The Captain relented.

"You must be hitting it pretty hard."

The boy's lips moved inaudibly toward the mike; it was hard to tell whether he was trying to speak or merely wetting his lips with his tongue in preparation for saying something.

"What you taking?"

The answer could not be heard; the lips could not be read.

"Speak up, son. Do you sell it too?"

This time the answer came faintly, from somewhere in cloudland.

"Once—upon—a—time."

"How's last Tuesday afternoon—is that once upon a time?"

The boy nodded solemnly, dreamily, with a slow-motion gravity all his own.

Yes.

Any Tuesday afternoon in cloudland was once upon a time.

A dwarf, with the head and torso development of a man of average height, was next. He stood two inches short of the four-foot mark on the black-and-white diagram behind him, and appeared to be in his early forties.

"What you here for, Shorty?"

"Pickup fer investigation."

"What kind of investigation?"

"I don't know."

"Do you know what you set seven years in Statesville for?"

"Suspicion."

"Isn't seven years on suspicion a little severe?"

The dwarf's voice was as shrill as a ten-year-old's.

"Yes sir. It *was* severe."

"Even been boosted through a transom, Shorty?"

"Yes *sir.*"

"Who boosted you?"

"A friend. He's still settin'."

"How many offices you rob that way altogether, Shorty?"

"Seven."

"I said altogether."

"Oh, altogether. Fifteen."

"A hundred 'n fifteen you mean. How much time you done?"

"Altogether?"

"Yes, altogether."

"Year 'n a day twice."

"You forgot Statesville."

"You said that one awready."

The women tittered their enjoyment of the little man's confession. A dwarf, standing between a seven-year-long shadow and a new shadow even longer. Perhaps it was funny, to be boosted so high. Perhaps it was like Mutt and Jeff in the comic strips. Perhaps it was just cute to be so little while the shadows were so long. Perhaps they saw no shadows.

Perhaps they saw no man.

"Ever tap a gas main, Shorty?"

"I done that too."

"When?"

"I don't remember."

"Then I'll tell you. 1927, 1933, and twice in 1935."

"I paid for 'em all."

"Wouldn't it have been cheaper just to pay the gas bill in the first place?"

"Didn't have no job."

"You been out of a job since you was born. You been a thief all your life. You got larceny in your heart right now. You're a dangerous man. Next."

The next man was a Negro of perhaps twenty-three, with one arm in a cast. His eyes were slanted slightly and his skin shone like tawny parchment.

"This is the sweetheart who shot Lieutenant Shannon Friday night," the captain explained. "Tell it to the people the way you told it to us, Memphis."

"I was out look'n fer somebody t' stick up 'n had my gun handy 'n he come along, that's all."

"Where was this?"

"South side of 59th Street. I was crossin' over t' the north side when I see Shannon, he wasn't in uniform."

"Did he call after you?"

"Yes sir. He say 'Hey Buddy, wait a minute!' 'n he had somethin' in his hand. It looked like a gun 'n I pulled out my pistol 'n stahted t' fire. He shot 'n hit me in the right arm 'n then I ran 'n tried t' find some place t' hide."

"You're sure you weren't out just gunning for Shannon?"

"Oh no sir."

"But you did know him from before."

"From a lo-o-o-ng time."

"And then he just happened by. Small world, isn't it?"

"Yes sir."

"You didn't know, of course, that he went home by way of 59th Street every day?"

"Oh no sir. He just happen by."

"You know he may die?"

"It was him 'r me."

"Not worried much about it, are you?"

"Him 'r me."

"It won't make any difference whether you were on the prod for him or just met him accidentally if he dies, you know."

"Him 'r me."

"How'd they find you?"

"I leaned on a mailbox, I was bleedin' pretty bad. I left stains on the box 'n some of my own people seen them 'n tol' an officer." The boy stood silent a moment, as though more saddened by that single detail than by either the imminence of Shannon's death or of his own. Like a melancholy afterthought confided to himself, repeated as though he had repeated it over and over, hour by hour, and was still unable fully to accept it:

"My *own* people."

His voice was heavy with shame for them.

"How do you feel about getting the chair, boy?"

Boy answered to himself, murmuring toward the mike without seeing the rows of white faces pointing so bleakly toward him.

"Don't care one way 'r another. Don't feel bad, don't feel good. Just feel a little low. But ain't scared of no chair. Chair's awright with me. . . ." His voice trailed off. Tenczara eyed him dubiously, as though there remained something not understood in his mind. Then he gestured for the moving of the mike. "What you here for, next man?" he asked.

This was a banty Italian, grinning out of self-consciousness. "Started a fire," he explained.

"Hell, that's no crime. In a stove?"

"No sir. In the house."

"Whose house?"

"My family's."

"What time?"

"About ten at night."

"Why?"

"I guess I was a little angry."

"You feel better now?"

"Yes sir. It burned to the ground."

"Was anyone home?"

"Just Father 'n Mother."

" 'Just Father 'n Mother.' What happened to *them*?"

"They got out. A dog barked."

"Ever have your head examined?"

"No sir."

"You should. You're a firebug. Next man, what you here for?"

"Wouldn't know that."

"Didn't anyone tell you?"

"No sir."

"Then I'll break it to you. You're strictly on the con. Isn't that right?"

"Not that strictly."

"Oh. You do other things too?"

"Beg your pardon?"

"Don't beg my pardon. Beg the pardon of the woman whose purse you snatched."

"I didn't snatch it."

"How 'd the officers come to find it in your room?"

"I stole it."

"Well, that's different. *Dis*charged."

The next man was a middle-aged Serb, splayfooted and over-sized, with the hands of a stockyards skinner.

"What you here for this time, Steve?"

"Neigh-bors com-plain."

"Again? What about?"

"I fight."

"Who were you fighting with?"

"Same ol' t'ing. Wid wife."

"Hell, that's no crime either. Next man, what you been up to?"

"Had whisky in my home."

This was a slender, high-yellow Negro in his early thirties, around the five-foot-ten mark.

"I thought they repealed that law. You weren't carrying a toy pistol, were you?"

"No sir."

"How about a real one?"

"No sir."

"Was there a gun on premises?"

"I wasn't nowhere near it."

"I didn't ask how close you were. I asked whether it was there."

"Yes sir. It was. But I wasn't nowhere near it."

"I see. You just had it handy in a drawer. Tell me, are you in love with a gun?"

"No sir. I'm in business. I got to have one."

"I thought you said it was your home. Now it's a business. Make up your mind, you can't beat both raps. Stick to the whisky story, it'll go lighter on you. If you don't look out we'll have you on both counts. What you using a private home for business for anyhow? *What* business?"

"Social club business."

"With five women?"

"That's the social part."

"I see. A mixed club. Good clean fun and lots of sunshine?"

"Yes sir. Meet in my home. Go on hikes into the country."

"Now it's home again. You're not selling whisky there then—I hope?"

"No sir. I give it away. They my guests."

"Which one of your guests filed the numbers off that twenty-two?"

"Nobody. I bought it that way."

"Now we're getting somewhere. Ever been in trouble before?"

"No sir."

"You're *sure* of that?"

"Yes *sir.*"

The captain shook his head sadly, to denote resignation at human mendacity. "You know, I'll begin to think you aren't telling the whole truth here pretty soon. You're down here for armed robbery in '36. That happen on one of your hikes into the country?"

"I paid a fine."

"You must have a good lawyer. Gets you off of armed robbery with a fine."

"It's what the judge give me."

"What about the year 'n a day in the House of Correction for carrying a concealed weapon?"

"I worked that one off."

"What about that telephone collector you stuck up in a hallway at 47th and Indiana on June 1, 1934—was that a bum rap too?"

"No sir. I just figured the telephone comp'ny always collectin', so I'd collect from them. I was collectin' too."

"Did you pay a fine for that no-bill for murder in '28?"

The high yellow started almost imperceptibly, as though he hadn't anticipated any recollection of events previous to June 1, 1934. The captain had reached him where he lived—in his courage. You could see him visibly trying to pull that courage together. You can tell when they're hurt if they try to smile. The high yellow tried.

It didn't come off. He had to answer instead.

"I didn't kill her."

"You know what I mean though?"

"It's a different case."

"You know what I mean though."

The captain's tone was final.

The Negro's face seemed burned rust-yellow, the color of a man's face being lifted out of the chair. He stared straight into the mike, his eyes two amber flares. He couldn't speak. But he had to.

"Yes sir," he said at last. And waited tensely for the mike to move. The amber fires began to die in the eyes; when they were faded to pin points Tenczara spoke leisurely, in the tone of a man with no place to go and the whole night to kill.

"Tell us a little more about it. We'd *all* like to hear."

Silence.

"If you don't tell it I'll read it."

The eyes were dead embers now. He spoke in a high-pitched monotone as though—at the first moment—with the dead woman's voice.

"We lived t'gether 'n we sort of separated 'n got t' goin' t'gether again. We were just drink'n t'gether 'n I wanted t' go home like we used to. Figured I'd bluff, teach her a lesson, scare her so's she wouldn't run off again 'n 'd always come home when it was time. I pulled the gun 'n leveled it 'n she grabbed at it 'n it went off 'n shot her in the stomach 'n when I went t' see her at County she took my hand 'n said, 'Honey, you shouldn't of done it,' just like that, 'n that was all they'd let her say."

The last man in line was Bruno Lefty Bicek; his cap in his hand and dried blood down the front of his shirt.

"You look like you been in a battle, son. Fightin' with the other prisoners? Where you live?"

When Bruno spoke there was blood on the front of his teeth. "No address. Just a pickup."

Then added reluctantly, because they wouldn't be taking the amplifier away until he'd said it:

"Suspicion of I shot at a old man."

"I heard you hit him."

"No sir. I missed."

"Lucky for you. You're in the clear in this town so long as you miss. We call straight murder a misdemeanor here." Before anyone had a chance to titter, Tenczara's voice turned hard. "C'mon down closer, gorilla, these people want a *good* look."

Bruno shifted from one foot to the other.

"Move, Lefty. You ain't manacled. So's these people 'll know you the next time they see you."

Bruno moved heavily down the two-step stair and around the platform, working his clenched cap with the fingers of his right hand.

"All the way, Lefty. You can move faster than that. There, that's far enough. That's as near as we want you."

Bruno put his cap on to shade his eyes, out of a burning embarrassment.

"Take off that cap. That's how he looks without a cap, folks. Now put it back on. That's right. That's how he looks with it on. Walk around, Daffodil. We want to see how you look when you walk."

Bruno began a dogged and deliberate pacing: five steps forward and five steps back. And turned heavily, at an imagined door. As though his life were a barred bull pen. Five steps forward and five steps back, head turned to find the promised escape that was never somehow there.

"That's enough of that, Bicek. Now stand still and turn around with your cap in your right hand."

Bruno turned, the sheen of his worn blue work shirt showing in the glare from above like light on a long-caged animal's hide.

"That's how he looks with his back turned, folks. Put your cap on, Lefty. No, don't turn around yet. That's how he looks when he's walkin' away with your money: he got his cap on then. All right Lefty, back on the platform."

Bruno returned heavily to his position before the mike. The line turned and scuffed restlessly through the door back to the cells. The overhead lights went out one by one, till even the tittering women were gone. And nothing was left in the showup room save the sounds of the city, coming up from below.

The great trains howling from track to track all night. The taut and telegraphic murmur of ten thousand city wires, drawn most cruelly against a city sky. The rush of city waters, beneath the city streets.

The passionate passing of the night's last El.

While his clothing and effects were being examined in the receiving room at the House of Correction, Bruno held onto his red sponge ball.

"It's to stren'then my right," he explained to the examining physician. "I got to make use of my time in here, I've gotta keep in shape for my career in the rope' arena."

He demonstrated, standing naked below a little light encased in a wire net, squeezing the ball with the right hand. The doctor was indifferent; but the relief at having his case finally disposed of had released Lefty Bicek's tongue.

"A pug can't take chances on bustin' his hands. Kid McCoy used to use rosin 'n brine, but that ain't legal no more. Joe Jackson you— he used t' keep his bats all winter in a barrel of oil by the 31st Street fire station. Of course that's differ'nt, that's baseball, 'n I ain't in that no more. It's the rope' arena for me, that's where the money is. Sometimes a guy is champ 'n he's fightin' some bum 'n busts his hands on the bum 'n the bum comes on t' win. Then he ain't champ no more. I can't take no chances like that."

His talkativeness was soon exhausted. When he saw the cells he relapsed into the sullenness that had become his customary attitude since he had passed through Tenczara's hands.

The cells at the House of Correction had not been cleaned in many years. To the corners of the cots bedbugs clung, one upon the other, whole generations clinging to the backs of the preceding generations while the next generation was being born above them. In clusters. Like grape clusters. In the shadowed corners on the underside of the cots they moved in clusters gently, swayed by an unseen hand.

The place was filled from morning to night with the sounds of human trouble: men moaning in sleep or cursing by day. No one complained about being in on a bum rap: they were all in on a bum rap. That was understood. But all were bitter at having to do their time here rather than in Statesville. There, it was said, the cells were clean and modern and bright, everyone worked, the food was varied and good, there were movies and teams and a chance to buy cigarettes—if one had the money for a pack—without paying a guard twice the package's price for himself.

"I'd rather do five years in Statesville than six months here," one youth asserted. There were none who thought otherwise.

Men with coughs, men with diseases, all ate at the common board. Bruno Bicek looked over the railing of the third floor tier on his way to breakfast, seeing the long tables set below. "If I was here for more 'n six months," he decided, "I'd take a flier."

To take a flier was to throw oneself over the rail headfirst onto the concrete below. That should spoil somebody's breakfast. And it had been done more than once. Bruno wondered, thinking it over, shuffling forward in the line, how it *was* done. Had the fellow had enough courage to keep his arms outspread all the way down? Or had his heart burst before he'd landed? In the gray light, with the numbing disinfectant over all things like a cloud, he determined that, if he ever had to do that, he'd do it by pretending that he was diving at the Oak Street Beach: he'd do it so gracefully that they'd go right on eating for a while. Then they'd talk about how much guts that Polack had had for a year after.

And maybe he wouldn't be hurt so bad either, somehow. Maybe

he'd land on his side sort of and just crack a couple ribs. Then people would hear about it and write letters and he would answer saying he was a professional fighter in because he wouldn't squeal on a pal, but he'd kept in such good shape that he was able to survive any fall, and pretty soon a guard who looked like Casey would let him out and he would be a contender again and every time he crawled through the ropes the house would cheer for ten minutes.

He was brought to himself by the odor of burned fat, and sat down to eat. The food wasn't much good, but it was good enough. And there was plenty of it. As much, and as good, as he'd been used to all his life. When he heard someone complain of lack of variety and lack of fresh meat, Bruno felt the fellow was just showing off. "He's just puttin' on a act to show he come from high-class people," Bruno would assure his cell mate. His cell mate would nod in order to avoid the slightest resemblance to an argument about anything.

This was a stout man who called himself Charlie the Dealer. He was doing three months for indecent exposure, and made a daily point of assuring Bruno that he had never sat on such a charge before.

"I done four times fer stealin', I never been in on such a charge like this."

He was proud of his thefts.

"I steal from the rich 'n give t' the poor. I'm Charlie the Dealer. Ask fer me around McGovern's on Twenny-Secon' when you make the street. They'll tell you about me. I'm Charlie the Dealer."

Charlie the Dealer talked a great deal, and during the day Bruno let him talk. It helped to pass the clockless monotony of the days: here where midnight was lighter than noon, where morning was no brighter than dusk. Where time went on without motion, through a corridor without end.

Charlie the Dealer was a conqueror, in his own right, by deception. Deception of the public utilities, deceptions of colossal department stores, deceptions of million-dollar movie palaces, and deceptions of vague, villainous personalities who constantly conspired to stop Charlie from taking from the rich in order that the poor should suffer a little less.

"I've beat every big-time outfit in the country," he boasted. Then amended the boast hastily. "Not the U.S.A. gover'ment o' course. I respect the gover'ment like my dear old mother herself. My dear old mother, I promised her on her dyin' bed I wouldn't do nothin' she wouldn't do herself. That's why I never chisel on the U.S.A. gover'ment. Though many's the chance I've had." A gleam of reminiscent satisfaction came to Charlie's eye, which was quickly blurred by the suggestion of a tear. "My dear old mother, on her dyin' bed she tol' me—'Charles, never bite the hand that's feedin' you'—" Charlie was too moved to continue for a moment. He daubed sheepishly at his eyes to cover his emotion. Then gathered himself bravely, being reminded once more of his conquests: he had also conquered a host of women.

Brown and white and yellow, gullible virgins, shrewd widows, cagey divorcees and over-sexed co-eds, housemaids and debutantes, chorus girls and haughty saleswomen—Charlie had seduced them all, had spent their money like water and brushed them off without a qualm and without an exception. Bruno listened.

"So she says she's mad at me 'cause she didn't meet me sooner 'n when can we start housekeepin'," Charlie recalled. "Imagine a woman that goofy to bust up her own home for another guy? Her old man was a slugger for the Yellow Cab, 'n plenty tough. So I fixed up a friend of mine with her who done me a bad turn once. I told him her old man was a crip. 'n it wasn't two nights later my friend bust a leg jumpin' out of the sec'nd story window into the courtyard, when the slugger come home early. Shot at my pal but missed, from the window. Then he seen my friend's leg was doubled up under him. So he come right down 'n lay the guy's good leg across his own knee 'n bust that one too. With the butt of the gun he done it. Boy, ain't some people *mean*?"

Bruno listened till, one visiting day, the lockup advised Charlie that his wife was downstairs in the waiting room. It developed that Charlie had four daughters and a son, by whom he had been long housebroken.

Nevertheless, Bruno envied Charlie. For not even Mama Bicek came to see Bruno B. And that night, when the sounds of the city were muffled and he could hear only the clatter of the night cars, Charlie the Dealer had to be still. Bruno heard a local curving west from the Loop. Its sound, half-asleep as he was, was that of a heavy-footed runner pounding down a million wooden steps; at every step the staircase creaked.

"A friend of mine I owed a bad one to once—" Charlie began.

"Shut up. I heard somethin'."

Above him the fat man sat up to listen too. "Is someone breakin' in down there?" he asked, sounding genuinely frightened.

But Bruno listened to the clattering beat of the Loop-bound local: between each beat of the wheels, as upon a descending step, a soundless footstep fell, within the thunder of the El. A lean man, down an endless stair; with every beat he paused, with each beat he was nearer. Bruno waited. For soundless laughter. Rolled over on his side, hands pressed to his ears.

Had she called "Next!" because she was mocking herself with the whisky in her? It seemed now that she had been mocking only him. If only they had killed her outright down there. If only that bullet had really bounced. If only the old man had been killed. Regardless of who had held the gun, Bruno B. would have been guilty; it wouldn't have been necessary to mention a woman then at all. Tenczara would have had him by the throat and who, in Tenczara's mind, he would have burned for, could have made no difference. For all his guilt was for Steffi R. Whatever happened to him now was on her account. He alone had killed her.

"What's the matter down there?" Charlie the Dealer asked.

"I heard somethin'."

"I heard nothin'."

When the next El came, and Charlie the Dealer slept, Bruno tried, for some reason obscure to himself, to hear those steps, that laughter, once more. But could not.

Down the cells someone began an idle tapping on a wall. Then began slapping the wall as though with the flat of the palm, slowly, regularly, then a little faster. Half in sleep and half in waking, he heard someone punching the bag at the far end of a gym, sounding at first like a featherweight hitting it.

Da-da-dadada da da dadadada . . .

A heavier boy took over, beginning slowly and working up speed ——

Braat—braat—barrat baatbaatbaatbaat—*rooof!* —as the bag whammed against the top of the apparatus like a bursting bomb.

It began lightly again, easily, skippingly ——

raat—raat—raat raat raaaaaaa—*rooooof!*

In the moment that the bag was silent there came the light rasp-rasp of a jump rope touching the floor.

A dream! Overhead smoke was floating past the lights, below type-writers were rap-tapping—and as though for an announcement of a windup, everything was still, there was nothing to hear in the world, no one, nothing, and yet he waited. There was no announce-ment. He was alone, in an empty park, beneath blinding lights. Heard a timekeeper's watch ticking and stood up: it was in his own pocket, he had come into the ring in his corduroys and relief boots. But no one had noticed, no one was here yet, and two tennis shoes waited by the bucket in the corner. He knelt there to change into them but the laces were knotted, he could not get them off; some-one had taped his hands too tightly, they were bound so that he could not undo the laces and he tore at them feverishly with his fingers, before the pressmen should see. Just as he got the tape of the left hand loosened, one of the lights overhead went out; then another. Then they all went out, one by one.

He stood up in the darkened ring and listened for the sound of men from the darkened rows. No one. Nothing. No one at all.

And wakened to the tapping down the tier.

Yet felt there was nothing. No one at all.

Bruno began to have long nostalgic moments for the life of the streets. Stood wondering whatever Casey and Finger and Corner-Pockets could be up to now. Who had Casey made president and treasurer in his place? Or were they all letting their hair grow back? And would they have a raffle for him when he got out, like they had had for Corner-Pockets when he had come out of St. Charles that time?

"I'll bet that creepy Catfoot thinks he's the Kingstuffer now," he speculated. "I bet he'll never get over how shrewd he is, haulin' Steffi up t' barber's that way. I bet he thinks 'cause he done five days fer milk stealin' that he done time. Wait. Wait'll I get out. He's got the bat 'n I'm shaggin' the flies right now, but wait'll I get out. I'll tell how me'n Mustang rolled a guy right *in* the clink. He'll be shaggin' then 'n I'll be battin'." He hummed a half-heard, half-forgotten tune he had once heard Catfoot sing.

> Stasha the Yashek down Division went
> With a priest from St. Agnes hot on her scent

Charlie the Dealer laughed when Bruno sang such songs. But always looked worried for a minute after when Bruno did not smile with him. And sometimes Bruno sang songs that did not make Charlie smile at all.

Charlie the Dealer was in time released. But half the day a whining rhythm continued through Bruno Bicek's head. He sang it leaning lonesomely against the bars, all to himself, with the cell to himself, in a flat, wooden voice.

> It's rainin' all the ti-ime

It began going through his head in a singsong even at night, in sleep; and always, to his own ears, no matter how hard he came down on "ti-ime," it rang clearly and true.

At the end of his fourth month he told himself that he knew, at last, what Tenczara had meant when he had told him he was well disposed of. "I get it now," Bruno thought. "He meant I was through."

Yet he persisted, occasionally, in his ambitions; once he scratched with his fingernail on the wall:

> Bruno B. loves Steffi R.

Then rubbed it out and wrote over it:

Bruno Biceps Contender
for the
Heavyweight Champeen

Charlie the Dealer was replaced by a rangy vagrant with a ptomaine eye. He came into the cell with his head in his hands and sat on the edge of Bruno's bunk for some minutes in this attitude. When he looked up, Bruno questioned him.

"Where'd *you* fall from?"

The vagrant did not reply. He did not speak all that day. But during the night Bruno wakened to the sound of his pacing, with the feeling that he had been pacing for hours. Bruno said nothing. He had barely fallen back to sleep, however, when the fellow spoke at last. To the whole tier.

"Let me out!"

Bruno jumped two inches off the bunk. The fellow was at the bars, the light from the corridor across his knuckles, his knuckles clenched on the iron, and the tier was in an uproar.

"Get out of that!"

The fellow turned hopelessly and the cells quieted with muttered resentments.

In the morning the fellow was still pacing. Bruno eyed him with disgust, following him with his eyes back and forth, back and forth. Abruptly the fellow came to Bruno's side, as though he had been waiting all night for him to waken.

"Have you got a belt?" he asked. "I'm going to hang myself."

Bruno pointed lazily to his trousers across the cell, depending from a projection in the wall.

"I never seen a guy hang hisself," Bruno encouraged him. "I seen a guy once by Oak Street, he was drowned. His belly was swoll. Go ahead—I'll put the belt back awright."

The fellow looked down at him with a long, melancholy, horse-faced reproach, as though waiting for Bruno to call a guard or advise him to think things over. Bruno eyed him without concern.

"Go it, guy. You're a done man anyhow."

The fellow spoke sadly, almost pityingly.

"You don't know who I am," he assured Bruno.

"Who are you?"

"I'm the man who's lettin' everythin' go."

"Oh. I didn't know. My name's Biceps. Bruno Lefty Biceps." He held out his hand, but the sad one did not take it. As though he had not heard the name of Bruno Lefty at all.

"Let them airplanes fly," he warned Bruno, his eyes rapt with some inner knowledge. "Let them race horses race. Let them bugs crawl. I'm lettin' 'em all go."

Bruno rose, dressed, and spoke no more. He lived on with this man with no further effort to impress him with the name of Bruno Lefty. And the man lived on in a perpetual search for himself somewhere within his remaining blood. At mealtimes other inmates took to asking him, at Bruno's instigation, who he was. His answer, always whispered, never varied.

"I'm the fella's lettin' everythin' go."

Sometimes he varied his tune, but the theme was always the same. And he spoke it like a prayer.

"Let them radios holler. Let them dice shakers shake. Let them boozers booze. I'm lettin' everythin' go."

He became known down the tier simply as the man who was letting everything go. And no one envied Bruno his companionship. That companionship endured two months, to the morning of Bruno's release. When Bruno's bundle was packed and the lockup had the keys in the door, Bruno offered him his hand again.

This time the fellow took it, shook it warmly and held it until he had finished giving Bruno a friendly parting word of advice.

"Let them monkeys jump," he cautioned, "let them lions roar. Let them telephones ring. Let them camels run. Just let ever'-thin' go."

Casey and Finger were waiting for Bruno at the gate, in the Chevie. After they had greeted each other, he climbed into the front seat and sat silent beside Finger, while Casey reassured him of his career from the back seat.

"First thing we got t' do is get you back in shape, Left'. I got two boys all set up fer you t' knock over, soon as you're ready. Soft touches, Left', just to give you the feel of the ring again ——"

"Who are they?"

"Vince Guerra 'n Cooney from the C.Y.O."

"I beat 'em both awready. Get me some good guy."

"I know, Left'. That's why I want you t' take 'em again—so's you'll get your old confidence back . . ."

"I got the old confidence back. What's the matter with Tucker?"

"Nothin's the matter with Tucker, Left'. That's just it. You been gone too long to step right into a match with him. People has forgot you was suppose to fight him, Left'. We gotta start where you was before that little trouble."

"What's in it for me?"

"Against Guerra you mean?"

"Against him 'n Cooney too."

"Not much, Left'," Casey admitted. "They know where you been 'n where you want t' go. They got to get a century each their-selves. That don't leave much."

"That don't leave *nothin'*."

"It leaves us Tucker, Lefty."

"What's in that for me?"

"Four 'C's. I'll give you my end of the purse, for takin' on Cooney 'n Guerra first. On account that trouble you set for was my fault. I shouldn't of throwed that gun."

"I don't want your end of the purse. I just want my own."

"We won't get nothin' but expenses fer Guerra 'n Cooney, Left'," Finger reminded him.

There was a long awkward silence as all three pondered the problem of Bruno's needs between this hour and the hour he would climb in a ring against Honeyboy Tucker. Casey answered the unspoken question as delicately as he was able.

"If you don't want to hang around yer old lady's no more, Lefty, you could give Mama T. a hand. Barber tol' me t' tell you."

"What's the barber's cut for *that*?" Bruno felt ready to fight.

"Not so much as he thinks." Casey nudged Bruno knowingly, and

Bruno felt better. That barber had done enough harm, but Casey's nudge had satisfied his question.

"Get me them soft touches right away then," he agreed. "I don't wanna hang around that whorehouse too long. I can't take no more chances on trouble. I got to go straight for real this time. One-Eye 'll pick me up fer nothin' now, if I don't watch it. If I get picked up fer somethin' now I'm done," he warned them both. And added to himself, "I couldn't stand another pinch if I had t' go back there."

And when Bruno thought this he did not think of the madman he had left in the cell, nor of the infested tiers, nor of the deadly monotony; nor of the callous gawks who had visited, out of the sickly curiosity peculiar to the safe and aging, in order to feel more sharply, in the very membrane if possible, their own security once they had returned to their own safe homes. For all these dimmed for Bruno Bicek after he was released.

A week later, bragging behind the barber's to the remnants of the Baldhead S.A.C., there was scarcely a picture of the Workhouse left in his mind. When he bragged of its filth he scarcely remembered its vermin; when he boasted of its diseased prisoners, he barely recalled one of them. But when he walked, beneath the shadow of the El or past Mama Tomek's curtained parlor, he saw before his eyes, black on white as clearly as though flashed on the screen of Schwante's Family Theatre, a square wall motto below a low barred window.

I   HAVE   ONLY
MYSELF TO BLAME
FOR   MY   FALL

To keep his vindictiveness always fresh.

BOOK III

OTHERS

I

The Hunted Also Hope

BETWEEN the police and the girls of the river wards an unceasing
battle waged. Captain's men and sergeant's men toured the river
wilderness: a wilderness of signal lights, abandoned earth movers
and boarded coalyards, of towering coal dunes and the city gasworks, with a red beam atop it. Of the little yellowish all-night bulb
burning within the fog of the funneled viaduct. All night, between
the switching engines, the slow smoke blew. All night, and overhead, across the wind, an all-night beacon passed: it swung above
a thousand miles of city track, searching the sky above the yards as
the Captain's men searched the yards. The Captain's men were the
hunters here; a hundred women were the hunted.

Sometimes a judge of the Woman's Court would be riding. On
such nights shades were drawn, and the hunted ones played soli-
taire. Or argued about nothing for a while and went to bed early.
Some evenings a citizen dress man came mincing over the tracks,
and then someone had to pay off. The women feared only "the
Heat" and disease.

The Heat came northward from the Loop or west from the Triangle's narrow streets. The Heat came by night, with headlights darkened. The Heat came noiselessly by noon.

Once a darkened car came up behind Steffi and a flashlight was full in her face before she knew anyone was near.

"Savin' overhead, Duchess?"

She had stood her ground.

"I'm on my way home now, Officer."

"What poolroom you callin' home now?"

"I got a home like anyone else."

"If you don't get into it damn fast you won't."

Money. They wanted money. They were by turns friendly and threatening, but, either way, it was for money. Any kind of money. The Heat took anything. A dollar. A half dollar. A quarter could get you out of spending a night in a cell as often as not. The jails were hotels, to the men who hunted in squad cars, of which they were the owners as well as the keepers: the hunted paid to stay out. That was what the hunted were for.

"I got no money to go to jail, Officer."

"Then move on 'n get some."

What was the use of arresting the tramp? Where was the payoff in that? By tomorrow night she'd have a dollar, perhaps two. They never forgot a face. They made arrests out of vindictiveness, feeling their man—or woman—was trying to evade payment. Arresting them taught the lesson that it was cheaper to pay off to a patrolman than to a bailiff; they were envious of the bailiffs.

Steffi had moved on, just fast enough to keep them following, but not fast enough to please them.

"Home" itself stood between the tracks and the river. Between the tolling of a switching train and the low moan of a river horn.

Now, in the heat of another summer night, she sat on the couch in Mama Tomek's parlor, a single passion-bulb burning above her. Its orange-red glow lit a dusty placard between the couch and the slot machine:

> This is no WPA project
> But you can get relief here

Beneath the placard six other women teased each other, bickered incessantly and fondled each other's rings; they slandered each other, affected one another's affectations, accused each other of jealousy and petty theft and duplicity and impiety and disease, while tapping restlessly with their toes. They rattled small change in their palms, their purses and their pockets, matched pennies and wound bubble gum about their tongues. They vied with each other in tinting their fingernails and dyeing their hair and toyed endlessly with eyebrow pencils, fingernail files and lipsticks; they picked imaginary threads off each other's clothes and sprinkled pink powder about aimlessly, from compacts or glass shakers like small saltshakers, some of it falling onto yellow, green, baby-blue and pink cleansing tissues. The floor was endlessly littered with Kleenex, Pond's, Chee-Kist, Venida and Kreemoff, with yesterday's horse tickets, last night's bus transfers, the morning's cigarette butts, half-empty Coca-Cola bottles, bobbie-pins and Tweek.

They forgave each other, apologized over and over, were truly *truly* sorry, had never meant to hurt so-and-so's feelings. Then tossed pellets, wadded out of tinfoil, gaily at each other.

The place seemed constantly filled with metallic sounds and rumors of sounds. Steffi became tensed waiting for the empty ring of the slot machine or the careless clatter of dishes in the kitchen or the faint clink of a tin spoon against a tin plate in the tin sink. When someone put a nickel in the juke after it had been emptied, the coin tinkled and dallied downward through a metal maze a full three seconds, struck bottom with a ringing metal twang and began spinning endlessly in a circle there till the tinny music began.

"That one went down into the basement," someone would remark then, "Maybe Snipes got it."

Under the tinny music the coin would be spinning still.

> The moon is a silver dollar
> Let's invest it in love

On one side of the juke were the Polish songs, on the other American. When someone wanted to play a Polish song, Fat Josie, who had just come to Chicago from Warsaw by way of West Virginia, would protest.

"No! No! American jiggy! Wes' Virginia jiggy!"

That and one or two other phrases was the only English Fat Josie knew. When asked a question in English she would reply with all the English at her command:

"T'ank you. Armour Comp'ny. Budweiser. Whobody say so? Good-by. Good lucky."

She learned English from the juke.

> Back in Nagasaki where the fellas chew t'baccy
> And the women wicky w-a-a-aaacky woo

A coal stove, with a coal bucket beside it, stood in the middle of the room summer or winter. A little Jew called Snipes tended it in fall and winter, and the girls sometimes stood with their backs to it, warming their buttocks in chilly weather. But summer or winter, the old-fashioned European stove looked oddly out of place between the American juke and the slot machine.

The girl called the Jockey spent hours yanking the slot machine's lever, giving the works no chance to come to a full stop. She played it for the mechanical diversion of yanking a lever, of seeing colored pictures of plums and oranges and lemons whir into one senseless blob of color, then slowly separate into distinct and understandable images once more. It seemed to the Jockey that sometime she might pull the lever and the wheels inside would start whirring faster and faster, the colors would whirl as senselessly as usual into each other —then the metal *pshdang!* as the nickel hit bottom would sound, suddenly, like a dozen nickels, like a thousand, till the whole parlor would ring with their spinning, whirring, circling sound—the parlor would go whirling till she could no longer hold on and the whole bright city would go whirling with her.

p-shdang! p-shdang!

Every time the pictures slowed down into sane-looking lemons and oranges and plums once again, she felt both an assurance of her own sanity and a faint disappointment in a world that didn't go whirling after all.

There were ripples below her mind's surface, where the girl believed in the slot machine implicitly—for five or ten minutes. Then back to the machine she would have to go, in order to believe again, even though it meant borrowing more nickels than she would earn the rest of the night.

And although there were always such compulsions in the darkened shallows of her brain, there were no secret things there: for the Jockey there were only things she did or did not do. She saw the other women grow restless when neither the juke nor the slot machine were going, saw that they too cared more for the noise the juke made in stopping and starting than for the songs it played in between. Silence, like daylight, brought them all back into themselves; like coming to in a stranger's room after a three-day binge. And all felt the need of being drunken. Of being constantly drunken.

Even women like Steffi, who just sat fingering a locket, felt this need all night; whether the traffic from the Loop was heavy or light. And the heavy drinkers, like Roxy, talked only of last night's drunk, tomorrow's gin, and today's hang-over. They resented nothing but those hours in which they must sit sober, waiting for sober company.

"Whyn't you quit when you're ahead, Jock?" Roxy would ask when the Jockey had won two or three nickels.

"I sure will, Honey—soon's I take off the winner."

She would put the winning nickel back in the slot and the lever yanking would begin anew.

P-shdang! P-shdang!

"If you *got* to toss off all your change, whyn't you put it in the juke so's we'll all get somethin' out of it?" the little Bohemian called Chickadee would suggest. The Jockey would obligingly borrow a quarter from someone and begin a restless slipper tapping before the juke, trying to decide what to play. A pink and green heart had been tattooed above her right knee and she would sometimes point to it and observe, "That's the *only* way t' really get somethin' for your money. What you got when the juke's done playin'? Now a picture right *on* you, there you got somethin' that's gonna stay with you. When me'n my girl friend Annie from Augusta was goin' to the World's Fair, she spent her whole World's Fair money gettin' tattooed on South State 'n never got t' see the Fair even. She got two snakes 'n a bleedin' heart 'n her mother's name 'n her boy friend's name 'n a Americ'n eagle you, but all I got was a heart. So I seen the Fair 'n she didn't 'n we didn't get along so good after that till she was took sick 'n I was tak'n care of her. 'Tattooin's like *in*surance, Jock,' that Annie used t' tell me."

Tonight, like any other night, number twelve was the Jockey's favorite.

> Now if you got a pussy
> You'd like to trade 'r sell
> Don't you let her wander 'r
> She might fall down a well

"God O God, listen at them records," Steffi would complain nervously. "They musta been dealed from below the deck."

"Why *Hon*, that's my hit-of-the-week heart-throb, I hope t' die gettin' raunched t' that song," the Jockey retaliated. The juke played five times for a quarter and she never wearied of tapping. Nor did she tire of the same record five times in a row; she was too indolent to select more than one number. The oftener she played a piece the pleasanter she found it.

"How can she take the same old piece over 'n over?" Steffi asked the parlor at large.

"I c'n take it because I like it, 'n when you like somethin' you sure c'n take it," the Jockey explained. And then, as though resenting questions from a comparative newcomer she asked Steffi directly, "Duchess, you like peanuts?"

To humor her Steffi answered, "Yes."

"You *monkey*. What has three legs 'n can't walk then?" she challenged Steffi further.

"You mean three *feet*, Honey," Chickadee interposed, "that's a yardstick. You told us that one. We heard all your corny riddles, Hon."

"What's the difference between a woman 'n a bottle then?"

Nobody in the parlor answered.

"A bottle you fill 'n then cork—get it?"

The lemons and the plums whirred triumphantly, signaling the Jockey's victory by jangling four nickels into the cup. She grabbed them, started toward the juke with them clutched in her babyish palm, and halfway across the parlor a fifth one fell. Roxy jumped up as though to beat the Jockey back to the cup. The Jockey whirled at the sound, half-stumbled and came up against the machine with her hand in the cup. Roxy feigned disappointment and reseated herself. The Jockey returned to the juke and put all five on number twelve. When it had finished playing the fifth time she went to Roxy trailing a greasy pink shoulder strap.

"Hon dear, tie me."

"The Jesus God, I'm tired of tyin' you, you're always pinnin' yerself 'n comin' apart. It never stays—whyn't you ever bother somebody elts? Who pinned you before I was around? Turn around."

"It ain't *my* fault, Hon dear. Don't bawl *me* out. It's the *material.*"

"Well, why you always buy such cheesy stuff?"

"Hon dear, it ain't *cheesy.*"

"It must be. It don't never hold."

"No, it's good material—*look.*"

She stood on one leg with the other crossed over her knee, trying to rend the cloth; she tottered, and could not tear it.

"Mary Mother, how can I tie you, you won't even stand still."

"Well, don't say *cheesy.* I ain't no *rat.*"

She giggled and stood rigidly till Roxy slapped her rump to indicate the strap was tied. Then she bounded halfway across the parlor and stopped abruptly, realizing she had no place to bound to. So returned to the crowded couch, where there might have been room for her between Fat Josie and Tookie if either had chosen to budge a few inches. "Where do I sit?" she asked them helplessly.

"On yer rosy rump," Tookie rasped in her whisky whisper, from behind a page of *Superman*; whisky had wrecked her voice and veronal her body. The Jockey seated herself cross-legged on the floor, alternately beating her throat with her handkerchief and tucking it beneath her chin, humming absently while reading the other side of Tookie's comics.

"I always read that *Superman*," she said when Tookie turned the page, "I read all that stuff. I believe it all too you," she tittered. "Only how does that sonofabitch fly gets me."

Her humming had something of the fevered patience that her slipper tapping possessed: the contented all-day humming in wards where mad women weave the same endless basket year after year. Here too the weavers met at the same time each day, year after year, smiling the same unsteady smiles in the same uncertain light. They sat in a semicircle in a carpetless room; each wove an endless basket in her mind's uncertain light.

The Jockey wove a colored basket, inlaid with plums and lemons and all the bright juke's colors.

Steffi wove a yellow basket, like an arc lamp's all-night glow, in which she wove, from time to time, the red carnations of the wall.

But Roxy's basket was mottled gray, the shade of a dead man's final wound. Roxy had died in the streets below, a dozen years before: now she sat on weaving still, contentment in all she did and said, preferred by the older men to the younger women; and knowing always that mottled gray was the best cloth of all for weaving.

The first parlor was darkened; the second, in which the juke and the slot machine stood, was bright. In a far corner of the first, shoved out of the way, stood an empty candy vendor displaying the printed advice:

5c * win a candy bar * 5c

"I wish someone 'd fill *this* gentleman up," the Jockey would hope wistfully, "I'd win a bar of Forever Yours the first time maybe." Fondling the lever, she paid no heed to another ad, a forgotten card thumbtacked above the vendor by some forgotten cynic:

Credit Department
Upstairs
Take the Elevator
Please

Talking earnestly to herself in the darkness, the girl recalled, as in a daydream, the path she had taken to Mama Tomek's.

"When I was in the Walkathon by the Coliseum my girl friend Annie from Augusta used to get froze stiff in fourteen hun'erd pounds from ice every Tuesday night. They even stuck a ad in the *Times* about her, her real name too, she was goin' to bust the world's record for bein' buried alive in a tomb of ice. Me'n her went to the Fair t'gether. She never did get t' see it though account of that tattooin' fella. She'd always have t' stop 'n say hello, 'n he'd joke her about gettin' stowed away in that tomb they called it, 'n then she was sunk. She liked to get ribbed a little about bustin' that record, I'd have t' go on to the Fair by myself. But she got a extra fin Tuesday nights for gettin' froze like that. My boy friend was a judge there, that's how I got on too. But he couldn't get 'em t' freeze me. All a judge had t' do was trip us up in the dynamite sprints."

No one paid the Jockey any attention. Such fragments of conversation, lumpish and unresolved, rose constantly here; and fell, like twigs on a falling river. Outside, even now, a week out of the workhouse, Bruno Bicek passed and repassed.

He wore a straw hat, bought for him by the barber, and the pavement-colored suit given him by the County. It was too tight across the shoulders, too tight in the thighs, and barely reached to the ankles. His wrists stuck out of it as though the sleeves had been fashioned for Bibleback. And yet he was self-conscious of it only because of its drabness. Despite the warmth of the weather he kept his collar buttoned and his tie in place, for his tie was orange, and that was the only color he had to wear. Save for the red sponge ball in his right hand, that showed through his knuckles as he pressed it, while walking. When he spotted a likely looking fellow he leaned his back against the arc lamp and nodded toward the parlor's curtained window as the fellow passed.

"They're tak'n 'em off in there now, fella—seven little French girls in the *ex*-treme nood."

When the women within spoke of him, all but the one nick-named the Duchess joined in. Even Fat Josie understood and would cry out "Good *majtek*! Good man! Good lucky!"

And Mama Tomek liked to say of him, "He's an educated boy, you don't know. Born 'n raised in this country too." She was inordinately proud of possessing a pimp whom she could boss; for her whole previous experience with the species had been one of subjection. To an odd dozen of them. So she let him carry a bottle on the job, where no one else attached to the house was so permitted.

On the first Saturday night of his freedom he came into the parlor and stood swaying in the middle of the room, fists clenched, as though looking for someone to beat.

"I'm Bruno Lefty," he introduced himself, "I'm keepin' things in order here." He looked about challengingly.

"Tell that to Sweeney, Murphy's dead," Roxy told him dryly, "You're out of order yerself."

His eyes found Steffi, sitting cross-legged in orange pajamas, cigarette in hand. He eyed her until she flicked the ash nervously onto the window sill and looked away. Then he opened his left palm and tossed a dime onto the floor at her feet.

"What's that for, Bunny?" she asked him.

"It's for you. It's how much you're worth t' me now. Pick it up. You." He spat between his teeth at the floor.

She felt no fear of him. Yet she stooped and picked it up and pocketed it and sat again looking at him without reproach. He appeared neither pleased nor triumphant at his easy success, only somewhat soberer; as though he had been, somehow, the humiliated one. His eyes sought the floor where he had spat.

"I'm disgusted of myself, what I'm doin' now," he acknowledged and shuffled off.

She followed beside him, anxious for him. "What more do you want?" she asked him seriously; feeling there was still more she might be able to give him.

He stood studying the thin-faced girl in the orange pajamas. Conscious of the pajamas, she hung her head before him. He lifted her chin up.

"You got no cause to hang *your* head," he told her solemnly, "you done nothin' wrong."

"I'm doin' wrong now. Every day."

"I know." His lips barely formed the words, as though it were a secret between just the two of them. "That's why I feel this way." He turned to go but again she followed. In the narrow hall, smelling always like a hospital hall, Bruno told her, "I ain't no good to myself this way. I'm beat every day of my life."

"You ain't no good t' me this way neither," she told him tersely. "Every day you're beat, I'm beat too. If you're truly sorry like you say, get after them to get you a couple fights 'n get me out of here."

"You mean pay off the barber, Steff?"

"That's what I mean. If you're *truly* sorry that is."

Down the hall Mama T. began moving toward them.

"Start gettin' yourself back in shape," Steffi told him, "You got to get back the stren'th the workie took out of you."

"I'll make 'em get me Tucker," he decided slowly, "I'll take that jig like Grant took Richmond." He flexed the muscle of his right arm and turned so that Mama T., arms akimbo, might admire it also. "That's the army," he explained.

"Tell Mama T. what the other one is too," Steffi asked, the lights in her eyes beginning to dance. He flexed the left biceps for Mama T. "That's the navy," he told her. "You want t' see my Detation Waltz?" Without waiting for Mama T.'s assent he drew himself back as though preparing to fire the world's fastest, straightest fast-ball, and came forward to end the pitch with one hand on his hip, woman-fashion, and the other tucking imaginary strands back into place behind his ear.

"He does it differ'nt every time, too," Steffi boasted for him, "It's his Detation Waltz he calls it."

"I hope he knows what he's doin' is all," Mama T. observed dubiously, "It looked queer as duck soup t' me."

Bruno whispered anxiously to Steffi, "Where's the phone book, Steff? Is there one?"

Steffi understood. He had torn every city directory in two that her mother had ever owned. She hurried off toward Mama T.'s desk to get the directory—Bruno'd show these farmers a thing or two.

Mama T. drew her back. "Honey-sweet," she began, confronting Bruno B., "You're gettin' two warm meals a day 'n liquor for gettin' customers 'n bouncin' drunks, not for clownin' for the girls. 'n not for takin' picks on 'em neither. You're here to keep trouble away, not to bring it in. Lord, a person can't tell what you're up to half the time. One minute you give me the willies, you look that mean, 'n the next I swear it's all I can do to keep from rolling on the floor. You should be on the stage, Hon—I only hope you c'n fight like you can cut up. But if you got somethin' against this girl, let me tell you now, don't you never try settlin' it in my parlor. I can't take chances like that, Hon, this ain't the old days no more. *Darling*, you don't know how easy it is to get in trouble in this town these days. Even after all the years I been runnin' a grade-A *re*-fined house. When someone puts in a complaint they slap it to me just as hard as if I was some Greek from Cincinnati up here tryin' to start up a chain. After all, Sweetie, it's only natural and you know it, I don't see why anyone should complain about a thing that natural. You can't go against nature, I tell them kind, so why begrudge others their fun? But when they get me on the carpet it don't matter how natural a thing is. They slap it to me like they didn't want to see folks enjoyin' theirselves.

"Another thing, Sweetie, you better not try roughin' that girl up anywhere else, either, the barber wouldn't care for that a-tall. If you want t' get that Tucker fight at the Garden that is. Duchess is the barber's so don't pretend you don't know. You brushed her off yourself, and in fine fashion you done it too I might add, 'n the barber tended her like a mother 'n put her back on her feet. You shoulda seen that girl like I seen her, the shape she was in. More dead than alive, I swear. 'n now look at her, a regular little lady, manners 'n all, she even sweeps up for the barber now 'n then, he's like a father to her.

"We don't have you here for nothin' but to keep you out of trouble so's you can get a fresh start, the barber wants you should stay out of jail after this. So you might as well ferget you ever knew that little trick. She's too good for you anyhow. So snap into it Sweetie, 'n lay off that bottle on your hip. You ain't brought the girls a decent date since you come out of the Beanery.

"He don't care for nothin', that one," Mama T. added when she had returned to her parlor.

"I'd like to see him go against that jig," Roxy hoped. "I'd like t' see the coon bloody him up."

The other women looked at Steffi, in the hope that she would take up Roxy's challenge. But the Duchess only sat fingering the locket she called her Heart-of-Jesus locket, and wishing the nights were not so long.

"He reminds me of my second boy friend, the tattooer," the Jockey was reminded, and when her tongue began chattering nobody seemed to hear. "We started goin' t'gether after my girl friend Annie from Augusta got so sick. She was his girl friend first, 'n then she got so sick. First she just lost weight, so I was his girl friend on the side, 'n she never did find out. She thought I was still goin' with the Walkathon guy. We kept it from her. Like in the movies you.

"Then they wanted me t' take her place gettin' froze, but my *new* boy friend wouldn't let me, he says that's what was doin' for Annie, he's tired of changin' girl friends. So I didn't take it."

She paused, where she stood by the vendor, as though deciding to tell them the story again whether they would listen or not; she seemed to relate half the incident to herself, silently, and then, in the middle, began, suddenly, aloud.

"It was just tak'n a little that croaked the poor thing. I worked for doctors so that's how I know. If you drink a whole bottle of it it won't hurt you, you just throw it all up. It's just tak'n a drop 'r two that croaks you. I learned how to short-arm inspect from doctors too. 'n that's just what done for the poor thing, 'cause most of it spilled on the bedclothes. She was that thin from being froze so regular, the last time I went upstairs to wash her I was afraid of touchin' her with my fingers. Scared I'd *hurt* her. So I got me a nice piece of cotton battin'. You know, she quivered all over like a cold puppy? Poor thing, quiverin' 'n gruntin' there on the bed 'n her room rent ten days overdue. 'n you know what our boy friend done the minute he come in 'n I told him how bad she was? He went right upstairs there 'n held her hand, thin as she was, 'n made a joke for her. 'You tryin' to bust the world's record fer stayin' in a tomb of ice 'r a *real* tomb, Honey?' he asked her. He was kind enough for anyone, that one was. He give up his tattooin' career just to work the doors for me after the croaker come for Annie. 'n there never was a time he wouldn't of give me his last crust of bread 'n butter either—that's how much *he* thought of me. See, Sweeties, you don't know. If she woulda took the whole bottle she wouldn't of croaked."

"Don't say 'croaked,'" Roxy objected. And her voice was cold as a cripple's kiss. "When I left my husband he said 'Before I give you a divorce you should croak.' So don't say it. I don't like it."

The Jockey sniffled contemptuously, as though silently comparing the man she'd had with someone cheap and vulgar, like anyone must have been who had married Roxy. "I've caught a cold from that goddamn tin fan," she said, "It's give me one cold after another all summer."

She paused, and in the momentary quiet someone said, "I heard you talkin' just when I was fallin' asleep. 'n Jeeze did it sound far away, so faint."

Then the Jockey's tongue was rattling endlessly on once more. She was a slight, streaked blonde with a small pointed face and a tenseness that made her seem always to be pointing at someone or something. "I always use *Venida*," she explained to no one at all, "the camphor kind—they're most as good as salts for breakin' up a cold." She slapped Odorono into her armpits and returned to the couch, where Fat Josie's departure had now left a place for her. "I seen Wallace Beery, boy was it comical you. He was a Indian scout 'n he needed a shave 'n the soap fell in the soup. Was it comical you."

"Don't talk so loud," Roxy directed her, "What are you—a public speaker?"

"If I was I'd have a better job."

" 'n don't say 'croaked.' "

"Well, get up 'n let me set. I had t' bounce with that one."

The Jockey feared Roxy. She rose humbly. But Roxy pushed her back onto the couch, her voice half-friendly.

"I was just kiddin', Hon. It's your seat, you're settin' on it. Only don't say 'croaked.' "

The Jockey went impulsively into her pocket for something with which to express her gratitude for the friendliness in the older woman's voice. And brought forth a nickel. She put it in Roxy's pajama pocket.

"That's the one come back late before," she explained, "It's really yours, you heard it come back first."

Mama Tomek insisted upon refinement. She instructed her women daily not to reply in kind when men became obscene. "We got some wonderful friendships here, but they all got to respect the girls," was the way she put it.

She usually sat at the head of the steps, between the juke and the slot machine, with her back to the women; so that Steffi R. sometimes passed a minute counting the buttons down her back. Mama T.'s back was so broad that none of the girls could see the little desk in front of her; nor could they see, for the spread of her hips, the little wobbly stool on which she usually sat.

On the evening of the third Saturday of Bruno Bicek's employment with her, she drew from her desk a paper package labeled Apple-Blossom Incense. She waved the paper about in the air a moment, till its odor hung vaguely about her. Then returned it to her desk and began counting the evening's change. She arranged five piles of dimes, ten in each pile, then counted out five brown paper rolls of nickels, twenty in each roll. She then began on quarters, four in each pile, and made three such piles; but there were two quarters left over and these, after a moment's hesitation, she laid carefully above a half dollar. And sat back looking pleased: Everything had come out even. Everything. For this night there would be only five little white piles left to stack.

From her apron pocket she drew forth a tiny light-blue box labeled Only One-half Grain. From it, concealing her motions from the girls by her elbows, she distributed a white powder into five neat rows between the quarters and the dimes, each an inch apart. She pinched a speck carefully from this pile and added it to that, until all five were equally separated. Then, without letting her eyes leave the little piles for a moment, as though by doing so they might melt into nothing or be blown away, she felt in her lap for her purse, found its catch, and brought forth a common drugstore soda straw. She stripped its paper off, passed it avidly along her tongue, and placed one end of it over the pile farthest to the right. Her eyes did not once waver nor wince: the large and luminous pupils fixed darkly on the piled dust. And fitted the straw into her right nostril.

Mama Tomek sniffed. And winced. Each time she sniffed she winced. When she had winced five times the little white piles were gone. And the pupils were shuttered, like the windows shuttered behind her. Her angular face grew softer and vaguer, till she crumpled the straw dreamily and let it fall, soundlessly, at last. Her face, which was pocked, no longer seemed so. Her lips moved soundlessly, till a smile strayed over them.

It was only in such moments that Mama T. spoke intimately of herself. And then only to the little Jew called Snipes. He fetched her heroin without knowledge of evil, and she repaid him with a single story, told over and over.

As though sensing that it was story time he came scuffling up the stair, holding the bannister with one hand, and crept into the chair beside her. His feet did not quite reach the floor, and his shapeless, colorless face was shadowed by an oversize derby into which he had pinned, buttoned, hooked and tied a dozen badges, buttons and pins: a milk-driver's union button for 1931 that Bruno had given him, a red-white-and-blue button with a picture of

Figura, candidate for alderman of the 26th ward in '36, upon it, and one which read around its edge: *A Big Brother to the Poor.* The rest were too rusted to read. Though his collar was buttoned tightly he wore no tie. His hands were covered, to the knuckles, by his coat sleeves, and gripped the chair's edge as though it were a great height to the ground.

He was happy to be up here near the women instead of below with the ashes and river rats. He saw, by the way she looked at him without seeing, that it was story time. He knew her story line by line, and her angular voice grew as soft and vague as her face in the telling; as soft and vague as the odor of incense about her. He recognized every line by its especial intonation, and his face grew anxious if she missed a line or changed its tone, or spoke too low for him to hear.

"Barber put me on the line long, long ago. That was around Chicago Av'noo 'n Noble Street, 'n Snipes was in the ar-my. Barber come from the old country so he shouldn't be in ar-my. He never laid a hand on me, but he put me on the line all the same. Had me scared to death them days, just like the Germans was scarin' Snipes. I was almost nineteen then, but almost no record at all. Only he'd act like I had 'n I'd do what he'd say I had to. I was that scared of coppers I took Barber's word that he had somethin' on me. 'n the first thing I know, he really did. It got so I couldn't get as much as sixty cents t'gether of my own then, but he'd get it off me. I went into the *Derby*, on Van Buren, just t' get rid of him. Was you scared too, Snipey?"

The buttons of the derby bobbed happily, the oversize sleeves clasped each other one moment—then raced back to the chair's edges for support.

"Then come the money years, 'n I got in the big one on Twenny-Second 'n Wabash, the Four Deuces they called it then. All a sudden I owed ever'body in the syndicate, I couldn't figure out why. They charge you five times over for ever'thin'. You got to pay for towels you never used, for music you're tired of hearin', for Lifebuoy 'n potash 'n dates who stay overtime 'n drunks who been rolled somewheres 'n start hollerin' they lost it with you.

For high school sprouts who come upstairs with two soldiers even 'n carfare 'n forget theirselves 'n put a quarter in the slot machine. You got to pay off the doc when he jabs you 'n sees you're sick, a sawbuck to let you off till Sunday mornin'. That gives you the chance to get it back. And a fin to the bondsman when the house is pinched 'n still you aren't sure you want to get out. Even when they need a hostess downstairs you don't ask for it. Because if you didn't make the grade you wouldn't have enough heart left to go back up. You wouldn't have heart for anythin' I guess. I guess you'd get blind drunk 'n blow your goddamn top. I figured I got to be careful. Are you always careful, Snipey?"

Snipes nodded solemnly.

"Always 'n always 'n always."

"See, you got to take a lot in my line, 'n the older you get the more you got to take. You gotta keep handin' it back, the tougher your comp'ny gets the tougher you got to be. The more they lie the more you got to lie, 'n they lie all the time. So you got to kid ever'body, mostly yourself. When you live like I done you don't believe *nobody*. When you kid yourself as long as I been it's too late t' stop. You can't no more stop than you could stop hittin' the bottle.

"I put a little money away, but it wasn't enough for no real hospital. 'n you know about County. They give you the black bottle. They cut up little dogs too, 'n make medicine from 'em 'n give it to you.

"Still I don't figure I'm mak'n no more of a fool of myself this way than any other. 'n someday I'll go to work for some Greek with a dozen houses 'n draw down my sixty-five per doin' just what I'm doin' here, keep'n track of cash 'n seein' that Lefty don't make trouble 'n the comp'ny don't swear. Just look'n after things you know, like havin' change fer the juke on hand 'n talkin' polite. I got real experience, I'm quick as a wink when I have to be. Well, where would I be if I wasn't? Say, I know every night sergeant this side of the river. I take care of myself.

"I'm just temp'rar'ly stranded is all myself. I've got friends, real pals. Boosters I bailed out, free-lance hustlers I paid their rent for—

I got a friend a precinct captain I perjured myself for. I c'd go to him t'night 'n he wouldn't even ask questions. Just, 'How much you need, Mama T.?' That's all he'd ask, 'n he got the whole precinct behind him. I just don't like to ask. The Republicans ain't so strong is why, since the alderman got into that little trouble.

"Anyhow I'm not down that far yet. I figure it this way: I got myself into this, didn't I? Well then, I'll get myself out. I take care of myself, I pay my own way.

"'n listen, I'll tell you, it ain't the hustlin' gals who always end up on North Clark—not the ones who been outsmartin' ever'body, just to live, since they was hardly babies you might say. The old mares holdin' theirselves up by the bar-rail at 4 A.M. cadgin' drinks 'n arguin' with the judge next morning 'n gettin' into fights with other dames in the tank 'n jumpin' off the municipal pier in winter —them's the ones been straight all their lives, till they got no resistance left. But the hustlin' gal's got a little racket all her own somewheres, runnin' a lottery or a house of her own in some nice country town, with a few chickens in the back. 'n goin' t' church regular as clockwork. Raisin' a couple kids too prob'ly—you never can tell—yeh, 'n raisin' 'em right, so's nobody won't make no suckers out of them. It's just like if you try t' walk straight down a crooked alley—you'll bump your puss on a barn or fall over somethin' for sure. That's how ever'thin' is, Snipey—ever'thin's crooked so you got to walk crooked. You ought to look where you're goin' all the time. You got to be careful where you step. Are you always careful, Snipey?"

Snipes nodded. Always.

"Oh I don't mean it's no bed of roses. It's bad awright, but it ain't no worse, take it all 'n all, than the next racket that girls without folks gets into. When a girl got nobody, one way 'r another, 'n she got to quit school in fourth grade like I done, she grabs at the first thing comes her way 'n you know what that is. It don't matter what line she goes into, she'll end up savin' snipes all the same. She can hire out to some college broad 'n scrub the kitchen 'n toilet, on her hands 'n knees even, 'r slice bacon at

Swift's like I done—it don't matter. She got to take her beatin'
sooner or later. That's the law of averages."

The doorbell buzzed and Bruno Bicek's arm could be seen, between the rails of the bannister, holding the door open for a customer. The customer came up heavily, a heavy man in a seersucker
suit.

"He's a friend of mine, treat him right," Bruno called up the
steps after him, to indicate he'd received a ten-cent tip from the
gentleman. For anything above that sum he called up, "He's a
pers'nal friend of mine—give him the works."

And once, when he'd gotten a half dollar: "Here's a king comin',
girls!"

Mama T. thumbed the seersucker suit into the parlor and resumed her story.

"You know, this railroad beat been my territory for years. I
know every window, every alley, every bust-out lamp, every car-
line, every newsie, every Polack cop, every cigar store with a
bookie in the back—I even notice where somebody tossed out a
cigarette 'r bust a milk bottle against a wall 'n the next day the
wind has blew the glass into the street. I've walked these corners
at 4 A.M. 'n 4 P.M., summer 'n winter, sick 'n well, blind drunk 'n
stone sober, sometimes so hungry I had t' walk slow so's not to
fold up on the pavement 'n get pulled in, 'n once with a month's
rent paid in advance 'n thirty soldiers in a spanty-new blue bead
bag under my arm. I was a proud one that day, Snipey, I tell you."

Snipes beamed, reflecting the lost pride of that lost day.

"I got that dough off a high school kid used to follow me around.
Turned out he'd stole it out a Mason jar he'd seen his old lady
hide in the back yard. I give her five of it back, poor thing, 'n we
called it quits. God, I've had men want things you wouldn't think
men outside a crazy house would think of. That's why I still got
t' be careful even though I don't work the doors no more. Only, I
got to be *more* careful, because now I'm *responsible*, 'n so do you,
Snipey. We're all responsible, 'n things 'r happenin' t'day that never
happened before.

"When I'm forty, next year, I'm startin' in church all over again.

Church people 'll take care of a person if she's their own. I'm not wearin' the cross again till I get back on my feet though. I won't listen to no talk against the church."

He nodded sleepily, and she touched his knee.

"Then there's your man, who steals 'n cheats 'n checks up on your comings 'n goings 'n has a key to your room. You leave it with him when you go downstairs for a shot, 'n he taps you on the shoulder in the booth before you're ready to go back up. 'Company's waitin',' he says, 'drink your shot 'n come on.'

"There was Carlson, who owned the hotel 'n acted like he owned me too. I was dirt under his feet in the daytime 'n still he come grinnin' to me soon as it was dark. Pritikin, him that run the sheeny delicatessen behind the viaduct, he overcharged me day in 'n day out for almost a year 'n then couldn't so much as tip his hat on the street. Because his Missis was along 'n whatever would she think. Don't think I ferget *his* kind. I can't stand no sheeny."

Snipes looked worried for a moment.

"Not you, Snipey," she assured him. "You're a *white* sheeny."

He smiled shyly in gratitude.

"I remember Max too, a old guy run the elevator in the *ho*tel. I was house-broad there. I been house-broad in some of our best hotels. He'd be in the back booth waitin' fer me to get pie-eyed so's he could get some younger guy to get me back upstairs. The young guy 'd have his way with me, after I'd passed out, 'n Max would watch. That was all he done. He watched. 'n tol' me about it afters, to rub it in. He'd tell the young guy he was my husband but I was too young 'n wild fer him, would he help get me back in the room? That was how it would start. 'n then that was what would happen.

"That joint was the only place where my credit was good. But I couldn't get drunk even there in peace account of that old man. Him 'n Collins, the night bartender, wouldn't let me be. Couldn't so much as get drunk by myself, far less sleep that way.

"Abe I had to have whether I wanted him 'r not. I'd of got beat up three times a week if he wasn't around somewheres. He got rid of Max 'n Collins for me, so I kept him around. Men just won't

pay a unprotected woman 'less they're scared not to. Goes against
the grain somehow. Abe was Abe White, his real name was Abe
Bloom, he used to wrestle at the Rainbow Fronton when we first
started keepin' comp'ny. They called him Chief Eagle-Feather
Friday nights 'n then he had t' wear moccasins. Ain't *that* a funny?
He wasn't so good at hustlin' me dates, but he didn't turn on me,
'n he let me put a penny in my purse. So long as there was enough
for hamburgers 'n beer Abe didn't care for nothin' else.

"'Abe,' I told him more'n once, 'You're the only white kike in
the business.' Them was my very words."

The little man was nodding, and she took him by the lapel,
threateningly: he wakened to cringe with a delicious and half-
feigned fear.

"I bet you think fellas are ones to remember a girl—don't you?"
He shook his head hurriedly, that he'd always thought that.

"Fellas have all the fun 'n she just sees one right after another,
so it seems like *he'd* remember her, better 'n *she'd* remember him,
only it works out the other way around. I ain't forgot one single
fella, all these years. But I bet there ain't *two* 'd know me from a
bag of bananas this minute. I'll tell you why *that* is. It's on account
the fella is more excited-like, 'n she's dead cool, that's one reason.
But the big reason is nobody can't forget anyone they got to get
the best of. 'n you got to start gettin' the best of a man before he
takes off his cap. You got ever'thin' at stake 'n he got nothin', that's
how you get to remember 'n why he forgets as soon as he's out the
door. A girl got her health in his hat 'n jail too maybe. 'n if she's
not real careful to get his money first maybe she don't get it at
all. But *he's* not goin' to miss no meal—don't worry about *that*.
'n nobody's goin' to arrest *him*. 'n even if he does have to come
along to the station, the chances are it's just in order to testify
against her. All it ever turns out, for him, is somethin' to tell the
boys in the back room about. But for her, it can turn out somethin'
that she'll never tell anyone about, all her life; she'll just remember
it: what the matron called her 'n how it felt to be fingered around
like a dog that bit somebody. 'n even if she stays out of that kind
of trouble, she still got to have her blood test regular Saturday

mornin', to make sure *he* don't get dosed Saturday night. Ever'thin's fixed for her to do the worryin'. That's the law of averages too, sort of.

"So there's no such thing as morals, Snipey. That's a act dames got to have to defend theirselves with. Morals ain't anythin' that's real 'n deep down, like havin' to be careful all the time. *That's* deep down, that's real. But not morals. That's a act, like havin' a racket, like why you better go to church 'r why you should vote Republican if your customers is Republicans. It's to get you by. Listen, I'll tell you, Snipey, 'cause you're different than any of them; ain't anythin' men won't do. Not *anythin'*.

" 'n they all belong to the law of averages is why. Ever' one of us is in the law of averages. Even sheenies, they got to belong too.

"That's why you got to start bein' more careful. That's one law we both got to watch out for. That's how come I'm right back where I started, with Barber.

"That's one bum rap can't nobody beat."

She leaned over and pinched his shadowed cheek. He flushed with pleasure at her touch.

When the juke sang rainbows moved down both its sides and voices could not be heard behind Mama T.'s back; it was a big bass box and the girls read each other's lips when it sang. When it paused the rainbows moved only down one side, and then their voices sounded unnaturally loud, there was a faint clanging of engines from the Northwestern yards, a chirr of crickets beside the tracks; the low murmur of Mama Tomek's voice confiding in Snipes again. The drone of the powerhouse all down Chicago Avenue to the river.

And the shuffling pace of Bruno Bicek's tennis shoes, walking his beat in hope of a fight. "If they don't get me a money one pretty soon, the barber 'r Casey, I'll pick me up one for free in the street by myself," he told himself.

The Duchess

In the pavement between the print curtain and Chicago Avenue the arc lamp had been planted, making the second-floor parlor half shadow and half light. Late on rainy nights of autumn the lamp's reflection in the sidewalk pools became that of an under-wave moon tethered by a single wavering cord; on windless midsummer midnights it brightened the dunes by the riverbank to the yellow of piled cottonseed: dunes of gravel, dunes of sand. Coal dunes, dark-by-daylight dunes, all were yellow by the arc lamp's light.

But inside, come winter flood or summer dust or windy nights of fall, all things remained half light, half dark; moving light and moving shadow. And this was so whether it were noontime in the city and the print curtain still quietly drawn, or three hours till dawn and everything opened invitingly.

All that summer a dry wind flapped the awning and banged the doors needlessly. The girls tapped on the windows with corkscrews or their room keys; when a door opened yellow newspapers blew in off the street or off the Northwestern tracks, where they had been held a while against the wheels of abandoned boxcars, or blew cigarette butts off the sills onto the floors. A reddish dust touched a little white table in the center of the second parlor, making tiny reddish drifts among boxes of powder, spools of colored thread, and bottles of red and green fingernail polish. The reddish dust from the river dunes settled over everything. And when the wind blew—midnight or noon or dawn—it raised one corner of the print curtain just high enough for the barber to see in from his hotel window directly across the way; and to let those within read the neon legend above the tavern below the hotel:

BROKEN KNUCKLE BAR
special today:
No Credit

An endless traffic from the Loop came off the great river bridges, endless images of men and machines turned the corner between the Northwestern viaduct and the arc lamp. Their shadows lurched downward, like the barber's, across the half-shadowed wall. Great tarpaulined trucks overburdened with fruit from the West, overweight women in slender sedans, newly married young men on new bicycles dangling shining silver lunch buckets and old hatless

drunks with rapt expressions, all waited by the arc lamp for the
traffic light to change. They waited also on the parlor wall, with
the same infinite, insane patience that the Jockey felt before the
slot machine: the wall changed from red to green and all jerked
violently forward like puppets yanked on a single wire: the tarpaulined trucks, the overweight women, the young married men
and the rapt, hatless wrecks. Each stumbled separately downward
into a darkness all his own. Or fled senselessly, each for himself,
across the reddened wall, the curtain behind ablaze like a sky above
a flaming asylum.

Steffi R. saw them all silhouetted so, sometimes with Bruno
among them: a helpless, hopeless, elbowing mob, mad and struggling. She killed time picking out figures resembling people she
had known in the world outside. "That's so-and-so. That's Udo
with a cue. That's Ben Bernie. That's Claudette Colbert."

She lifted one end of the curtain surreptitiously, to watch the
bar of the Broken Knuckle below. She slept with the barber above
the Broken Knuckle and each night heard the beating, through
many walls, of Ryan's three-piece band. Traffic was light tonight,
yet she watched with shuttered eyes. An express whoomed past, its
boilers making a red lightning over the thousand nameless weeds
between the tracks and the viaduct. East-bound, on the other track,
a broom of light began spreading itself wider and wider; by it she
saw a man come to the black- and white-barriers. He stood beside
the LIGHTS NOT WORKING sign facing her, his head cocked to one
side as though alert to count the cars; when the caboose had passed
she saw he was a youth on a crutch, his left leg severed at the
knee. The barriers lifted and he lurched toward her eagerly; but
passed, with a peculiar skip and bounce of the good leg, entirely
different than the barber's lurch toward her, and with averted eyes.
The juke behind her taunted him.

> You say that you're sorry
> Well ain't that a shame

Steffi sighed in relief that he had passed. Even in the brief moment of passing he had wearied her; now there was just one cripple the less in the world to deal with. Let there always be one less and one less in the world forever. Until this moment she had not known it was possible to be so tired that the sight of men passing into open hallways or turning corners out of sight or hurrying absently past in cars, of empty schoolrooms and abandoned churches and darkened bars with the chairs on the tables, boarded windows, for-rent signs on deserted streets, weed-covered walks and windowless places, could give her a twinge of pleasure: for each time she felt she had one less man or car or darkened bar to contend with. They were all trying to cheat her here.

In moments when the shadow-traffic on the wall disappeared, leaving the parlor empty of all movement, the load of anguish in her heart lifted and she would feel rested a little. But always it was not enough: the juke still whined on nasally, like a tired and ill-tempered Mama T. still taunting, forever, all those who had ever passed so from her sight:

> You say that you're sorry
> Well ain't that a shame
> 'Cause I got a brand-new picture
> For my picture-frame

And would she, too, end counting quarters for the barber somewhere? So wondering, she drew the curtain together, picked up wads of Kreemoff left scattered and stuffed about the couch, shut off the tin fan, slipped her frayed coat over her flowered and faded pajamas and saw that it was three o'clock. The others all had gone, it was her night to stay late, clean up a little and lock the doors. Hoping that the barber would be playing till morning, that he wouldn't show up in the room till noon—when she left it—she crossed under the arc lamp to the Broken Knuckle. When she came to the foot of the uncarpeted stair a breath of the place came down to her, like a urinal fouled in the heat, a little like the barber's breath. She turned into the bar to see if Bruno B. was there. He had just left, so she had a short beer alone, without a collar; along the long bar mirror a price list had been chalked:

Hard-boiled eggs .... .01
Rooster fee .... .01
Defense tax .... .01
Wear & tear on hen .... .02
                                        ———
                                        .05

She left by the family entrance and turned down the rutted street
that went, forever narrowing, down to the moving river.

On either side great mounds of trash and garbage smoked and
smoldered all night long. All night, and in the valleys between each
mound sunflowers crowded, slender and bent; their petals glinting,
in the dull copper light, like petals of wetted metal.

In one such valley wild corn grew. Almost as high as the smoldering mounds. Deep in the valleys the river frogs gossiped.

Over the metal sunflowers lay a pall of coal smoke, blacker than
the Illinois night; trailing without movement in the windless August
heat. Steffi saw, through the smoke as through fog, the high-piled
lights of the Loop on the other side of the river.

Then the river itself, black and sluggish as though coming out
from under the dumps, from under the coal-smoke sky.

A darkened barge moved noiselessly in midstream. When it came
under the lights of the bridge she discerned tiny figures working
noiselessly about its deck and surmised these were the men who
were raising a government tug that had sunk three days before,
where the river's mouth opened into the shoreless lake. They would
be in shoreless waters by morning, they would labor all day in the
summer sun. Steffi promised herself that, once back in the barber's
room, she would listen for the moaning of its river horn when it
reached the lake. There would be a whiter fog on the river then:
in midstream in August it was cool as May. Where the shoreless
waters were.

She stood one moment studying the foolish red tassels of her
slippers, imagining flood waters seeping silently over them till the
bright cork heels were out of sight and then running over the edges
and down into her stockinged feet; she fancied the coolness of the

first mud under the balls of her heels and turned hopelessly toward
the barber's room.

Despite the heat of the staircase she felt a chill going up. And
when she came to the pavement-colored carpet that led to No. 24
she drew the frayed coat more tightly about her, fearing anew that
he would be home.

He was out, but the room was littered with drying gobs of
snuff spittle; the cracks of the floor were stained with the brown
and drying remains of bugs exterminated during the day. She left
the door ajar while undressing, using the light from the unshaded
bulb in the hall to save the barber electricity. It seemed to her,
with the naked light on her and the door ajar and the sounds of
men at the bar below, that she had done nothing all her eighteen
years save to undress beneath the unshaded lights of this public
place. An uncovered light and an unclosed door had been her life.
She had been in a hundred corners with a hundred men—and
now—so soon—it had all come suddenly to no more than this, on
a night toward the end of summer.

Had it been only a year since the night at Riverview? It seemed
like twenty. And yet seemed no time at all, but only the natural
ending to the same night. Or to any night that begins with lights
and music.

In bed she watched the thin column of light between hallway
and door. The hotel filled slowly with noises and rumors of noises:
tap-tap-tapping of water from a faucet down the hall, then a sudden curving up-wall sweep of a thousand microscopic legs; a civilization of roaches lived in the walls. A woman on the other side
of the flimsy partition began turning something slowly in her
throat, like a marble of mucus rolling lopsidedly from side to side—
she felt her own breath clogging at the sound and sat upright
trying to cough; then lay back swallowing emptiness.

The enormity of being accessible to any man in the whole endless city came to her like a familiar nightmare. It was true. It was
really true. It was true of herself, truly true; it was to herself this
had happened and to none other. It was true.

The room grew hotter and closer as the night wore on, till she felt the night itself was a room. A little, dark, windowless, doorless room with no carpet across the floor. "I got a touch of fever," she said aloud and gravely, as though explaining herself to a family doctor, "feed a cold 'n starve a fever."

She passed her hands down the white bow of her loins; her hips were filmed with a cold perspiration and her finger tips felt chill to the touch. She shut her eyes tightly and tried imagining they were Saint Teresa's finger tips, cold and purifying, and healing too. Whatever they touched—they healed! The room swam away, and she was sitting on an endless bar swinging her legs in time to a song that was familiar, but which she could not somehow identify in her mind; it came from a juke behind numberless walls and it played the juke's favorite tune. Over and over.

I see a new horizon

She hummed to herself, kicking her legs—

My life has just begun

A man in an immaculate tuxedo with a butterfly collar began bending at the waist, formally before her. He kissed her hand lightly and formally, a movie actor's kiss for a movie actress, and offered her a drink from a tiny wineglass. But it was empty when she tilted it, her throat felt drier than ever and it was all a joke on her, like his bowing; for he had not shaved for many days, his tuxedo was only a sleeveless blue work shirt, open at the throat. She put the glass down gently so it would not break, feeling vaguely disappointed in everything; the bar swayed beneath her and she stirred, feeling the roughness of the shirt like a steady weight pressing her breath and her body evenly inward, and she was home on her mother's couch. Somewhere in the room a fly without wings was beating at a pane, till the beating was a storm of wings and then a storm of rain. It began smashing in sheets at the frame walls, first one side and then the other, growing less like the rain's pounding and more like that of a bass juke behind many doorless walls; behind the flimsy partition the sleeper coughed at last the way Fat Josie coughed, and the girl wakened: the partition was throbbing with the all-night beating of the band below and the column of light between hallway and door had widened with the beating till the naked bulb of the hallway shone directly into her eyes. She shielded her eyes with her arm as though to ward off a blow.

Warm, so warm. She went barefoot across the scarred floor, toes turning with distaste of the soiled wood. Her outstretched hand touched metal thin and hooked, slid down it and then stood with the iron jet in her hand and so remembered: the open transom above her, the hundred nights behind her. Closed it swiftly and shut the door softly; and her fingers felt all the heat of the day trapped in the iron. It required both her hands to open it, and suddenly, just as it was quite wide, the beating below stopped abruptly; and there was no sound anywhere in the whole hotel. Nor in all Chicago, for she listened to hear. She fancied she heard the dark barge moving steadily downstream, and a cricket's brief chirr. But the beating of the band below had stopped forever.

"I'm gettin' so I just can't *stand* that juke no more," she told herself. In her mind's eye she saw the juke with its rainbows moving down both its sides. And working swiftly, stuffed the stained sheet beneath the door, then waited on the window sill behind the smoke-filmed pane, looking down at the Northwestern yards. A copper-red shimmering ran down the rails, she looked up to see what arc lamp cast such a glow, and it was the moon. It was the moon, as large as a sun and crossed twice by city wires, glowing sullenly in the coal-smoke sky; and so motionless in the heat that its stillness was part of the sleeping city's stillness. Beneath it stood the abandoned hotels and boarded fences of the river front. She looked farther, at all the houses and all the factories and all the parked cars and all the darkened dime-a-dance halls; and there was no one, nothing left alive, not a man nor a woman nor some forgotten child to waken and cry fear of the night. She heard the rushing of city waters hissing beside a moving barge. She smelled: nothing. Closer: nothing. There was no gas in the jet, and she had to get out of the barber's room.

She slipped down the hall in her chemise, a city woman with her hair in two dark-brown braids about her head, to the door marked ESCAPE. There a crimson cage held a wavering flame, and the door was already just so much ajar. But she could open it no farther and feared to make a noise by forcing it. She peered out, and no moon showed; only great billows of darkest coal smoke, one above the other and unmoving in the heat. Now the city itself, in this final summer hour, was a smoldering dump beside the Northwestern rails. She caught a glimpse of a pale purple neon sign, and a great shower of sparks plumed upward from some buried street. With the fall of the sparks the city seemed to crouch, the darkness to grow like a burden upon it. And over all things lay an airlessness that felt like a single indrawn breath: the city's million sleepers were holding their breaths in sleep together. She went softly back down the hall, past all the half-open doors.

Each door stood numbered in bright bald tin. The sleeping women stirred as she passed.

On the bed she lay on her stomach, shaking with fever, drawing her own breath in; thinking thereby to be like all other sleepers. Yet each time she breathed anew the springs made a faint moaning beneath her, like a child's moaning, and she cast aimlessly about in her mind to know whether the child was far away or near at hand. And why should the fading night be troubling it so? Awake so late? So early in the morning heat when it should be so long at rest?

Abruptly she forgot the child altogether and listened intently for a new sound, a single sound, from above or below or near at hand. Such a sound would be important, like a long-expected knock. So important she must not sleep, must scarcely breathe; lest she miss it and it never come in her life again. And heard a single raindrop splash against the smoke-filmed pane. Then—another. And one by one they fell as though they were being counted; so Steffi counted too. "I'm countin' too," she told herself wistfully, as though counting were a privilege only a few enjoyed. "Each one. My whole enduring life. God has more than He has spent. Each one's a bead on a rosary." For each brought daylight nearer.

The rain was God's rain. For bringing daylight nearer. It ceased, and began, and ceased again. Once the woman behind the partition turned on her springs and fell again to sleep. And it was all so long, so long. Everyone went through the streets of the world alone, averting the eyes and avoiding other faces, disdaining other hands. The world was a street like Potomac Street, with shuttered windows on either side. And only a smoldering dump at either end. All men, all women passed in darkness, like the shadows on the parlor wall, each on a separate journey. Each hurried, anxiously or eagerly, through narrowing streets to his own small and final place beside the city dump. A final place that was lightless: it was doorless and windowless too. A sign over a door would say PRIVATE, so that each could be always alone. She heard the river barge moan, in a white fog as in sleep.

Then sensed someone moving down the stair. A door slammed, and slippered feet came slipping down the pavement-colored passage: a woman like herself, who had been in a hundred corners, awake before morning in Chicago. A woman with a voice and eyes and hands that moved like her own hands. That loved the city's light at noon and worked the city's doors by night. She had a quick conviction that this woman was a familiar friend to whom she could—any moment—go like a friend. She put off going for just a moment.

And so slept. Toward the end of summer.

Chickadee

Chickadee had a thin olive face, with the harassed look about the eyes one sees too soon in the women of the poor. She was dark-eyed and dark-haired, and had tried to henna her hair unsuccessfully. It was merely streaked here and there, and made her look dissatisfied, which she was; she appeared ready to pout at all times.

She did not carry a handbag under her arm like the others, she had lost and misplaced so many that way. Instead she wore a small brown leather change purse with a bright tin border, depending from her waist by a short metal chain. On busy nights she jangled and jingled from room to room, and the listening women pretended to follow her movements, behind closed doors, by the jingling.

"Listen to them dimes of that bohunk's," Steffi would say, "Her date must be marryin' her."

"Maybe that wouldn't be such a bad idea at that," Tookie offered challengingly, for Chickadee was her friend.

"How about *her* though," Steffi apologized. "Ja see that guy? I'd rather marry my dog."

On quiet nights, when traffic was casual, Chickadee would grow as restless as the Jockey; but she was too frugal to go to the juke or the slot machine. Instead she would sit fingering the cheap leather of the change purse, clicking it open and shut and then swinging it in an off-center circle about its chain. Sometimes she would go to Mama T. and change her nickels into dimes and the dimes into halves and the halves, eventually, back into nickels. Mama T. humored her in this, always making the needless changes gravely and patiently.

"Just to have somethin' to *do*," the girl would explain with a distressed sort of giggle when others taunted her good-naturedly on her change making. Her face was expressionless even when she giggled, as though its muscles were paralyzed. She giggled unhappily almost constantly, as though she had a store of energy which had no outlet in speech or movement here. A slight, willowy girl, she had been an acrobatic dancer in East St. Louis taverns, and expressed a little of her restlessness by back-bending. "This is how the niggers do," she would say suddenly, and start shagging. "They got a differ'nt idea of shag down there 'n they have up here."

If a customer mentioned that he had been in St. Louis, she would throw her arms about him. "Were you ever at *Danceland*, Hon? Do you go to The Grove? How's *Danny's Inferno* doin' these days? Wish I was *there* t'night!"

She spent much of her time picking out the flute, the cornet, the sax and the piano on the juke, and frequently remarked that she planned to dye her hair, which was blue-black, to platinum blonde.

"But where does Li'nel Ham'ton *go*, Hon?" She would complain— "He used t' be at the Monty Carlo but Larry Clinton's there now. Wasn't he at the Kokonut Klub?—Well, who *is* there then? Benny Goodman's at the Rose Room, that's in New York. Which one's the

King of the Vibra-Harp? I always ferget." Her life was troubled by the restless journeyings of half a hundred band leaders; she seemed always to assume that, once she could place each in a definite location, she would be troubled no further. So that when one whom she had fixed in the Panther Room of a Loop hotel was heard broadcasting from Hollywood, she felt vaguely displeased with him. Her mother in East Alton assumed she was working a swank Chicago night club doing back-bends on roller skates.

"Who starts out like this?" she would ask anyone, clucking her tongue resoundingly and slowly, and then would answer herself in a shout of discovery: "Tommy Tucker Time!" And add earnestly, "Who starts out like *this*?"

She kept track, too, of the marital fluctuations of screen stars, through the newspaper columns. "Margo Standish's keepin' comp'ny with Tyrone Taft again," she would announce, like announcing the engagement of a personal friend. "Lili De Lee 'n Greg Hart 'r bustin' up, 'n Mary-Jane Martin keeps comp'ny with Johnny Grant, only she's pinin' for her husband 'n Sharon Sheely is going with that Manny Rivkin, only he ain't divorced." When no one appeared to be listening, she whiled the time by imitating, with a spoon against glass, the rhythmic tinkling of water against glass. "That's Skip Gordon's signature," she would explain.

Every evening a little yellow dog came down Chicago Avenue. Chickadee had named him "Pimp." "You're my pimp," she would tell the pup, and fondle his ears while expressing many opinions to him. "Honey, they got a different idea what a pimp is up here," she would confide to the dog, "Up here a pimp's just a fella hustles dates for his girl friend. Like that drunk Polack pug. But down *my* way he takes all her money 'n slaps the crap out of her. That's what *I* call a pimp." She had no man, and took this indirect means of expressing a feigned contempt for all Northern Illinois men in general and Bruno Bicek in particular. But if he took such a generalization personally, she would reply smugly, "I wasn't talkin' to you. I wasn't talkin' to no one but my honey-pimp here." And would lay the dog's cool muzzle against her own cool skin.

"Chick gets tickled so easy," Tookie liked to say of her—"sometimes she just looks at some date 'n starts right in."

Actually Chickadee laughed easily only with Tookie. When with a man her least conversation was as measured as her nickels.

"I imagine this is a rather boring existence," some shoe clerk would offer, and she would not reply. "I just mean," he would explain, "the same old thing day after day. No offense." She would be silent, and he would persist. "Or don't you really think so? Disagree with me if you want. Ain't it *really* boring? Ain't it *awful* tough?" He would catch her eyes shifting to him, hostile as a trapped animal's, in the cracked dresser mirror.

"*I* don't think so. Why should I? Fellas are different. There's always some excitement. They're nice. If they aren't they can't come back." She never expressed dissatisfaction to a man, as one does not concede humiliation readily to any enemy. There was nothing any man could say that was not, to her, a means of getting at her, of humiliating her further or of cheating her out of a quarter. Shoe clerks commonly remained silent after a while, and the sooner they were silenced the better Chickadee liked it: the whole business was an unpleasant triviality, a tolerable sort of routine, a function to be accomplished as swiftly and safely as possible.

All in all, as lives of women go, she was moderately content and had no wish to exchange her way of living for any other routine existence. She would have giggled unhappily anywhere.

"This is my *line*, Hon," she explained to Steffi. "It's my field, what I'm *best* in. But when I was a kid I wanted to be a nurse all the time. I fixed dolls for all the kids on the block—they'd pretend one got hit by a auto 'n bring her in t' me 'n I'd put her back on her feet in no time. I don't know what kids think they're doin' anyhow. I even tried fixin' a little sick sparrer he couldn't fly yet, but the sonofabitch died on me. That's what killed the nurse idea. When I got to be a waitress though I was always bustin' the cups.

"Every line you go into you bust things a while before you get the knack of it—you got to pull boners 'n have fellas put things over on you 'fore you can catch on. That's when you get experience. We all make mistakes, we're all just human. Every time you make a big mistake you get just that much more experience. Some girls make mistakes by not goin' to school, like you 'n me, 'n some go so long they get crocky." She giggled her unhappy giggle— "Some dames got too much get-up in 'em 'n some ain't got enough. Like you, settin' 'n mopin' all the time, you ain't got enough. But I kind of enjoy it I guess, at least I don't mind it so much. In a way it is like bein' a nurse after all, sort of.

"In this field you meet new people, you'll find out. All the time. I like gettin' out 'n meetin' new people. It's hard work but it's sort of fun. Gee Honey, sometimes I hardly know what I want any more, but I want a fur coat all right, I'm savin' up this year." As she talked on she became half-distressed. "Anyhow, why try a field you ain't cut out for? I'm goin' to get me a little chicken farm somewheres—I love little chicks they're so *fluffy*. Honey, did you ever notice that ad with the egg 'n the little fluffy chick steppin' out of it 'n it says right underneath, 'ain't scratched yet'? I'd like t' get a picture for my wall like *that*, Honey. Honey, where do you *get* them pictures? I asked Rox, but all she does is go 'cheep, cheep' like that instead of tellin' me. 'Cause I asked her so much I guess. She calls me Chick all the time, that's why they all call me Chick. Sometimes they all go 'cheep! cheep!' But I don't mind, I like nicknames, if I kept little chicks I'd have nicknames for every one of them soon as they're born. Hon, are they fluffy like that when they're *born*?"

The ad with the newly hatched chick would have helped Chickadee's wall. She had nothing on it save a yellowing cutout of Tyrone Taft scissored from a tabloid magazine, and a doctor's certification of her good health. Of the latter she was quite vain, and, when drunk and alone in the little room, would read it to herself and feel a rising pride.

TO WHOM IT MAY CONCERN: this is to certify that I have this day inspected Miss Chickadee La Rue and found her free of gonorrheal infection.

Meyer Shapiro, M.D.

That was all. But every Saturday forenoon Meyer Shapiro, M.D.,

appeared, inspected, ignored Bruno Bicek, and added a date to the
certification. And every addition, in his fine cramped hand, added
to its impressiveness for the girl. She felt personally grateful to
M. Shapiro each time he so obliged her; as though he had brought
her an intimate sort of gift. For it was her diploma, her place in
the city and her degree. It showed men that she was something
more than just another whore. It showed them that in the scheme
of things she too mattered. So that when Roxy mocked the old man,
by quacking like a duck at his approach, Chickadee turned bitterly
on her.

"You hush that, Roxy, you respect this man. I don't mind you
cheepin' at me but I won't put up for no sound like that at Doc.
Respect this man." Roxy hushed.

But no one could hush Bruno B. His name for the old man was
as simple as his announcement over the old man's shoulder as he
plodded up the stairs with his instrument case in hand:

"Here comes the sheeny croaker, girls! Spit out yer gum!"

Shapiro was a hulking immigrant whose capacity for pity was
larger than his capacity for medicine. He had lived on the curette
till his clumsiness had cost him that livelihood as well as his professional standing; and, since, had lurked in the twilight land between medicine and quackery, where his clumsiness had room
enough to be redeemed by compassion.

He was more gentle with the women than their mothers had
been; not one of them, even the youngest, felt embarrassment before him. Even the youngest forgave him. For he dispatched their
blood to the Board of Health weekly and had it analyzed there as
coldly as though it were blood from so many cows.

He did not have to apologize; their forgiveness bordered on
condescension.

"We know it ain't your fault," Chickadee told him. "Nobody's
blamin' you, Doc."

But M. Shapiro blamed himself. He had other sins on his soul.
And found expiation by assuming, silently, a burden of guilt not
his own.

"Were you ever inoculated?" he had occasion to ask Chickadee.

"You mean knocked up?" she asked. Then went on complainingly: "That dame at the clinic hurts me—she just *jabs*. If you could fix that . . ."

The plea remained unfinished and unanswered. There was nothing in Chicago that Meyer Shapiro, M.D., could fix. Once, when he was about to leave, he saw Chickadee sitting on the edge of her bed with a colored comic strip across her knees, her lips moving in solemn absorption—oblivious of everything save what Secret Operative 77 was confiding to his girl friend; the old man went down the steps that time feeling troubled to learn that Miss La Rue wasn't a woman after all, but a child whose pain was a child's pain, as sharp as it was bewildered.

That, to M. Shapiro, was infinitely the greater outrage.

He nodded, reluctantly, to the plank-shouldered pimp leaning against the wall, as he came out onto the street. For, when he passed Bruno B. without recognition, the boy followed him a dozen steps quacking like a sick duck. The nod of recognition was worth the price that such an embarrassment had occasionally cost the good doctor.

Helen and Tookie

Chiney-Eye Helen was a dark, spare girl who painted her eyes to resemble those of Myrna Loy and neither smoked nor drank. She couldn't understand why others drank, she said, instead of eating with their extra change. Her prejudice against whisky was purely gastronomic.

"We were just talkin' about that the other day, tryin' t' figure it out," she would say. She had become a prostitute through a man with whom she had lived only a few months and who, she claimed, had been a Hollywood stunt flier with a five-hundred-thousand-dollar trust fund. But he had lacked money for a meal on the very day she had first met him. He had carried a picture showing himself standing beside a plane, and had assured her that he could go to any air field in the country and take a plane up on his credentials. Any plane he picked out. And if she wanted him to prove it, all they had to do was to take a streetcar out to the municipal airport. But he had lacked streetcar fare, a crooked lawyer was keeping him from getting his hands on the trust fund just when he needed the money most.

They had never gotten near enough to a plane for Sherwood to prove himself, Chiney-Eye Helen admitted. She had given him money for a meal and he had spent it on whisky and returned to her drunk, demanding money for the meal he had planned to get, accusing her of not really believing that he was hungrier than ever. They had lived together, in furnished rooms and under these circumstances, for six months; each day of which she had given him money to eat with, and each day of which he had gotten drunk on an empty stomach. Now, five years after, she sat at Mama Tomek's missing him and showing the faded photograph to all who would look. And hungry herself much of the time.

The trust fund, in which Sherwood had given her a fifty-one per cent share, was no remote hope to Helen, but an imminent reality. He would return, probably by plane, they would perhaps be married in a plane, and after he had flown her back to their Hollywood home she would tell him that he did not need to give her her share in cash, that she trusted him for it, that money wasn't everything after all.

Her waking life was a confused daydream in which avarice and romance were merged; when interrupted in either thought of money or thought of love, she was irritable; and so was irritable most of the time.

"Comp'ny ask'n for you, Helka," Mama Tomek would tell her gently.

"My name ain't 'Helka,'" the girl would snap; and remain sitting.

"Helen then, Honey. I'm sorry."

"My name ain't Helen."

"What is it, Honey-Sweet?"

"Don't 'Honey-Sweet' me. It's Heléna."

And Mama T. would have to say it just like that: "Heléna."

But when Chiney-Eye Helen was especially cross, her right name was "Heléne." And on such nights Mama T. would be eager to see

Sherwood's photograph; she would be careful to praise the man's features as though she had never seen the picture before.

"Heléne Honey, if I didn't know how truthful you always are, about everything, I'd say you were kidding me—if this guy ain't Jack Holt's double then I never saw a movin' picture."

"But Mama T.," the girl would say, at once pleased and impatient, "I told you, he *does* double for Jack Holt. All the time."

There was little in the world about her that Chiney-Eye Helen understood, beneath her artificial lashes and blue mascara and slanted, penciled brows.

"She just ate a pound of round steak, the dog," Roxy remarked, "'n she's still hungry. She eats more'n Josie 'n you could still wash out a pair of stockin's on her ribs."

"I weighed a hunderd thirty-four before I entered the Life," Chiney-Eye Helen recalled, using a phrase she had read in a magazine, "the Life 'll give me the t.b.'s yet."

Sometimes the juke cut a piece short, sometimes it ran over and kept grinding until someone stopped it. When it stopped short Chiney-Eye would rap on the window to get Bruno's attention. "Honey!" She would tell him helplessly when he came in to see what the trouble was, "It done it again." He would bang heavily on the rainbows of the box till the wheels inside stopped, reluctantly. "Why don't you sit down 'n rest a minute?" She would suggest to him then, "Your back must have a crease in it from leanin' against that lamppost." He would leave without reply. He never touched the women of the house.

Although she was neither pretty, like Chickadee, nor fat and friendly like Josie, nor handsome and ice-cold like Roxy, men sometimes liked the way Chiney-Eye sat waiting, stiffly upright, always a little apprehensive, elbows pressed to her sides and her school-girl's handbag before her on her lap, contrasting with her matinee make-up. Beneath the lipless, haughty line that marred her mouth, and the single relentless stencil that lengthened her brows, they all saw a brainless innocent, movie-struck and moon-struck, and dressed too early for her first real date. She appeared to have over-rouged herself feverishly from a borrowed compact while listening for her mother's footstep on the stair, and seemed worried that her date might be standing her up at the last moment.

Her exaggerated efforts to achieve arrogance, hauteur and the appearance of callousness, were piteously betrayed: they all detected her humility beneath the mascara, they read her fear of being mocked. And because she was so easily hurt, the younger men preferred her to such a woman as Tookie, whom no man, old or young, would ever reach again. When a man nodded at Chiney-Eye Helen she could not help feeling a little flattered; but when one nodded at Tookie, he seldom did so a second time.

Unless he returned, half-drunk and vindictive, for more of the same. For while all of the others were closemouthed with all men, Tookie spoke freely—in order to slash.

She was—only once—slashed lightly in return.

A heavy fellow in overalls came up the stairs, looking as if he had just rolled off a Santa Fe boxcar, where the cars slowed toward the Loop. As he spoke he chewed an end of some sort of sausage, so that the string of it dangled from his mouth.

"I'm Broadway Jack O'Neil," he offered the parlor at large, brushing wisps of straw off his elbows as he chewed. "The Polack with the army haircut sent me up. He's done some fightin' too he says. So I give him a tip 'r two, I like to see a kid make his way like I done. Never mind my real name, you'll be readin' that in the papers. Just call me Broadway Jack." He looked about and fancied gratitude on every face.

It was largely in order to deal with this type of vagrant that Bruno B. was kept near at hand. Scarcely a week passed but one of them entered under the illusion that, since he had traveled two thousand miles on Southern Pacific brake beams, or had reached the Eastern seaboard twice, therefore everyone along the right of way had come to know and envy and revere the legend of Broadway Jack. Or Smilin' Dan. Or Fargo Red, or Tennessee Slim. Or Dusty Rhodes—"from everywhere but Memphis 'n I won't be here long." They left their names on boxcars, in jails, scratched on rock by the water tank or burned on a discarded tie in the jungle. They dramatized their harassed, helpless, hopeless lives into gay and heroic legends of the people. And died at last, as famous as ever, beside some abandoned filling station or under the sunlit wheels.

Broadway Jack wore, unwittingly, a boutonniere of spittle; to go with the *salami* string caught between his teeth. He was a man well over forty and didn't feel so well as he once had. Nor did he look so well. There was a chicken-car smell to his overalls and Sterno on his breath. The girls wrinkled their noses and the Jockey bounded off to the juke; Chiney-Eye Helen gave him her matinee stare and Steffi looked the other way with studied deliberateness. Fat Josie alone looked undismayed; but his eye caught Tookie instead.

"What's your name?" he asked, his hands behind his back as if about to confer some pleasant little surprise upon the lucky girl.

"I'm Queen Marie, Stupid," she answered, and began adjusting her hairdo so that he wouldn't muss it.

He seemed to be weighing a great decision in his mind, one which might well alter the courses of many lives.

"You'll do," he decided irrevocably. "But I oney got a dollar to spend."

"Hell then Honey, let's spend it," Tookie urged.

But once inside the room he saw she was not as young as she had seemed in the parlor. After she had gotten his dollar she moved indifferently under the light, and he saw.

He saw, first, that an old eczema pitted her left cheek under the powder. He saw her mouth to be pinched and piteous. He saw her eyes; and felt for a moment that she did not see him clearly when she looked at him. For Tookie saw nothing clearly any longer; no one. Heard nothing, no one. Remembered nothing. No one. Asked no man's help, no woman's mercy, pitied no one, asked no pity. Without hope as she was without wonder, she avoided herself along with all others. Had lived on only to avoid the pain that others brought her. Till there was nothing left to bring her and nothing left to return.

He saw she was closer to thirty-five than to the nineteen he had first taken her for. "Do you like Hawaiian music?" he asked for some reason, while attempting to resign himself. After all, he wasn't any apple-orchard virgin himself any more. And she had the soldier packed into her slipper already. "You're mighty young to be in this game," he added hollowly, watching her preparing herself and feeling no more pleasure in the spectacle than she felt shame. "*Mighty* young, I'd say."

Splashing of water.

"*Mighty* young. *Mighty* young."

Splashing of water.

"Been prostitootin' long, sister?"

They often asked something like that, hoping she'd say ten days or two weeks. A professional billiard player had once given her an extra half dollar to struggle against him as though she were being raped. She felt too tired for that sort of thing this night.

"Plenty long, Boy Friend. Been hustlin' my bustle between here 'n Baton Rouge goin' on fourteen years now. Had a chance to go to Cuba once but heard about it in time. Almost ready to quit. Caught my first dose the week Harding died. Been dosed three times since. No worse than a bad cold though, once you get used to it."

That was how Tookie felt this night.

"How'd you get started prostitootin' in the first place?" he persisted.

"I often wonder about that myself. So far back I can't hardly remember. Now let's truck on down to the candy store, we can't wrestle here all night."

"Well, don't you want to get out of it?"

He sounded impatient, a little put out.

"There's worse things."

"What?"

"Givin' it away. That's worse."

"Oh. But the first time. How about *that*?"

"Another kid done it to me a little. Get that *salami* string off my chin. It tickles."

"How do you know it's from *salami*?"

"I can smell your breath."

"Do you still *enjoy* bein' a prostitoot?" He tried to take that back. Even her lips went pale. She shoved him and sat up.

"Prostitute! Prostitute! What a *fancy* word! What do you want for a dollar?" Then the mascara was running beside her eyes and the artificial lashes were suddenly wet and she was pleading to be let be.

"Can't you say 'girl' just once? Just *once*?"

He was grinning down at her. He'd gotten his dollar's worth. Tookie closed her eyes, feeling neither anger nor self-pity in the bottomless well of a fresh despair.

It had once been Tookie's hope that she had at last touched the bottom of her hopelessness: that there no longer could be anything below. "Fellas don't know what they're sayin' half the time," she complained, "There ain't no bottom to hit. There's a roof, but there ain't no bottom." But as certainly as she began to feel that she had touched the final depth, a new one opened beneath her. Now, now, if this could be the last, the very last.

"Listen," she asked, "Don't mind me at all. It's your party. But let's not wrestle."

Tookie sighed with fatigue, watching the slanted shadows of the bed slats through his armpit; a tiny trickle of perspiration was sliding, an inch at a time, down his side, and its progress diverted her—would it tickle him? Above the barren dresser hung a faded photo of a faded blonde, signed in a struggling, self-conscious hand.

> *To the Frolics—Just a wonderful place to work*
> —Bébe L'Amour

Tookie wondered wanderingly now, as she had wondered often on this bed, what Bébe's real name had been, how the picture had found its way here in the first place and where was poor Bébe now, after all these years? What kind of a joint could the Frolics have been anyhow, that it was so damn wonderful just to work there?

She had once invented a real name for Bébe, feeling a need for knowing the real name—a name that sounded so convincing that she had only to say it to herself to feel satisfied that it was Bébe's real name, just like Steffi was the Duchess's real name. It was more real to her than the real name ever could have been.

"Poor Beulah," Tookie would think solemnly to herself, "I wonder how that poor Beulah O'Brien is gettin' along these days." The string from the naked light hung down to the small of his back; it was tipped with a little luminous bell, and she hoped that would tickle him too. The shadow of the little bell scurried like a bug across the wall whenever he moved above her: across the carpet and up the wall and back across the bed.

When he was dressed she asked him for a quarter for luck, but he only looked dour and muttered something about being on the stem himself. She waited by the dresser while he laced his shoes, to see that he didn't lift the ash try. Migratory men were fond of picking up little knickknacks as fetishes or souvenirs, something that lent them a sense of attachment to someone who always stayed in one place.

"You see this little wood tray?" Broadway Jack could say to Fargo Red over coffee a hundred feet from the tracks—"The best-lookin' little blonde whore you ever lay eye on gimme that in Chicago to remember her by. She picked me up in New Orleans on the Desire Street wharf 'n followed me clean up to Chi—imagine a quail like that? 'n then she was mad at me 'cause I hadn't come around earlier. Fin'lly I put her on the line up in Polacktown, I can't be burdened with no woman the way I travel. I go places 'n do things too fast for that. I wanted to get shet of her anyhow. Could've stayed on, pickin' up eight 'r ten toads a day just layin' around smokin' her cigarettes. But I got to keep movin', I got wayfarin' in my blood. Not cut out to live off no woman, though many's the chance I've had. Nice kid she was to, though somethin' terrible jealous. Could'd help herself about that I suppose. May go back there some day when I feel more like settlin' down. She said she'd wait for me, in case I changed my mind about her." And the little wood tray would be in his hand to bear him out.

Tookie guarded it, studying herself in the cracked mirror to see if she ought to give up platinum blonde and go back to just plain blonde for a change. The reason she kept it as it was was because Mama Tomek felt one platinum blonde in the place was enough, and Fat Josie was already making Polish-American noises to indicate that she felt that she, rather than Tookie, should be the chosen one. "I'll keep it this way t' spite the fat hog," Tookie decided with a pang of pleasure, "I got the better right, I was born in this country, I got the seniority. 'n beside I'm closer to it naturally."

Broadway Jack left, chewing the *salami* string dully. At the head of the steps he paused, looking like the lonesomest man on earth. He shook the slot machine there furtively, thinking no one was watching.

Sometimes a nickel came down late.

The hours were so long at Mama Tomek's, the lights so bright, that after the first months there it seemed to Steffi R. that she had been nowhere else all her life. She ceased to remember the outside world, no longer visited her mother with the pretension that she was doing housework that required her to stay overnight with only Sunday afternoons off. The widow knew. She had learned from the half-smiles of her poolroom patrons. Not many of them came around any more; those that did racked up their cues with half-smiles.

By day Steffi slept in the room above the bar, by night she sat in the curtained parlor. There was no outside world.

The world was a curtained brothel.

The streets below were so dark, and the lights inside so bright, that nothing of the streets could be recalled in her mind, night or day. She ceased to go down to the pavement at all except for early Sunday Mass at St. John Cantius. The world was a street one never went down to. The world was a wall, like a sealed-up room. The world was a room like the barber's room. Like an inside room in some exclusive madhouse.

The city itself was a sealed-up room; the city itself was a madhouse.

The world was a madhouse where everyone was refined.

How many women had abandoned themselves in this small place? Steffi wondered. How many with the natural carriage of old-world women had lain here staring straight up into the light, while the breather above them became convulsive and finally floundered, spent and gasping? They let him lie till his breath returned, their eyes on the dun-colored ceiling.

Till the pride in the eyes hardened to a burnished dime-store stare. And the carriage was gone, and the only pride left was in lack of shame, and the greatest respect went to the most shameless, the most drunken, the most foolish, the most cruel, the most treacherous: the women with death in their eyes were envied by those still half-alive.

Steffi had learned how, overnight, everything could be lost to a woman. A woman could go to sleep with all things before her, and waken with nothing left but a useless youth snoring beside her. When that happened a woman's face hardened and turned cold.

And whoever wanted it so? The barber wished only not to be cheated. Bruno? He wished only to be a man. Benkowski? Catfoot? Mama T.? The laundryman or the housekeeper, the little Jew who hauled out ashes or the judge of the Woman's Court? They were all careless of what became of the place, not one of them wished it to be so in their hearts. They were all trying not to be cheated.

"I like it here," Chickadee told her, "This is my line." Yet Chickadee was distressed all night, sleeping or awake. None of the others even feigned to want it so. They spent their money like water on cheap clothes, paying half again the prices that housewives paid. The Jockey flittered around the slot machine with her savings and Mama T. spent hers, and more, on small piles of whitish dust. The barber bought salvation at St. John's regularly, and Tookie spent hers on faintly tinted gin. The little Jew spent his extra dimes on horses as completely burned-out as the ashes he hauled. And Bruno Bicek assured Benkowski he was saving his money for "trainin' expenses" at the very moment the two of them were drinking up their last dime over the Broken Knuckle Bar.

Girls came and went. Some worked a week and quit, to go back to six-dollar-a-week drudgery selling cheap cologne at Gold-blatt's or housekeeping in the suburbs; or to running an elevator where you were asked to smile for eight hours straight; or to selling Father Philip's Vanilla or Father Andrew's Cough Syrup or Father William's Liniment from door to door. Some stayed on for months because the money was easy and all doubts were solved readily by the Board of Health. You didn't even have to take insults here, as you did on other jobs, without being paid on the barrelhead for being insulted first; nothing said after the money was on the line was really an insult, for it cut both ways then: the customer had paid for the privilege. Here, at least, you always had change in your slipper and a decent dress to walk down Division with; you had your own racket, like everyone else. And when you had a racket you had your own rights: it was nobody's business then, as it was the boss's business when you didn't get to the six-dollar job on time, where you were last night. Here you didn't have to haggle, either, with a housewife, when you came in after your half day off and found the sink full of dishes, so that you knew you hadn't gotten a half day off after all.

Another difference was that if you were scrubbing floors, or packing candy, or slicing bacon, or selling subscriptions, you had to make out you never drank a drop: the lower the wage the greater the morality demanded of you off the job. In such jobs you had to keep on your toes even if you had overdone it the night before, and your knees were buckling. It was a cycle: the tougher the job and lower the wage, the greater was the desire for drink in the off hours; and the more you drank, the tougher it was to hold down the job. But here at Mama Tomek's you could sit back and tell the others, tell anybody who came in, what a binge it was and where you'd picked the guy up and the wild way he'd talked, till the both of you had been thrown out of the place. And if you felt like it you could always go upstairs to the hotel and sleep it off. It was all so much easier, so much simpler, so much more sensible. Especially if you could tell those who accused you of taking the easy way, that you'd already tried the hard way.

For the hard way didn't work for the women of the poor. The hard way ended against a warehouse wall.

Steffi thought nostalgically of places where beds like hers were never rented and sheets were changed twice a week: Polish homes, set amidst gasworks, churches, grammar schools, taverns and factories. Men and women who worked by day in order to sleep together by night. If it wasn't for that they labored, what then was their labor for, she wondered. To sleep together. In a place of their own. Yes, that made sense. But in what way then was one like herself held to be so different? Because it was not her own place, but the barber's? She felt swiftly bewildered by a sense of furious struggle, among men and women, all for *that*. It was so brief, it was so soon over, it meant so little— Could it all be just for that? She passed her hand over her eyes, feeling unwell at her own thoughts. Yet that was why the barber paid the alderman for protection, why he suspected all others and why she herself was here. Two cigarettes lay on the window sill, and when she was finishing the second someone set the juke to singing lightly.

> The blues that I got on my mind
> Are the very meanest kind

On some days each song had a yellowish tone. For on some days her fever persisted. Although she walked about freely and smoked cigarettes and kept correct account of her earnings by the number of tokens Mama T. gave her for money, yet something inside her was changed irrevocably. Behind their laconic grins and casual chatter she wondered whether the others lived, like herself, in a fleeting yellow fever, like the yellow she had dreamed of, filtering in through an unfamiliar transom. If they too felt to themselves, each as she, that they had become something that no other woman in the world before had ever become.

She became concerned with imagined illnesses: fear of tuberculosis made her give up cigarettes for three days. Fear of catching pneumonia, of bronchitis and pleurisy and wind on the stomach and every other complaint she had ever heard or read of that came from cold or dampness. Across from the bed was a tilted mirror. The tilted mirror was her other room.

Once she asked Mama Tomek for a key to her door, that she might lock it when she had company. For its hinges were so loosened that often it would slowly swing wide. Then, with the light from the parlor across her pillow, it would be like a public hall: passing men, and sometimes the women of the house, would glance in.

"Honey," Mama Tomek told her, "There ain't no keys in here. The barber don't believe in keys."

"What does he believe in?"

"Honey, he believes this ain't no damn *Ho*tel Ritz-Somethin'. That's across the street. This is a Polack cat-house 'n there ain't no keys. Honey, *why* don't you get back t' work?"

And everyone was so refined.

Looking down at the street from a corner of the curtain she would assure herself that this was the last night she would see it so: the street light flooded the gutter, where punched-out transfers, yesterday's horse tickets and yesterday's relief stamps lay. Light lay on the rails where the streetcars ran, clear down to the viaduct's unlit mouth. After the parlor was closed she returned to the hotel. There, while others slept, or bickered, or persuaded themselves that a long one was due in the fourth at Empire City, Steffi assured herself, fingering her locket, that by morning, somehow, she would be dead. She would watch the face of some man or woman waiting for a car in the arc lamp's light, feeling confident that this was the final face, the very last, of all the faces of her life.

For every face Steffi R. saw was the last, and she planned her own death fantastically. And as she dramatized herself so, it followed that she dramatized the days and hours: each was the last, the final hour. She would be dead without having lived, and that tragedy would weigh on Bruno Bicek all his days. Then she dismissed her thoughts by awarding herself, in the tilted mirror's reflection, all the peace that he had denied her. She studied herself there, pretending that the reflection was the wife of Bruno Bicek, gave herself a contented expression, and did her hair up in a bun at the back because he'd once said he liked it that way.

Then she would turn away, her heart for make-believe gone, and again convince herself that her life was over, that there was no further meaning to it. Yet she felt so only out of a greed for life. She fought greedily for every moment of it, would not be denied even its worse moments, and begged others not to buy liquor for Bruno, lest he catch cold while drunk and develop pneumonia also. During the very moments that she planned her own death she would be fastening a muffler about her throat in order that the fan might not give her a chill; and realizing, dimly, that it was life she desired. That that desire in her was too strong for the lifeless place she must live in, that what she told herself was a desire for death was actually a desire for life. And knowing this well in her heart, her only true plans were plans to regain her life.

On rainy nights she thought of the absurd habits of the poor: of her mother's faded underskirts hanging out to dry back of the poolroom, hanging there through rain and sun, four or five days before being taken in; of the washings hung on fire escapes, of laborers who tried to keep sheep in a tenement basement, or chickens in a kitchen, or a goat in a two-by-four lot. When it rained she recalled her mother's gas radiator, that could only be lit by thrusting a flaming piece of paper far underneath; a match would not reach. She hoped Udo would do it always for the widow now. And when it rained she watched the pale purple neon shimmering in the pavement. Heard the cold, derisive rhythms of

the rain all night. Listened to it wandering, lost and alone, all
night through the Triangle's unlit streets.

She thought of the men and women together in the Triangle's
tiny rooms; carpetless places above darkened vestibules. She
thought of those all over the city, on unpainted benches in leafless
parks, in back-room dance halls and curtained beer flats or in the
balconies of ten-cent burlesques; in overnight tourist cabins or
the littered alleyways of the South Side: white men with white
women, white men with brown women, brown men with white
women, brown men with brown women. But always and forever
the same: locked, and panting.

Even men with murder on their minds wished to be loved to
the last; even women with larceny in their hearts could give themselves freely.

An Italian fruit vendor came in, speaking indistinctly. The paper
came off a package of cookies he was carrying and while he re-
wrapped it he told an obscure story of a policeman who had taken
a banana out of his basket, had eaten it and then given back the
peeling, saying that he didn't have to pay because he had eaten
only the core. Then he had paid anyhow, because the policeman
was his great good friend. He hovered a moment over the slot
machine, a bandy-legged man with a basket under his arm, played
a nickel and saw a plum and two lemons come up; that reminded
him of a schoolgirl who bought a lemon from him every day:
he pantomimed her, how she sliced it and went away sucking
it between her teeth.

Listening to him, Steffi felt there were only two kinds of women
left in the world: those who sat before a bar and said, "Buy me
a drink, buy me a drink, buy me a drink," rolling a cheek against
the drinker's to sell him a package of cigarettes or brushing off
his coat in the checkroom or counting dice behind a "twenty-six
board"—and those who, like herself, sat waiting for company from
the Loop after midnight. These were the only women left in the
Real World.

And even these sometimes seemed unreal to Steffi.

Just as the men who gathered around Bruno at the barber's

table sometimes seemed unreal, although they were the men of the Real World. She called them—Bruno and Casey and Catfoot and Kodadek and Finger—the Real Sports. Half asleep, she recalled a sign she had once seen in a Milwaukee Avenue spiritualist mission:

THE BLOOD

Night after night she heard the iron rocking of the bells of St. John Cantius. Each night they came nearer. Till the roar of the Loop was only a troubled whimper beneath the rocking of the bells. "Everyone lives in the same big room," she would tell herself as they rocked, "But nobody's speakin' to anyone else, 'n nobody got a key."

Everyone was alone, trapped in the same vast beer flat forever; making the same endless plans for escape, repeating the same light songs to pass the time and inventing the same false gossip; like convicts living in the same cell for years together. All were in on the same charge, and the charge was a bum rap for all of them. Everyone was in on a bum rap; not one would be paroled.

"God has forgotten us all," Steffi R. told herself aloud, "He has even forgotten our names."

The people of the streets and walks, of the furnished flats and rented rooms, those straphanging toward the Loop and those coming home from it: the girls posing in shaky tableaus at the Rialto, the conductor taking transfers all night long, the usher with change for a quarter in his eyes, the aged paralytic and the poolroom patriot with the cigarette cough. God had forgotten them all.

On her knees in the barber's room she prayed to St. Teresa: "Why can't a fellow as much as wash his hands for a girl? Not even be clean for a girl? They hang their dirty caps over my locket on the bedpost— Why can any fellow in the whole city just hang his cap over my locket the same as dropping a post card in the corner mailbox? Everyone does or says what he wants to a girl— Why do fellows always knock a whore down so?"

There was no answer. But the answer could have been that the young men were too quick. At the slightest friendliness they became overly familiar, and made demands that turned her stomach. There was no bottom to their depravity, and she wondered dimly whether there were any who made no such demands. The more respectable they appeared the deeper their depravity, she soon learned. And a strange thing, which she learned gradually, as Tookie had learned it, was that there was always a new depth below that to which they would have her descend. There was no stopping place for the quick young men. No place at which to say, "This is the greatest sin of all." There was always another, a yet lower depth, a greater sin. And no satisfying the best of them.

Steffi sensed that there was no real limit to their demands, save what she herself imposed, and drew back from them as by instinct. They themselves at first drew back, sensing an endless chaos, degradation upon degradation, hopeless evil upon hopeless evil, beside which the commoner perversities appeared normal. There came unspeakable suggestions to their lips and into their eyes: in the eyes the desire remained, for there were no names for their desires.

For there were no such things as they desired.

Yet the nameless lusts obsessed their senses no less fiercely for being phantoms: the quick young men were driven by phantoms as furiously as by any real and namable desire. They lived with shadows across the back of their brains, and their brains were crippled by the city streets; crippled shadows, no less real for being shadows. To Steffi the terror of them lay in this: that they went to work and joked and lived sensibly with their mothers and saved their money and married and grew conservative and cared for their health by day, while practicing, all their lives by night, the madnesses of the streets as though their madnesses were the reward of being virtuous by day. They went about as though their real selves were the mad selves, as though to be obsessed by drink and depravity was—between themselves—the normal way to be. She heard them speaking innocently of innocent things; yet heard always, behind their voices, the tone of men locked in for life. They too were doing time on a bum rap: not one would be paroled.

She dreamed one night that she walked, as a child and alone, through Lincoln Park; saw flames above the trees and, running toward it, saw the small-animal house ablaze. All manner of strange small animals scurried past her toward the safety of the trees about the lagoon; they brushed past her legs, half monkey and half dog, pale catfaced things that limped as they ran, blind bird-faced rodents that wriggled like lizards as if in pain, and white-bellied, hairless things that leaped like frogs. As they passed she saw that some had tiny faces, like some tiny young man's face, pale and unshaven, the lips half-open and the eyes ablaze.

When she wakened she held a picture in her mind of another place: a great stone penitentiary with all the exits barred and no sign of smoke or disorder without, no sound of crackling flame; but only the steady murmur of the machine shops within. Guards paced the wall steadily and regularly so that no one in the whole outside world could guess that the cells within were blazing, tier upon tier within the very stone, that the smoke was in the lungs of a thousand chained men. That the very bars they grasped were melting within the stone.

There was no horror in the quick young men, no named nor nameless horror. And in this lay the girl's own dread. In this, to Steffi, lay their greatest unnaturalness: that they spoke of the unnatural, and acted unnaturally, as though it all were so natural. For in this they became alien to her own humanness. She did not fear their depravities, she could protect herself against those; but against a lack of humanness she had no defense. It was something beyond her feeling and her understanding, and when she sensed such a lack she feared the man as she would some monster.

Now it was evening and outside the door someone was saying to a drunk, "But Honey, if you're all right why don't you let me examine you?"

"I didn't come up to no damn hospital. I didn't come up here a-tall, a fella sent me . . ."

"Go home, Honey, you're drunk."

"I won't come home to no damn hospital," the drunk asserted.

" 'n I don't blame you a bit, Honey."

Steffi heard his steps downward to the street, walking as though he thought he were going upstairs.

The big frizzly blonde called Josie looked constantly for nickels beneath the slot machine and behind doors where they might have rolled and been forgotten. Sometimes she held a nickel of her own while counting, in Polish, the times others played the slot machine; she would not risk hers until it was time to pay off. "There goes that greenhorn jack-pot sneak," Tookie would say then.

Josie had little knitted purses, and kept change twisted into her stocking top. When men's footsteps sounded, going upstairs or down, she listened with the oval of her head cocked to one side.

"What you listen for, Josie?" Steffi asked.

"I listen for drop some'tin'. Nickels. Dimes."

She was good-natured, indolent and phlegmatic and was imaginative enough to fancy that no American man would stoop to pick up a coin he had dropped unless it was a silver dollar. During idle hours she sat on the edge of her bed and tossed small objects over the partition into the barber's room. Bobbie-pins, fingernail files, a spool of thread or a beer-cap. Anything she could get her hands on that had no immediate value to her.

"Josie, don't throw things," Steffi would ask, "Why you throw things, Josie?"

"I play lipfrog wit' t'ings," Josie explained obscurely.

There had been no games in Josie's childhood. So that now, in her early womanhood, she played child's games by proxy: Hide and Go Seek with three nickels and a token for whoever was It—hiding the coins about her dresser and making the token find them; Run Sheepie Run with comb and brushes.

"What you're best at though, Hon," Tookie told her brutally, "Is Red Light. That's *your* game."

None of the women knew anything of Josie; but she bore stretch-scars on her stomach from birth-giving, and wore a ring.

"I t'row somet'in' new ever' day," she promised Steffi, like promising a gift.

Once, in the barber's room, Steffi watched a roach come out of a crack in the floor and pause at each crack he came to thereafter, like a nearsighted man on the right street but uncertain of the address. He peered to the right, feelers waving, then crossed and finally disappeared under the radiator. His disappearance, somehow, depressed her. Just as seeing where someone had stuffed a snipe in the keyhole, for no reason at all, depressed her. And the whole soiled, ruined aspect of the place came to her in a single sickening wave.

"I want t' go home," she thought miserably.

Sometimes the little Jew janitor came upstairs with newspapers under his arm, to play a game with Josie. He would whisper some nonsense in her ear as though gossiping about someone, then would whisper to Steffi, as though slandering Josie in turn. They all tolerated him, he was harmless.

Few men came to the head of the stairs with any decisiveness, and many left out of sheer uncertainty. Others shifted from one foot to the other, or stood looking furtively at the seated women while pretending to be absorbed in the slot machine or the juke; or inquired of Mama T., with gentility, "whether this is the place that has disorderly rooms."

"C'mon in 'n get disorderly, this is it," Tookie invited them all raucously. When one pretended that it was the juke or the slot machine he had really come up for, as a way out of his inability to select, Tookie would ask him directly, "Ain't you gonna play Hide-the-Weenie, Hon? C'mon, Slim, let's slam it around."

And everyone was so refined.

When she was away from them all, and the barber was out, Steffi read from *Explanation of the Baltimore Catechism*:

Sepulchre is the same as "tomb." It is like a little room. We call such places vaults and you can see any of them in any cemetery or burying-ground.

The passage fascinated her. She read it over and over. And

one night dreamed that her room was such a vault. Doorless, and sealed forever. Within her dream she heard, guarding her escape, a ceaseless shuffling of shoes on stone.

Outside, an arc lamp wavered behind a gray print curtain. Like a flame held unsteadily in a rising fog.

The room, like the city's, was everybody's and nobody's. It belonged to anyone and to no one. It held a bed, a straight-backed chair, a saucer bearing a burned-out cigar butt under a dresser light, and a shallow pan of lukewarm water.

Steffi never forgot the red carnations of the wallpaper, the green checks of the linoleum, the red buttons down Mama Tomek's back, and the little hissing sound a cigarette made when snapped accurately into the cuspidor; and the marks about the cuspidor where cigars and cigarettes had burned out on the floor. She remembered the subdued voices, after Mama T. had been scolding: those strange quiet times when even the juke was still; remembered, too, the smell of Mama T.'s incense in the passageway. And, when traffic was light, the slap-slap of cards across a wooden table, if Bruno and Casey and Finger were playing the barber and the barber's boys below.

"Catfoot 'n Fireball," Steffi told herself solemnly, as though for some reason she mustn't forget it, "They're the barber's boys." That was because they had neither to pimp, like Bruno, nor run errands to the City Garden, like Benkowski, to make Bonifacy put out money. They were the barber's boys. Once the barber let her stand behind his chair while the five of them played seven-card poker. Finger and Casey and Bruno sat on one side of the table and Fireball and Catfoot on either side of Bonifacy. The barber did not deal himself in; but when a pot was over a dollar he caught a nickel between his middle fingers and worked it absent-mindedly toward the wallet on his lap; he was careful to keep his earnings out of sight, in order not to make the players sharply aware of the percentage they were playing against.

Steffi stood avoiding Bruno's eyes. She sensed that the barber would be cheating, as he cheated at everything; but she could not see how, though she tried. It was none of her business who was rooked, she told herself: Bruno knew the man as well as anyone. If he wanted to take chances, that was his affair.

She felt, also, the hostility of the three across the table toward the three whose backs were toward her. She had learned that the barber held a fear of Benkowski getting Bruno into a windup at the Garden on his own, leaving the barber out. She had heard Catfoot tell him that they could get five hundred dollars for a match with the negro Tucker. Five hundred dollars—split between Bruno, the barber and Catfoot—or five hundred dollars for Bruno, with fifty or seventy-five of it for Casey and twenty for Finger. He'd have four hundred left! She understood his sullenness: the barber wanted him to take a beating for a hundred and fifty dollars, and he'd be letting Casey fix it instead, in order to leave Catfoot out. In the moment that that surmise came to her, she caught the flash of the second card: the barber had slipped the first and given Catfoot the second. He turned up three threes and Bruno turned up two pair, kings up, and didn't look as if he suspected a thing. For half a moment she looked up, but he did not raise his head to catch her eye. So she dropped her eyes once more, as though dropping them forever.

She lived with downcast eyes, fingering the locket of simulated gold at her throat. And had taken to washing her hands every half hour or so. When she wished to light a cigarette she always sought a matchbox with but one match left in it. Once, on a street-car, a strange woman beside her rose and took another seat, next to a window. Steffi knew that that was because the woman had sensed, somehow, what Steffi was, and didn't wish to be seen near her.

When she saw people bending with laughter she fancied, for a moment, that they were weeping at some final disaster.

And hung the locket on the bedpost, when company came, and would not wear it till she was alone once more. Doing that loaned her the feeling that nothing real had happened since she'd hung it on the bedpost: everything was the same as it had been before company had come.

It's raining all the ti-ime

the big juke sang

I'm weary all the ti-ime

Sometimes she tapped, in time to the music, with her cork heels, until Tookie told her to stop. She would sit then, instead, beating the empty air with her foot and wondering why it was that, whenever any of the card players sought one of the women, none of them ever sought her. Not one. Not even Catfoot. Not once.

"They think they're too good for me now is why," she decided.

She spent whole hours picking out the petals of the metal carnations of the wallpaper of the barber's room. She was occupied in this, one Sunday morning after Mass, when Bruno walked in as though to see the barber. Finding him out, he asked her to walk with him, and she left the shabby safety of the place wondering what he had on his mind. Was he too good to talk to her too?

He said nothing, and they boarded a Chicago Avenue car to the lake and walked together around the curve of the Oak Street Beach. This was late in the last of summer; the lake front was abandoned save for an occasional faded Cracker-Jack box and a few faded leaves. But the sun was catching the glint of white-caps the other side of the breakwater. It had rained, and the sky was drenched with running colors. Steffi thought of the fancy five-cent post cards in the rack at the corner *Apteka*. A post-card sunrise, and all her own. She felt the lake breeze: that was like the fan that gave Jockey summer colds on nights when traffic was heavy and the juke played *La Cucaracha* all night long. Bruno walked without touching her hand, avoiding her eyes, till she wondered whether it was because he wanted to know, from her, whether the barber had cheated him. She determined that, if he asked, she would say that she had seen nothing. But he did not ask. Was it because he had come to distrust her as he assumed she must distrust him? She could not tell. And she could not tell him of the barber's tricks. Though she had not yet found it in herself to distrust him: there was no betrayal that could make her doubt him.

"I still trust you," she told him at last, thinking that it may have been that he was wanting her to say. He only shook his head unhappily. Then answered sullenly. "You do but I don't. I don't trust nobody. Not even myself no more. I don't trust nothin'."

They spoke no more.

Back in the room she told him to go, she didn't want the barber to find him there with her. "He don't trust nobody neither," she added, and he left without saying good-by.

"Thanks for the car ride, Bunny," she told him over the bannister, and he waved his hand without looking up.

That night, beside the barber, Steffi dreamed she was being hunted. She had to hide, and forever in some degrading posture: on all fours in the alley behind the poolroom, between the telephone pole and an open refuse can. Cans were strewn about in puddles. It was after dark, in March, and all the day the late snow had been thawing. She felt its wetness against her knees, but could not rise. And the hunter knew where she hid, where she always hid; he passed and repassed, in an arc lamp's light, pretending to have no idea she was near. In order that the hunt might last till morning. Till the last arc lamp had faded and the last tavern had closed? Or because he knew, as she knew, that the night would be forever, the lamps would never fade, the taverns never close, morning would never come again; in order that, all night long and endlessly forever, he might be about to catch her at last.

For this walker wished only for her to be always on all fours in a littered alley, her knees against damp stone.

In a fever she saw herself in her mother's kitchen. She was turning from the wooden sink to reach for a dish towel, and when she faced the sink again there were no dishes, but only a pan of soapy water with a bar of blood-red soap at its bottom. She looked closer, bending, and saw that the bar was really a red tin number and there, on the wall above the sink, hanging loosely by a single nail, was the same red tin number. She wondered uneasily, twisting as she slept, feeling that in some way the number pertained to herself, worried that the nailer had been so careless. Behind her a voice, that was both her mother's and Mama T.'s, explained everything:

"Put a penny in your pocket Dearie, 'n some bread in your purse."

So she knew then that her real mother was Mama T., and was oddly relieved to find this so. The reddish number blurred before her eyes, and the aging voice went on and on.

"Haircut! Haircut!" it kept calling, till Steffi turned and saw the barber's crazy parrot with a red tin number about its neck for a bloody crucifix.

Yet not a crucifix after all, but a perfectly round and red-framed mirror reflecting, in a glittering blur, the scarred eyes and battered mouth of Bruno B. She saw him as from a great distance, rocking himself in a straight-backed chair as though in pain, his hands manacled across his chest. He was clutching a red sponge ball in his right hand, there was blood on the front of his shirt. And he was watched casually by a woman searching aimlessly about for a red-bordered towel that hung directly over her head. Then his eyes were closed at last, there was a strong light from somewhere, and the woman was hanging the towel across his eyes to conceal his identity from someone who sought him. But he sat too stiffly under it, without rocking at all, so that the woman took the towel away. And drew her hand back swiftly, for it was no towel, but a sheet over his dead face. And he sat with the manacles gone for good, clutching only a red sponge ball.

Steffi saw herself sleeping, dreaming of Bruno Bicek dead. Saw herself waking, in the dead of night, in a room where vigil lights still burned. Many others had been here, the hoarse sounds of their drinking still rang down the hall; they had left her alone with the burning candles. And a long desire to cry.

To show he was dead to her? Had that been the dream's meaning? Below her lay the city wilderness; and it was warm, so warm for so late in the year. The poor, still sleeping on the roofs, or any floor near an open window, were strangely still in the heat She watched the shadows along the viaduct, like those of men and women fleeing toward the lake after work or returning reluctantly from it in order to be on time for work. Children had opened the fire hydrant beneath the viaduct and, though none of them were near now, the water splashed soundlessly and made motionless pools all down the gutter: in one pool, beneath the viaduct light, the light's reflection wavered like a little tethered moon. She saw Bruno walking with his eyes down looking for something. They had tricked him: she wanted to call out, to tell him there was nothing to be found, that the whole thing was a trick on the two of them; but her voice would not come. She saw him as through the small end of a pair of field glasses, walking lamely, and there was a smell of antiseptic like a low cloud everywhere. A watch began to tick behind her and she turned: a click, and someone had locked her door from the outside—Mama T. had a key after all! Had locked her into the barber's room, as into a vault forever! The door went up to the transom in the old unfamiliar fashion and the transom was half-open: light came filtering through, from a place she had never seen.

The door opened easily for her because of the special way she turned the knob, that Mama T. knew nothing of, and down the hall a small woman whom she knew well but could not place, was walking down a doorless passage away from her bearing a pan of soapy water in one hand and a great half-eaten cinnamon cookie in the other; a woman wearing some light sleazy stuff with one shoulder strap dangling. Steffi came up close and saw a small mole, at the point of the woman's v-shaped garment, with a single brownish hair stemming out of it. The water began slopping over as she walked, but the woman seemed neither to notice nor to care. On either side of the passage were half-open transoms and the odd yellow light filtering uneasily, like yellowish soot. The water kept spilling as the woman kept walking, never growing more distant, down the endless corridor; till she turned, and it was herself who walked, and the fever passed into a dream, and the dream passed into a windless waking.

"A few more days 'n I'll be ravin'," the girl told herself aloud. "I don't know when I'm awake 'r dreamin' no more."

The next morning was Sunday and she rose while the barber still slept, before light. Still feverish, she lit a candle for prayer, and it wavered in the bluish air. She knelt, listening for an angel's wings. And heard the occasional thunder of the El. Somewhere below a drunk was trying to get into the Broken Knuckle, and Tookie was abusing him from the second-floor window across the street. Then everything was quiet at last, save for the barber's labored breathing. In sleep he breathed as if he were walking, lurchingly.

She knew an indulgence prayer for the first, second and third day of a novena. The barber had given her a little worn booklet:

Behold at thy feet, O Mother of Perpetual Help! a wretched sinner who has recourse to thee and confides in thee. O Mother of Mercy! Have pity on me. I hear thee called by all, the Refuge and the Hope of sinners; be, then, my refuge and my hope. Assist me for the love of Jesus Christ; stretch forth thy hand to a miserable, fallen creature, who recommends herself to thee and who devotes herself to thy service forever. I bless and thank Almighty God, who in His mercy has given me this confidence in thee, which I hold to be a pledge of my eternal salvation. It is true that in the past I have miserably fallen into sin because I had not recourse to thee. I know, too, that thou wilt assist me, if I recommend myself to thee; but I fear that, in time of danger, I may neglect to call on thee, and this I beg, with all the fervor of my soul, that, in all the attacks of hell, I may ever have recourse to thee. O Mary! help me. O Mother of Perpetual Help, never suffer me to lose my God.

Then she felt that a room above a bar was a blasphemous place for prayer, and rose and dressed. Wrapped in her threadbare coat, the collar up, she walked the abandoned streets till she came to St. John Cantius. No priest was there and no candle was lit for her. She had expected none. She wasn't good enough for them now. She knelt in the aisle alone. Once someone behind her opened a door and let it close itself slowly: a chill wind swept the aisle, and she drew her coat closer about her. Her fingers showed their tinted nails through the open ends of her gloves.

Father Francis came and himself lit the altar lights. He peered at the little white face beside the first pew and came toward her, and blessed her, thinking she might wish to speak. But she shook her head. No. She had nothing to ask. He turned, and she called him back.

"Father. As you did at Confirmation."

He understood, and slapped her lightly on the cheek. He saw she was unwell.

"God has more than He has spent," he told her.

Later little girls with bright head scarves, shepherded by their mammas, filled the middle pews. The old men came after. She stayed on, Mass after Mass. The church warmed and grew brighter: the painted windows showed glints of the autumn sky. But her fingers grew as cold as her heart, here where her own were praying.

The poor were praying. The poor in heart and the poor in substance. Stirring restlessly, feeling a rocking in their hearts when the great chimes rocked overhead. The old men, the old women; the boy crouching at the end of the pew with cap in hand, crossing himself hurriedly. Steffi knelt, beating the knuckles of her right hand against her heart whenever she kissed her beads.

I confess to Almighty God, to blessed Mary ever Virgin, to blessed Michael the Archangel, to blessed John the Baptist, to the holy apostles Peter and Paul, and to all the saints, that I have sinned exceedingly, in thought, word, and deed, through my fault, through my fault, through my most grievous fault. Therefore I beseech blessed Mary ever Virgin, blessed Michael the Archangel, blessed John the Baptist, the holy apostles Peter and Paul, and all the saints, to pray to the Lord our God for me.

May the Almighty God have mercy on me, forgive me my sins, and bring me to everlasting life. Amen.

May the Almighty and merciful Lord grant me pardon, absolution, and remission of all my sins. Amen.

Then she said one Hail Mary and ten Our Fathers for Bruno

Bicek's troubled soul. She prayed that he might achieve all his desires and gain peace of mind. And as she prayed so, beneath the peal of the organ, she heard the clinking of small change into the money nets. The poor were giving. The poor were always giving. Once Bruno had said that the priests, the politicians and the police were all in secret league against the poor; and she had been afraid of such talk. "Better a good peasant than a bad priest," was the saying. Yet she feared not to pray and not to give. Was not everything her fault? Her own most grievous fault? *Mea culpa,* she crossed herself in fear of her very question, and forcibly made herself think: *Mea culpa, mea maxima culpa.* The ushers came first with yellow baskets for bills, then with dark green nets for dimes and nickels and pennies from the little blonde girls in the bright head scarves. The poor were giving. The priests were taking.

She watched Father Francis handing the holy water to the altar boys, saw him coming down the aisle to bless the poor who gave and the poor who did not, with equal gestures. In a moment of silent contemplation she tried to think of her sin with Bruno Bicek again, for which she was being punished daily now; it must have been a very great sin, even greater than she had feared, that its punishment should be so unremitting and so long.

She looked at the pictures of the saints, and the inscription beneath the tortured figure on the cross: I. N. R. I. And the little red lights, as the chimes began again overhead, far up and slowly, slowly.

She tried to feel as humble as the catechism had warned her she must, and clasped her hands before her with the effort.

But hardly felt humble at all.

She must be bad at heart and all the way through, not even to feel humble here, she decided. And now she would tell herself once and for all that she was being punished justly for the sin into which her own willful frivolity had led her. "I got only myself to blame," she murmured, "God my dear, God my dear."

The boy at the end of the aisle with his cap in his hand ducked out, still in a sort of half-crouch, as though he had time today only to have half his sins lifted but would be back with some whoppers tomorrow sure, and was gone. When the chimes faded Steffi rose, blessed herself with holy water, and walked past her mother's poolroom with her collar turned high. Just to see how things looked once more.

II

The Law of Averages

IN THE barber's room, above the Broken Knuckle Bar, another poker game was beginning. The place was filled with cigarette smoke, the cards slapped softly or sharply down; sometimes a brief oath punctuated the bluish air, like a little colored balloon bursting above the players' heads. Sometimes voices came up from below. Sometimes the dealer sang.

Bonifacy the barber was the dealer. And he was taking no nickel cut tonight. For tonight he dealt himself as well as the others and if he won—he promised—there'd be beer for all before they left. On his one side sat Finger and on the other Catfoot N. On the other side of the table, on either side of Bruno Bicek, sat Kodadek and Benkowski. In front of the barber lay a half-peeled orange, and behind him, as always of late, stood Duchess Steffi, to give him luck. Although her eyes were wide and unwinking, they seemed somehow to be defending her thoughts rather than seeing others tonight. Each man dealt two hands, then passed the deal on, and when the deal came to Bruno he snapped on a green eyeshade. Could it be that he wished to take no chances on catching her eye? She wondered, then saw him shift the shade ever so slightly. Just enough to see her mouth. She pursed her lower lip, as though about to say "No"—then let her face go blank and expressionless, to read the barber's cards.

The barber stacked nickels among the orange peels before him, and Steffi picked out the peels for him. She was carrying them in her hand across the room, to throw them in the sink, when someone knocked. Lightly and timidly.

The players looked covertly into each other's faces after the manner of men with a common fear. Catfoot put his hand on the barber's hand and the hand stopped with the six of clubs caught upright between the pale and aging fingers. Steffi opened the door, but there was no one in the hall: only a small blue gas jet flickering in the windy passageway. She stepped, uneasily, into the passage; the house used electricity only in the rooms and in the bar below. Now the long hall smelled to her of years of gas flames and transient men in second-hand clothes. A cold draft swept the players. The barber called her impatiently.

"Dumb t'ing! Close door!"

She stepped back and the knocking came again.

This time she looked behind the door after opening it and saw Snipes, in a faded army overcoat that fitted him like a burlap sack. He whispered on tiptoe to reach her ear, trembling as if something in the passageway had frightened him into knocking; he feared any group of men, and he drew aside from the players now. He had been a thief in the railroad wards in his boyhood.

"I was p-peekin' t'ru th' keyhole," he confided in Steffi, "I seen the p-poker cards."

Every game where money lay in the middle of a table was "poker cards" to Snipes.

He had become a professional dealer, in his young manhood, before the first World War. Now, of all the games he had dealt, in a dozen silver-dollar houses between Reno and Cicero's Rock Garden Club, he recalled nothing save the single phrase "p-poker cards." He called Steffi "Sarah," the same name he had for all women; and seemed to distinguish between women only dimly. He stared up at her through double-lensed tortoise-shell glasses a moment, then drew a greasy nickel from a big, intricate wallet bearing a faded gilt-engraved legend:

Forty-Second Kentucky Derby.
Louisville, Ky.

He held the nickel up before her eyes as though she too were almost blind. He often showed nickels or pennies to women, and sometimes they would feign to steal the coin from him, holding up one of their own and saying it was his. But he knew they were joking then, and only pretended to be worried at his loss by looking hastily through his pockets for his own coin and turning the elaborate wallet inside out. Yet he never played this game with men. If Casey or Bruno or Catfoot, or any man, as much as held out a palm demandingly to him, he became truly frightened and pleaded indistinctly to be allowed to keep his coin.

"Match?" he asked Steffi now, showing her the coin. "Match-match?"

"Look," Steffi called, hauling him into the room on her arm, "Stirnuts wants to match nickels. He just win ten 'g's at Washington Park 'n he feels like matchin' to relax hisself a little."

The players greeted the little man with half-murmured laughter and without lifting their eyes; he retreated into the corner where, in winter, the radiator hissed comfortingly. He fumbled with his sleeves there, trying to get his hands free of them to warm them above imagined steam; he put the greasy nickel safely back in the wallet and squinted at the players through the foggy lenses. They all seemed a little familiar to him, they all looked alike; and they all looked like a thousand other always-losing players he had watched through trailing cigarette smoke on other early October nights.

"If I had my good ol' helt' like I used t' have, I got a system on the dice you'n me c'd make ten 'g's, 'n stash it all away too," he assured some long-dead sucker. Then, sensing that the sucker was no longer listening, he grew bolder and said loudly, like a child alone in a long-empty room: "One 'g' fer me 'n one 'g' fer you, one fer Sarah 'n one fer Lou." He gestured with his index

finger against his thumb as though dividing dollar bills with someone across the radiator. Steffi nodded, knowing it was herself
with whom he divided, and he wetted his thumb and began
counting all over, as though two bills had stuck together. Immediately he felt he could never get them apart—reliving some
incident of reality—and moaned just loud enough for Steffi to
hear and waited, watching her helplessly: he didn't want to cheat
his Sarah and he didn't want to cheat himself but there was no
use in his trying to get them apart himself. They were stuck for
good and Sarah would be angry. Till Steffi nodded, and so they
weren't stuck any more—and—what was even better—he could
have them both for himself now. His gratitude strayed across his
lips, a smile shy as a child's. All the buttons but the top one
had long fallen off his overcoat, and this last he kept tightly
fastened, threads dangling from the sleeves over the red-enameled
radiator. The deuce of hearts fell face up before the barber, and
a misdeal was called. Steffi twisted the fabric of her skirt between
forefinger and thumb as though resisting an impulse to yank
the zipper down. The barber was doing most of the winning.

"When I was a boy," Snipes told himself, "I lived on South
Wells. One night I was a-sleepun 'n up come a rat-thing 'n I was
a-sleepun. Ever'one was a-sleepun." His face looked long and loose
through the smoke, like a face distorted by a trick mirror; to Steffi
it seemed to waver and change shape a little. "'n up he runned
'n—zzzzzzzzz—bitten off my little piggy."

"How'd they let you in the army then, Scrumble-Bug?" Catfoot
asked absently, watching Bruno Bicek's draw.

Snipes looked about, searching blindly for the one who had
spoken. He had already forgotten what he had told and returned
to fumbling the frayed sleeves without yet getting his hands free
of them; only the darkened and broken nails ever showed, giving
the impression that the arms were too short for the body. Catfoot
began a swift humming rhythm to the cards as they flashed out
of the barber's hands, fingering his green silk tie.

"Barber," Catfoot observed, "he likes to deal one-handed." And as he spoke his humming seemed to take the place of the barber's idle hand.

> I'm a ding-dong daddy from Duma
> 'n you oughta see me do my stuff

Barber continued taking most of the pots, till Finger stood up and shoved his chair toward the table. He was through. Kodadek, thinner than ever and his eyes like two wet black olives, shifted into the empty chair with his back to Steffi R.

"Let me rub some of that luck off you, Barber," he said, scrubbing the barber's back with his knuckles. For some reason Snipes began clapping his hands. Loosely, the palms meeting mostly by luck.

Abruptly as a wind that veers in a single moment from west to east, the cards began falling against the barber. Bruno, whose losses had been steady, won four hands running. He began concealing his hands in front of his chest as though fearing that someone was peering over his shoulder.

The barber's head began wagging from side to side, like some puzzled professor's.

"Send the scrumble-bug down for a Cincy-Ky.," Catfoot asked Steffi, sounding worried. Snipes understood orders only from women. She gave him exact change, whispered in his ear, and he left repeating her words over and over, in order not to forget by the time he got to the bar below.

"They're startin' t' blow my way," Bruno warned the barber, and tilted his eyeshade a fraction further. With the next pot, raising the barber's bet without looking at his cards, he won without having to look at them. The next deal the barber called him and he turned up a five-high straight.

When Snipes returned, with the bucket of Cincinnati beer and a pint of Kentucky whisky, the players took time out to drink. Benkowski took advantage of the pause to draw a small stack of calling cards from his pocket, and laid one against each player's glass. Then he handed one to Steffi and even gave one to Snipes.

The barber could not read English and looked suspicious of every-one until Steffi read it for him:

Bruno Lefty Biceps
contender for the heavyweight championship
of the world

Conqueror of Greek Christophor, Vincent Guerra, Turkey Johnson,
Ink Martin, Nash Cooney, etc., etc.

Casey Benkowski, Magr.   Finger Idzikowski, Trainer

"Who do you think *that* is?" Casey asked, flushing with pride to the very roots of the bristles of his skull.

"It's him all right," Catfoot said at last, looking first at Bruno and then back at the card as though comparing the reality with a photo-graph. "It's him all right." Then even Catfoot and Fireball looked half-pleased, and Finger grinned from ear to ear. Only the barber looked annoyed. "Only alderman should have such cards," he said. "What kind of a fighter is, he gives out cards?" he asked Benkowski.

"My kind of fighter," Casey answered, and added needlessly, "This is a pudding you don't get a finger into, Barber. My boy is signed against Tucker."

The barber's eyes went to the stack of nickels and orange peel before him. He had not known of this, and he would not reply now. Catfoot looked at Kodadek and then both, by tacit agree-ment, sat silent. Benkowski had pulled it behind their backs after all; they had only to look at Bruno, trying to avoid everyone's glance at once, or at Finger, who was bursting with pride in both Casey and Bruno, to know it was so.

"You shoulda seen what we done t' the Greek," Finger boasted. "We ain't losed a fight. Me'n Evil-Eye Finkel got perfect records. The time we fight the Omaha Dago we would've lost except I got the old presence of mind—I switched the whammy to the judges 'n pointed them 'n then switched it on the ref 'n sure enough, just in time, Lefty got the duke. That's 'cause I'm psychopathic, I tell what's on their minds."

"Why don't you hex Hitler, Polack?" Steffi asked.

"I'm doin' that too," Finger answered readily and good-naturedly, "'n what's more, I'm doin' the Chinks too. For free. O' course it ain't like hexin' a Omaha Dago who 's there right in front of your eyes. I can't make direct pers'n'l contact—but awready I got 'em worried 'n it's the beginnin' of their end. Adolf knows the Finger is on him on account people have writ to tell him."

"How you do it, Finger?" Steffi teased him, in order to cover up the dead silence that Casey's announcement had provoked. She felt that, if someone didn't keep talking, they'd be at each other's throats.

"I go into single confinement in a dark room twenny-fours before each fight," Finger answered as soberly as he was asked, "I go there t' get in harmony with the spirits."

"Dumb t'ings!" the barber suddenly demanded, "No talk! Bad lucky! Bad lucky!" He brushed orange peel off the table, picked up the deck and began dealing hurriedly. In his eye-slits little red veins were shimmering, and each time he looked at his cards, Steffi saw his fingers trembling. Win or lose, there would be no free beer for the Real Sports this night.

Hand after hand now was played between only two, for Bruno began forcing the game to the barber. He knew the barber for a player who played well when out in front, with others on the defensive; but when put on the defensive himself, anger and fear caused him to betray his hands, suspicion deprived him of accurate judgment. A current of challenge charged the air when he laid down an ace-high straight. The others knew, then, that he was playing for more than poker stakes. Bruno showed three jacks and a pair of treys. That took the last of the barber's earlier winnings, and his grizzled neck began turning in its collar. Because his eyesight was growing poor he had to hold the cards under his very nose, and the more he lost the looser his neck seemed to become; it waggled and twisted and gulped and writhed. Steffi unbuttoned his collar for him, and then the folds of skin on his neck hung down like a turkey's wattles. He lost pot after pot and plunged ever more heavily. A wind went past the windows, like the first wind of winter, and the room grew colder. The players put on their sweaters and vests. The barber's stiffly starched collar began jabbing the underside of his jaw.

Steffi stepped into a clothes closet, shut the door modestly behind her and came out wearing a faded yellow turtleneck sweater of the barber's that bore the abbreviation MGR down the left sleeve, in red lettering; it was a relic of the days when he had been getting fights for Benkowski. She went to the barber now and stuffed a muffler between the stiff white collar and his neck. His eyes remained glued to his hand as she tended him.

After half a dozen more hands he sat back. "You quit now," he told them all.

Bruno shoved back his chair. "Guess I had the luck t'night, Barber, it's all part of takin' care of number one though. I need the dough for trainin' expenses."

"On South Wells where I lived once a rat-thing eat'n my little piggy off," said Snipes, "He bitten it off when no one was a-watchin', the Big-Rat-Thing."

The barber rose, his broken knuckles whitening on the table's edge. Then his face bunched oddly, and he put his full weight forward on his good leg.

"I got nice big i-dee," he said. "You cheat me, somebody." His tiny eyes searched Finger's for confirmation.

"I seen nothin'," Finger mumbled, and shoved his hands down his empty pockets. Then he arranged himself behind Bruno and, with Casey leading the way, the trio filed past Catfoot, Fireball and Bonifacy, to the door. At the door Bruno turned.

"I couldn't see nothin' goin' on, Barber," he said earnestly—"I had on a eyeshade."

And they were gone. Those left in the room heard their footsteps on the stair and the final slam of the outer door. They had cheated him. They had cheated him twice. They had taken away his fighter and then they had taken his money. He eyed Catfoot and Fireball, trying to figure whether they had helped cheat him. "I didn't see nothin', Barber," Fireball said.

Snipes began clapping his hands over the radiator, till Steffi waved at him, and the foolish sound stopped.

"He was watch'n 'n watch'n," Snipes mumbled resentfully.

The barber turned.

"Who was who watch?"

Snipes shook his head. He wouldn't tell. The barber shifted his weight to face the little man directly.

"Who watch?"

"No."

Catfoot took a single step toward him, but the barber drew him back; he didn't want to frighten Snipes out of his memory. He held up a nickel for Snipes to see.

"You tell. I give."

Snipes shook his head.

"Won't tell on Sarah."

Steffi's lips began a "No," then she stood a moment with widening eyes; Bruno had left too soon. She knew he had left too soon, yet felt, in one moment, happier than she had in many days: he had not walked out on her this time. He had left without knowing she would be found out. She knew, beyond all doubting, that this time he would have stayed; against Fireball, against Catfoot, against the barber. Against them all. She knew, and that knowledge was all she needed, hearing Catfoot and Fireball leaving. They closed the door softly behind them, as though planning to listen to the barber beat her.

Let them listen then. She stood before the old man without fear and said "Yes" to his waiting eyes. He slapped the word back into her teeth with the heel of his palm and slipped, catching himself on the point of the elbow against the table without attempting to straighten up for the moment. Steffi's hands came up slowly to her mouth, and Snipes' frayed sleeves followed hers to his own lips, as though he himself had been hit.

"I didn't tell," he assured himself inaudibly, "I told on the rat-thing."

The door slammed faintly three flights below, and the hall door swung open a little, as though uncertain of itself. The cold draft from the passage swept in: the barber felt trouble for someone coming in at the wavering door. Trouble, nothing but trouble. None of them stayed by a man in trouble. This was his last woman and his best. But she would not stay, she would cheat him too. He leaned on the table, studying her and breathing heavily, thinking: the others were all gone and let them go; but let this one remain. For all the others who had cheated, he would cheat them, in return, ten times for their once. But let this one not cheat; in order that she be uncheated.

Now there was only the little Jew left, in this room with the littered cards across the floor, and a woman he himself had broken. He saw her sit on the edge of the bed, her head flung back so that a single thread of blood moving from her mouth divided her chin and started down the pale pillar of her throat. Or had he broken her after all? Had she not broken him instead?

He lurched to the bed and stood above her. If he had not broken her yet, he would break her forever this night. He would break her before another might touch her.

"You cheat," he said simply.

The blood came down the hollow of her throat into the hollow between her breasts; the yellow of her sweater became stippled with red like a Chinese design, and she daubed ineffectually at her lip with a crumpled Kleenex. Snipes came out of his corner holding out the end of one sleeve, to help. And ran into a backhand fling of the barber's left arm that sent him whimpering, as much for the sudden reproach it carried as for the sudden pain, back to his radiator; there he promptly forgot the blow and began fumbling his hands above the valve. Steffi stood up. She was two inches taller than the barber, for she wore her hair like an auburn helmet. She put her hands against his cheeks and smiled knowingly into his eyes.

"They're like ice, Honey. Just feel." She nodded at Snipes and added, "Everybody got cold hands t'night."

He slapped her hands down, and she affected a pout.

"Never mind cold hands," he warned her. "You cheat me?"

"You treat me so rough, Barber," she evaded him coolly. What was the use of telling him that Bruno never touched her? Let the old man worry about it a while, maybe he'd get to appreciate her more after. "Bunny's so kind. He wants t' marry me, Barber."

They would even cheat him out of her then, this last living thing that his life had left him. They would cheat him out of his life before they would let him go.

"In the jailhouse he'll marry you," he told her. "Right back where he come out of."

She eyed him steadily. "Bunny did his time," she said. Her defense of him cut the old man. He came up to her so closely that, for a moment, he looked to her like his own bleak-eyed parrot; all beak and eyes and age.

"Not for rape he do no time," he told her.

"For rape he doesn't have to," she said, feeling that the old man was holding something back. "I won't testify."

A white film winced across his eyes, like the wincing of a bird's eye.

"Law make you test-ify."

"I'll bring your own boys in it if I do. 'n you'll be in it too." She shot him a glance full of triumph, that he should have played into her hands so swiftly. But saw no defeat in his eyes.

"My boys not in. I not in. Just Lef-tee in."

He drew the side of his hand across his throat.

Something she had known and yet had not known, something rumored and implied and withdrawn and forgotten and brought back to a rumor once more: what had happened in the alley above her?

"What's he in, Barber?"

"In for kill. Catfoots know. I know. For kill a Greek, what all boyz see. Catfoots know, I know. Catfoots good boy. You like Catfoots?"

She felt her innards sag with the weight of her fatigue, but somehow remained standing before him, searching frantically in her mind for something with which to stop him. Why was there never anything with blood on it to name the old man for, when he lived by blood every day?

"Remember how you won from him last week, Barber?" she said weakly— "Remember you slipped Cat the second card?"

The barber laughed at the very weakness of her retaliation.

"I talk kill, you talk card game," he told her smugly. Then his mind reverted to the evening's card game, and any card game loss no longer seemed something small enough to be smug about. His face clouded with his sense of being outraged by her.

"Twenty-two dollars you cost me!"

"That makes you about even-up from the last time then."

"No."

She saw him calculating, getting his money back. "No," he repeated, "I lose not'ing. You lose. You lose coat. Winter coat I promise, now you not get."

"But you're so *rough*, Barber. Bunny's so *kind*."

"Don't call 'Bunny.'" He made as though to strike her, and she ducked, needlessly and wildly. He shoved her by her shoulders back onto the bed, his fingers digging into the thin stuff of the sweater. The stained points of his old-fashioned collar jutted yellowly, as though they were parts of his stained throat.

"You're hurt'n me," Steffi told him.

"You like," he assured her. "You like hurt. He hurt, so you like."

"Not like you he never hurt. He didn't mean it that time, you mean it all the time. He don't want to hurt, he wants me. You don't want *me*. All you want is hurt, hurt. Just hurt. Why pick on me all the time? 'Cause you got somethin' on him is why," she answered herself—"The others won't let you hurt, they tell you go hurt your dog"—she began a dry sobbing despite herself, knowing that even that pleased the old man—"'n I'm such a damned fool, I let you get away with it too." She raised herself to a sitting posture and pried at his fingers on her shoulders. He banged her above the right eye with the back of his knuckles.

"*Kurwa!* Whore!"

She shielded the eye with both hands, observing him balefully with the other.

"You made me one," she accused him, like a child accusing its mother even at the risk of another blow. "You told me I had t' stay a couple days, the police was lookin' for me, there'd be a stink about it in the papers 'n my Ma 'd find out from the neighbors 'n have Bunny arrested. You told me Mama T. went to see her to tell her I was keepin' house for her, 'n Mama T. didn't go a-tall. 'n then I couldn't go, then I had t' stay, then I couldn't face Ma. I c'n hardly face her now." She buried her face in her hands, seeing herself as it had been all night, in this same room with the one door locked, stripping herself for the three of them: Catfoot, Kodadek, and the old man. First for Kodadek, then for Catfoot. She hadn't understood why they had made her dress herself anew each time, only to strip before them again. Now she knew.

"You like go home for stay?" he asked, his voice all considerateness. She shook her head miserably. No. She could believe his offer or she could distrust it, but she had tried to leave once before. She could take him at his word, and it might be that he would not bother her for several days. But back to him then she must come. Catfoot would come to tell her, and there was no way of not going back; unless it was to the police.

And she had no money for the police, she knew Bruno had no money for them. And at the barber's she was, at least, protected from them. With Tenczara it would be either the workhouse or money on the line. As well as the police for Bruno again.

Nobody had money but the barber. She thought of Bruno, with twenty-two dollars of the barber's money in his pocket, and was gladdened. Money could get people like herself and Bruno out of almost any trouble, because it was usually just through lack of a ten-dollar bill that they'd gotten into trouble in the first place. If Bruno's twenty-two were two hundred, perhaps that would be enough. But she did not know how much was enough; only that, whatever it was, it was more than she'd ever fancied having in her life. Too much for Bruno to get. He couldn't get that much with a gun, he had told her despondently. Could he get that much by fighting? A warm hope went through her with the realization that that may have been what he'd been thinking of in cutting the barber and Catfoot out of his end of the purse. She looked up with her heart bounding, as though such a hope were actually true.

"Yes. I go home," she told him, falling into his argot, "I go home for stay."

He stood before her without letting her rise.

"You stay by *rajfur* you mean? By Pimp Bruno?"

"He's not *rajfur*. He's a white hope. The paper said."

"I don't want to hear. Not Hope. *Rajfur*."

"You better not try callin' him that after he wins Monday."

"Won't win. Is *rajfur*."

He saw that the word was infuriating her, and repeated it, linking her name with Bruno's. "*Kurwa! Rajfur! Kurwa! Rajfur!*"

She smoothed her skirt down over her hips and spoke with finality. "I don't need you. Bunny'll take *good* care of me."

Deftly he inserted a forefinger into her left nostril and pulled her off the bed as though his finger were a hook. In the corner Snipes began hopping excitedly about and pointing to the pair, as though telling the radiator to look too.

Steffi gaped, her jaw going slack; he smashed at it then. Left side, right side, lurching as he swung, till he sprawled above her on the bed. Then he cleaned his finger across her cheek and regained his feet. She sat up rubbing her jaw reflectively; then the back of the neck at the base of the skull.

"Now I wouldn't take your muckin' coat if you give it to me," she told him.

"Don't wor-ry. You not get. Twenty-two doll-ars."

"Quit talkin' Polish."

"Ain't Po-lish. Is Eng-lish."

"By you it sounds Polish."

Snipes hopped on one leg between them, pointing anxiously at the open door as though someone had been peering in.

"I been too good to you," Steffi said. "I used to feel sorry for you sometimes, you'n your gimpy leg. 'n now look where I am—listen'n to you cryin' for twenny-two bucks after you took a thousand out of my flesh. Twenny-two bucks—" She glanced up, dry-eyed with hatred, and for one split moment he saw her as she should have been, a good woman in a quiet home on her own bed.

"Go ahead," she encouraged him, as though seeing the brief picture in his mind and trying to keep it there— "Hit me all you want, you got me where you want me, you can't do more t' me 'n you done awready." She thought she read something of pity trying to surmount the suspicion of all things within him, and it touched a chord within her that left her without hate for anyone. "I'm so *tired*, Honey, I don't know what I'm sayin' any more. I got no heart in me for this business, Barber. The heart's all out of me."

She flung herself face downward across the bed, her arm across her eyes and one long silk-stockinged leg still touching the floor. His eyes followed its lines; it was so, drunken and sleeping, he had first seen her. Something of that first time aroused him now; her very helplessness before him, as she had been helpless then, aroused him. He touched her shoulder.

"Is all right," he said. "I buy coat."

Her head turned haughtily toward him, and he wondered what it was now that he had said that had not pleased her. He saw a pride in her eyes he had never noticed before, a kind of confidence in herself he could not fathom and did not like. Then saw her old contempt for him, the greenhorn barber: she wove a bitter little smile for his age, his accent, his greed and his uncleanliness. A smile that never failed to excite him.

"You know what you can do with your coat," she told him.

He knew.

He went to the door and closed it quietly. She saw the trembling of his hand on the knob and sat up very straight, her discolored face looking angry under the lights. She'd make him eat his own heart tonight, as she had so often eaten hers, awake in fhe dark while he slept well beside her. When he returned he asked her humbly, as though for the last time:

"You not fool wid Lefthander no more, *Stasha?*"

"Don't *Stasha* me. My name is Steffi R."

He did not plead. It was time to tell her:

"You fool wid Lefthander, I fix Lefthander now. I give free trim again."

"I don't need no greenhorn to tell me who to sleep with," she heard herself saying. "I don't need no double-dealing yashek to tell me the score. I don't need no small-time fence. . . ."

She stopped, feeling, of a sudden, that he could kill her without passion and be done with the business of forever suspecting her; she felt he was going to kill her. She felt it was time someone did that, and that it should be him. It was the least he could do for her. And there was no immediate dread in her; only a long fatigue at the endless waiting. He hit her under the heart, she felt the knuckled fist and then a half-sickening, half-pleasant faintness as fear came up her throat at last. In a tightening fog she felt his fingers ripping the front of the sweater down and tried to remember the sweater's precise cost; the fog distorted his face till only the eyes were real. And these were fixed, the pupils dilated as with shock. She closed her own: to see a yellow sweater in a five-and-ten-cent store aisle, ripped down the middle with a price tag still on it. Till her mouth filled with tears or blood, and she pushed feebly against him, blubbering in dismay for the ripped sweater. Her nipples and finger tips felt so cold and the room was so cold and no room where she would be would be warm again for her ever.

And everything was so wrong. So hopelessly and forever wrong. Always to be alone, in the wrong room always. She felt her brain clearing and thought lucidly, as she felt at last what he was up to: money. What she needed most was money. That was what made everything so wrong, that was what made all rooms so wrong. To get out of this bed, out of this room, away from the always curtained parlor. Nothing but money, and Bruno, could do that. Money from Bruno or for him, but money. If he couldn't get it she'd get it herself. Was that what was wrong with him too? What was wrong with everyone?

"Close the door," she asked, feeling a draft. But the door was already closed.

"I never have fun, Barber," she told him placatingly, "I want fun once in a while too."

"I can have fun too!" Snipes piped from somewhere like a small solemn echo.

She felt the barber's muscles tightening about her, and felt so old in those arms: then they tightened tenderly.

Snipes limped to the corner and squeezed between the radiator and the wall with his back turned, clucking his tongue at the yellow walls. He wanted to look but felt ashamed.

"Barber," she said gently, "you're hurtin' me."

Snipes peeked covertly through his fingers. The naked light was on them. He turned to the wall and did not dare to look again.

"Rany boskie. Jestem wniebie." He heard her moan a little. Then they lay quietly, his passion spent. After all, she reflected dreamily, at least he was jealous. That was something. At least he meant it.

The barber lay on his back wondering what he'd gotten so excited about. It all seemed for no known reason now. Sensing his passivity, she said, "I'll take your goddamn coat."

"You not want."

"I want."

He laughed, pleased at her acquiescence. Then his old caution told him to stop laughing and think: she'd sacrificed her right to the coat, he could claim a return for giving it now. So he remained silent, thus putting her on the defensive. It was her turn to bid and his to weigh.

"Sleep now," he advised, as though he wished to dismiss further talk of a coat. But he was calculating— What could she give him greater than her fidelity?—a fidelity uncompromised by her hours in Mama T.'s rooms. There was a fidelity she could give him in his own room. Yet even that could be secondary.

"Don't sleep, Barber," she asked.

He snored gently.

"Barber . . ." she shook him, sensing that by morning the coat would be gone for good.

"Barber!"

He stirred.

"I been straight with you, Barber."

He rolled over on his side with his back to her.

"Barber."

"Ugh."

"Turn over. I want to talk."

He grunted, returning to face her reluctantly.

"Don't fake, Barber. I want the coat."

"You want. You not want. Forget altogedder."

"No. I want."

"I want too."

"Oh. Whyn't you say? What you want?"

"I want you be straight."

"I said that."

"Then you show me."

"Show you what?"

"Show you not like *raffur* no more."

"How I do that?"

The barber had it ready and he gave it to her fast.

"You let him come see you. I not be here. You drink."

"I get drunk with him?"

"You make *he* get drunk. Sunday."

"He fights Monday night—he won't drink Sunday."

"Celebrate. Little drunk. Little more. He forget."

"Then what?"

"Then I take care."

She lay a long time gathering courage to ask the next question. He waited for it tensely. She asked it softly.

"You gonna wreck him, Barber?"

"You like I wreck him? He wreck you, you wreck too. Nice?"

She asked herself whether she wanted that: she saw Bruno clearly, without love, a duped hoodlum who had kicked her into the gutter and let her lie because others might laugh if he helped her up.

She saw it, yet saw it so only for a moment.

"He didn't mean it bad. He just don't have no guts. Don't wreck him, Barber. Not for no coat."

"Is not for coat." He snorted contemptuously.

Steffi understood. Not because Bruno would be making money now, and the barber would be getting not a penny of it, for all his shirt ripped halfway down his chest. He had lost his coat, and the rain had left great drops, like tears, on his throat. He had been beaten about the eyes and stood, weaving, showing her the knuckles of his left hand. They were bruised blue; he shook his head slowly from side to side as he looked at them.

"I couldn't see in the dark," he was mumbling. "They kept comin' at me. Now look what they done."

She was helping him down an uncarpeted stair, where puddles of water remained in the hollows. He wanted to leave her, he said, because people were saying he'd killed her. "You mustn't leave in such a rain," she told him. "The Jew is dead, so Barber won't know who cheated."

It was Saturday afternoon, so everything must be clean for the evening. He leaned too heavily upon her, yet she must get him down into the basement, so the barber would not find him and yet he would be always near. She had to clear an old plush couch of newspapers, piled there for years, forgotten by everyone. Beneath the last yellowed sheet, with the yellow viaduct light across his face, lay the wizened body of Snipes: they had all forgotten to bury him. They had all forgotten his real name, so he could not be buried ever. They had forgotten his name. As God had forgotten theirs.

"The Devil killed him," she explained to Bruno.

He was curled up and shrunken to a baby's size except for his head, which seemed swollen and lay on an oversize wallet for a pillow. She slipped the wallet from under his head carefully, for a nickel to play the juke, and his tiny index finger reached out and touched her skirt. When she tried to draw back she saw she wore no skirt, but stood before him only in her red-tasseled slippers, her high black-mesh hose and a pink lace brassière. And he was smiling dreamily to himself because of his mocking finger that she could not draw back from.

"That one ain't worth five cents," Bruno B. whispered to someone behind her back. They were all fully clothed, behind her there, women and men; she stood stiffly, to hear what they were saying about her. They were nudging each other and laughing derisively; half-muffled laughter, as though a door were being opened and

trouble. Not even because Bruno had cheated him at cards. But only because she had helped him to cheat. That was it. He really meant it. All the way down.

"You think he'll win Monday, Barber?"

"No difference. He fight. Get in money."

"Big money, Barber?"

"Pretty soon big money."

He spoke with anxiety—did he already fear that big money for Bruno meant that Bruno would take his girl back? Did he mean it that much?

"Won't Casey cut you in?" she asked, pretending, along with him, that there was nothing involved in his vindictiveness but dollars and cents. The barber answered angrily. Who was Casey to do any cutting in?

"I make cut. I give Casey supper money. Good enough."

"But if you'd split with him 'n leave them other two cliff-apes out maybe they'd let you in."

"I make cut. Supper money. Catfoots good boy."

"Supper money for Bruno too?"

"I buy him beer too," he conceded.

She felt his greed sickening her, this man who had to have all or nothing.

"Supper money for me?" she asked, teasing and serious.

"For you, coat."

"And if I don't want no coat?"

"Then po-lees."

So that was it. He'd rather have her in a cell than with another man. He'd rather have Bruno in the electric chair than to lose her. He had her and he had Bruno. He had them both as completely as he had Mama T. He had them all.

"I'll take the coat," she told him, deciding to make the best of a bad bargain. Why cut off her nose to spite her face?

But he misunderstood. He misunderstood her fear of the police for vindictiveness toward Bruno.

It was growing light outside the window facing Mama T.'s before he slept. When everything was still Snipes tiptoed out, closing the door carefully behind him, like a well-taught child, so as not to waken the sleepers. In the hall he trembled, drew his overcoat collar about his neck and spoke earnestly aloud to himself all the way down the steps; but was careful to mutter in a whisper when passing the second floor. For there the girls slept, and he must not waken them before noon. When he reached the basement he had to be even more careful and go even more softly, for Bruno B., when drunk, slept on newspapers there. He made his way blindly toward the back and lay down himself, on papers piled a foot deep in the faucetless bathtub of the washroom.

Snipes had dim recollections of war. He had been shell-shocked at Cantigny Ridge and had later served four years, for conspiracy to defraud, in the workhouse. It was there that his mind had failed. And six months in the workhouse hospital hadn't, somehow, improved it. Now he took out ashes in a whorehouse and kept a barroom basement clean. There were nights when his childhood fear of rats returned, and he would say softly in the dark, "Go away, Rat-Things," or shout aimlessly at nothing. Sometimes he dreamed of them and, waking, failed to distinguish between his dreams and reality: he would go busily about setting traps or spreading poison to catch a dream rat; and when he caught one thus, in reality, his sleep would be untroubled. When he caught one in sleep his waking hours were freed of his fear.

When one of the girls gave him a dime he put it in the oversize wallet and kept it there until he'd accumulated fifty cents. Then he bet it on a horse called Royal Jackpot, fifty cents on the nose. The horse had never won a race in five years of trying. But once, against a cheap field, had gotten a call and only missed the show money by a photograph. That afternoon Snipes had been a hero, the women had vied with each other to tell him how close he'd come: that if he'd bet the half on show instead of to win, that he would have gotten five and a half dollars back. At first Snipes didn't believe, but their insistence convinced him, until he was no longer certain whether he'd won or lost that day. Although it felt as though he'd won. He had saved the ticket in the wallet's folds, and every forenoon gave the women confidential tips which never came true.

Royal Jackpot had become a sort of wonder horse in his mind. "If you was his jockey he'd never lose," Steffi told him.

Snipes would look at the tattered ticket, when he was told that, and smile shyly.

Upstairs the naked lights burned on above the naked sleepers.

Five brunettes and a platinum blonde slept on, each in a separate room.

Below them the chairs of the Broken Knuckle were stacked along the Broken Knuckle Bar; the light above the twenty-six-board was out and the sign above the cash register read NO SALE. "You have an honest face," a sign above the register read, "but we can't put it in here." And an arrow pointed downward toward the register.

Downstairs Bruno fought the barber in his sleep.

Within the windings of his dream, Bruno led heavily with his right, then threw the left, like a weight, into the short ribs to the waist. Great lights were blazing overhead, the papers piled beneath him squeaked as he tossed about. "Left t' the body 'n right t' the head," he said aloud in sleep. And little Snipes, hearing, thought the words were for him.

"I'm goin' t' bed, Rat-Things," he assured the voice, and climbed into the tub in the dark.

Above, the barber too lay dreaming. Dreaming that he was playing twenty-six at Ryan's Bar. The twenty-six-girl was pock-marked like Mama T., but was young and wore her hair in dark-brown braids. He was playing with a beer in one hand and picked up a dice-box with the other, annoyed that she should go on pretending not to know him. "The thunder killed a devil," he was telling her confidentially so that he would always win at everything, and then dashed the beer, instead of the dice, across the green baize of the twenty-six board: it slopped across the knees of her skirt and she jumped up dismayed, swearing at him in Polish. So he was glad he had done that, for he had known it was the Duchess all the time. He wriggled his head with pleasure in his sleep. The barber had strange dreams.

Beside him, the sallow, rain-washed light across her face, Steffi dreamed of Bruno Bicek. He appeared before her in the rain, his

closed constantly upon them. Then the unseen door closed softly forever, making of their derision the faintest of tittering, and she went to a window to get farther away, as far away as she could go.

And looked out upon a bright, cloudless afternoon of some October she would never know. The street was familiar, yet subtly changed: she had seen it often years before, had forgotten it forever long ago; yet it was all so strangely new. As forgotten as the yellowed papers: as new as yellow sunlight.

And he was gone, as he'd wished to go. In a long-forgotten rain.

On Sunday evening Bruno B. walked into the barber's room. Steffi was alone. He sat in the straight-backed chair holding a bag of bismarcks in his hand; the bag had grown greasy from them, he had carried them two miles.

"They're day-olds," he apologized, "from the old lady's. You want 'em?"

"Put 'em on the dresser for the barber, Hon. That pack-rat 'll eat anythin'."

He noticed that her eyes were red-rimmed, and found himself hoping that someday she'd be able to sit down and cry for a week.

"Don't you like bismarcks no more?" he asked. "You used t' like 'em."

"Somethin' I like even better now," she told him mechanically, "that certain thing."

"You don't have t' talk that way t' me, Steff."

"Why?—Are you different?"

She turned her head away; her face looked anguished with fatigue. The corners of the ceiling were black with soot.

"I didn't come up for that. I come up to ask you t' wish me luck. I'm fightin' t'morrow night."

"I know. Good luck."

"Is Barber sore?"

"I wouldn't know that. You can bet you don't have no job around here no more though."

"I won't need it. Are you sore at me too?"

"I got nothin' left in me to get sore at you about. All I wish is you was dead. All I ever got from you all my life was a beatin', 'n you ask me if I'm sore."

"If I beat that jig t'morrow you won't wish I was dead, Steff'. I'll make it all up to you then. We'll have somethin' to buck the barber with then. We'll get out of town t'gether if you want, Steff'."

"I like it here."

"I mean married, Steff'—ain't it time we get married?"

"You think I was born yesterday?" she asked, her voice full of suspicion.

"No. You was born nineteen years ago, almost."

"Did you know me that far back, Bunny?" The suspicion faded from her voice.

"Almost. I knew you fourteen ago."

"You mean when we moved on Cornell, in that old shack?"

"Only it wasn't Cornell them days. It was Chestnut."

Powder from her compact spilled on the floor, and while he sat rubbing it with the sole of his shoe she saw herself on a forgotten doorstep, one roller skate on and the other in her hand. She had loved to skate to the library and look at the books with the brightest pictures, and skate back carrying the pictures in her mind. She saw herself skating boldly up to a stranger, one skate dangling over her shoulder, and passed her hand over her forehead and held her locket tightly: each time she permitted herself some recollection of childhood her fevered mind tricked her into some monstrous confusion with the present, till she feared the past as fully as the future.

"Give me the money first, Hon," she solicited the stranger in her mind. She looked up: Bruno had twisted the paper in his hand as though he had followed her thought as reluctantly as she had pursued it.

"You oughtn't t' cut the sleeves out of your shirts," she told him irrelevantly, to cover the steaming fever in her brain.

For a minute there was no sound in the room save that of Bruno scuffling his tennis shoes. He waited for her to caution him again about his sleeveless shirts, to enjoy her concern. He pointed at the toes of the shoes diffidently. She looked at them without interest.

"What's the holes in 'em for, Bunny?"

" 'cause they're my Helt' Shoes."

"I remember. Like your cap." She rose and offered him a bottle of "Kentucky Cream" that the barber had left for the purpose on the dresser.

"I—I can't, Steff'," he apologized. "I'm in trainin'."

"He isn't so sharp as he used to be," she thought. "He used to be sharper than me. I see through things faster now." And added aloud. "Well, I'll have to drown the worm alone then."

She drank slowly, watching him furtively over the bottle's rim to see how soon drinking like that would remind him of the last time they had drunk from the same bottle together. His eyes dropped, and she knew. Knew that that night had been with him every night since. She felt the liquor hit her and thought, "This 'll be another night he'll remember a spell."

Outside the rain began, tapping derisively at the pane.

"Don't need to knock on no window t'night," she told him. "Rain does it for me."

She spoke deliberately, provokingly, putting all her hard-won hardness into her voice. "I'm hard as any now," she assured herself proudly.

He had once seen a woman in front of a line of men at a police line-up. They had manacled her and she had stood silent even after the amplifier had been moved before her.

"What's your name, sister?"

Silence.

"What's your name?"

Silence.

"You better talk, sister. It's your only out."

She had spoken then. Hard as the manacles on her hands.

"There ain't no out. You shut the doors already. You'll send me back there, right or wrong. Whether I talk 'r whether I don't. You want me t' tell how I been half-killed there, so's you can kill me the rest of the way. But I won't. I'll just look at you till you finish me off. *Coppers.*"

They had moved the mike away.

"Don't talk tough, Steff'," he asked, remembering. "It ain't nice. You ain't that kind."

She looked at him in genuine amazement. Then she saw that he meant it, that under his pretense of toughness he was still that soft. He looked ready to cry.

Well, she'd wanted to cry too and couldn't. Let him try to get something out of his system like she had in hers. It couldn't be done.

"What do you think I'm doin' these days, talkin' t' me like that?" she asked. "Keepin' track of the towels?"

He gulped. She looked at him sitting there looking so big and foolish.

"Steff'—I. I'm sorry."

He would say no more. It had been a struggle to say that much. She looked away to defend herself from his eyes. They were trying to tell her that there was nothing, now, he would not do for her. And his physical presence, the animal smell of him, the full deep breathing of his chest, all reached toward her to plead for her forgiveness. She reached blindly for the bottle thinking, "He beat me with the bottle once, I'll need it to beat him tonight. He had his way with me once—I'll have my way this time." She mustn't believe in him again, she warned herself. "For my own sake, I mustn't believe in him."

She no longer cared for what the barber wanted. She wished only to defend herself. He had kicked her into the gutter once, he'd kick her back if she trusted him for a moment. She drank off four fingers, as if it were the last one she'd ever drink. And he took a small one with her.

"You never quit thinkin' you got ever'body in the world on the ropes, do you?" She lashed out at him. "You think all you have to do is say 'sorry' 'n I come runnin' for another beatin'?"

He took her hand without reply and she could not pull it away. She shoved at his shoulders with the other and they resisted her without effort.

"Steff'," he asked, "don't push me. I feel bad all the time. I want to make up for what I done . . ."

"Don't feel sorry for me, Bunny. That's the worst yet. You give me every kind of beatin' there is in the books, but don't do it that way too. If you think you got somethin' t' make up for, go t' church 'n do it."

"I didn't mean sorry that way. I meant make it up for both of us. I meant make it like it used to be. . . ."

He let her hand drop and she smiled up at him, the dry, wry, bitter little smile she had gotten from her contempt of the barber.

"Like it used to be, Bunny? Ain't it a little late?"

"No."

She looked at him first with disbelief, then with genuine impatience, half-turning from him. "What the hell *is* the use of talking like that? When somethin's done it can't be undone, you can't just fix things by sayin' they didn't happen." She turned back to him. "What the hell *is* the use, Bunny?"

There was no fear of him left in her voice; only the fullness of her desperation at the past was in it.

"Go away," she asked him. "All you do is make me remember."

She reached for the bottle and his hand stopped hers upon it. Then she was in his arms, her memory of everything blurring at being there again, as though she had never been anywhere else. And there was no fear in her for anything, save that he might let her go. He rocked her gently, feeling no need of any bottle; feeling only the need of her small mouth on his own.

When he kissed her he saw that her lips were full and red, as he had not seen them for over a year.

"I don't know what I want no more, Bunny," she told him. Yet even as she spoke she felt herself taking strength from him. "I been sick in the head 'n now I feel better. You make me better."

"I still got twenty bucks of the dough we won off the barber," he told her. "I been savin' it. I ain't had a drink in a week. Get your clothes 'n we'll go to your Ma's. She's been askin' 'n askin' how you are 'n why you don't even visit. She knows, Steff', but she's scared to ask it. She won't ask nothin' if you come back. We'll tell her we're gettin' married. We'll do it after the fight. I'll make them gimme a hundred in advance, just t' be sure. A hundred bucks—

Steff'—we'll set up housekeepin'. I'll be makin' that much every month now. Maybe more." He looked down at her solemnly, to tell her something he thought that, perhaps, she didn't yet know. "I can lick anybody, Steff'," he assured her with no shade of doubt in his mind, as though he were telling her his name.

She buried her face against him, ashamed to show her joy. "Your old lady can come t' live with us, Bunny—she's too old to work." Then she remembered something and added lightly: "I was s'pose to get you drunk t'night. I was s'pose to get you drunk 'n the barber's boys was s'pose to come in 'n fix your clock. He ain't so mad about gettin' cut out of your purse as he is about my still lovin' you."

"I thought somethin' was up," he said. "You was offsteerin' me."

"I ain't offsteerin' you now,' she added seriously. "You better clear out 'n I'll tell 'em you didn't show. We won't have time to pack 'n I ought t' be here anyhow when they come, so's it won't look funny. I'll come with Casey to the fight 'n wait for you afters. I ain't never seen you fight, Bunny. Where should I wait?"

"With Casey. You stay by him 'n you'll see the Chicago Av'noo Powerhouse hisself. I'll kill him fer life, Steff'—" he led cautiously with his right—"I'll bring him in like this"—he packed his head behind his shoulder and chopped the left into the teeth, giving his man no chance to get set. She folded her palms about her locket, a rich tingling going through her.

"Is it like that, Bunny?—Is it like that?"

The door behind her opened a foot, and half a foot farther, and Kodadek stood in the opening, lean as tuberculosis. Bruno came up grinning from cheekbone to cheek. It had been long since she'd seen him smile like that. Then she saw the smile going and looked where he looked.

Kodadek. Catfoot. And a short man she had never seen before, in a light green pencil-stripe suit and polished patent-leather pumps; as though he had just stepped off the main ballroom of the Happy Gardens. His face was powdered pinkishly, as though he had just shaved and had used a woman's compact instead of after-shaving talc. Under the powder, a face she had seen half a hundred times.

And yet had never seen it. She stood staring as at a face in a
dream, familiar and yet unknown, seeing the razor-crease of the
trouser and the false carnation in the lapel, exactly like one of the
false carnations of the wall. That she saw each night in dream.

It did not occur to the man that the girl was staring because she
could not place him. Everyone knew the Tiger. Everyone. He took
her glance for admiration of his suit, and spoke with embarrassed
pride.

"It's my Linc'n Park Suit. The one wit' the stripes in. A gag
you. Hah!"

Steffi saw a yellow label on an open whisky bottle.

Pultoric.

"We don't want trouble," the picture-face said. He looked as
though he were wearing a two-by-four across his shoulders.

And came forward in a mincing loose-kneed shuffle, his eyes without color or light. She saw Bruno put his back against the dresser
and get the bottle there into his hand. From the doorway Catfoot
spoke.

"He got a bottle, Tiger."

"Gimme the bottle, Bud. It got my pitcher on it."

"This one got *my* pitcher on it."

Pultoric stood squinting, hands hanging loosely, knees mincing
loosely.

"Let's see."

"You can see from where you're at," Bruno said, and felt his own
eyes narrowing.

Pultoric's face saddened oddly as he studied the bottle.

"No pitcher," he said thickly, and turned to the two near the door,
helplessly. "No pitcher."

Steffi looked about at her company, bewildered. Was the fellow
that punch-drunk?

"Gimme the bottle anyhow," she heard him say, and the thick-
ness was almost out of his voice.

"I'll take the bottle," she told them all, and, as though he had
expected that of her, Bruno handed it to her without taking his
eyes off his man. She heard Catfoot closing the door, and, as she

turned her head, caught the break of Pultoric's shoulder and he was in, swinging loosely into the body. She saw his head rock back and Bruno going to the left with both hands cocked. The two at the door stood unmoving; she clenched the neck of the bottle with one hand and gripped her locket with the other. She saw Bruno's left snap out and back, with a sound like a splashing. Pultoric was standing before him, his hands at his sides, his nose bloodied, grinning. He extended one hand.

"You're real sharp t'night, dearie—'n let's call it quits."

"It's quits," Bruno said, without either taking the hand nor lowering his left. Pultoric laughed over his shoulder at the pair at the door. "I'm gonna need help here, he's feelin' mean." She saw Kodadek's hand fumbling in his pocket, find what it sought and he came shambling forward with the hand in the pocket. When he was four feet from her she leaned the bottle across the back of his head with all her weight behind it. He spun, and as he spun she saw Bruno knock Pultoric aside with his elbow. He was on Kodadek and Kodadek was on the floor. She threw herself in front of Pultoric, yanking at his coat, saw his heavy features mildly amazed at seeing her there, and felt herself slung against the wall. She steadied herself against it and saw Bruno on his feet, his back against the dresser where he'd started, and Pultoric trying to get Kodadek to his knees. In Bruno's hand was Kodadek's knife and he was breathing like a bull.

"Get him out of here. Throw him down the steps. I'll give you till I get my breath. Then I'll cut."

Kodadek sensed his desperate need of getting onto his feet. When he reached the door he banged against it blindly, blocking Pultoric. She heard the front door slam faintly: Catfoot was far in front of them both. Then a sound of excited voices down the hall, and Pultoric's hoarse urging of Kodadek. It sounded as though he were half-carrying, half-hauling Kodadek down the staircase. As she closed the door behind them, Kodadek coughed. From the bottom of his stomach.

The knife lay open upon the dresser.

"I been scared of that stabber all my life," Bruno said without looking at the knife, so that she did not know whether he meant Kodadek or the blade. Then she saw he was rubbing his hand. The knuckles were already swollen.

"The hand," he said below his breath, "the hand."

She brought cold water in a pan, and he rested the knuckles in it.

"I gotta use it to set him up t'morrow," he told her.

When he took his cap to leave, Steffi held him a moment in the door. Then watched him leaving, walking away from her with cap in hand as once before, toward a poolroom door, he had walked away from her. As though leaving forever, without a word. She called after him, "Bunny! Bunny!"

Then put her hand to her mouth as though to stop her voice, for she had nothing to call him back for.

He turned, waiting to hear what she wanted.

"Keep your chin out of the way," she told him airily, "'n your pants off the floor."

She saw him smiling in the dark. A wide white grin.

Everything was going to be all right after all.

BOOK IV

TOWARD EVENING LANDS

THE sons of a Polish baker and a mulatto pigsticker crouched across the canvas from each other, the Pole in a blue robe and the Negro in flaming red: two splashes of color in the depths of a pit peopled in black and gray. The crowd, packed steeply uphill about them, stirred restlessly; but the robes sat without motion. Two clothing-store dummies at the bottom of a human well. A low and ceaseless murmur came down across the ropes and was returned across it.

The Pole, in worn tennis shoes, sat with lowered head. The Negro stared steadily at the light on the brass ring post behind the Pole's shoulder. Between them a slim young Italian in a dark suit, looking like a night-club M.C., was speaking into the public address system.

"Interdoosin' to you, from Chicago's great South Side, fight'n out of the Savoy A.C. at one-hunert-eight-one 'n three-qwatahs poun's—the forma STATE LIGHT HEAVY CHAMPEEN in the black 'n red trunks HONEYBOY TUCKA!"

Tucker half-rose, threw his right glove lazily over his left and sat down again, unimpressed.

Scattered applause. Catcalls. A North Side crowd and a white man's evening.

"*What* state? Road Eye-lund?"

"Where'd you get the sun-boin, Tucker?"

" 'n in this cawneh interdoosin to you a great boy some of you

260

seen before, from Chicago's great Nawth'est Side in the green 'n white trunks weight one-hunert-ninety 'n a half, a boy who never been off his feet inside a ring—the great new contenda fer the heavyweight champeen—BRUNO LEFTY BICEPS!"

"How about *outside* the ring?" someone whooped.

"When they let *you* out, Lefty?"

"Hey Bicek, I tawt they hung you!"

"You get the clip in the workie, Bicek?"

"Hey Lefty! Them trunks got stripes!"

The announcer intervened, as the jeers seemed gathering in number.

"Kin'ly refrain from smokin' durin' this featcha bout of the evenin'. Ill'nois Box'n C'mmission rules. Count'n fer knockdowns Nat'n Han'nstein house physic'n Dr. Frank Catanese ten roun's thank you."

Bruno heard the white men give him a hand then, for being white too, and turned toward the darkening rows to scrape his shoes in the rosin. He spotted Steffi and looked down until he saw Casey climbing in from the other side and the ref behind Casey. This was Westside Spector, brother to a long-dead hoodlum who had dominated the Twenty-sixth ward before Twelfth Street was Roosevelt Road. Spector motioned the bright robes into the center of the pit and stood between them, both half a head taller than himself, both with heads bowed like penitent monks; the clipped blond skull of the one almost touching the greased and glistening wool of the other.

"Now I want you boys t' realize you're responsible in this ring t'night before the sportin' world. When I tell you t' break I want you t' break 'n ——"

Casey ran his hand over the mulatto's skull.

"Get that grease off 'r we don't fight."

He reached for Tucker with his towel, but the boy rolled his head easily, letting his own handler swab off the outer coating of oil. Westside Spector went on mechanically.

"All I demand is a clean fight." And paused dramatically. "Is that askin' too much?" And answered himself. "No."

Tucker pounded his gloves together tensely. He had been jabbing his left six rounds a day for three weeks, and every nerve in him screamed now for release—to jab, jab, like something with a life of its own in his wrists. Jab. Everything in the world is a target. Jab. He felt his whole torso tautening with the effort to restrain himself a few more seconds; his handler, sensing his need, massaged the left shoulder gently. Nobody was listening to Spector.

"Watch the body-punchin'—you both know the rules in this state, one low blow c'n be the differ'nce between vict'ry 'n defeat, if you foul I'm gonna take away the round off you. No buttin', no heelin', no back of the glove, no rabbit, no kidney, keep your gloves closed 'n laces tied—now go t' your corners 'n come out t' give us a real ex-bishun."

Casey grabbed Bruno's left glove and packed it firmly beneath Tucker's navel— "How's this Spector—when we get him here is it legal?"

Westside Spector flared, "Now you fought here before, you know the C'mmission's rules."

A single agonized cry came over the ropes:

"What's dat—*cabbage*?"

"All I ask is a clean fight," Westside repeated— "*Is* that askin' too much?"

"Get out from d' ring 'n let 'em scrap!"

With his arm about Bruno's waist, Casey had the last over-the-shoulder word:

"Don't give *us* that hustle. You never seen this boy throw a low one in yer life."

"All I ask . . ."

The lights went out all over the house, and down to the cockpit of the ring came the constant and indistinct rumor of voices: from mouths behind cigars, pipes, cigarettes, veils, mustaches, neckties and half-murmured wagers. From the troubled salesman behind the sucker bet and the frayed collar, the housewife getting in secret debt to the dead-pan sheet writer beside her, the jobless youth rejected by the navy and hoping to make the army, the ex-middle-weight from Fargo with a restaurant and a daughter who wouldn't

wait on trade, the linotyper whose wife sat invalided on a suburban
sun porch and waited irritably even now in its shadows for his
return, the professional blackjack dealer's mistress and the poolroom
idler, in on a pass, doing most of the cheering and all of the booing
in his section.

"Oh that face! Where'd you get them *ears*? Hey Westside, are
you his old man? Hey Biceps when you shave last? Slug him when
he shakes hands Biceps—NOW! NOW! Oh you Polack jerk that was
yer last chance—Hey! Westside! You got a share in the place yet?
Give us King Levinsky!"

In the moment before the bell Bruno stood pulling at his trunks
as though they were trousers with a fresh crease, his new mouthpiece protruding, hearing Casey's last-minute instructions un-
willingly.

"You got t' get to him right off, Left'. You ain't in the shape t'
stay with him. He goes fifteen wit'out even breathin' hard—ruin
him before he gets set 'n we got him. The left in the gut—always
in the gut. Ferget he got a face even." Casey, seeing the stubborn-
ness in Bruno's expression, began pleading, "Fight my way just
t'night, Left'. Fight yer own way the rest of yer life, but fight my
way t'night. Just t'night. Just the first two rounds then. That's all
I'll ever ask. All I ask is ferget his jaw fer two rounds, Left'—
Do that for me? Do it for me?"

Bruno chewed his mouthpiece into place. "I got my own technique," he said without looking up. Casey shrugged his shoulders
helplessly, patted Bruno on the back timidly, and crawled through
the ropes talking below his breath.

"It's awright," Finger consoled him. "I'll put my Cosmic Whammy
on the jig. I been savin' it up two years." Finger got up off the stool
below their corner. "You set down, Case."

But at the bell both rose, with their chins on the apron of the
ring. They saw Bruno cross himself mechanically and turn; heard
the kissing sound of the gloves as they touched.

Tucker, looking cool and grave, feinted his man into a mis-
lead, slapped a light right to the head, and brought Bruno's guard
down just to see if he could bring it down that easily. Tucker

blocked an attempt to the body, shifted the left to the head and came in hooking. Bruno rolled and tied him up. They broke of their own accord.

"Tie him up wit' the ropes, Biceps!"

"Don't fight, boys—we don't expect it!"

"A little music wid dat waltz!"

"Hey! You guys must be on a project!"

Tucker's mouth made a perfect "O" and his brows went down toward it in a "V." Bruno stepped inside a left, chopping upward against the stomach's grain, Tucker countering to the kidneys; Spector let them fight their way out of it. With his left tied, Bruno slammed his right to the navel and heard Tucker grunt. They spun each other around to get free, Bruno started his left from long range and let it fall off. They tied each other up once more, this time in a sort of human bridge, skull to skull, while the crowd booed for action; they were tied up at the bell.

In his corner Finger began splattering the sponge over Bruno; he swung his head away in irritation.

"Lay off. I ain't even got up a sweat."

There was a single thread dangling from the top strand of the rope in Tucker's corner, and that annoyed him too: he wanted to get up and pull it off neatly. Casey, leaning through the middle rope, slipped the mouthpiece out, ducked it in the red-white-and-blue bucket and held it, a tiny pink horseshoe, about his middle fingers, gesturing. Bruno eyed the bucket at his feet, feeling less irritable, even in this hurried moment, at seeing the blue letters of his name encircling the white stripe of the bucket: BRUNO BICEK. A nice job, that bucket; the Finger was good for something after all. He stood up and let Finger take the stool away.

"Don't get hit, Biceps! You'll eat milk 'n crackers a mont'!"

Tucker tried a left lead along the face, crossed the right and followed through with the left into the stomach's pit; the impact tossed him back onto his heels and Bruno was after him hooking hard. Two inches, an inch, then half an inch over the belt. A flash bulb exploded in the corner as though it were part of his hooking hands, splattering tiny glass triangles onto the ring's apron.

"Go away with that Brownie!"

He pumped in a right as Tucker backed, felt the belt give with the blow, packed his man into the ropes and swung from the balls of his feet to the jaw. To find the jaw blocked, the ribs and kidneys covered by the elbows, and the head pulled into the shell of the gloves. He swayed before Bruno like a headless turtle till he felt the ropes behind him, then slipped his head under the top rope and leaned out backward over the apron.

"Don't get hit, you boogie."

"Make him eat hair now, Lefty—you wiv too!"

"You ain't got wire hair like him!"

"Iron them kinks out, Biceps!"

"Show him you come from the gas station, Lefty—give him service!"

"Ah you jerks, you fight like I useta."

Tucker slipped back in weaving a fresh shell about his chin. Bruno, fighting straight up because Casey had told him to crouch, waited for him to pop out. He popped, and Bruno threw the left wide. His head still buried in elbows, Tucker went four inches off the canvas under the left, straight into the teeth with a stiff-arming right, and back into his shell. Bruno blinked, backed, and spat; a tooth zipped in an arc through the light into the blue-gray fog about the ring. Some mouthpiece.

And the bell. Casey was all over him with the towel before he sat down, swabbing his mouth inside and out.

"You want to bust the hand altogether? If you hadn't been wide with it you woulda jammed it for sure. Can't you understand, Left' —the hand ain't no good on his head t'night? You're gonna bust it as sure as you catch him with it. His jaw ain't rubber, Left'." Bruno lifted his head, seeing Westside Spector picking up the pieces of the cameraman's bulb. "If I catch him with it it won't matter if I bust it," he said sullenly. "He'll be out fer a week. Don't worry, I know where the money is."

"What if you catch him too high?" Casey wheedled innocently. "What if it bounces off his forehead instead? Then what? Where's the money then?"

Bruno had no answer; so Casey told the answer to him.

"He ain't even gonna feel it, but you'll bust it all the same. This ain't the only fight you'll ever have, Left'—we'll fight every month after this, we'll need that hand. For Christ sake, Lefty"—losing patience—"Low, fer God's sake keep it low. They can't do no more'n take the round off you."

"I got my own——"

"I know what you got. You got a skull 'n elbows, but you ain't usin' 'em. Get on to yerself. Give him the works. You're gonna lose if you don't weaken him fast. He fights in a gym, Lefthander—'n you're fightin' his way. Now go out there 'n get him out on Noble Street. Make him fight it your way."

Bruno tilted his head far back and half-closed his eyes; at the ten-second siren he opened them and Tucker was standing in his corner, his mouth already going into an "O" and his brows into a "V." His legs went up to his torso hiplessly, and his shoulders spread in a slope, like an open umbrella. All shoulders, legs and arms. Behind him a line of little orange and green bulbs were strung across a corner of the Garden as though they had been left from Saturday night's Halloween dance; he thought vaguely of other strung lights and another fall night. He stood up, impatient for the bell; and as he did so the bell rang twice.

"Oh you spider!" A woman shrilled at Tucker as he came out, sounding to Bruno a little like Mama T.; and added gaily, to encourage Bruno, "Step on the spider!"

A white man's evening.

Tucker came in as though his right hand were heavier than his left, the back of the glove almost touching the floor while the other still rolled protectively about his jaw. Bruno jabbed him off balance and felt the wind of that right hand go by.

"Take him, Biceps—he's all yours!"

"Stay out of them corners, Bruno!"

He felt the ropes burn his back and trapped Tucker's head under his arm, Tucker pawing blindly to catch Bruno's gloves. Westside Spector came between, pulling at Bruno's gloves as though Tucker's gestures had called his attention to them.

"Who you pushin' around, Spector?" someone called.

"Is that what they pay *you* for?"

"Hey, I tawt this was yer aggressive night, Biceps! The paper said so!"

"Step aside 'n let 'em both fall, Spector!"

"Give it to him on a blue-plate special, Biceps!"

"The ol' laces—*you* know."

"The ol' el*bow*!"

Bruno saw Tucker's belly dipping deeply for breath, got inside over the eye lightly with the right and drove the left from the shoulder straight into the very point of the jaw. The impact brought his own right foot into the air: then came forward behind the blow and Tucker was waiting for the left, his mouthpiece half in and half out, to catch it again without rolling, without fading, without falling away, and the house came onto its feet like a single man to see the boy holding on without strength—Bruno shoved him off, cool and deliberate as he had never been in his life, and measured him. "I got all night," he assured himself. Then the surge of the mob's voice came over the ropes.

Seven thousand whites in the dark, watching a single brown one in the pitiless glare of the lights. Trying to get his hands up like trying in a dream. He swayed, in the center of the ring, with his mouth unhinged. Bruno snapped his head back with his right held high like a balancing pole and the left back of his ear like a club.

"*Do* it *do* it *do* it *do* it!"

They'd stood up in the rows here before to see this slope-shouldered Pole come in for the kill; they had learned to like the way he had won before, dropping his man face forward and stiff as a board as though—who could tell—he were out for keeps with an inquest and all. Hadn't Baer killed Frankie Campbell, and remember poor Ernie Schaaf? Bruno threw the left like a center fielder pegging a ball into home. It skidded off the forehead, he felt the knuckles crumple as though he'd hit a bag of steel marbles. And the uneasy dust came briefly between.

Behind the dust Tucker faded at last, moving shakily to the right, shaking the circulation back into his head. A slow freight hooted, in a long melancholy boo as it passed; under the lights Tucker's eyes were clearing.

In a fresh flurry Bruno forced him from rope to rope, hooking blindly in a rage at letting his man get away, swinging like a drunken street fighter without letting himself get set. Tucker held, burying his chin in his man's shoulder and swabbing the thumbs of the gloves into Bruno's eyes until his arms were tied behind him. Then he held Bruno's wrists there with his own until Westside banged the wrists free. Bruno shoved him off contemptuously and Tucker stood for one moment tilted backwards on his heels, knees unbent, spine stiff against the ropes. Bruno sensed him stretching them to gain momentum, yet stepped in to meet him, head down and hooking. For a split fraction Tucker held Bruno's chin cupped in his gloves, swaying it gently from side to side. Then he smashed it with a curving right, his right shoulder curving to the waist behind it.

Bruno felt himself going down through a basement floor: they were all far above him, watching him falling on a falling elevator; he spread his hands within the gloves to stop the sick feeling. And felt the floor under the gloves at last, bracing him against canvas. Each glove was a ten-pound weight and he shook his head slowly, feeling the beginning of the pain along the nape.

At seven he got onto one knee and at nine rose heavily, mocking Tucker with a fixed smirk to show he wasn't hurt after all. But Tucker knew, for his mouth made a determined "O," and the crowd knew, for they remained standing. He poked, snorting, at Tucker's nose with his right, fighting out of a fog, moving as in a nightmare. Sensed Tucker getting set and poked him off balance again and came in with the left under the heart. The pain from the nape went along his elbow with the blow; yet he felt Tucker fall away. And the bell.

He stood in the middle of the ring, smirking fixedly, till Casey and the Finger pulled him back to his corner, onto the stool, and shoved ammonia up his nose. He pushed it away as it cleared his head. "I got my own technique," he told them both, "I know where the money is."

Blinking and groggy, he saw a streetcar's cable flinging green lightning over the top row of the bleachers, showing momentarily a line of small green faces under felt hats, a few leveling field glasses. "I'm a white hope," he informed Casey solemnly, and from somewhere out where the green flare had passed, a gleeful tenor answered him.

"Another year 'n you'll be in the nuthouse, Biceps!"

"It's awright, Left'," he heard Casey saying. "You done like I told you fer a while anyways. Then you fergot. But you drew blood on the bugger. Stall him now till you get yer stren'th back."

Bruno looked across the ring and saw a handler painting Tucker's left cheek, and he couldn't remember doing that. Good. He felt Casey dipping the broken hand into ice water, and saying nothing. Good old Case.

"We get blood out of him, Case?" he asked.

"Sure did. Under the eye. Poke it open first chance you get. He'll be blind by the sixth."

"What's comin' up?"

"The fourt'. Lotsa time."

"What's in?"

"Nine 'n a half 'g's. You're on gravy, boy."

"You got somethin' on me too, Case?"

"My end of the purse 'n Finger's. Punchy 'n Knothole threw in with us too, ten apiece."

"We get blood out of him, Case?"

"Under the eye."

At the siren Bruno felt Finger slipping the mouthpiece between his teeth. Casey was going now. Finger was going too. Dumb Kunka and Poor Bogats were long gone, they were all long gone and going.

All but Westside Spector marking a score card hurriedly and worriedly with one foot on the lower rope, using his white-slacked knee to write on, breathing hard in a red shirt. All Spector had to do, Bruno reflected dimly, was to point at the Judges to take a round away from Bruno Lefty. A rage at Spector began filling him. He better not. And the bell.

Bruno felt the spark coming back with his anger. He flicked his left to the face, then crossed the right. Tucker went away with the cross and Bruno tapped out at the little pink horseshoe-shaped scar at the tip of Tucker's bridgeless nose. The scar reddened pleasantly. He missed with the right at long range, stepped in and burned the boy skillfully against the top rope and heeled him hard as they broke. He chopped up at the gut coming in and, straightening, splayed Tucker's ear with his left; for a moment it glowed like his nose. Tucker stung him with the back of his glove.

"Pound his head soft, Lefty!"

"Stick yer thumb in his eye!"

"You want Spector t' hold him up for ya, Tucker?"

"Go ahead, Tucker—he can't hurt us."

"Down in front!"

Bruno got set for the dig, watching Tucker deliberately lowering his gloves in the hope of bringing him in. He started his left and delayed it, to bring the boy's hands up where they belonged: they came up fast enough, so he knew Tucker's corner hadn't caught on that the hand was broken, and shifted his right into the side. Caught Tucker's left on his shoulder and planted the right again, came up with his left shoulder and knew by the plashy sound he'd caught the boy's bad eye again. With his head in the boy's gut, he felt the trickle of it coming over his shoulder and Tucker's nose rubbing into the hollow of the shoulder: the boy was giving him some of the blood and tying him up at the same time. He got his left free and threw it into the gut to test it. It hurt. And heard Casey pleading frantically below him.

"The right! The right! The right! The right!"

Couldn't the jerk see the way the right was bound up? When he stepped back he felt Tucker sag, for one moment, then come in to stop that left into his liver. Something began going around in the back of Bruno's brain: "You got blood out of him, Bunny. It's awright, you got blood out of him." He backpedaled, trying to remember better: why had she called "Next! Next!" like that? He mulled his man mechanically, listening to hear her call again. Tucker's bloody face bobbed before him like that of a dream fighter

whom you couldn't beat and yet couldn't quit fighting. He stalled
him, without heart. "You got blood out of him, Honey!" And the
bell. It would have been best if he'd killed the old man. A hand
like a house brick smashed into his temple, he spun half around and
saw Casey above him.

"What happened?"

"You dropped yer hands too soon." He felt Casey loosening the
left lace. "Lash him when it works out," Casey told him.

"Cut the eye for me, Case," Bruno asked. "It's swellin' tight as a
drum."

He closed his eyes when he felt the knife: then the loose wetness
of the blood down his cheek and the cool touch of collodion as it
began to freeze over. He sat then, his eyes watering and his mouth
dripping from the sponge, with the towel about his neck, looking
like an oversize baby on a stool about to blubber for oatmeal. The
announcer climbed over the ropes and spoke into the amplifier.

"Is Dr. Morris Pechter in the house? Dr. Pechter, please call
your office. Is Dr. Pechter here?"

"Is that fer him 'r me, Case?" Bruno wondered.

"Not fer neither. You ain't hurt. Fer some croaker in the house
is all."

Bruno looked out wonderingly, hopefully, into the dark and
listening rows for Morris Pechter. Wouldn't he ever come? But no
one replied or rose.

Only a chorus of boos and jeers as the announcer persisted in
trying to find his man.

"Quack! Quack!"

"Get off the air!"

"Bring on them bloody gladiators!"

"*Is* Dr. Pechter in the house?" the announcer pleaded.

Finally, from the bleachers:

"Aw hell, lemme stay fer the wrasslin'."

The announcer retired, at the warning siren, a beaten man.

And at the siren Bruno could feel, by the way he was working,
that Casey had caught the crowd's excitement: he was working to
beat the bell, holding the belt away from the waist with one hand,

dipping the mouthpiece with the other; it came out of the bucket looking like a tongue. Bruno knew Casey should be out of the ring now, but he stuck the bottle between Bruno's teeth and Bruno filled his throat and he jerked it away. He closed his eyes and spat, a tiny reddish stream, in a curve from his closed lips onto his chest. Then he raised his head and spilled the rest into the bucket in a bloody string. Water dripped off his head onto the ropes, off the ropes onto the floor, and off the canvas onto the apron. Were they giving him extra time because he'd been hit after the bell? Casey breathed into his ear with the smell of sen-sen on his breath. That meant he had been drinking. "I c'd use a hooker myself," he told Casey. But Casey was gone.

At the bell he missed a left lead and fell away. Tucker followed. Bruno open-gloved him around the ring and came up fast, in close, with his shoulder. It missed the eye, but the cheek split like a melon. He felt the lace come loose and lashed the boy across the eye. Spector came in and tucked in the open lace while Bruno stood looking tough and Tucker wiped his face on his gloves. Spector glanced at Tucker and gestured to a white-haired man who could have been the announcer's father. He came through the ropes creakily, while the mob screamed and bellowed at him, with no jesting in its tone.

"Let 'em fight!"

"Wipe his face 'n get out!"

"He can dish it out! Let him take it!"

Bruno thought pleasantly, "They'll murder the sheeny croaker if he stops it now." It was good to feel the house behind him, the whole white man's house. It was good to know, in that single outraged roar, that it was all for him and nothing for Tucker: that there was nothing he could do now that could mean more than losing a round or a point or two. He was in. Old Casey had been right again. The boogie had fought Biceps' fight and now he'd have to finish it that way. There wouldn't be a ref this side of Madison Square who wouldn't let Bruno Lefty win it his own way now. He saw the old man lift the lid of Tucker's eye perfunctorily and wait while Tucker's handlers stopped the bleeding. The sight angered him a moment; then he turned to the ringside seats and grinned. And heard a deepening undertone in the mob's cry: the added note of approval. He was their man. The undertone of encouragement, he felt without even hearing it clearly, without thinking, only sensing it, was for him; as the shrill derision in it was for Tucker and the doctor.

"Slip a gimmick in his glove now, Doc!"

"Pat him on the cheek why don't you?"

"Wipe yer own nose, croaker!"

"Pull his eye out, Biceps!"

"Knock his head! You wiv too!"

They touched gloves as the ring was cleared and Bruno stalked him. Tucker did a little jig, to keep his legs from going dead and came in with a folding motion. Bruno met him coming in and they fought on a dime in the middle of the ring. The rest had done the jig good, Bruno felt, and clamped Tucker's head under his left arm to stop him; he held him, then hooked the right hard into the liver. Spector straightened them up and Bruno felt Tucker sagging. His v-shaped brows clouded with pain; in close again he ducked into his elbows and brought his forehead up sharply: Bruno felt the eye open and then spill over.

"Looka that claret! I'll take mine in a small glass!"

"Will I be sore tomorrow!"

"Awright Cue-Ball—bust it up!"

"Hit him from behind now!"

He saw Tucker's head in a red mist, bobbing like a great red sponge ball, reached for where the arms should be and felt a flat-iron smash in under his heart. Felt his heart turn over and sink, felt himself sinking with it. He swung his head slowly till the red mist cleared: through it he recognized the floor. Wasn't there ever a bell any more?

He was on all fours, one hand outside the ropes, and Tucker was in his corner with both hands across the top rope, and the single loose strand was in reach of Tucker's glove but he wasn't going to reach for it until Bruno Bicek got up. Nobody would reach for it till Bruno Bicek got up. He looked around hopelessly, searching for that Bruno B. with one eye. But Bruno B. was in jail, it had to hang there till he got out. He got onto one knee without hearing a count. Then slipped back to all fours.

But there was something he had to hear: a bell, or someone calling "Next!" He listened hard, to hear her again, and saw the shadow of Spector's hand across the canvas, and Spector's voice calling from behind a partition down an endless hall.

"Nine."

The shadow mustn't come again. He used both knees this time, got both feet under him, and fell sidewise against the top strand. Now it was all right. He'd done it. He felt himself going again and gripped the rope in his right hand. Saw the great red sponge ball bouncing at him and threw the left, timing the ball to catch it on the bounce, without letting go of the rope. The ball stopped dead in mid-air, Spector banged his right hand free, and he fell forward onto Tucker, holding like a vise. Tucker's left slipped wetly around his body and a flood of perspiration, down his chest and stomach, felt like a flood of blood.

He returned to Benkowski holding his head back, to show everyone how fresh he felt. But his legs went out from under him and he collapsed on the stool. When he came around again it was to the pricking of a cotton-wrapped toothpick, soaked in iodoform, that Casey had up his nose: Bruno closed his eyes while Finger swabbed the tongue. When he opened them to spit the lights were up full and ushers were hurrying toward a far corner of the stands. A fight had broken out and the house was standing up and stretching to see the milling pair.

"Put 'em in the ring, they're ruinin' business," someone called.

Then the lights were down forever, the ushers were hurrying back to catch those trying to move nearer the ring, and the ten-second siren sounded under Tucker's stool. Bruno felt his strength returning in a hot wave and realized dimly that Finger had been swabbing his tongue with something stronger than water. It felt good, and hot. It made him laugh a little inside. He noticed, for

the first time, that the white lettering on the back of Spector's
red sweat shirt said simply:

CHICAGO

He pounded his gloves together and looked down: Casey had
cut the inner edge of the right one. Good.

He saw the doctor's black suit before him. The croaker was trying to look good tonight. But he'd given them time, Bruno realized, to get patched up. He felt the old man's timid touch and
rolled his eye up to the white to help him. Let the old boy try
to stop it. It'd be the last fight he'd ever stop.

"If it opens again I *got* to stop it," the old man said sadly.

Bruno saw Casey grinning his toothless grin into the old man's
face; Casey's jaw was out a foot and his fists were clenched against
his hips.

"You ain't stoppin' nothin' from this corner, Dago. You didn't
have the guts to stop it over there, did you? Who give you yer
job, a white man 'r a jig?" The old man turned humbly, Bruno
watched his trim tan-and-white oxfords mincing away. I must
be ahead on points, he calculated, for Casey to run him like that.
As though answering his thought Finger said from somewhere:
"The money's on you, Left', the gamblers won't let the doc stop it
now. Just stay in there 'n you got the duke. You're the ol' white hope
t'night."

He stood up to let Finger take the stool away.

"Don't let him butt you no more, Left'," was Finger's parting
word. "Anythin' goes, Left'."

The crowd greeted both men at the bell in the hope of seeing
the fight finished within the round.

"We want blood!"

"Quit savin' fun'ral expenses, Lefty—lay down."

"Hold him up another round, Tucker!"

"Hey! Chicago Av'noo! Give yerself up!"

"C'mon Daddy!"

"Hey Biceps, next time yer down there pull up yer sock!"

"We want blood."

The ring posts wavered, like four small tethered flames; and along the upper rope lay a cord of rainbow-colored light. And Casey was gone and they were all gone. All the boys from the barber's and all the boys from Ryan's Bar. They were all going home in Finger's Chevie and leaving Bruno B. to take a Chicago Avenue car and get home alone as best he could. He felt certain, somehow, that Steffi and Casey were leaving together, along with everyone else he used to know. That there was only Honeyboy Tucker and himself left, and the newspaper men who always wrote why was it that everyone feared Tucker so?

"Quit the jitterbuggin' 'n give us a fight!"

"Use that patent Polack Paralyzer!"

"Get a toe hold, Tucker. Throw the switch!"

The white band of Tucker's glove began working in and out like a wrist-watch band.

"In the kitchen, Tucker!"

"In the basket!"

"The Sunday punch!"

Tucker came forward crouching behind his left shoulder. He shuffled, bobbing and weaving forward. Behind him the loose thread on the middle strand seemed to be hanging an inch lower.

"Get him where he lives!"

"Oh that face! Don't look by the photographer!"

"They get you by Dollar-Day at Goldblatt's, Biceps?"

Tucker came in low and fast, to miss with a left lead. Bruno nailed him with a right cross that rocked his head back, then followed with the left to the heart. It was no good. Tucker didn't even grunt; and the shock of the impact sent a line of fire back into his shoulder. That was the last, he knew finally. He wouldn't use it again. Spector came pulling importantly at Bruno's left glove; found the open edge and crossed the ring for the shears. While he cut the glove off the garden filled with catcalls.

"Oh you gladiators!"

"Oh you Polish ham!"

"Slip a gimmick in it for him!"

"Get Harry Thomas!"

"Where's Jimmy Adamic?"

"Throw 'em *both* out!"

"What stopped your glove, Lefty?"

Spector wrapped the new glove on: Bruno watched his face when he saw the taped knuckles, swollen till the tape was bursting off. Not a flicker. A dead pan. No wonder they called him Westside. Casey watched the binding beside Spector, and Tucker's handler watched from the other. The new glove was almost red, while the old one was olive-colored, Bruno noticed. Then he shut his eyes and listened to the jeering.

They thought he was going to get it. They were all so sure he was going to get it. That he was going to get it now. The barber and Fireball and Catfoot and that pansy heel Pultoric. Well, he'd taken a lot around this town, and he'd dished it out once in a while too. He could still dish it. "I can take care of myself," he thought stubbornly. They had come all the way from the Triangle, he felt, all the boo-boo birds way back in the bleachers, telling each other on the way out that they wouldn't mind betting fifty cents that that dumb Potomac Street hood would get it tonight. He had it coming, and they'd be laughing to themselves a little all the way home, recalling a right that had staggered him or a left that had made him buckle. He was that kind of a fighter, he knew, and that kind of a man: the crowd had come out to see Biceps kayoed, they were all here because he was going to get it. Casey thought so, Finger thought so, Steffi thought so, they all thought so. And Tucker thought so too, leaning against the ropes still looking fresh, now shoving his gloves up against his ears to shove up an imaginary head-protector, now turning his back to talk to his handler. Bruno saw a yellow back, speckled with great freckles, like a backful of brown butterflies. Well, he wasn't going to get it. The jig was going to get it.

"*Grzmoty zabili diabla,*" he thought slowly, "*diabla zabilia rzyda.*" He had it now. Now, in this moment, he knew what the barber meant.

He stalled Tucker with his left and was short with the right; then clamped Tucker's gloves to his ribs just in time. He clubbed at the base of the neck with the ball of his wrist. Then the elbow into the gut. Tucker swerved at the break, shaken, and Bruno was on him. He threw the right onto Tucker's left glove and let it bounce into the groin. Tucker grabbed him about the hips and went down slowly, his hair tickling Bruno's belly as he slipped and scraped toward the canvas. Then he sat, fully conscious, his trunk bent forward to ease the pain. At eight he got onto one knee. He rose in a fog of cigarette smoke pyramided from the four ring posts into the lights. There were four green candles burning steadily in each corner for Bruno, where the ring posts used to be, each looking like a vigil light at St. Bonifacius.

"How'd you like it, Tucker?" The boo-boo birds were asking. "We want blood!"

Tucker came in snorting blindly into his glove, in a crouch to ease his pain. And got his own right in, fast, four inches below the waistband and two inches into the groin. Got it in close up, from the floor, with three full feet of swing behind it. And straightened up dancing like a college fighter.

Bruno backed, sagged, crossed his arms feebly over his groin, and coughed. Here and there the crowd coughed with him. The whole house had seen it. And sat paralyzed as though struck, each man of them, himself. Then the booing began, a long sick boo, half fear and half glee. Spector shook a warning finger in Tucker's face and wiped off the Negro's gloves.

"You're as dirty as yer color!"
"Now it's *your* turn, Lefty!"
"Give him the same, Lefty!"
"Do it, Bruno! Now! Do it!"

Spector shook a warning finger in Tucker's face and wiped his gloves. The gamblers were earning their money this night, Spector reflected cynically. And stepped back, motioning the men toward each other.

Bruno tried with his right, to show he wasn't hurt, and felt Tucker's left sting his cheek. The bleachers muttered and sat down, more pleased with every foul and hoping for just one more.

Bruno tried with his right, to show he wasn't much hurt, and felt Tucker's left sting his cheek. He grabbed Tucker mechanically and pressed close, till the damp mattress of the boy's chest tickled his own and he caught the sour smell of Tucker. There, snuggled deep against Tucker's breast, nuzzling blearily into its warmth, he held like a chain, making Tucker grunt to get him off; then he felt the breast going away and clamped harder onto the arms. And the roar of the crowd was in his ears relentlessly. The arms were slippery with perspiration, they were getting harder to hold onto all the time—if it just weren't for somebody always dragging him off, he knew he'd have his strength back soon. He knew he could last it, even though he had to hold those arms by their very hairs. He felt Tucker folding his gloves firmly against his shoulders to shove him off and leaned his weight farther forward and more heavily—Tucker released him fast and Bruno slipped heavily, covering automatically as he did so. Tucker threw his right into the body, then the right again, taking his time but getting his shoulders behind each swing; with each swing sweat splattered off his gloves in a spray. He stepped back, as over-cautious as he had been overanxious before. Then he came in.

Through a fog of pain Bruno saw his red waistband weaving in, rising and falling before his eyes, and the roar of the crowd was in his ears relentlessly. He felt himself falling forward toward Tucker, felt his right glove scraping the floor, and lifted himself off the floor behind it in an arc, his spine arched with the effort. It hit something that felt as though he'd driven his hand through a wooden wall. A falling away, a crumbling. He caught himself, off balance, half the ring away from Tucker and against the ropes. That was all. He knew it was all. Tucker could come and get him now. He had nothing left to throw and nothing left to try. He had thrown everything and tried everything and he was done. He closed his eyes and felt himself going, so opened them again and tried to find Tucker with them.

He was there, rocking and drunken, for Bruno to get. Bruno saw him drop his hands and walk unsteadily along the ropes, tapping them absent-mindedly and smiling unsteadily down at the judges and newspapermen, who smiled back. Bruno stared.

So that was what they were yelling about. He lunged halfway across the ring with his right hand cocked to club him out: Tucker's back was toward him. He came up behind the boy and swung his right under the right armpit flush against the jaw with the sound of a baseball bat splitting against a fast-pitched curve. Tucker went face-forward till his chin caught on the second rope. He hung there as though he'd been decapitated, till the lights came up like morning. And then kept on hanging stubbornly, smiling vacantly, till his handlers hauled him off: Bruno saw them hauling him, trying to pull his feet after him, feeling faintly proud that he could still hit that hard, guarding his heart against the hope that the boy would be all right. He felt Spector taking his wrist and pulled away, spinning Spector around; Spector kept his hold, his toes almost off the floor.

"The winnah in two minutes forty-eight secon's of the eight' roun'l"

The bleachers howled like a winter wind through an empty shack. Bruno, suddenly relaxed, squatted and threw his legs out in a sort of crazed Russian dance.

"No, Lefty, no," He heard Casey tell him, and let himself be led to his corner.

The crowd saw his wrecked mouth and his drunken grin and booed happily. The Polack had made it a white man's evening after all.

"Wipe up the blood, Lefty—you spilled it!"

"Re-match! Re-match!"

The way back to the dressing room was lined with the little greenish faces under straw hats. He put his head back as he walked, trying to look like a winner but somehow not yet feeling like one. Once a white-coated vendor brushed past him shrieking, "French-fried p'tato chips fresh 'n butter like roast chicken!"

Down in the dressing room a featherweight from Gary and an aging featherweight from Juarez lay on training tables on either side of the single row of lockers. The veteran from Juarez had never seen the boy from Gary. Yet each knew the other's personality, his record, his strengths and weaknesses, his mannerisms in the ring and the way he liked most to win; now only a single row of tin lockers and a ten-second warning were left to keep them apart. Bruno stretched out on his own rubbing table, letting the Finger take the tape off his hands.

"You were great out there t'night, Left'—two more like that 'n they'll give you the big fella." He had brought a bucket of ice water and talked as he sat, dipping the broken hand in it. He touched the hand tenderly. "The bones is jerked out of place," he concluded professionally, "It'll heal in a week. Need a shot, Left'?" He pulled a half-pint off his hip with three inches left in the bottom. Bruno drained it, lying down, without taking his lips off the bottle. Finger put the empty beneath the table and wiped Bruno's mouth with his towel. Bruno felt his strength returning.

"Say it the real way, Finger," he asked. He had not asked that since he'd gotten out of the workhouse. Finger grinned, and announced the fancied headlines softly, while working alcohol into Bruno's torso and breast.

POLISH WHITE HOPE KAYOES LOUIS! CHAMP DECLINES RE-MATCH!
Bruno listened with eyes half-closed. The bell for the first round of the featherweight windup came faintly to him.

MODERN KETCHEL TO RETIRE UNDEFEATED!
"I'll show that jig what buttin' is, Finger, if he tries buttin' me like that one did t'night. I'll butt with anybody. No man in the world c'n take a Biceps butt 'n live. I'll hit him so hard he'll have a bellyache fer a year you. I'll fool 'em, Finger. He'll think I swing at his head. But I'll do what Case tol' me, I'll bust his belly, then I'll be the heavyweight champ of Illinois, I mean from Illinois, I said it, didn't I? I never knew I c'd punch like I can, Finger. If he'd 've got up I would've killed him fer life, fer Christ I would. I know where the money is now." The tape off his left hand was dragging on the floor and he gathered it up; then cupped his hands before his eyes— "I'm sweatin' on my hands, Finger— what does that mean? Better tell Case right away— Where's Case?"

"Wait'n upstairs with the widow's kid. It's too hot fer him down here, he says."

A little man with a straw hat in his hand ducked his head in the door and waved the hat at Bruno. Bruno saw that a program still stuck in the hatband.

"Still with ya, Lefty! You're a pug, Lefty! Wanta go home in a car, Lefty?"

Finger moved him back out of the door. "We got a car," he told him, "a Chevie." Before the door closed on the fellow Bruno heard two vendors bawling their wares past the door at the same moment: "Get yer double-jointed peanuts here! Poipah! Al Capone goes mad!"

Circles of steam swam about the pipes above him. He flopped over on his stomach and pillowed his face in his arms. He closed his eyes and felt himself drifting passionlessly toward unconsciousness. Then slept for long minutes, deeply and untroubled. When he wakened it was with the full realization that, at last, he had won. His good nature began returning with his strength.

"That nigger got good heart, Finger," he said, "Ain't nobody can take that off him." He sat up to let Finger tape his eye and heard a low humming near at hand.

> I'm a ding-dong daddy from Duma
> 'n you oughta see me do my stuff

Catfoot stood smiling in the doorway as though he'd been watching Bruno sleeping for minutes.

"You don't have t' hang around the door, Cat," Bruno assured him. "C'mon in. Have one on me. Where's the bottle, Finger?"

"There ain't a drop left, Lefty," Finger reminded him, "We drank her up." Bruno shifted to let him work on the shoulder, and Finger began working too fast on it. Bruno lifted his left hand out of the bucket in order to point out to Catfoot a lump, the size of a darning egg, over his left eye.

"Ain't it a beaut, Cat? It's where he butted me."

Catfoot smiled faintly. It was a beaut all right. The door behind him opened noiselessly.

Tenczara.

In plain clothes.

Something flopped coldly in the pit of Bruno's stomach, then lay too still there: he felt it drawing all his blood down as it lay, making a sick and silent whining through his veins. He touched Finger with the back of his hand to make him stop rubbing the shoulder.

Tenczara came forward, his face half-shadowed by his hat. When he reached Bruno's side he leaned on the rubbing table and brushed the hat onto the back of his head; and spoke looking straight ahead, his voice so low that none but Bruno could hear.

"Got you for the Greek, Lefthander. Two witnesses. One boy seen the body 'n the other seen you do it. You remember Bible-back, Lefthander?" Bruno heard the crowd on the other side of the door surge forward in an approving roar: the old Mex must be taking a deadly beating out there. The Mex's feet didn't follow his punches any more, they said. He was on his face out there, the roaring told him.

"Gonna come along, Lefthander?"

"'n if I don't?" he asked Tenczara as quietly as he had been asked.

Tenczara lifted the first link of the manacles from his pocket and let them slip back in. "Come along quiet," he pleaded, "I won't walk you around like the other time."

"'cause you don't have to," Bruno told him.

Tenczara flushed. "That's right, Lefthander. I don't have to this time."

"I got friends waitin'," Bruno said absently, hoping for the bell to save the old Mex.

"Well, you don't want t' say good-by to them with links on, do you?"

For reply Bruno dressed deliberately and slowly. Tying his orange tie in the tin mirror on the wall, he saw Catfoot leaving, and felt relieved for a moment. Behind him Finger came up, looking pale and choked, with Bruno's steel-tipped street shoes in his hand. "Gonna change, Lefty?" Bruno shook his head, aware that he still wore his tennis shoes.

"Keep 'em for me, Finger. The tennis ones is more comfortable."

When he had adjusted the tie carefully he turned steadily to Tenczara.

"That's how I want it all right," he decided. And extended his hands with the wrists touching.

Tenczara hesitated.

"Go ahead. Put 'em on," Bruno challenged him, "that's how we both want it. That's how you'n me always been wantin' it. We'll go right down the middle aisle."

When he felt the Finger's arm across his shoulder he spoke softly, looking down at the air holes punched between the toes of the outworn tennis shoes.

"Knew I'd never get t' be twenty-one anyhow," he said.

And the bell.

ALGREN'S INNOCENCE

IN A way, in all his work, Nelson Algren was writing about innocence. Regard the girl, Steffi, and Lefty Bruno Bicek in *Never Come Morning*. Yet all his life Algren dealt with people who hardly were innocent. Regard Otto Preminger. It was Algren's dealings with Hollywood that first got me to talk to him. We talked for more than a year, about everything, and late in 1964 published *Conversations with Nelson Algren*. Many of our talks revolved around—when they were not warily circling—Algren's allegedly naïve exposure to Otto Preminger's powerhouse Hollywood of 1955. But Algren was not naïve, and I was trying to find out what had happened. How could he have sold *The Man with the Golden Arm* for a pittance; and then, when Preminger got control of the book, and asked Algren out to talk about a script, how could he have been bushwhacked by agents, lawyers, and pipe-smoking Yes-men? Three days after their first meeting, Algren handed Preminger a twelve-page treatment for a film version of *The Man with the Golden Arm* wherein the dramatic climax would have Frankie Machine—ultimately Frank Sinatra—intone, "White Goddess say not go that part of forest." They did not meet again. But their lawyers did. Algren had wanted John Garfield to make the film. Garfield had agreed; but then he had died. Algren most wholeheartedly did not want Preminger to have anything to do with the film. His agent at the time had not protected Algren on this. Algren said he was innocent about such things then. He spent half the money Garfield's people had paid him earlier—$15,000 for the book, $4000 for a complete script—on lawyers. Algren lost. Then, soon after, he sold another novel, *A Walk on the Wild Side*, to Hollywood for $25,000; and on the advice of friends never went to see the eminently forgettable Jane Fonda film. So he had lost again.

It was some loss. For writers of Nelson Algren's generation (he was born early in 1909) there were two inventions of the Western culture that had smote them into strict attention just as they reached maturity: the worldwide Great Depression and talkies. Earlier writers had scorned the silent "moving pictures," aiming instead, like Thomas Wolfe, at the serious stage. But from Al Jolson's "Mammy!" was born the serious writer's wish to reach and stroke or jar millions of moviegoers; and Nelson Algren had that fervent desire. He tried twice, innocently he said, and twice failed, not to try again. Dreiser, Faulkner, and Aldous Huxley had gone to Hollywood to take the cash, letting the credit go. They had succeeded. Another of Algren's heroes, Hemingway, had made millions on his own books and short stories. He did not try to work on his own fiction for films. In the '50s the literary world spread that very word: Do not try to work on your own stuff. Algren knew all of this before he went to Hollywood to ride around in Preminger's "red Caddy." Then Algren saw the film— which to him was among other things "my war with the United States as represented by Kim Novak." So of course I asked him all about it.

Did I get answers to my questions about his innocence? Perhaps. Other questions kept arising, sometimes hanging us high, like Spanish moss; at other times, as one can see below, they popped out brightly like morning glories, the strangler. Word was, for instance, that Algren, your friendly anarchist, the man the Communists lost because, among other things, they tried to tell him when to drink and whom to bed, word was that Nelson was a political naïf. Perhaps. But that political naïf caused this Kennedy-liberal (compared to him: a conservative square) to wonder about that when, while waiting in Chicago's North Side Riccardo's for two attractive women, he leaned over in the middle of one of our political arguments and—looking me straight in the all four of my eyes—sweetly said, "I'm not saying the Rosenbergs weren't spies. All I'm saying is that we shouldn't have burned them." He said *we* and that is what he meant.

But he did not always say what he meant about innocence because he did not always know what he meant by innocence. I was surprised that he cared, at all, about the booby-trap notions behind that complicated word, carrying as it does whiffs of theology, of primeval purities, of highly improbable hope; a lush pampered conceit for the fortunate, destined to swiftly shrivel in the desiccated world Algren knew and so piercingly described. The idea itself arose Phoenix-like from talk about the reasons for his core sense of personal, professional, cultural loss. Of the two of us, 'twas I who was the more naïve because, although like him I came from factory people, it was small industrial Trenton, N.J., the outskirts of town with mongrel border collie and the old swimming hole that cuffed me about, while he was raised in the grinding viscera of World War I and Roaring '20s Chicago. But innocence for me went the way of all prides, as Divinely ordered, at First Communion, after which one could officially sin, no longer needing to worry about the long wait in Limbo on one's faithful way to unhurried heaven. (Limbo is gone now from Mother Church's estate, along with St. Christopher and fish-on-Friday, among other things.) Innocence was like one's first set of teeth: You got it, you lost it, then you went on with a better rack. So I was surprised to learn that innocence was important to him in his work. It was no religion for him. He was tougher on suckers than Barnum and W. C. Fields combined. I only hope he knew (I can see and hear him sardonically relishing the fact) that the Pope who infallibly legitimized torture for The Inquisition was called Innocent.

Why was innocence important to him, along with the innocent word, loyalty? Loyalty made him move. He had held onto an early agent when other writers (and even editors, who do not mind incompetent agents) warned him she had grown inept and parasitic. And as he was working James Baldwin over in *Conversations*, I wondered why, not asking, letting him go, knowing he was neither racist nor homophobic. After publication a literary historian scoffed at my ignorance: Baldwin had accused Algren's friend, Richard Wright, of being an Uncle Tom. The liberal literary world often can be a very un-nice illiberal place, when it is not paying off positive dues via mutual message games, such as book dedications.

Algren's first book dedication was an act of familial love. *Never Come Morning* was "For Bernice," his hard-working sister, the first person to help push him out of the car repair shop (where his father kept telling him police would never, ever break the law). Bernice helped get him to college (where he no longer would be embarrassed by his mother's inability to pronounce words). Bernice helped him to read, to write, to travel. On his travels he mingled with Jean-Paul Sartre *et aux*. Like gangster Joe Gallo in the New York City theatrical world, he loved it—until he was no longer needed. The London edition of *Never Come Morning* is dedicated to Jean-Paul Sartre who translated it into French. (I could not convert Nelson to the side of the less totalitarian-minded existentialist Camus, primarily because at the time—he said—Camus was greatly admired on American college campuses.) Sartre's unofficial *ux*, Simone de Beauvoir, being something more than a dutiful daughter to both men, dedicated *The Mandarins*, her best-selling *roman à clef* to Nelson Algren. In her novel, Catholic-educated Beauvoir was gushingly explicit (for 1954) in her descriptions of their love affair. For instance:

> From head to toe, his hands were learning my body by heart. Again I said, "I like your hands."
>
> "Do you like them?"
>
> "All evening I've been wondering if I'd feel them on my body."
>
> "You'll feel them all night long," he said.
>
> Suddenly, he was no longer either awkward or modest. His desire transformed me. I who for so long a time had been without taste, without form, again possessed breasts, a belly, a sex, flesh; I was as nourishing as bread, as fragrant as earth. It was miraculous that I didn't think of measuring my time or my pleasure; I know only that before we fell asleep I could hear the gentle chirpings of dawn.

Algren was hurt. His fiction writing was fiction. A writer should not, he said, "dig up his own garden." This believer in innocence must have been confused by the "pact" between Beauvoir and Sartre ("Procurers," he would write, "are more honest than philosophers"), and by the fact that Sartre had asked her to remain in the United States with Algren so that he could continue his affair with "M" in France, an affair that drove Beauvoir to drugs. Yet Algren dedicated *Who Lost an American?* to her in 1963, as well as permitting her to use some of his letters in another book. In 1964 she came out with even more gushings about the two of them and their intercontinental time together. Part of his response was technical. Algren, the writer, cannot be surpassed as a reporter. "The guy [his character in her book] was a preposterous proletarian in a clean shirt," he told a news magazine. Then, as many innocents do, he released his sorrow with a laugh: "She ain't Heloise," he said, "and I ain't Abelard," adding, as he no doubt covered his loins, "I hope." Still trying to shrug, he closed it out by saying, "I have the old-fashioned puritanical idea that some things are private."

In our literary world? He was not that naïve. Or was he innocent? Did he have some kind of vested emotional interest in maintaining innocence? How was it connected to his work?

The 1963 edition of *Never Come Morning* is "For Candida Donadio." Algren and I dedicated *Conversations* to the same woman, our mutual agent. Her name means "Bright Gift of God," and at the time she also represented such writers as Joseph Heller, Phillip Roth, Nancy Mitford, William Gaddis, and Thomas Pynchon. She reorganized Algren's career—he had accepted advances from different publishers for works not delivered—saving it. Once in 1962, while doing *Conversations*, a *Paris Review* party had moved to an East Side bar (Managing Editor John Train had thrown us out), where a well-intentioned socio-literary critic, a raving Algren fan, was commiserating with him about the publishing business, which never paid good writers such as Algren anywhere near what well-connected hacks got. Then the critic-fan got on agents, all of them, including, by name, Donadio. Algren began to grin.

Now, I knew Algren did not grin. He could scowl or (rarely) laugh out loud. He might produce a friendly mischievous frown, or—if particularly gratified by something breathlessly inane or insane—a fine grotesque Kabuki mask. But few grins. So, with some physical effort and much whispered cajolery, I got him out of there. The cajolery was quiet because he had begun to scream dreadful threats at the surprised critic, who did not know why Algren was acting that way. Defending his friend who happened to be his agent, Algren was so angry he forgot to bat me out of his path, which he could have done, being a large man, tough in his fifties at the time, which he had to be, going where he went, seeing what he saw.

In his later years he lived modestly, as usual, near the wealthy literary Long Island Hamptons. Friends gathered round. His culture that he so fervently criticized gave him honors, but hardly any money. His last book, *The Devil's Stocking*, about the black boxer Hurricane Carter and his murder trials, had been, as they say, partially funded by an agency of the United States Government—the National Endowment for the Arts, an occurrence designed to give Nelson Algren nothing but the deepest sense of ironic hilarity. At seventy-two this atheistic Jew was buried in a properly kept Long Island cemetery—Protestant. He was innocent of that, but he would have loved it. In *Conversations* he reports about going to a relative's funeral. She had been a member of the American Legion Auxiliary, was also Jewish, and received a very thorough Christian planting. He loved it.

Everyone likes to remember Algren laughing. Many know him as the polemicist and keep that Algren for their very own. Many know him for the underpaid master worker in a world of rich mediocrities; they brag about him, swinging him from their social totem poles. (Behind his back, in true sophistication, some snicker at this representative of a world they, having helped make, at their peril must still go on trying to avoid. One such lovely, rich and pampered lady sweetly opined that Algren, though amusing, still had "the stench of the boardinghouse about him.")

But those who read his books may come closer to the truth of what he was, what he tried to save, to preserve. Why should one write such a book as *Never Come Morning*? Naïve Steffi and Bruno. We go with them to their fates, via a road called naturalism, or realism, through a world of innocence and loyalty where, for them, there never was any. Half a century later, Steffi and Bruno are still happening.

As we read Algren on innocence in the excerpts that follow, taken from a context of talk about his other values—sentiment, for instance, and commitment—we should remember the writers he admired and why he admired them. They were realists, to be sure, and sometimes as severe as he. They range from Flaubert, to Hemingway, and especially to William Styron. They were and are what Algren, from his unpampered high school days wanted to be. They exemplify what he became, as he preserved a certain kind of innocence in order to become it—a writer telling the truth, in a finely tuned, unself-conscious, beautiful writing style.

H. E. F. DONOHUE

New York
May 1987

INTERVIEW*

QUESTION: O.K. Now I'm going to ask you specific questions about the writer, about innocence, about failure, and about money. O.K.?

ALGREN: Yeah, yeah.

Q: I've got the feeling that when you went out to Hollywood the first time, you were just looking around and that you learned some things. When you went out the second time, though, I have the feeling you thought you were going to fail; almost as if you expected to fail. . . . Am I wrong in thinking that?

ALGREN: Oh, I didn't have any belief any longer that Hollywood would seriously make a movie that was true to a book that it took. I went out to see if I could get some of the money that I knew they were going to make, that was all. Preminger had some money coming.

Q: So you actually did not fail when you went out to Hollywood because you did not expect to succeed, right? Or is that too—

ALGREN: I didn't expect any real belief in the book, but somebody had gotten hold of a property that had much more value than I thought and I wanted to save some of it if I could.

Q: But if it had just been left to you and your agent, nothing would have been done in Hollywood to get *any* part of your book into a movie, right?

ALGREN: Yeah, that's right.

Q: But a man whom you dislike and distrust, a series of men you dislike and distrust, got something of your book onto the screen.

ALGREN: Yeah.

Q: So weren't you wrong abut the capacity of Hollywood to produce anything good?

*Donohue, H. E. F., from *Conversations with Nelson Algren* (New York: Hill & Wang, 1964). These excerpts were edited by Mr. Donohue for this edition.

ALGREN: Oh, I know Hollywood can. There are producers in Hollywood who have produced good movies.

Q: Those are the heroes, those are your heroes. But even men for whom you have no respect saw more in your work than you did. They saw a greater possibility of producing it.

ALGREN: They saw more than I did the possibilities of making money out of it.

Q: Did you think you were particularly innocent when you went out to Hollywood to talk to Preminger? . . .

ALGREN: There's no question about it. I mean we weren't talking about literature, we weren't talking about human values; we were talking about how you go about borrowing money from a bank and getting somebody to write the script, and about how you get an organization together—about how you make a production using the title of a book and how you get the money. I was totally innocent of all this. I mean, I've never given it any attention. It wasn't where my attention was focused.

Q: Can an innocent also be contemptuous of the people who are not innocent?

ALGREN: They don't let you feel anything else *but* contempt. I would have liked to—I reached around to *find* some way of respecting the man. I mean you much prefer to respect somebody. It's a lot more trouble to feel contempt.

Q: But can an innocent feel contempt about anything? Isn't that a rather uninnocent human thing?

ALGREN: No, I don't think so. Of course, you've got to put some limitations on innocence. We're not talking about the kind of innocence you have from not coming into contact with the world, the sort of innocence of a recluse or of someone who's taken monastic vows. I'm not talking about that kind of innocence. I'm talking about the innocence that comes *through* contact. Innocence is not just the *lack* of something. Innocence is an achieved thing. You can't be unworldly without first being worldly. I mean anybody can be unworldly, I mean just duck the world. But to be an innocent in the best sense is to have the kind of *un*worldliness that comes out of worldliness, to be able to see how people waste their whole lives just to have security.

Q: But you did go out innocent in a sense, and I don't mean ignorant.

ALGREN: I went out innocent in the sense that my attention had been given to just one aspect of society and there's no more time to be more than one person, and that absorbed me. So far as what is going on in the business world or in the financial industry—well and good, but I'm not interested in it. . . .

Q: But innocence for most writers and for you is something to be nourished and maintained, isn't it?

ALGREN: I think there's a distinction between a creative writer and a journalist because the journalist is conscious of what he's doing. He knows just what he's up to and proceeds to express it in an orderly way, because he simply is working out of a conscious plan and this never comes to anything more than most journalism because the only things that last are the things that are done when the writer doesn't know what he's doing—that kind of innocence. Faulkner didn't really know what he was doing. He didn't know what he was doing because he was working out of a compulsion. He didn't know and he certainly would have defended himself against having it broken down. He knew that much about it. He had a drive. Certainly Hemingway, in this sense, never knew what he was doing. . . . A writer who knows what he is doing isn't doing very much.

Q: . . . I want to know whether or not you think you should have failed, and whether or not you wanted to fail.

ALGREN: I have no doubts about it: I've never had *any* desire to *fail*. I have a strong desire to *succeed*.

Q: And you've written to me that you begrudge every penny made by others from your written work.

ALGREN: Yeah.

Q: Well, what about going out there and being fooled by these people, twice? Didn't you once tell me that your friend John Ciardi,
the poet, asked you, "How come you're back in that same box?"

ALGREN: Ciardi said, "Why don't you protect yourself?" He said I've
been in the world long enough to know that it's full of people like
Preminger and that they're going to take you, that the world is full
of people who want something for nothing and if you expose yourself, they are going to take you. His mild reproach was, "You're a
man; you've got to take care of yourself." And my story is that you
can't do two things, that you're entitled to protection if, in writing
a book, you're preoccupied. I mean you should be entitled to have
a total preoccupation, you should be entitled to innocence. Let me
put it a different way. About ten years ago I am talking to two
addicts about *The Man with the Golden Arm*. They had both read
the book. There were two schools of thought going. The addict
sitting on the right-hand side says, "It's a hell of a book, it's a good
book." The other addict isn't enthusiastic about it. I said, "What's
the matter with it?" And the guy on the right-hand side asks the
other junkie, "Why don't you think it's a good book?" The other
junkie says, "Well," talking about me, "he's a square." He can't
understand talking to me. He knows I can't understand him. But
he'll talk to the other junkie on the right-hand side because the
other guy can understand him. He says to the other guy, "You know
it isn't like that," he says. "I come on and I read three or four pages
of the book this guy is telling what it's like." You know the part
where the junkie in the book, Frankie Machine, is talking, drama-
tizing the thing. This guy says, "Well, you know it isn't like that.
We don't talk like that about junk." The other guy, the guy who
liked the book, agrees that the junkie in the book was a phony.
"Yeah," he says, "that's right. But if this guy knew what it was
really like, he couldn't have written a book. He'd be out in the
county jail. He'd be on junk. You can't write a book when you're on
junk. It is the best thing that a square can do." And the other guy
says, "Oh, is that what you mean? For a square. All right. It's a

good book for a square." And that settled the argument. But in the same way, if you have enough guile, enough distrust, to deal on an equal plane with Preminger or any of them, I just use Preminger as a name, with this whole pack of make-believe people, if you could deal with them, then you wouldn't be able to write the book.

Q: Any book?

ALGREN: You wouldn't be able to write a particular kind of book which is based on, which has innocence. I mean, if you really had any real distrust, if you really didn't believe in the world, if you didn't believe in people, if you thought basically people are shit, if you wouldn't sit down and knock yourself out for two or two and a half years to write a book like that, or to write any book. As *you* know, you work on it every day and you work out of belief. Nobody is going to sit down in a society where he can do something else and write a serious book about people unless he had a really deep belief in people. You can't stop that. A belief carries over from the book. I mean you develop innocence.

Q: Are you saying that this developed innocence should be maintained for the sake of your work?

ALGREN: I say *entitled* to innocence because not everybody makes it. You are very fortunate if you come along that far and can develop a belief in people. It's something that happens.

Q: But you are less innocent about Hollywood now, aren't you?

ALGREN: Yeah, yeah.

Q: And it has not detracted from your work. As a matter of fact, you can now do a little writing about Hollywood, can't you.

ALGREN: Yes, I suppose. But it certainly detracted from my will to work because I would never sit down now and work for two and a half or three years. As a matter of fact, at the time I finished *The Man with the Golden Arm* I thought, well, now I know how to write a book and I've got enough of an economic foundation—I can work at my own pace—and I'll spend five years, that's what I figured, working on a particular novel about a woman. I wanted to do it just line by line, day by day, just making every sentence count. I believe I would have been very happy to do that. It means a pretty rigid life, but no more rigid than the things that actors do when they do just nothing else but try to learn how to act. It's a very, very rare opportunity when somebody is given by accident, by a hundred different accidents, a chance really to do something that is serious, when everybody else is doing something they don't believe in at all. I can say that at the time I was the only person I know of in Chicago who was doing something that was actually worthwhile. I didn't know anybody else. I'm sure that later in Paris and New York, too, you do find people who are totally preoccupied with something important, with something that has something to do with people. They're plugged into our society. You go around now and see somebody knock himself out with a public relations outfit or something—all this advertising and all the hokum that people use to get by—they don't believe in it themselves—they don't believe that it has any importance—they have to do it to survive. But once in a while somebody's extremely fortunate and gets his work all cut out for him. And there's really nothing else for him to do. It can be sculpting or acting or singing or something, but that is a really privileged person. So, in that sense, in losing that opportunity, I think the experience with Hollywood was very distracting. I don't think it was good for me.

Q: Why not?

ALGREN: I think it's a lost opportunity because I would never do that now. I would never put in the three, four, five years to turn out a book that has a chance of enduring.

Q: Why not?

ALGREN: Because I'd get nothing out of it.

Q: I don't understand that.

ALGREN: I mean you have to have a reward. You have to believe your work is *wanted*. After all, *The Man with the Golden Arm* wasn't

my first book—it was about my sixth. I was willing to go through
that.

Q: Aren't you going to go through that again?

ALGREN: No, no. I wouldn't do that again. You don't have to do this to
get money. And you've lost two or three years. There's a lot of
money. You can get money much faster than by doing it this way.
There's no point in doing it for money. You'd do it for the real
satisfaction—you'd assume—that it's wanted. But the real deception, the real disappointment is that actually it's not wanted. The
work is not wanted. Maybe this goes along with that innocence we
were speaking of, but I really believed that *Never Come Morning*
and *Neon Wilderness* and *The Arm* and that story you liked, "A
Bottle of Milk for Mother"—I believed that these were close
enough to our society. I mean if total strangers write to you and say
that they got something out of this, then the money thing is secondary. I think anybody, anybody, if given the choice, would always
take the privilege of having his work wanted by other people rather
than the privilege of having more money than anybody.

Q: But haven't you received letters about your work from people?

ALGREN: I receive a letter now and then.

Q: And a million people bought the old paperback edition of *Never
Come Morning*, right? Why did those million people buy it—just
to pass the time on a train?

ALGREN: Yeah.

Q: They could have selected many other things. How do you know
your work isn't wanted?

ALGREN: That doesn't mean it's wanted. People buy Mickey Spillane
by the seven millions, by the ten millions.

Q: How do you know when your work is wanted?

ALGREN: You feel that.

Q: Are there any other indications besides your feelings?

ALGREN: Nobody's work is absolutely wanted. But the point is—do you *believe* it's wanted, or not.

Q: Do you believe your work is wanted?

ALGREN: No, no. I don't know. I certainly did then.

Q: When?

ALGREN: Oh, up until the time and for a short time after I finished that *Man with the Golden Arm*. The fact that it may not be wanted isn't important. The fact is you believe it.

Q: And your Hollywood experience made you feel that it was not wanted?

ALGREN: As one aspect of the whole experience. All I'm saying is I don't have the belief.

Q: But did the Hollywood experience lessen your belief that your work was wanted?

ALGREN: Oh, sure. The Hollywood experience and the New York experience, too.

Q: What New York experience?

ALGREN: Because I didn't find any real difference in the values of the publishing world than in the values of the studios. It's the same thing. Their values are: get something that sells; get books into the presses and then promote them.

Q: Do you agree with Robert Louis Stevenson that everyone lives by selling something?

ALGREN: Well, yeah, but—

Q: Then what's the matter with Hollywood and Madison Avenue?

ALGREN: Hemingway was selling something. Hemingway was selling vitality.

Q: Why shouldn't Hollywood and Madison Avenue sell?

ALGREN: They sell sterility.

Q: So it is the product they sell that bothers you, not the process?

ALGREN: It's what you sell. Sure, everybody sells.

Q: What about you and money? Do you know the value of a dollar?

ALGREN: I am very good with one dollar.

Q: Do you know the value of two dollars?

ALGREN: Yeah. Oh, the questions are getting harder now. That was a tough one. What's the next one? You're leading up to three, *four*, FIVE!

Q: How about a million dollars?

ALGREN: That's a real head-scratcher! That's a *lot* of money.

Q: Is it too much?

ALGREN: No. It ain't enough . . .

Q: Are you worried about selling out?

ALGREN: Selling out?

Q: I know some young writers who are worried.

ALGREN: I don't know if I'm in a position to worry.

Q: By young, I mean under thirty.

ALGREN: Maybe they are flattering themselves that they've *got* something to sell out.

Q: But you are worried about it, too, aren't you? In your Hemingway article you wrote: "The hard-bought American belief that literature can be made only by a willingness to take one's own chances was sold piecemeal by individual surrender. . . . Honesty among writers had meant a willingness to take the kind of personal risk by which, if it fails, one fails alone; yet if it succeeds, succeeds for all. Now the writers began to subserve, rather than to stand against, the businessman's world." That sounds to me, Nelson Algren, like the protest of a writer who's worried about selling out. How much did you fear, if you have a fear of selling out, how much did that fear figure in your work when you went out to Hollywood or when you talked to publishers?

ALGREN: I've never been afraid of the accusation of selling out. Nobody makes it but those with nothing left to sell and I'm not accountable to them.

Q: No one has ever accused you of selling out. But have you ever been *afraid* of selling out?

ALGREN: Well, you see, I'm trying to think of just what it means.

Q: It means what you accused most other writers of doing.

ALGREN: If you don't keep producing, it's kind of a sellout.

Q: I don't mean that. I mean a sellout to the bourgeois, square, moneyed world. Can our culture produce writers who make a million dollars who have not sold out?

ALGREN: Sure.

Q: Is it conceivable that you'll make a million dollars sometime?

ALGREN: I don't think so.

Q: What if *Never Come Morning* as a play runs for a year on Broadway and you sell it to Hollywood for a couple of hundred grand plus a percentage and your script approval condition is met and the film makes a lot of money? Is that conceivable?

ALGREN: It's conceivable but a little dubious because everybody carries a certain price tag on them immediately and it doesn't necessarily have much to do with his worth. The price tag is what his agent sets. To be more specific, Irwin Shaw put himself down as a *very* unavailable, *very* high-priced writer *immediately*. I give him full credit for that. Irwin Shaw is always extremely hard to get. He's very high-priced. He did this way back in the thirties and he stuck to it. I happen to have had an agent who hung a very low price tag on herself— which was appropriate for herself—but she wrapped me into her crackerjack box. I'm the tin whistle of American letters.

Q: You're speaking now of the past?

ALGREN: The past still pertains. James Jones gets three-quarters of a million dollars, Algren gets a free train-ride to New York. They know what the price is. This is the price category I happen to have been put in. That's why I mention my present agent, my new agent, because she understood right away and saw that the problem was how to get me out of this free train-ride league.

Q: But *you* got the new agent, which means you were no longer willing to put up with the old price standard?

ALGREN: The world of those standards doesn't exist any more.

Q: Yet, in terms of a senior high school psychology course, your evaluation of yourself has gone up because you got yourself a better agent.

ALGREN: My evaluation of myself has never varied. It's very high. I'm a solid-gold whistle. I'm a platinum saxophone.

Q: Then your own estimate of your own *monetary* worth has increased?

ALGREN: Oh, yeah, yeah. Just look around me. I know that if James Jones, who is a fourth-rate writer, if Jones is worth three-quarters of a million dollars, then I must be worth Fort Knox.

Q: But how come the time that you are taking better care of yourself financially is the same time that you feel your work is not wanted?

ALGREN: Well, the work that is wanted is not very well paid, and the stuff that is not wanted gets paid very high.

Q: Isn't that a pretty good definition of a writer's innocence?

ALGREN: I don't know what you mean by that. What *I* mean is the highest price goes to the most useless stuff, the most unwanted stuff.

Q: Do you *really* feel that?

ALGREN: Well, I don't know.

Q: Is your best work behind you?

ALGREN: I'm not prepared to answer that because I don't know what's coming.

(The next day, after listening to the taped recording of this whole conversation, Algren made the following comments.)

ALGREN: In listening to this discussion about money, I remembered our last conversation in Riccardo's when you quoted Camus to me, to the effect that a man is what he does. And then, of course, five minutes later I took exception to that because it could be that a man turns out to be not what he does but what somebody else does.

Q: To him?

ALGREN: To the world. I think you have more of a belief in Camus than I have.

Q: I mentioned him only as a bona fide representative of an idea I thought you also held—that it doesn't matter what a man says he'd like to do, nor what he hopes he can do, but what he actually does.

ALGREN: I agree with that, but I don't share the common reverence for Camus. I believe he was a man of conscience, but I don't believe he was at all a profound man. Leo Durocher said, and I am *not* trying to be funny here, Leo Durocher said the thing just as profound and he's not the man of conscience Camus was, but he did say the classic thing, you know, when he said, "Nice guys finish second." He said, you know, "I like my mother, but if I'm playing second and she's trying for third, she goes down." In other words, either you win or you lose. You come to bat in the last of the ninth with one out and two men on and you're two runs behind, and you hit a drive over the third baseman's head—a direct smash into the left-field seats. Both runners start moving home. But the ball ricochets off the flagpole into the outfielder's glove. He throws it to second, doubling the guy off there and catches you coming into second. The game's over. You didn't win four to three. You lost three to one. You hit into a double play, that's all. You hit a flagpole, that's all. So as far as these movies go, especially *The Man with the Golden Arm*, it turns out that it is not important what was in the book, because this is what was done to it, and according to the reviews you showed me about *Walk on the Wild Side*, both of these books I did turned out on film to be flagpole shots. How many times did I say that? Shall I proceed?

Q: Yes.

ALGREN: In the same way that a thing turns out depending on whether you hit the flagpole or not, the same thing happens with money. We spoke a great deal about money. Well, money is what whoever has it is. Money is no specific thing. To one man, money is safety, his total security, but to somebody else money is music. It depends whose hands it's in. My identification with money is almost identical with writing. I've never believed in writing directly from imagination. If I had the imagination maybe I would. But this kind of work is good for Immanuel Kant or Marcel Proust, who stay in one room, you know. This kind of writing can be done very rarely. My kind of writing is just a form of reportage, you might call it emotionalized reportage, but—as *you* know—the data has to be there. Compassion has no use without a setting. I mean you have to know how do the law courts work. You have to know how many bars there are in a jail cell. You can't just say, "The guy's in jail." You've got to *know*. You've got to know there are different doors—there are solid doors, doors without bars. Some cells have one bar left out in the middle for a little shelf there. You have to know what that shelf is for. Actually it is used to put coffee on, or a little Lily cup of milk or something when the prisoner gives money to the matron or the screw—they go out and get coffee or milk and put it on that little shelf. Or if the prisoner comes in late at night, it is a little pantry. They use that. And you have to know do they get blankets or not. You're talking about a jail in Texas—

well, how do you know if the cot is iron or not, or if the blankets
are cotton, or whether you get blankets, or whether you get a
mattress or not. Some jails have mattresses. The reason I've never
read Jack Kerouac is because the first book of his I picked up says in
the first sentence that the guy was lying in a gondola. Well, I
stopped to think: a gondola is a coal car and the bottom opens. You
can't lie in a gondola; you'll hit the track. He doesn't know. He
doesn't know what he talks about, so why read him? But if you
read one sentence, if you read the first sentence of John Cheever,
then you know Cheever knows. If you are a serious writer, you have
to find out more than anybody else. For me this takes money, a
little money so I can move around for the data, for the stuff you
make books out of. I'm just trying to explain what I consider
money to be. For instance, I remember a morning, about four in
the morning, when I was with an addict, a guy, a six-and-a-half-
foot drummer from Arkansas. He's an addict. I wanted to go
home. It was getting late. I was broke. He wanted to make a stop
somewhere. He wanted to go into some little restaurant and just
wait. I was tired of it and he said, "Well, you don't know what it's
like to have a monkey on your back." This is pretty stale stuff by
now, this phrase. It's been used in a dozen hundred paperbacks. It's
common language now. But at that time in 1949 I don't believe this
phrase had come into the language of articulate people. It was
something that musicians, that drug addicts said. I happened to be
there and I repeated it. I knew it was good. I used many things like
that. If I found something like that, I'd go home. That's what you
make books out of . . . I recall at least two writers of the thirties I
met briefly—Ignazio Silone and Albert Maltz. At that time there
were many writers who were merely writing out of an intellectual
pattern, but these two guys, my feeling about these two guys was
that they were writing out of an almost Christlike feeling, out of a
real heartfelt concern, really concerned with the world. And I
don't think they needed any monetary reward for that. . . .

Q: In this unpublished manuscript which you were kind enough to
let me see, as you have been kind enough to let me see a number of
things, a manuscript called *Things of the Earth: A Groundhog*

View, you wrote: "Thinking of Melville, thinking of Poe, thinking of Mark Twain and Vachel Lindsay, thinking of Jack London and Tom Wolfe, one begins to feel there is almost no way of becoming a creative writer in America without being a loser." You wrote this in 1950 about the time you were dealing with Hollywood. Now you do think this is true today? Do you have to be a loser in order to be a creative writer in America today?

ALGREN: No. We have examples of good creative writers who aren't losers. It can happen.

Q: Do you think that Nelson Algren must be a loser?

ALGREN: Oh, yeah, yeah. Yeah.

Q: Why?

ALGREN: I'm trying to connect this with your question before when we talked about the loss in Hollywood. That was a bad loss because you have to take money for your purpose. The loss is that there isn't any place now to do what guys like Silone and Maltz were doing— they were working out of straight compassion. This don't work. The loss is the loss to make the connection with humanity. . . . The loss I am speaking of is in the shifting of a writer who's plugged in one way, the good way, to our society. Now the only way I can be plugged in again is on this money thing. That's the only thing by which you can get respect. . . .

Q: What about innocence and anger? Many people think of you as a terribly angry man. They do not know any other side of you. You have a reputation for being a very tough guy and a very angry one. Are you angry? Do you express your anger as anger or as innocence?

ALGREN: Oh, I don't go around being angry. Nobody who is *really* angry goes around *being* angry. As for innocence, I think it is a very lucky thing if it's an achieved innocence, if it's something that happens to you. I think Brendan Behan had innocence. I think Dylan Thomas was an innocent. You have to go through the world to get to that sort of innocence. I mean there's no trouble for a woman to be chaste if she's never been tempted to sleep with anybody. The really chaste woman is the whore. There is nothing less whorish than an old whore who hasn't gone down the drain. She's not a whorish person. The whorish ones are the prick-teasers, the middle-class prick-teasers, who run in and out, who play with sex. There's much more whorishness there.

Q: You've made other notes there. Do any of them still interest you?

ALGREN: Well, for some reason I wrote down something of Henry Miller's where he says the writer's got to go all out. That hooks up with something I said before about how the only good writing is done by people who don't know what they're doing. They just go all out. Like Hemingway and Faulkner, they were working out of a compulsion. There were things they had to do for their own survival which was expressed in their writing. But it had to be total. It goes all the way.

Q: What about your comment that "there is almost no way of becoming a creative writer in America without being a loser"?

ALGREN: I don't think the American writer is necessarily damned.

Q: But you also keep quoting that thing by Scott Fitzgerald. Over and over again you quote it: "Why was I identified with the very objects of my horror and compassion?" Consider, if you will, the possibility that a writer must *always* identify himself with the objects of his horror and compassion, and that this is one of the things that F. Scott Fitzgerald never found out. It was too late when he started asking himself that question. He couldn't cope with it. Do you believe that?

ALGREN: It just jives with what I was saying—that it takes a total commitment. Fitzgerald identifies himself. He was as good a writer as he was because he identified himself so closely.

Q: But did he? He didn't say "Why did I identify myself . . . ?" He said, "Why was I identified with the very objects of my horror and compassion?" Implying that he did not wish to be so identified.

ALGREN: He was a writer despite himself. He didn't want to—

Q: But haven't you identified yourself with the objects of your horror and compassion?

ALGREN: I hope so. I don't know, but I hope so. If you lose that identification, well, then you're just a journalist.

Q: What about the possibility that because Fitzgerald could not identify himself with the objects of his horror and compassion—

ALGREN: He didn't want to, but he did.

Q: You think he did?

ALGREN: Well, he felt something had been done to him, but actually he did it himself, out of his compassion.

Q: Do you do these things to *your*self? Much of your critical writing sounds as if you do, but I have been talking to you and—

ALGREN: If I did it, I would be identifying myself.

Q: It would be under your control, though, wouldn't it? Under your commitment and your wish?

ALGREN: I think that's important. I don't think anything has been done *to* me.

Q: This makes you and Fitzgerald different then.

ALGREN: Well, I can see there's a difference.

Q: When he speaks of a writer being a loser or how a culture doesn't understand the writer, you would have to feel then that this didn't apply to you. Now you've written about Wolfe and his troubles, and Lindsay. But you are no Wolfe, nor a Lindsay. You are different there, too. You write often about Chekhov. What about you and Chekhov?

ALGREN: I have a liking for the guy's personality, what little I know of it.

Q: You keep quoting him about how when he was at home all by himself, everything was fine, but as soon as he walked outside his door, life became horrible.

ALGREN: That's not exactly it: "When one is peacefully at home, life seems ordinary, but as soon as one walks into the street and begins to observe, then life becomes terrible."

Q: But do you agree with that? Why should he be surprised by what was outside his door? Do you think life is *that* hard?

ALGREN: Oh, yeah. It's the same thing that Tennessee Williams knows, or that Sherwood Anderson knew about. There is no such thing as a normal life. It's never lived that way. A critic in Chicago once got tired of Tennessee and wrote, "Why can't we get back to writing about plain old workaday Sunday folks?" Or that other critic saying, "But why don't we ever read about happy marriages?" Because there are none.

Q: Has Hollywood stuck pretty close to what Tennessee Williams intended?

ALGREN: They made a better movie out of *Streetcar* than it was on the stage. I found it more moving than the play. . . .

Q: You write poetry, don't you?

ALGREN: Sometimes.

Q: Is your poetry wanted?

ALGREN: No.

Q: Then why do you do it?

ALGREN: Because I want to and I like to and it's fun.

Q: Isn't poetry the hardest kind of writing?

ALGREN: No, no. Novel writing is the hardest because it's drudgery. Poetry is fun. To write a novel, you have to just do this single-minded thing. . . .

1962–63